Off-limits has never been so irresistible.

FORBIDDEN

KATRINA SNOW

Enjoy the adventure! Katrina Snow

Cover Design by WGoulet

Shutterstock.com Image Credits:
Passage to Mysterious Castle by Melkor3D
Woman in Gown by Conrado
Aurora Borealis by Serge
Dolomites Alps by Wjarek
Malachite Ball by Nadezda Boltaca

Flying Dragon Stock Photo by Andrei Gurov
Stock Photo of Bushes by Goffaux Denis

Cinzel Decorative Font by Natanael Gama

Published by KL Andersen
PO BOX 7452, New York, NY 10150

ISBN-13: 978-0-9970024-0-9
ISBN 13: 978-0-9970224-1-6 (MOBI)
ISBN 13: 978-0-9970224-2-3 (EPUB)

First Edition

www.KatrinaSnow.com

*For Mom and my sister, Becky,
for their endless encouragement and
for loving everything I write.*

ACKNOWLEDGMENTS

I have been fortunate to have a wonderful collection of people in my life who have supported me as I've taken this long, occasionally disappointing, always exciting journey to publication. My mother has cheered me on from the beginning of this crazy dream, and I'm grateful for her constant enthusiasm, as well as the times she bandaged up my bruised confidence when rejections struck a little too deep.

On Mom's heels is my sister, Becky, who has cheerfully read everything I've written numerous times—and I mean *numerous* times—and still managed to catch the tiniest issues. She's brilliant and my secret continuity weapon. While I'm at it, I'd also like to thank the rest of my family, both extended and close, including Greg, Nick, Alex and Holly, for believing in me. I didn't learn until recently that because I was always writing and her Mom was often reading my stories, my niece, Holly, grew up thinking I made a living as a writer. How fun is that?

I must also take a moment to thank Louise Knott Ahern for rescuing me when my first editor fell through. Her insight and enthusiasm were indispensible. Sometimes fate leads you to the people you need at just the right moment and I know that happened with Louise.

I've also been privileged to develop some fabulous friends in the writing community and to be part of many terrific writing groups, and I'm grateful for all of the support, encouragement and wisdom they've shared. In addition, I'd like to thank the Romance Writers of America for providing opportunities for budding writers to improve their craft, meet amazing authors and learn the ins and outs of the industry.

Lastly, I'd like to thank YOU for reading this book. You are the final piece of the dream and I hope you enjoy *Forbidden* as much as I enjoyed writing it.

FORBIDDEN

CHAPTER ONE

Land of Astonia, Kingdom of Cragmont, North Cove – April 6, 1594

"I won't do it."

Kate jerked her arm from Lord Sylvan's grasp as he forced her into her bedchamber.

"I won't be your magikal slave. Or any *other* kind either," she added, just to be clear.

In mocking disrespect for her wishes, the guard slammed the door behind them. Kate darted for the handle. A heartbeat before she latched onto the knob, a familiar boom echoed as the crossbeam crashed into place outside. Bolted in more securely than a castle keep, she turned her attention back to Lord Sylvan.

The man's hard eyes took a leisurely stroll through the room, lingering on the lit candles, the books on her desk, and the untouched knitting basket before coming to rest on her face.

"The wounds healed," he said in his eerie accent. "The deed is done."

"We can undo it."

"It's irreversible." He moved to the hearth, not a hint of sympathy, empathy or even acknowledgment that the *irreversible* act had been horrific.

She glanced at her hand, just as she'd done a dozen times over the past hour. And just as she'd confirmed the same dozen times, the skin looked whole. The bloody gash was gone, as if the barbaric rite had never happened.

"Didn't your uncle explain the nuances of the spell?" Sylvan asked, stoking the fire.

"Of course," Kate said, flooding the words with sarcasm. "Moments before the blessed ritual, dear Uncle Morten pulled me aside and said, 'Kate, I'm going to seal you against your will to a fellow sorcerer. You won't mind will you? Obeying his every command forever?'"

Sylvan chuckled coolly. "No, I don't suppose he said that."

None of it made sense. Aside from the jarring revelation that the myths about genies were real, Kate couldn't comprehend why Morten would give her to this man. To any man. Using her powers for his aims had been his favorite obsession for half her life.

"Are you holding something over him? Did he give me to you to appease a debt?"

"No," Sylvan said, placing kindling on the hot embers in the hearth.

Morten wouldn't tie his boots if it didn't forward his plans. "Did you pay him something—a kingdom—in exchange for me?"

"Are you worth that much?" he asked, adding a log to the pile.

"Is that a no, then?"

Another log went in. "He thinks I'm going to command you on his behalf."

Thinks?

Not *knows?*

Did the man have other aims? An unsettling energy stirred within her. She'd never met a Zafarian who'd dare cross Morten, but Sylvan certainly wasn't like her uncle's other advisors. In appearance alone he stood apart from the herd.

Where the other sorcerers were wrinkled and wiry, this one was tall and broad-shouldered. And he didn't sport the usual patchwork of gray often adorning Morten's confidants, but thick locks the color of flame. In short, he was *young*, maybe eight and twenty—only a handful of years older than she was.

"Thinks?" she asked. "As in he *thinks* you're going to help him, but you aren't?"

As he shifted the burning wood in the hearth, the fire roared so high it warmed her across the bedchamber.

"Are you ready to part ways with your uncle?"

"Part ways?"

He glanced over his shoulder.

She stared.

"Would you like to leave?"

The word, the promise, the trap hung in the air between them. "Is this a trick? If I say, 'Holy gods, yes,' you'll tell me to be a good genie and you'll take me away someday?"

He dragged an unwelcome gaze over her, hair to boots. "We leave today."

Today? Her heart hammered so loudly, she was sure the guard heard it in the corridor. Having been conned a time or twenty by her uncle, Kate reached out to confirm the declaration. Opening herself up, she drew in his feelings.

The moment his energy touched hers, a brew of hate and vengeance coiled around her heart like a snake twisting up a tree. Holy gods, he despised Morten as much as she did.

As she breathed through the biting emotions, she zeroed in on his intentions, his desires. He needed her for something, wanted to use her powers for something, but overshadowing all, she felt his burning ache to return home. As if he couldn't get there fast enough.

"Unless you're more fond of your uncle than you're letting on," he said, rising.

"I'm more fond of liver cakes."

His brows inched up.

"They don't stay down," she added.

One corner of his mouth hitched.

"What do you need me for?"

"Does it matter?"

Perhaps not. He wanted to use her Gifts, but she could use him instead. She could go with him, even make him think she was pleased about it, then break away from him once they were safe from her uncle. Sylvan was handing her the best chance she'd ever had at escaping Morten's hell.

A sensation rippled through her, one so foreign it took a moment for her to identify it as hope.

"Where would we go? Where are you from?" she asked, mortified to discover she'd started shaking.

"Far."

Of course it was far. His sharp accent and unusual attire whispered of distant shores. And for the first time, she realized the rhythm of his walk and conviction of his talk screamed nobility. And not the sort trailing off a feeble branch. His people were of the trunk…and the roots.

As she envisioned a long voyage and her uncle seething on the other side of the world, Sylvan said, "You'll need a hooded cloak that will hide your hair and eyes. They make you too easy to identify."

Yes, the black hair and pale eyes helped her blend in among the gypsies, but she suspected they weren't who she'd be staying with. Not this time.

"The bigger issue is my Gifts," she said. "And yours. Morten can track those far more easily than anything related to my appearance."

"We won't use them until we're out of his reach."

And he snuffed out her budding hope with one simple phrase. Sylvan's plan would fail. He didn't know what they were dealing with. She could work the spell to curb her Gifts, but if Sylvan thought it was safe and used his, there would be no escape.

"I thought you knew what he can do. It doesn't matter how far we go. He can sense our Gifts anywhere."

He glanced around the chamber again, as if looking for something. "My land is guarded. His Gift won't reach us there."

A guarded land out of Morten's reach sounded like a fairytale. But Sylvan's tone indicated he believed it, and no sorcerer who valued his life would cross Morten if he couldn't get to safety. Was it possible there was such a place? Was it possible she wouldn't have to curb her Gifts forever? Was it possible her life had finally taken a turn for the better?

"Ready the cloak and pack anything else you wish to bring."

When she didn't move, he fetched her cloak from where it hung.

"Now. Pack now."

Kate had no choice but to trust, as alien as that was to her. She quickly set down the cloak, threw open a large traveling trunk and began gathering up her few precious belongings.

The satchel with the spell's ingredients went in first, then a small blade with a moonstone handle, two heavy books on Zafarian sorcery, her mother's brush, a collection of figurines from her father's travels, two chemises, stockings, her favorite blue gown and a sturdy one of dark green fabric that wouldn't show the dirt on the journey. Finally, she tossed in a couple of hair ties and a cake of lavender soap wrapped in linen.

To think, she was finally going to be free. Holy gods, was she humming? As she laid the cloak over her stash, she caught Sylvan removing the rapier from its mount above the mantle.

"The workmanship is excellent," he said, inspecting the intricate handle.

"My father had it custom made. The stones are rare and spelled to bring the bearer good fortune." Although that hadn't worked, had it? Maybe it would bring luck in a new land.

As he tested it out, slicing the air with the long, thin blade, something shiny caught her eye from the hearth. All four bronze candlestick holders lay engulfed in the flames, along with the hearth

5

tools, her knitting basket, and what looked like the quills from her desk, the latter turning to ash before her eyes.

A cool sweat crept over her body.

"Do you know how to use it?" he asked.

Well enough to win bouts with the stable hands more often than not. Her father had arranged that as well, insisting she learn so she wouldn't need to rely on her Gifts to defend herself. But she couldn't say that, could she? She hadn't missed the fact that the items in the fire could all be used as weapons.

"I'll take your silence as a yes," he said, then tossed the rapier in with the rest.

"No!" she cried. "There's no need to destroy it. I'll go with you." And he did want to go. She could still feel that in him.

"I need to take care of a small matter first."

"What small matter?" she asked, quelling the instinct to call the blade out from the flames. While Morten didn't fuss about her empathic abilities, he'd be on her like gulls on a carcass if she summoned an object.

"The final rite of the Binding."

A final rite? They'd already drawn blood, what more could it require? When he glanced toward the bed, her skin prickled as if jittery spiders had decided to torment her as well.

Backing away, she said, "You told me it was finished."

"I said it couldn't be undone."

She glanced at the weapon in the hearth.

"Don't do it unless you want Morten to join us."

Reaching out again to read him, she looked inside the man for anything she could use.

Pushing hard, she sifted through his tangled psyche, past the rage, behind vengeance, and under other dark emotions adrift in him like a shattered ship on the sea.

Fear hitched up her body. She'd missed it before. Where gentle feelings should have been, Lord Sylvan had gaping holes, as if a great storm had washed away any pockets of goodness he'd possessed. A strange sense hit her. She couldn't quite place it.

"Something damaged you," she said.

"Do not read me."

Another wave of emotion turned her stomach. "What happened to you?"

"Get out of my head."

While he hadn't answered her question, he must have thought about the event, because his next surge of emotion made the room spin before her.

Struggling to steady herself, she grabbed onto a chair. "Holy gods, it was horrific."

Fury exploded from him so tangible it propelled her backward.

"I told you not to read me!" he roared, then vanished the same alarming way he'd done before the Binding. One second he was solid before her, the next vacant air. But his essence clogged the space like the pungent odor on the docks.

"Lie on the bed, Kate," his voice demanded.

With her belly roiling, she glanced at the bed, then darted for her trunk and the small blade inside.

"I command you to stop!"

As if possessed by another, her feet instantly anchored to the floor.

"Now, I *command* you to lie on the bed."

"No. There must be another way," she cried as her legs obeyed, carrying her across the room.

"Not one that you'd like any better."

She fought every step, but it was useless. Her feet kept moving. "You can't do this. I'm a lady. My father was a Duke, my great grandfather a king."

"That merely makes you a genie with a noble pedigree."

With ugly promise in the air, her body climbed onto the bed. "Maybe I can help you. Heal you," she said desperately. "In exchange for my freedom."

"You think you can heal my soul like one of your mangled pets?" The whispered words sent shivers up her neck.

He was right. It wouldn't be like any healing she'd done before. Could she do it? Would it kill her? Even as she thought it through, her body rolled back onto the bed. Fortunately, the moment her head hit the linens, her limbs were her own again.

Jerking up, she said, "Why not let me try?"

"If you really wish to help me," he said, invisible fingers moving up her leg, "then lie still while I finish the Binding." The cushions dipped at her feet.

"No!" She kicked out, slamming her shoe into something solid. His ribs? Stomach?

With a growl, he pushed her down, his heavy invisible body smothering her.

"Show yourself," she demanded, fighting to break free. "This is sick."

"As you said." He yanked her skirts to her waist. "I'm damaged."

She frantically gestured toward the candlesticks in the hearth. They instantly obeyed, sailing across the room, across the bed, and missed, smashing against the wardrobe.

As he tried to force her legs apart, she wrenched up her body, shoved him lower and thrust a knee where he'd feel it. His heavy grunt told her she'd hit her mark.

She scrambled across the bed, but he latched onto her ankle, hauled her back, and pinned her again, his legs between hers.

An icy tremor rattled her bones. Were the gods so cruel? Would they help her find the means to escape Morten, only to tear it away?

As she twisted and fought, the bed curtains came loose, boxing them in. With a desperate flick of her finger, she brought down the panels, covering Sylvan in moss green brocade.

Cursing, he thrashed about trying to free himself.

With another quick motion, Kate sent the fabric whirling about him until he was rolled tight like a rug.

He began shouting.

She knocked him hard onto the floor.

"Kate, I command you—"

With another swift wave, she toppled the wardrobe over him.

Silence.

She leapt off the bed terrified he'd awaken.

"What's going on in there?" a booming voice carried through the door.

She hadn't much time.

"Lord Sylvan needs help," she cried, snatching up the cloak and the satchel from the trunk, quickly shoving in the blade, brush, and soap.

Running for the door, she willed the beam from its slots on the other side. Throwing open the door, she crashed into an oversized guard with a wary expression.

"The wardrobe fell on Lord Sylvan," she cried, trying to pull the mammoth into the room. "You need to lift it off him."

The man didn't budge, but looked over her head to confirm her claim.

"His Grace said you might cause trouble," he said, not alarmed in the slightest.

"Would His Grace want you to let Lord Sylvan die?"

"Looks like you can ask him yourself."

She whipped her head around. Near the bed and her fallen master, green mist billowed out into the room. Morten had arrived.

"Oh, for the love of the gods, move!" She stepped away from the guard and sent him flying into the room.

Darting out, she slammed the door, dropped the beam into place with another gesture, and bolted down the corridor.

"Bluebell?" Morten's lilting voice echoed. "Come out, come out…"

Clutching the satchel closer, she skipped down the steps two at a time. Darting out the side entrance, she sprinted around the back of the manor toward the path that led down to the docks.

Her feet slid out from beneath her when she glimpsed the harbor. The fall and the realization equally painful.

Morten had cleared it. Even the crippled ships were gone.

Panic gripped her around the throat. As she scanned in vain for any sign of a boat in the cove, a distant glimmer of light caught her eye.

Castle Cragmont.

If she could get there, she might find a place to hide and, most importantly, a ship to freedom.

But first she needed to do the spell.

Before she used her Gifts again.

Before they found her.

Turning toward the sea, she scrambled down the path to the caves.

CHAPTER TWO

Castle Cragmont - Eight Days Later

With her pilfered candle well beyond half-mast, Kate crept through hidden passages in Cragmont's drafty stone castle. During her first day or so in the walls, rats and mice darted out of her path with squeals of terror, but now they behaved as if she were one of the pack, scrambling around her feet as she crept along. Perhaps their mutual need to go unnoticed created a strange camaraderie.

With her feet crunching on remnants of critters past, Kate turned down the narrow corridor to Victoria's chamber. Thick cobwebs and dust garlands blocked the way like drapes of gray silk. As she swiveled the satchel to her back and used the candleholder to cut a path through the webbing, thunder clapped so loudly it seemed as if the walls rattled. She'd never recalled a week of such storms. It was as if the heavens didn't pause to catch a breath before assaulting the cove once again. The upside to it, the storms provided good cover and no one heard her creeping around. The downside, it prevented all arrivals and departures of the seafaring kind. Nearly all by land too.

The Florian princess and her two attendants had been the only visitors. They had arrived the day prior and were soon to be departing, if the gossip beyond the walls was to be trusted. Kate's only chance of hitching a ride with that caravan was Princess Victoria, and Kate hoped she could convince her cousin to orchestrate a way.

Kate paused at the secret panel to the princess's bedchamber. It still bore the markings they'd carved into it as children—a soaring hawk and a sun with rays covering half the door. As Kate ran her fingers over the wings she'd created years ago, the voices of Victoria and a maid carried into the passageway.

The latter prattled on about a deathly illness that had struck the visiting princess's maid and lady-in-waiting. Victoria asked questions, but provided little fuel for the conversation.

When Kate heard bathwater splash and a call for a lavender soap cake, she leaned against the door to wait until the maid left for the night.

Sometime later, after she was certain Victoria was alone and long after her candle burned out, Kate rapped on the back of the panel.

Nothing.

Kate knocked again, harder this time, causing a sharp sting in her knuckles.

The rustle of fabric and soft footfalls were followed by her cousin's no-nonsense, "Hello?"

"Victoria, it's Kate," she said through the panel.

Silence again.

They hadn't seen each other in nearly eight years, but surely she hadn't forgotten her.

"Kate?" The word sounded more suspicious than friendly.

"Lady Katherine Isolde Durant? Your cousin?"

The sound of scraping wood echoed in the passage. The panel swung open.

Kate blinked against the light.

Victoria's gaze swept over Kate, soot-covered gown to web-covered hair. "You look horrid."

Same old cousin. To the point and unemotional. Thank the gods. Kate needed the calculating cousin she remembered to help her calculate a way out of there.

"You look beautiful," Kate said. Not that she was surprised. The auburn curls Kate had longed to have as a child had grown more vibrant and full, flowing well past the waist of the princess's plum-colored dressing gown. And sharp eyes, so much bluer than Kate's, shone from an alabaster face that would stir sirens to envy.

"What are you doing here? And in there?" Victoria asked as a firm knock sounded from her bedchamber door. "Oh, for the love of…" Victoria muttered. "Just a minute," she whispered, shutting Kate back in the dark passageway.

"Yes?" Victoria said loudly.

A hinge creaked, followed by the quick clip of expensive shoes moving at a rapid gait. Kate had heard that same pattern through the walls numerous times over the past six days. Victoria's sister-in-law had come to call.

"The lady-in-waiting and maid are taken care of," the queen said, her voice tight.

"I wondered if you'd had a hand in their illness," Victoria said, her tone accusatory.

"They'll be fine after the festival is over."

The remark sounded so dismissive, Kate could almost see the woman waving a hand.

"What festival?"

"The festival to win Princess Rachel's brother."

"Win her—"

"Without her attendants, she'll be grateful to have you in her carriage. That will give you three days to gain her aid in winning Prince Edmund's hand."

"I didn't enter," Victoria said in a chilly tone.

"I sent a letter to the Florian King weeks ago, declaring your delight in participating in the competition."

"I and my ladies-in-waiting are not prepared for such a journey. We're not—"

"They will remain here with me," the queen said. "You may take a maid."

"They won't wish to stay."

"If they choose to go, the illness may strike them as well. You wouldn't want that, I'm sure." After a heavy pause, the queen added. "This is my castle now. *My* throne. Your brother has spoiled you long enough."

"Alexander didn't spoil me, he needed me," Victoria bit out. "My father needed me."

"And now your father is dead and Alexander has a wife. Neither needs you now," the queen emphasized, as if Victoria wasn't bright enough to catch the meaning. "You are five and twenty. You should have wed ages ago."

"No one was suitable."

"Suitable or not, if you don't win the competition, you'd better find yourself a husband before you return."

"Or?"

"I will arrange one for you," the queen said using the same chipper tone Morten used when he'd cornered a victim.

"Who?" Victoria's voice was as hard as stone.

"My cousin's second wife recently passed and he's inquired."

"That lecherous old buzzard? Alexander won't—"

"Alexander is fond of my bed and wants heirs. He will do as I wish," the queen said. "Which means you will too. Understood?"

Silence.

"I didn't quite hear you."

"Yes." Cold, crisp, final.

"Good." The clipped steps nearly skipped away and a latch clicked in the distance.

Kate waited to be sure the queen didn't return before carefully pushing open the panel. The bedchamber looked much as it had on her last visit. A canopied bed large enough to sleep four princesses stood at one end, ten feet or so from a grand stone hearth. Shimmering tapestries of garden scenes and seascapes adorned the walls, and thick woolen rugs covered the wood flooring. Near a dressing screen and a towering wardrobe sat a deep tub, full and inviting. Two high back chairs and a small desk piled with books sat before three tall paned windows dressed up with brocade panels the color of sapphires.

And at the center of it all, her back to Kate, stood Victoria. Although hail beat so hard at the windowpanes they threatened to shatter, the princess stood as still as a statue, hands fisted at her sides.

"Victoria?" Kate said tentatively.

Her cousin spun around. After taking a visible breath and uncurling her fingers, the princess's gaze fluttered over Kate once again.

"You look like you've been living in a cave."

"I did. For one night," Kate said, not volunteering that the grime was more likely due to the nights in the forest, the pig farmer's barn and the sooty castle walls.

Victoria nodded, as if estranged cousins showed up every day. "When was the last time you bathed?"

"Before I fled my uncle."

"Which was when, a month ago?"

"Nine days," Kate said. "I need your help, and it appears you may need mine as well." She gestured toward the door.

Victoria stepped over to the tub. "Alexander doesn't see what she is." She dipped a hand in the bath water.

"Your brother was always soft when it came to maidens."

"Yes, but I think this one bewitched him," Victoria said. "And not with her charms."

"You can't be implying she used sorcery. Because—"

"I know, I know, it's forbidden." Victoria waved off her objection, sending water droplets flying. "I'm not saying she's a

Zafarian, just that she uses magik. I'm sure a lot of people do."

Kate wouldn't say *a lot* was an accurate assessment, but the count was certainly more than *none*, which it appeared her sharp cousin had ascertained.

Victoria's eyes found Kate's with alarming speed. "Can you put a hex on her? Render her mute or something?"

Not without one of Morten's spell books. "No," Kate said.

"Really?" Victoria's steely gaze bore into Kate's. "Rumors say your uncle practices."

"Do they?" Kate said, feigning innocence.

"Yes, the gossips say he smells of sulfur from working spells, and tortures animals, and can disappear leaving only a cloud of green smoke behind. Is none of that true?"

Holy Gods, had the gossips been living with us?

"It could be," Kate said.

"Come, you need a bath," Victoria said, motioning for Kate to shed the gown.

Happy to oblige, Kate set her satchel on one of the chairs.

"You've been his ward for twelve years and you didn't pick up anything?" the princess asked, starting on the gown's side ties.

"Why would I keep fleeing if I wanted to learn from him?" Kate let the filthy garment drop to the floor.

"That doesn't answer my question," Victoria said, lifting the gown with her fingertips.

And Kate wouldn't, not with answers that could lead to the burning stake. Too many had perished for far less than what she knew and she couldn't take the risk that Victoria wouldn't say something. Just one hint to the wrong person could be deadly.

"I can't do what he does. And I won't try. But the gossips are correct about him being dangerous."

Victoria tossed the dress into the hearth.

"Has he abused you?" Victoria asked, eyes dropping to where Kate was rubbing at her palm.

"In a manner."

"We should speak to Alexander. We can ask him to intervene, to have you live here."

While Victoria's suggestion was touching, Kate couldn't stay. She'd be far too vulnerable so close to Morten's manor. Her uncle would surely find a way to take her back. No, her only hope was making certain he didn't know where she was. Lord Sylvan, too.

"There's a little more to the story," Kate said, pulling off her boots and stockings.

An auburn brow arched.

"Uncle Morten gave me to another man," Kate said, losing the chemise and stepping into the bath. The water was still slightly warm and as close to heaven as she'd been in ages.

"*Gave* you?" Victoria handed her a soap cake. "To wed?"

"To keep." Kate let the implication settle in the air.

"Nine days ago?"

"Yes, and they will both be looking for me," Kate said, lathering up. "I had hoped to secure passage on a ship, but the storms have conspired against me. No one has sailed since I arrived."

"You realize Florian is landlocked. If Lord Morten and this other man follow, you'll have limited means of escape. The Zafarian Divide marks its entire eastern border and nothing lives beyond that. To the north—"

"I realize it isn't ideal, but unless you can produce a seafaring solution, this is my only hope."

Victoria nodded.

"I'll do whatever you need me to."

"You'd make a much better lady-in-waiting than one of the maids," Victoria said, pouring half a vial of lavender oil into the bath. "But if we do this, you must stay with me until the winner is crowned."

"How long will that be?" Kate asked, breathing in the heavenly scent.

"Marriage festivals usually last a fortnight or so. It could be three weeks."

Three weeks in one place! How could she manage that with Morten and his men hunting her? But was she any safer in Cragmont? It was only a matter of time before he came looking for her at the castle. She'd didn't have a choice. She'd have to do it. Go with Victoria. She could plan her next move from there and leave as soon as the competition concluded.

"Fine. I'll stay with you until it's over," Kate said. "I'll even help you win the prince if that's what you wish."

"According to the queen, what I wish is irrelevant, but at least I'd have some help getting what I need." Victoria pulled a long cobweb from Kate's hair. "What will you do after the festival?"

"Disappear," Kate said. "Abroad or as a servant somewhere in the kingdoms."

"A Durant shouldn't be forced to disappear," Victoria said. "Or work in service."

"No, but what should and shouldn't be is irrelevant, isn't it?" Kate said. "We both must deal with what is."

The princess nodded and padded toward the wardrobe. "You'll need some gowns and things."

Kate dunked her head under the water, silently thanking the gods for finally intervening on her behalf.

* * *

Kingdom of Florian - Three harried days later

The gods obviously had a wicked sense of humor. Kate should have waited for the next merchant ship—or pirate. She should have found a dinghy and faced the sea herself. She should have bribed the gypsies to take her. Again.

She should *not* have attached herself to a royal caravan replete with not one, but two spoiled princesses. Runaways needed to hide. To blend in. Kate had never met a princess who could blend. They attracted attention and trouble in equal measure and at frequent intervals.

Case in point, had Kate not been in a traveling carriage with Princesses Victoria and Rachel, she'd not be facing bandits…if they were bandits. Admittedly, if they weren't what they claimed, but Zafarians on the hunt for her, the princesses would be the least of her worries.

"How could they be bandits? Aren't we a stone's throw from the castle?" Victoria asked, mirroring Kate's thoughts.

"Oh, I'm certain they're harmless," Princess Rachel said as if they were discussing a litter of puppies. Perhaps Florian's princess hadn't met the other kind yet. The non-harmless ones. Although it wouldn't have surprised Kate to hear that ruffians of any caste turned docile in Rachel's presence. Even with disobedient locks that refused to stay braided, the petite princess had the sort of blonde, ethereal beauty that men fell on their swords for.

A seasoned guardsman rode up to the window, his horse dancing in circles. "Pardon me, your highnesses," he said, looking to Rachel for a reply.

"What is it, Stiles?" Rachel said.

"We are unable to conquer the bandits, and their leader demands a favor for safe passage."

Victoria, unaccustomed to playing second princess, even if neither coach nor guard were her own, asked, "What sort of favor?"

"His price is a kiss," Stiles said.

Kate felt certain she had heard the man incorrectly. Outraged gasps from both princesses testified otherwise.

Bandits overtake a convoy laden with finery, jewels and two princesses, and all they ask for is a kiss? The ludicrous request had her once again fearing that they weren't bandits, but her uncle Morten's men or the sorcerer himself. But Lord Morten could not have tracked her. Thanks to the spell, she hadn't used her Gifts once.

"Your highness?" Stiles prodded.

Rachel's fair complexion paled further.

"Offer another bounty," Victoria said, shooting a stern glance at the man.

"Perhaps the silks?" Kate suggested. "Those should appease true bandits."

"You don't think they're bandits?" Rachel said as Victoria caught Kate's eye.

"Offer the silks," Victoria ordered.

As Stiles raced to deliver the message, Kate stretched out the window to catch sight of their captors. Unfortunately, the men were beyond the bend in the road and the forest was too thick to see through.

"It isn't him," Victoria said.

Kate darted back inside accidentally landing atop her cousin and dislodging a book from Rachel's lap.

"Take care before you crack your skull," Victoria said, pushing Kate back onto the seat across from the two maidens.

"Who do you think it is?" Rachel asked, retrieving the book. "Or *isn't*?"

"Kate's guardian." Victoria spread an embroidered handkerchief over her lap and set two rings—one ruby and one pearl—in the center.

"Kate? I thought her name was Hildegard," Rachel said.

The problem with an alias is that people had to use it. And despite insisting upon and inventing the thing, Victoria couldn't seem to grasp that part.

"It's my nickname for her," Victoria said with a grimace in Kate's direction.

Rachel nodded and said, "And why would Kate be concerned it's her guardian?"

"She left Cragmont without his blessing."

"Would he pretend to be a bandit?" Rachel asked.

"Of course not," Victoria said, adding earrings to her stash.

"Which is why it isn't him. But that doesn't mean I think they're bandits either."

Kate's stomach pitched as if being tossed about by unruly waves. Could they be Lord Sylvan and his men?

Stiles returned. "Your highnesses and milady, I have presented your counter offer, but their leader insists upon the kiss."

"Is he a drunkard?" Victoria asked.

"Or missing a few spokes?" Rachel said.

"No, your graces, he has his wits about him," Stiles said.

"Why don't we offer him ale instead," Kate suggested.

"Do so, Stiles," Rachel said with a dismissive wave.

Once again, the man charged off to deliver the message.

"Now, back to your theory," Rachel said. "If they're not bandits, who do you think they are?"

"I think it's subterfuge," Victoria said, struggling to undo the clasp of a woven gold bracelet.

"Subterfuge by whom?" Kate asked, welcoming any ideas that would counter her own.

Victoria looked at Kate as if she had to explain why ships needed sails.

"From my competition, of course," Victoria said, holding out her arm and gesturing for Kate to remove the bracelet dangling from it. "Have you forgotten that six other royals have entered the festival to win Prince Edmund's hand?"

"Ten," Rachel said. "Papa is overjoyed that my brother has drawn such interest. Our older brother Stephen is the heir, and he had only five at his marriage festival."

"Ten," Victoria said gravely. "Even more reason. If this bandit tactic manages to send one competitor home, the strategy is a success. It's brilliant."

Brilliant, but there was a slight hole in her cousin's argument. Handing over the bracelet, Kate said, "If thwarting you is their aim, why would they demand a kiss?"

Rachel and Victoria studied Kate for an awkward moment before Rachel said, "A diversion?"

"Exactly," Victoria said, removing the last of her jewelry—a golden broach—and adding it to the rest. "A diversion. While we are kissing bandits, they will steal my jewels and gowns, which will put me at a disadvantage in the competition."

"As interesting as your theory is, I find it impossible to believe anyone would resort to something so sinister," Rachel said. "Don't you?"

Victoria must have thought it best not to illuminate Rachel about the true dealings among royal maidens with the same aim, and Kate was not about to school her on how sinister people could be.

"In case they *are* bandits, you should try to look less appealing," Victoria said, tucking the loaded handkerchief inside her bodice. "Rachel, you should hide your jewels and muss up your..." Victoria trailed off, eyes locked on Rachel's hair, which was already in wild disarray.

"Fortunately, I only wear a couple of pieces when I travel," Rachel said, removing a bracelet and oblivious to Victoria's stare. "It's too easy to misplace them."

"Kate, you already look mussed, but you should take off your locket," Victoria said, vigorously shaking her head until several curls sprang free.

Kate's quick review of her attire confirmed Victoria's assessment. The single dark braid down her back was likely as unruly as Rachel's hair, and her borrowed blue gown looked several days shy of fresh. Everything about her appeared rumpled, worn and tired. As Victoria hinted, the silver locket was likely the only thing that would draw anyone's attention, but it would take a lot more than the threat of bandits to persuade her to remove it. It was not only her last tie to her mother, but her talisman rested inside—a coin-sized slice of polished malachite as green as summer grass and as necessary to her future as air.

Without the stone, she wouldn't be able to renew the spell blocking her Gifts. Without it, Lord Morten would track her. Without it, she would be doomed to the life of a genie.

As Kate tucked the precious possession under her bodice, Stiles returned yet again.

"Their leader refused the ale as well," the guard said. "He instructed me to announce he isn't interested in breads, cheeses or trinkets either."

"Are you sure they're bandits and not Zafarians?" Kate asked.

"They're not Zafarians milady. We've encountered them before," he said.

"Then fight them," Victoria said.

"They outnumber us three to one," he said.

"I cannot believe two dozen royal guardsmen are being held captive by a bunch of grungy bandits," Kate said.

"They're heavily armed."

Victoria flipped open a small wood box of jewels and pulled out a garish broach—thumb-sized mother-of-pearl petals arranged in the shape of a daisy and set in copper. It was the kind of broach you'd see on, well, no one with a hint of taste.

"Give this to him," Victoria said, handing the piece to Stiles.

Following his path once again, Stiles disappeared.

"A gift from the new queen?" Kate asked.

Victoria nodded. "Designed to torment me."

"Do you think he'll accept it?" Rachel asked.

"Probably not," Victoria said. "But I've been hoping to lose it for ages." The thought drew a rare laugh from the princess before she sobered and said, "In truth, if we are to pass, we'll need to go back to Cragmont for help. Our guards won't mind a fight."

"Surely, going back isn't necessary," Rachel said. "As you said, we're a stone's throw from the castle."

"We're not going back," Kate said vehemently.

With matching regal expressions, the princesses turned her way.

"No?" Victoria said, raising a brow. "Are you now giving the orders?"

"They will just overtake us as we flee," Kate said, shifting under the weighty gaze. Cousin or no, Kate knew she'd overstepped. "Please, there must be another way."

Victoria nodded. "There is one last solution."

Kate and Rachel both waited for the pronouncement.

"We will grant their request," Victoria said.

A dainty gasp came from Rachel's camp. "You're going to kiss him?"

"Kiss a lice-ridden bandit?" Victoria said. "Of course not."

"You can't think I will," Princess Rachel said.

"No," Victoria said, turning her lovely eyes in an unfortunate direction. "Kate will do it."

While Kate had agreed to tend to Victoria's every need, that did not extend to appeasing bandits. "Kiss him? Oh, no. I have no intention—"

"I didn't think so," Victoria said, then leaned her head out the window. "Driver! Tell the guards we're going back for reinforcements."

Going back wouldn't lead Kate to reinforcement, but to enslavement.

"Wait! Wait," Kate cried.

CHAPTER THREE

Stiles, not Rachel, rounded the bend yet again. The lass was sure milking the moment.

"What are they offering this time?" the bandit asked. "Pottery? Parchment? Poetry?"

"A broach," Stiles said, tossing the offering to him.

"It's hideous." He laughed, turning the frightful ornament in his palm.

"She doesn't know it's you," Wolfe said again.

"Of course, she knows it's me. She's playing along."

"The last time we arrived, she ran all the way from the pond to greet you. The time before that, she didn't even change out of her bedclothes. It's been half a year. If she knew it was you, she wouldn't be in that carriage."

"Ah, hell. Stiles?" he asked, hoping the man would support his side.

The guard's face pinched like he'd bitten a sour apple. "I believe she and her guests—"

"Her guests?" he said. "Isn't she riding with Lydia?"

"No. She is accompanied by the princess from Cragmont and her lady-in-waiting. I think they are of the mind that you are bandits."

"Ah, hell," he said again, starting up the road. "Why didn't you tell me!"

"I believe I did," Wolfe said, falling in next to him.

Before they'd eaten up a dozen strides, a gypsy-haired maiden marched around the bend. Her blue traveling gown clung to her curves in a way that would make any man stare, but it lacked the usual glittering embellishments that the princesses of the kingdoms seemed to demand. And her hair wasn't twisted atop her head like the royals wore it, but draped over her left shoulder in one long black braid.

The lady-in-waiting.

He hadn't realized his feet had ceased moving until she stopped in front of him. Near enough to assess, too far to touch.

"Are you the scoundrels halting our progress?" the maiden asked, her sharp gaze gliding from him to Wolfe to their comrades.

"Some of us are scoundrels, milady, others are misunderstood," he said, drawing her gray eyes back to his.

"I'm sure I can guess which camp you fall into."

Laughter rumbled among the men.

What a contrast. Eyes cool as ice and wit hot as fire.

"Derek Wolfe," Wolfe said with a quick bow. "Often the latter, occasionally the former."

"His accent causes all the trouble," he said.

"I doubt that's the only cause," she said, dark brows hitched expectantly.

She awaited his name, no doubt.

He should tell her the truth. He should end the charade and let her pass. But shoulds were so damned boring.

"May I present—" Wolfe began.

"Bregovi," he said. "Bregovi the Bandit."

More laughter among his men and the guards threatened to give him away.

"Bregovi?" she said, rolling the word over on her tongue. "I've heard that name somewhere."

Bregovi could almost see her brain shaking the rafters for the answer.

"Tales of my exploits?"

"Perhaps," she said.

"May I ask *your* name?"

"You may ask, but the answer is not your concern."

"Not yet," he said in a tone that had coaxed numerous wenches out of their corsets.

She ignored the tone and the insinuation, and looked over his men instead.

"I've never seen bandits in such fine attire. Matching even," she said.

"There's no need to be slovenly," Bregovi said. "Even in bandit trade."

"Banditing isn't a trade," she said.

"You give a kiss. I give passage. The bargain sounds like a trade to me," he said with a wink.

"Why not demand coin or jewels?"

"Like this one?" He held up the broach.

"Yes, even that hideous thing would do you more good than a kiss."

"I think you underestimate the good a kiss can do."

One of her dark brows hitched up. "You obviously don't have much practice with princesses."

"Why? Don't they kiss well?"

"They don't play with bandits in the woods."

"And their lives are poorer for it, wouldn't you agree?"

"Hardly."

"Well, what do you suggest, my lady-in-waiting? How would you direct a bandit who merely wants a little affection? Someone to tend to his less monetary needs?"

"Oh, for the love of the gods," she said in a delightfully

exasperated tone. "Barmaids from here to the wetlands would line up to tend to your *less monetary needs.*" As if she'd not intended to say as much, her face flushed as pink as a sunrise.

"And why would that be?" he asked.

"I've heard they like arrogant rogues," she said, her eyes glinting.

Laughter burst from him. He couldn't remember the last time a maiden had sassed him. "Perhaps you could steer me in the direction of such a wench. Until then, my demand stands."

She turned to the guardsmen. "Surely, you can overtake them."

The men shot uncomfortable glances between her and him.

"Anyone?" she said. "Are you all cowards?"

The men shifted, no doubt wanting to correct her on that.

"It's just one kiss," faithful Stiles said, shooting warning glances at his men.

"What if they demand more? If he—"

"I won't," Bregovi said as Wolfe cleared his throat loudly.

"If he does?" she asked Stiles pointedly.

"My men will intervene, milady," Stiles said.

She wiped her hands on her gown as she glanced among his men again. Some of the bravado had left her. Ah, hell, she looked scared. He'd have to tell her. Wolfe nodded as if indicating he was about to do the honors. Then...

"One kiss and we pass?" she said.

What was that? Had she agreed to a kiss from those berry-ripe lips of hers?

Ignoring Wolfe's louder cough, Bregovi said, "You have my word."

"That's as comforting as an executioner's last assurances," she said, studying their surroundings, perhaps looking for an exit.

He waited. Letting her decide the next move.

Finally, she took in a long resolute breath as her misty blue eyes pinned him in place. "Very well, collect your kiss."

* * *

Bregovi's left brow shot up, then a smile crept across his face. Kate worried he had caught onto her plan, but his lazy step forward reassured her he had not. Reaching as if to embrace him, she quickly pulled his rapier from its sheath.

Men on both sides cried out in alarm.

Bregovi grinned. She wished he'd stop doing that. Smiling at her. On her sixth escape attempt, she'd met a dockworker with a sharp jaw, powerful build and grin that sparked wicked thoughts. No man had ever topped him. Until now. The bandit had the kind of face and form that drove sculptors to marble and maidens to sin. How annoying.

"Still want that kiss?" she asked, circling him, rapier at the ready.

"Absolutely," he whispered in a husky tone, starting a slow circle of his own.

An unsettling wave of pleasure washed over her, causing her to misstep. The emotion was not her own. It appeared that while the spell successfully blocked her from using her Gifts, it did not prevent others' emotions from reaching her unbidden. She had also felt a surge of anger when the brawl had broken out at the inn the day before, and her mood had not matched it.

Could this new emotion have come from the bandit? His eyes were alight with something akin to fascination, and the word had been soft on his lips. Full, ripe lips. Suddenly her stomach pitched as if she were at sea.

Addled. The spell must have hindered her senses too. Or perhaps it was the taste of freedom. And at the thought of tasting, her bent mind contemplated what flavor his lips would hold. *Completely addled. He's a bandit. He has probably eaten raw trout with those lips.* It was the most disgusting image she could envision with his green eyes dancing before her.

Taking a breath, she reminded herself he was keeping her from her future. "I suggest you and your band of cretins depart." Staring square into those sparkling eyes, she tested the blade with a few elaborate swipes, then tapped his arm before he'd even seen it coming.

Guards and his men jumped forward.

He raised a hand to stop them. "If we do not?"

She gave him her most devious grin and brought her weapon to sparring stance. Delicate pink stones adorned the hilt in an ornate rose pattern. Obviously stolen.

He nodded to Wolfe. It fit that the two were associates, for the foreigner had the confident manner of a man who got whatever he wished and a face that guaranteed he'd get *whomever* he wished as well.

"You can't mean to fight her," Wolfe said in his odd accent.

Bregovi motioned for the weapon.

Wolfe tossed him another rapier, which Bregovi caught by the handle with ease.

"I hope the hellcat takes you," Wolfe said.

"Traitor," Bregovi replied as he rested the thin blade on his shoulder. "May I propose jousting rules?"

"Which would be what exactly?" she asked.

"The first to pin the other with blade or strength wins the bout and their boon," he said.

"I and my party get passage?"

"I get that kiss."

"Fine."

Kate positioned her body with open ground behind her to ensure he didn't have the initial advantage of forcing her into brush or trees. And through a gap in the forest, she caught a glimpse of Florian's castle gleaming in the distant sunshine, sprouting turrets like giant trees reaching for the heavens. Truly a stone's throw away.

"Magnificent. I would ask you to clasp hands on it, but I doubt you'd oblige. I suppose I will have to rely on your honor. Can I trust in that?" he said with a wink.

Her honor? Infuriating man. She sprang forward, her blade meeting his with a quick tap. He blocked each strike as she forced him backward toward a cluster of trees.

"Impressive," he said, then, in the space of a blink, spun to her right.

She turned to keep him in her sights, but the man was light of foot and had her twirling in circles before she knew what he'd been up to. After freezing her steps to halt the dizziness, she felt the firm smack of his blade on her bottom.

"Is this how you fight all your opponents?" she asked, trying to locate him again as he stepped behind her at each turn.

"Only the beautiful ones," a warm voice said in her ear.

Spinning the moment he spoke, she latched onto his tunic with her free hand. As mischief danced in his eyes, a long-forgotten memory bubbled to the surface. A childhood game of blind man's bluff with her father. He'd always been full of mirth and had teased her much the same way.

"Perhaps you'd be better employed as the court jester," she said.

"You may be right. I'll inquire about the position the next time I see the king."

As if he'd ever met the king. Stepping back, she brought her weapon around once again. He blocked blow after blow as she forced him toward a huge elm.

"I will disarm you," she uttered through gritted teeth.

"Dear lady, you disarmed me long ago." He said it with such affection, such warmth, it caught her off-guard, and her blade lowered a fraction.

At that precise moment, he twisted his weapon with hers, swiftly whirled her around and pinned her against the tree. They were both out of breath, bodies pressed against one another, their rapiers pinned between them, the back of his fingers resting against her right breast.

Hoping he hadn't noticed the intimate placement of his hand, she struggled to break free.

His hold was solid.

Her mind raced. If she could use her powers, she'd draw a knife in an instant, or pull down a tree, or command a rock to—

"You smell like lavender," he whispered, his eyes inches from hers.

"You smell like—" She took a whiff, expecting something repugnant. Instead, spices and mint filled her senses. She could almost taste cinnamon, and her mouth started to water.

"I smell like what?" he asked, his eyes teasing.

Kate was not about to tell him he smelled delicious. "I didn't know bandits bathed."

"We are not all as you would expect." He winked and devilish dimples popped on both stubbled cheeks. "I believe I have won the point, fair lady. Do you concede?"

The idea of kissing him was becoming far less disagreeable, but she refused to give in. She struggled again to no avail.

Easing up, she said, "It appears I underestimated you."

He smiled.

She smiled back.

He relaxed his grip. Exactly what she had counted on. Mustering up her strength and a knee, she shoved him off. As he struggled to regain his balance, she rushed forward, caught his blade with hers and executed a move to free it from his grasp.

In expert fashion, he recovered and countered with a twist of metal and will. Her weapon flew through the air, leaving her without blade, breath or speech.

Kate looked around at the men, the sword, Bregovi.

"Considering another play, fair one?" he asked.

"You agreed. Safe passage." She could not be considering this.

He bowed in acknowledgment and threw the borrowed blade back to Wolfe.

"The bargain stands."

"Yes, well, we've already discussed my view of your bargain."

"A misguided view, indeed," he said, his voice dropping to a whisper. "For I promise to do all in my power to ensure you are satisfied with the exchange."

Satisfied. The word hung in the air. Taunting her. She wondered just what ensuring her satisfaction would entail and grew dizzy—either from fear or excitement, possibly both.

Whichever the case, she had little choice and once again uttered, "Very well, collect your kiss."

He smiled lazily, started forward and halted. Reaching down, he slid a dagger from his boot and tossed it away. The men laughed and she couldn't help but join in.

"At least you learn from your mistakes," she said.

"Always." He stepped closer.

Her knees wobbled.

He moved nearer still.

Kate drew in a breath and something fluttered in her stomach.

Guards and bandits cheered.

Bregovi smiled at their audience, then turned full attention back to her, a grin playing at his lips.

His eyes were full of magik and spells and mystery. Emerald pools flecked with gold. He held her gaze. Intimate. Intense. Hovering just a step away.

Waiting, while his lips and eyes beckoned.

Waiting, while a hint of spice teased her nose.

Just *waiting* until the suspense mounted to an unbearable degree. Unable to withstand the infernal tension another moment, she rushed forward to get the blasted kiss over with.

Unfortunately, she misjudged the distance.

Her lips crashed into his with such force she knocked him backward. But instead of toppling over—as she would have done under a similar attack—he grabbed her arms and softened his mouth over hers.

Kate had not expected his lips to be so gentle. Or so warm. She had not expected to kiss him at all beyond a short peck. But he had kissed her. He *was* kissing her. Quite thoroughly.

Rather than protest, as any lady would, she not only let the marauder invade, she latched onto his tunic. And instead of releasing her, as any gentleman should, he not only claimed his kiss, he enticed her to join in, luring her toward dark, unknown waters.

The moment she considered letting the tide take her, his mouth left hers.

Dazed, confused, and slightly disappointed, she realized it was over. As the fog cleared, she concluded the spell must have blocked her good sense along with her powers, for she never would have allowed such liberties otherwise.

Then his hurried breath whispered over her as he leaned in and kissed her again.

She forgot all about spells and liberties.

His bewitching lips gently pillaged, cunningly teased. Persuading. Coaxing. Inviting. Torn between *want* and *should*, she tightened her grip on his shirt to steady her legs.

Completely unaware of her plight—or perhaps keenly aware of it—the man's hands moved to her back and drew her closer. Too close.

As he nibbled on her lower lip, an unsettling excitement began to build. The man knew kisses like she knew magik.

In an effort to create a safer distance, she slid her palms to his chest.

He sucked in a breath.

She wavered.

Then his heart jumped under her fingers, and she forgot her purpose and leaned toward him instead. As his nimble tongue swept over hers, delicious warmth washed through her. If there was a reason she was supposed to resist, she couldn't recall it.

Finally, she let the current take her.

Sinking into him, she boldly accepted his invitation, teasing and tasting in return.

His grip tightened, her morals loosened, and their wicked kiss deepened. Steamy. Claiming. Endless.

While his mouth deftly made love to hers, her mind whispered that the mischievous man would be an entertaining companion. In her countless fantasies of a life free from Morten, she'd never imagined it could include passion and laughter. Was it possible? Could a chance encounter with a rogue lead to more? Had the gods finally intervened?

Her heart grew light at the possibility. Her uncle would never look for her among bandits. Could she convince Bregovi to hide her? Would he? Contemplating the boon he'd likely ask for such a favor started a tantalizing ache low in her belly.

While the debate raged on in her brain and thrilling sensations swirled through her body, she became faintly aware of whispers among the men.

"Edmund?" It was Princess Rachel's voice. Surprised. "Edmund!" No, not surprised. *Scolding.*

While her brain came into focus, Kate glanced over her shoulder and caught sight of Rachel and Victoria at the turn in the road, the former looking joyful, the latter puzzled. The pieces jolted into place.

"Edmund?" Kate said, darting her gaze back to the man still pressed against her. "*Prince* Edmund?" Embarrassment raced up her neck and charred her cheeks.

"I was thinking of a kiss on the hand," he said with a sheepish grin. "But that was much better. Well worth the duel."

"Insufferable," she said, shoving him and her foolish fantasies away just as Rachel leapt into his arms.

"Why didn't you tell me?" Rachel cried. "And poor Kate! You must apologize."

Zafaria would grow grass before Kate would give him that opportunity. She hadn't let sorcerers get the better of her, and it riled her that the prankster prince had managed it. Holy gods, she'd let him goad her into kissing him. In front of all those men. The kingdom guards no doubt. She should have bit his impudent tongue.

Approaching Victoria, Kate said, "Are you sure you want to win a prince who plays bandit charades in the woods?"

"No," Victoria said quietly. "But I could do far worse."

"Come, Edmund," Rachel said. "You must meet Princess Victoria and render that apology to Kate."

"Perhaps you'd rather wait in the carriage?" Victoria whispered.

"Finally, a good idea," Kate replied, fully intent upon avoiding the man for the duration of the festival and the remainder of her days, for that matter.

Fortunately, the festival royals and guests aided in her cause. With constant arrivals at the castle, she managed to disappear into the shadows, a skill well-honed over the years with her uncle.

* * *

Two Days Later

"When can you leave?" Wolfe asked as Bregovi took aim at the deer figure. "My ship and crew are ready, and I need to check on the carpet makers in Khadmar."

Bregovi's arrow flew across the archery field, striking the wooden beast on the shoulder.

"The carpet makers. You claimed their workmanship was inferior to the Dojian's." Bregovi studied Wolfe's stance as the man aimed at a soldier-shaped target. Stiff. Resolute. They had never repeated a route in less than two years and Khadmar was twenty months shy of that.

Bregovi wondered at Wolfe's true purpose. It certainly wasn't the carpets. Most likely, he had some secret trade in mind. Or a secret woman. His friend had never lacked when it came to feminine affections, with wenches and nobles succumbing to his attentions with equal abandon.

They claimed the unusual accent drew them in, but the man's blond mane and tall, muscular build didn't hurt his cause any. And

Bregovi suspected that cause was at the root of Wolfe's focus on the Khadmar port.

"Where would the course take us?" Bregovi asked.

"Westor. Trevina," Wolfe said.

Ah. Trevina was a stone's throw from Madora. "You sure your intent isn't to check on the merchant's daughter?"

Wolfe's arrow sailed toward the soldier…and missed entirely.

Bregovi shot again and embedded an arrow in the deer figure's back flank.

"If my memory is sound, Angelina bested you at your own game and sent you on your way without a nod," Bregovi said.

Rather than the expected retort, Wolfe chuckled. "That she did, but she won't win the rematch." The man shot again, striking the wooden soldier in the stomach.

"She could be off on a trading errand for her father. Or wed."

Another faulty hit by Wolfe. "How soon can you leave?"

"Whoa, are you thinking about marrying this one?"

"Of course not, but I'd like another round with her before her father pairs her off," Wolfe said. "What are we looking at?"

"If I can get out of this ludicrous festival, I can sail in two weeks. If not, somewhere around a month."

"What are the odds your father will release you from the contest?"

"I don't know. It isn't as if removing my hand from the winnings will damage our relationships with the other monarchies. These matchmaking festivals are held in several kingdoms each year, and with or without me, half will be betrothed by its conclusion."

Bregovi aimed for the soldier and maimed it somewhere about the knee.

"The main issue is funding. Since Father severed mine unless I wed, we'd need to find other means." His father used the perfect tactic to force his cooperation. The journeys to foreign lands fueled his soul as surely as food nourished his body. While he loved his family and his home, being trapped in Florian suffocated him.

"Of course, we could avoid all this by sailing to your land and asking your family to support the next expedition."

"Not possible," Wolfe said as his arrow struck the mark on the soldier's chest.

"Not possible or not pleasant?"

"Both."

"One day you're going to tell me where you're from." Bregovi hit the wooden deer again, this time near the tail.

"Why would I do that? You love a mystery more than I do." Out of arrows, Wolfe headed toward the targets. "I'll wager that's why you are so intrigued by Kate. Is she still dodging you?"

"Yes, the maiden is more difficult to find than the isle of Caligo."

"Caligo is mythical."

"Mythical, yet you could find her." Bregovi pulled an arrow from the deer figure.

"Only if compelled, and you won't compel me to find your maiden," Wolfe said, wiggling an arrow from the soldier target.

"You won't need your Gift to find her," Bregovi said. "Your instincts or intuition or whatever you use will do well enough."

"My price is Madora," Wolfe said. "If I deliver Kate to you, the port marks the first stop on our next voyage."

"We were set to search for the Crystal City next." Bregovi added two more arrows to his quiver.

"Madora." Wolfe strode toward an arrow protruding from the grass behind the targets.

"You'll locate her before sunset."

"It's a fair bargain. You will have your lady and we sail for mine."

Bregovi did want to *have* his lady in so many ways. "Fine." The sooner he found her, the sooner he would win another kiss and more.

As they headed back toward the firing line, Wolfe handed over his arrows and bow.

"Conceding victory so soon?"

"Angelina awaits." Wolfe strode toward the castle with the gait of a man determined to capture his quarry.

"If Kate manages to evade you this afternoon, look for her tonight at the ball," Bregovi shouted after him. "Check all the dark corners."

Wolfe waved an arm in acknowledgment. Bregovi felt as if the task had already been accomplished and decided it was time to strike another deal.

CHAPTER FOUR

As the plush carriage jostled over the rutted road, Sylvan again wished he'd taken a horse instead. Riding would not only have afforded a smoother journey, but a more peaceful one.

"Chapman," Lord Morten Durant, Cragmont's over-pompous duke, shouted toward the window.

"Yes, your grace," came the steward Chapman's eager reply.

"How close are we?" Morten asked.

"Not far, your grace," Chapman said, peering in from his mount. "The scout advises it's just beyond the next hill. They're holding a celebration of some sort. They haven't noticed us."

Morten nodded as he stroked the gem-studded serpent ring twining around his fingers. Sylvan could almost see the wheels spinning in the man's brain. The duke's hair loss and niece were likely the only things he couldn't bend to his will. And while he appeared to have accepted the former, accomplishing the latter fell into the murky territory of obsession.

"Instruct the driver to halt outside of their view," Morten ordered. "And fetch our steeds."

"Yes, your grace," Chapman said before disappearing from sight.

"Do you think she's here?" Sylvan asked.

"Not if she's thinking clearly," Morten said. "But when she's on the run, she rarely thinks clearly."

"You should have told me she has a tendency to flight," Sylvan said.

"If you hadn't bungled the final step, her tendencies would be a moot point," Morten said. "You'd be able to summon her back anytime we wished, and we wouldn't be on this merry hunt."

Irritated hairs pricked up the back of Sylvan's neck. Her escape was not his fault. If the duke hadn't been so secretive, so arrogant, Sylvan would have known what he was dealing with and taken proper action to ensure her cooperation. Or he would have proposed an alternative she wouldn't have been threatened by.

"We should have performed the marriage sealing, instead of the genie binding," Sylvan said. "If her Gifts are as you say, I'd have her powers now and we could accomplish your conquest without her." Not that Sylvan cared much about the man's conquest.

Morten's complexion grew unnaturally ruddy as he studied Sylvan's face. "If she passed on her abilities to her husband, as her parents did to one another, then she'd also gain *your* powers. Kate's Gifts already make her the most talented sorceress in the kingdoms. If we added invisibility to the mix, my tracking ability would be useless. More importantly, since I don't have her empathic Gift, I'd have no idea if she were lurking about."

Point well made. Invisibility gave one the opportunity to hide. To sneak. To spy. One could learn a man's secrets—his vulnerabilities. The delicious Gift had allowed Sylvan to study Lord Morten for weeks, learning exactly how to infiltrate the man's ranks and, ultimately, how to fool the Order Master—the land's most powerful sorcerer—into believing his newest supporter was not only a common lord, but a Zafarian.

Morten's gaze pierced him for a frigid moment. "Or is your true desire to increase *your* abilities?" Gripping the Zafarian dagger resting on his lap, the duke slowly leaned forward across the carriage. "If you have plans to usurp my power, I assure you, I can undo this spell before you gain a fingerhold."

While possessing Kate's Gifts would certainly help him to reclaim his kingdom, neither gaining her abilities nor Morten's hoped-for throne were Sylvan's aims. The maiden herself was the key.

"I do not wish to take what is yours—or soon to be yours—but your threats are hollow," Sylvan said. "We both know you can't reverse it."

"Perhaps not, but there are ways to transfer a genie to another master," Morten said.

As death of the existing master was the only way to facilitate such a transfer, Sylvan felt the full weight of the threat.

He didn't like it. The sole reason Sylvan tolerated the relationship with the man was because he needed Kate. He wished to all the gods she were connected to another family, for he'd like nothing more than to dispatch with this power-hungry, throne-usurping sorcerer.

"If you wish to continue to serve me, your concern should be how you are going to seal the spell," Morten said. "The only two options are consummation or to spill her blood. As you blanched at the latter, I suggest you accept my assistance with the former."

Blanch wasn't the term Sylvan would use for his reaction. He needed Kate to fulfill the prophecy, and the seer had made no mention of the maiden in a spirit form. He needed her alive.

"Once we recover her, you may fill the bedchamber with Zafarian minions if you wish," Sylvan said.

Morten's snide smile indicated he'd like nothing better.

As the carriage halted, Chapman reappeared with two horses. "Your mounts, your grace. The gathering is around the bend in the road."

Lively music from flutes, strings, and other instruments greeted them as they rode into the gypsy camp, and the rich odor of roast boar set his stomach rumbling. From the dancing, laughter, and the sight of a couple adorned with flowers, Sylvan deduced they'd interrupted a wedding festival.

Like a wave on the sea, the reveling ceased as Morten, Sylvan and the guards passed by. Adults held their ground in stony silence while children scattered to peer out from behind trees and wagons. Holding up a hand to halt his men, Morten stopped in front of a tall, raven-haired gypsy of bulky build.

The gypsy approached, motioning for his people to move back. Tattoos twined up the man's thick arms and around his neck, and scars across his right cheek and shoulder indicated he'd faced his share of foes.

"Lost her again, I hear," the gypsy said.

"Simply the usual cat and mouse game," Morten said. "She so enjoys the hunt."

"Then why not let her hide a hair longer?" a crackled voice said from behind them.

With the grace of a lioness on the prowl, a silver-haired gypsy woman took up a position near the tattooed man.

"Why, I fear for her safety," Morten said congenially. "One with her abilities could meet with mobs or worse, those who would use her to forward their own ambitions."

"None are worse than you," the woman said and spat at Morten. The spittle hit the sorcerer's boot.

"Control your elderly, Vance, before she insults me," Morten said, his tone eerily serene. "I'd hate for one so frail to meet with harm."

"Frail!" This time, her wet sentiment hit Morten's knee.

The bridegroom stepped forward, eyes fixed on Morten. "Come, Selena, Lady Katherine would not wish you to bring an ill fate upon yourself again." Taking her arm, he led the still-muttering Selena to a tented wagon several paces away, where she turned and watched with beady eyes.

"Is she here?" Sylvan asked. "Do you have her?"

No one spoke.

"Kate," Sylvan shouted, spinning his horse. "I command you to show yourself."

No one stirred.

"It appears your commands are useless here," Vance said.

"Where might she be?" Morten calmly asked as if the two were sharing a smoke.

"If the gods are just, she's where you'll never find her," Vance said, matching the duke's tone.

Morten chuckled. "You must know by now there is no such place."

The breezy banter blew Sylvan's frustration hotter.

"Enough," Sylvan said. "I shall look myself!"

Inhaling the element of air and exhaling his material form, Sylvan rendered himself invisible. Screams echoed about them, invigorating him almost as much as the invisibility itself.

As the material world faded slightly, another level of the camp revealed itself to him. Elves, wood sprites, and other faeries perched on branches and wagons. Fae musicians, most likely there for the wedding festivities, played and danced to a lively tune as if nothing was amiss. A couple of brownies lurked at the outskirts of the wagons. And near the wedding feast, a stout goblin with a wicked grin appeared on the verge of mischief.

All but the musicians watched the scene as attentively as their gypsy friends. And all seemed keenly aware of and, from the sound of the chatter, amused he had joined their midst.

In his own land, the veil between the fae and human realms was much easier to breach than in Astonia. But from the volume of the faerie host in their midst, Sylvan suspected the gypsies had also mastered the tricks of interacting with them.

"Where is my genie?" he asked the closest elf.

The elf grinned and danced away.

A pixie hovering near Selena giggled. "She's far and near. Hidden and in plain sight. Safe and in danger of being discovered."

"And exactly where would that be?" he asked the pixie.

The creature buzzed around him, giggled a bit more and flew off.

"If you're not going to say something useful, you might as well tell me to sod off," Sylvan grumbled and dismounted.

"Sod off," Selena said and spat again.

Insulting as the gesture was, Sylvan would let Morten deal with her in his own time. More important matters beckoned. As the sorcerer continued his genial conversation with Vance, Sylvan investigated the camp with a train of fae musicians in tow. *Playing.* His experience with the fae told him they wouldn't interfere. Thankfully, they were usually more intrigued than concerned with the dealings of humans.

So, ignoring his entourage and making no attempt to be discreet, Sylvan threw back tent flaps and checked wagon homes at will, hoping to drive Kate from her hiding place.

While he discovered formidable supplies, more fae folk, and a couple heating up a bed of straw, the search did not produce his genie. As he wove through the camp on his return to the duke, he passed two young girls peeking out of a wagon and slowed to listen to their whispers.

"Mama had a vision about her," the smaller of the two said.

"What did she see?" the other said.

"Lady Katherine was in a fancy carriage with other maidens."

As Sylvan crept closer, the conversation shifted to how Kate had taught one to braid her doll's hair.

While they were content to stray from the tale about the carriage, he was not.

Drawing so close he could smell the honeysuckle in the girl's hair, he whispered low in her ear, "Tell me what your mother saw."

The girl gasped and tried to duck into the wagon, but he caught her arm before she succeeded.

"I asked a question of you, did I not?"

The girl's eyes narrowed as she tried to make out his form.

"Tell me what she saw," he ordered with enough menace to make any man quake.

The child, not more than six years strong, glanced around the camp and dared to utter, "No."

"No?" He tightened his grip until he could feel the ridges of her tiny bones. "This is not a demand you can refuse." When the child's eyes grew dewy, he squeezed harder. "Tell me what she saw."

"No," came her choked reply.

Sylvan growled and hauled the informant out of the wagon, for which she kicked and punched in protest. When her boot delivered a sharp jab to his shin, he threw the brat under his arm and took her to Morten.

"This one has information but has forgotten her manners and won't share it."

"Well, let's help her find her tongue," Morten said, turning his steed to face the girl.

Sylvan released her body, letting her feet hit the ground, but kept that same steady grip on her arm.

As the gypsies visibly pulsed forward, Vance drew a blade.

"Back," Sylvan shouted. "I've a knife at her throat."

The girl screamed and he tightened his hold. Lovely thing, invisibility. One could claim any number of threats and, unable to disprove with their eyes, people were forced to believe. At least the humans were. The fae gathered around him knew better and snickered at the deception.

"What does she know?" Morten asked.

Sylvan relayed the sliver of news.

"She didn't say where Kate was going?" Morten asked.

"No," Sylvan said.

"She doesn't know," said a slender woman with coal-black eyes and lavender buds woven into her hair. Drawing recklessly near, she added, "I didn't see where Lady Katherine was going."

"You lie," Morten said. "You protected her last time. Delia, isn't it?"

"Yes, but I speak the truth. I did not see her destination."

Squeezing harder still, Sylvan drew a whimper out of the girl.

"Please," Delia said. "Take me instead. Hannah has done nothing."

"That's precisely the problem," Sylvan said.

"She's an innocent," Delia said. "If you release her, I'll tell you everything I saw."

"The way this works is you tell us everything you saw and *then* we let her go," Morten said.

"I have your word?" Delia asked.

"Do not trust him," Selena cried. "Remember his last visit. He cursed us all. Even those who answered his demands."

"That's right. You did," Delia said, growing noticeably frantic, but no closer to divulging the information.

Pulling a dagger from his belt with his free hand, Sylvan scratched the blade against the girl's throat just hard enough to draw a small trickle of blood.

The girl began crying.

"Wait. Wait," Delia said. "Lady Katherine was with a blond and a redhead. Royal, from the look of it."

"From what kingdom?" Morten asked.

"I didn't see crests," she said. "But they were on a journey through a wooded land." She glanced between Hannah and Morten. "Please, I promise I didn't see more than that. Won't you please release her?"

"That's up to Lord Sylvan." Turning in his direction, Morten said, "If he's feeling merciful."

Mercy and its benevolent cousins weren't emotions Sylvan had felt in ages. Reason would need to dictate. While killing the child wouldn't hinder his sleep, the mother had cooperated. Then again, the girl had denied him, and disposing of her would send the message that he and Morten weren't to be trifled with.

As he contemplated his choices, the host of gypsies pled for her life and the fae watched in indifference. All except one.

He hadn't noticed her earlier. Had she been there all along?

Elves and fae musicians parted as she passed through their midst, iridescent colors swirling about her, wavy midnight hair floating on the breeze. His eyes instantly recognized the amethyst hues of hers and the ridge of freckles dusting her cheeks and nose—a feature she'd earned in the many hours he'd helped her to appear in her human form. To the fae, the trait flawed her, but he'd always found it one of her loveliest attributes. And while endearing emotions eluded him, a whisper of longing tugged somewhere near his heart.

"Elliana."

Other than in dreams, he hadn't seen her since he'd left Viridia months earlier.

"Sylvan," she said, pausing within arms reach. "This is not your way."

"It is now."

"The truth has been spoken. The mother knows nothing more."

"You know where she is, though. Don't you?" he asked. "The maiden I need."

"You seek the one you need, but what you need isn't always what you seek," Elliana said.

"More riddles. Speak plainly."

"You will find the one, but not here. Release the child. Her destiny is not yet fulfilled." Elliana reached out and rested a gentle hand on his cheek.

For a moment, a foreign sensation swirled through him like the colors swirling about her. Back in the recesses of his mind, beyond the fall of his kingdom, beyond the slaughter of his family, beyond the curse, his memory recalled what it was. *Love.*

Marveling at the long-forgotten feeling, he stared at Elliana, yearning for another time like a man thirsting for water in the desert.

"Did you come to save me?" Hannah asked, eyes wide.

"I've come to save him," Elliana said, her gaze never leaving his.

If only she could.

"Are you showing yourself to everyone?"

"Just the girl."

"So I'd know this isn't a dream."

"So you'd know."

"Are you a faerie princess?" Hannah asked.

Elliana's lips tilted in a crooked smile.

"She's a faerie goddess," Sylvan said.

And his faerie blushed. Just as she had every other time he'd declared her as much. The yearning grew to an ache. Would he ever return to his kingdom? His home? To her? He needed to find the maiden from the prophecy. He needed to find Kate.

But for now, Elliana was with him and that was enough.

He released Hannah, who ran to her mother. Cheers rang out around them, and fae musicians started a lively jig.

He reached up to place his hand over Elliana's and caught a hint of her familiar scent—honeysuckle, willow leaves and sunshine.

"I'll do it," Sylvan said. "I'll find the maiden and save the land."

"I know," she whispered. "Remember what I told you. About the one you seek."

"Remembering won't make me understand it. Can't you simply tell me what you mean?"

Slowly, she pulled her hand away. It was as if her touch had been the dam holding back the darkness. For as soon as she'd let go, all the good in him washed away, leaving him bereft and empty. Just as one couldn't describe the taste of a favorite meal, he knew the moment had been good, but could no longer recall the essence of it.

"You will find her when the time is right," Elliana said.

"Is the timing prophesied too? If so, it would have been helpful if the seer had mentioned it."

Elliana's eyes danced with that one. "Some things cannot be accomplished without a measure of struggle."

"I promise you, there has been plenty of struggle."

That brought a laugh from her glistening lips.

"Sylvan, are you finished being invisible yet?" Morten bellowed over the cheers and the fae music. "We've a genie to hunt."

"Farewell, my love," Elliana said.

As the words pierced through the darkness, the mist of colors swirled brighter around her and she vanished.

And so did his longing for her.

Holstering his blade and retaking his visible form once more, Sylvan remounted his steed, piecing together the clues they'd received. He didn't yet know what to make of Elliana's riddle, but the information about the maidens with Kate could be helpful. While he himself had red hair, he hadn't seen many in Astonia with the same.

"A redhead shouldn't be too difficult to find."

"Kate's cousin Victoria has auburn locks," Morten said, a satisfied smile spreading. "*And* she's royal."

Their best lead yet. "Shall we pay her a visit?"

"Absolutely. It's been too long since I checked on my relations at Castle Cragmont." Turning his attention back to Vance, Morten said, "If you harbor my dear niece, I'll not be as lenient as last time. It'll be one life for every day she finds shelter with you."

Vance's jaw clenched, but he kept his retort to himself.

As they rode back toward the coach, Morten uttered an incantation under his breath. At its conclusion, Sylvan heard several screams from the gypsy camp. When he glanced back, he saw the old gypsy woman convulsing on the earth.

"That should cement the message," Morten said with a wink.

* * *

Bregovi found his father on the balcony outside the man's study. The view extended to the formal gardens behind the castle, and the king appeared to be lost in the scene.

As Bregovi stepped up next to him, his father nodded in acknowledgment. Since returning to Florian, Bregovi had noticed the monarch's hair had grayed considerably, and his bold frame had taken on a weary stance. The blue eyes remained resolute, however, as he turned them on his son.

"I will not release you from the competition, Edmund. We need this marriage."

"I disagree. I can fund my expeditions by other means. I will sell some of the goods I've brought back and charge passage to royals on our journeys."

"The goods belong to the kingdom and are not yours to sell," his father said, watching Rachel and two maidens in the rose garden. "Charging for passage to increase your purse and reduce Florian's costs is a sound idea, but the funding is not the reason you need to wed."

Rachel glanced up and waved while her companions dipped in eloquent curtsies. The men nodded in return.

"If the kingdom isn't short on funds, why are you forcing the issue? Stephen is the heir, not I, and he married well and has already produced three sons. The monarchy is sound."

"I am not concerned about heirs, I am concerned about the kingdom. Florian needs alliances," his father said, disappearing into the study.

Bregovi followed. "Alliances?" War hadn't touched Astonia in ages and the monarchs were all on good terms. Perhaps the man's memory was faltering. "Our relations with the kingdoms are strong. The remedies I've brought back have ensured that."

"I know your efforts have garnered good will, but we have threats besides illness. There have been attacks in the north and near the western sea. My advisors say the Zafarians are resurfacing."

"Surely you don't believe them."

"I do. As do many others. The majority of those entered in the competition are here without the royals from their kingdoms. The monarchs stayed behind to protect their lands."

Zafarians? In the years Bregovi had spent obsessed with the secret society, he had never found evidence any had survived the last witch hunts. "But Zafaria remains a wasteland, and the last sorcerers were wiped out a century ago."

"The sorcerers may have burned, but the blood of The Ten flows through nearly every family in the kingdoms. Like their brown eyes or copper hair, the tendency toward magik can surface at any time. Unfortunately, all we can do is cull them from the herd once they show themselves."

His father motioned to a map spread over a large table. Red figures dotted areas to the north and west.

"Half the kingdoms have reported incidents. The sorcerers have targeted those with Zafarian artifacts. It is only a matter of time before they strike here."

No time at all if they learned of his collection.

"Marriage alliances will bring armies that will aid us over others," his father said. "For the good of Florian, you need to wed. Rachel too."

If the account was accurate, the Zafarians did pose a lethal threat to many lands, but marriage alliances and larger armies were not the only solutions. Nor the best ones.

"What we need to do is to capture their leader," Bregovi said. "According to legend, an Order Master directs them."

"It is impossible, son. No one knows who the man is. Those who have been caught won't divulge his identity."

"Are they using magik?" Bregovi asked, more intrigued than he dared admit.

"Witnesses report they have been blatant about their abilities, probably trying to instill fear among the people. I know you find sorcery fascinating, but there is no honor in setting a house afire with a word."

"I admit magik interests me, but I have never doubted the Zafarians were dangerous. The fact that they destroyed every living creature in Zafaria demonstrates as much. That is why we need to stop them now. Before they gain in power. I have volumes detailing their history and rituals. Let me try. Let me do this for the kingdom. And if I succeed—when I succeed—let me win my freedom as a reward. Rachel's too."

The king studied the map of the land and then Bregovi. "If pursuing this mad quest will appease you, then you have my consent. But it must not interfere with the festival. You must attend to your duties here."

"I will. Thank you, Father."

"Be careful, son. And be prepared to marry when you do not locate the sorcerer."

Bregovi understood his duty and would do what was required, even if it meant marrying a maiden he had no affinity for. But for the first time in weeks, he had hope of avoiding that duty just yet and of doing something to benefit Florian in the process.

He needed to speak to Wolfe. Bregovi would set him onto the Zafarian immediately after the man located Kate, which he suspected had already occurred if Wolfe was on his game.

At the thought of the maiden, another brilliant idea sprang to mind.

"Father, have the commoner entries been determined?"

"Yes, we decided this morning. The smithy and a barmaid."

"May I suggest another choice?"

"You aren't fancying a servant, are you? We need an alliance with a kingdom, not a commoner."

"Of course not, I merely wish to bestow a favor."

His father studied him for a moment then nodded. "Speak to Randolph."

"Thank you." Bregovi felt like he'd outmaneuvered a wily fox— and he wasn't referring to his father. With Kate entered in the competition, her reclusive days would be history. He needed to find Randolph before the maids cajoled the names from him.

"Son," his father's stern voice halted him near the door.

Bregovi turned, hoping his eagerness to depart hadn't altered the decision.

"Enjoy her," his father said, rolling a red figure in his palm. "Better yet, *bed her.*"

Now, does one agree with one's father about bedding a woman or dive for another topic? *Unquestionably the latter.* As Bregovi grasped for any idea to replace the image of Kate in his bed, the man's unwavering eyes met his.

"Do anything you wish with her, but make certain she does not win."

CHAPTER FIVE

That evening, sitting on the throne next to his father and Rachel in the Grand Hall, Bregovi scanned the throng for Kate and Wolfe. Making his task nearly impossible, the room overflowed with the entire population of Florian as well as an enormous contingent from abroad.

Randolph blew a short horn burst, and the crowd quieted to hear the introduction of the next competitors. Standing stoically at the base of the center staircase, the elderly crier held up a parchment and read with a voice far larger than his stature. "Presenting Sophia Rose Scarcella, Princess of Westmont, escorted by Lord Nicholas Fredrick Gryffin, Earl of Sydmore."

The blond princess wore a silver gown that glittered with every step, and the stately earl looked sharp in a tunic decorated with golden emblems. Smiling to all, they started down the stairs.

"Princess Sophia's kingdom is rich with sapphire. Her interests include the viola, croquet, and of course, gemology. Lord Nicholas's kingdom is home to twenty mineral springs of great medicinal properties. He is a jousting champion, hunts wild game, and is fluent in ancient tongues."

They paused at the bottom of the stairs, nodded toward the

thrones, then gracefully joined their rivals on the dance floor. As did the ensembles of many of the other entrants, Sophia's gown shimmered with a flagrant display of gems. They could feed a small country with the value of the gowns whirling before him. He would wager Kate wouldn't be so frivolous. Her dress in the forest had been simple, but her curves had ornamented it better than any jewel could.

As he remembered the feel of her pressed against him, his pulse quickened yet again. Their duel had been nearly as thrilling. She'd managed the rapier *and him* with skill unheard of for a woman. Where had she learned to wield the weapon? And why? When most maidens were studying an instrument or the arts, she had spent hours sparring with men.

To calm his budding jealousy, he reasoned she must have been taught by a brother or father. If she had been as determined to learn to duel as she was to defeat him in the woods, they hadn't a chance. Hell, he'd consent to instruct her on every weapon in his arsenal to see the sparks in her eyes again. The devilish grin she'd given him when he'd asked if she could use the blade could have set driftwood aflame.

He resumed his perusal of the hall, determined to find her and draw another smile or biting remark. Either would delight.

"How do you feel about being in the same room as your future bride?" Rachel whispered from across their father.

"Claustrophobic," he whispered back.

The king chuckled.

A dancing couple paused before the throne to offer a curtsey and a bow. The royals nodded in return, and the couple continued on.

"How do you feel about being in the same room as your future husband?" Bregovi said.

"My husband?" Rachel quickly glanced around. "Did he write to Father? Has something been arranged?"

"He?" Bregovi said. "Who would write to Father?"

Another couple stopped before the throne, following the example of the first. Once again, they exchanged smiles and nods.

"If no one wrote, how can I be betrothed?"

"You haven't told her?" Bregovi used the disappointed tone his father usually reserved for him. The man's face grew ruddy, but he held his tongue as Rachel glanced between them.

"Told me what?" she asked, her voice rising in pitch and volume.

"I hadn't found the right moment," their father said gruffly.

"I suggest you make this the right moment, before she hears it from Randolph," Bregovi said.

"Papa?" Rachel said, latching onto their father's arm. "Have you made an arrangement for my hand? Please say you have not."

"I have not made an arrangement."

"Oh, thank the gods—"

"At least not with one man."

Her face froze. His father swallowed what Bregovi hoped was guilt. Then Rachel looked his way, her gaze imploring him for an answer.

"Your hand is up for the winning this year as well."

"Mercy, no." Rachel sank into the cushions of her throne. "But there is no time. It has already begun. Why did no one tell me?" She choked on the last word, tears pooling in her eyes.

As Bregovi leaned toward her to assure her he had a plan, Randolph announced the last couple. "Presenting Victoria Millicent Euphrenia Durant, Princess of Cragmont, escorted by Lord Sebastian Elliott Grey of Brandish."

Rachel gasped and glanced up to the pair. Bregovi had noticed Victoria's beauty when she had arrived, but she seemed even more ethereal atop the stairs. The skinny, red-headed nobleman on her arm looked kingly by association. Victoria's eyes caught Bregovi's as she descended to Randolph's recitation. The Brandish lord also gazed their way, a silly grin taking up the whole of his face.

"Princess Victoria's kingdom claims the deepest stone quarry and the largest shipping fleet in Astonia. Her interests include poetry, dancing and historic conquests. Lord Sebastian's kingdom boasts the highest peak in all the land. He is accomplished at archery, sailing, and of course, mountain climbing."

Upon reaching the bottom step, they curtsied and bowed, then took their place among the others.

Before Rachel remembered her plight, Bregovi thought he'd distract her with a turn around the room. It would also allow him to search for Kate from another vantage point.

"Would you honor me with a dance, dear sister?"

"I would be delighted," she said, leaping from her throne.

He was no expert at reading women, but if he had not seen the tears moments earlier, he would assume Rachel was overjoyed with the arrangement. She took his arm as he led her to the edge of the dance floor.

"You appear to have overcome your shock," Bregovi said, whirling her into the throng.

Rachel merely nodded in return, searching for someone among the competitors.

"Have you set your eyes on a groom already?"

"Of course not," she said, her blush indicating otherwise.

He couldn't help but laugh.

"Stop it. You do not know everything."

"I do not know half of everything," he said. "Whatever the cause, I am glad you are more at ease."

"Papa should have told me. This could have turned out horribly."

He wanted to know how she was so certain it wouldn't yet, but did not want to ruin her good spirits. As they crossed the room, Victoria and her partner danced closer, and it occurred to him if anyone knew where Kate was, the lovely princess would.

"Are you ready to pair off and meet some of your suitors? I see a maiden I would much like to talk with."

She followed his gaze and the color in her cheeks deepened. "Yes, I think so."

* * *

As Sebastian led Rachel in the couple's dance, she looked everywhere but at him, grappling for something intelligent to say.

"The musicians are among the finest I have heard," Sebastian said.

"Yes," Rachel said as they spun past the double quartet. "They are in high demand throughout the kingdoms." *Not especially brilliant.*

They took another turn around the floor in aching silence.

"And the weather in Florian is quite temperate," he said.

"Indeed. Spring is my favorite season here."

"I see why."

Spring is my favorite season? Lud, it's everyone's favorite season. A nursery babe has better conversational skills.

They traversed the full length of the room again without utterance. *Will it always be this awkward?* Perhaps he had only been writing to humor her. Not out of genuine fondness. Still, his palm felt sweaty against hers, and he had stumbled more than once as they moved about the floor. Chancing a glance at his face, she caught him concentrating on their course.

He had grown since they had last met. At least a head taller. And his freckles had faded a bit, but not, she was pleased to discover, altogether. He looked boyishly manly, or manly boyish—some combination of the two—and she found it charming. She wondered if his eyes were still as blue. She had seen them so many times in her dreams, she thought her imagination may have embellished, but when he turned to her, she discovered it had not. They were as bright as the morning sky, exactly as she had remembered. He smiled at her, a little lopsided grin. She remembered that too, and some of the awkwardness faded, although not all.

"Why didn't you write to tell me you were coming?" she whispered.

He waited for a couple to pass, then whispered, "Why didn't you write to tell me you are to be matched? Did you not wish me here?"

She sucked in a breath. "No!"

"No, you did not wish me here?" he asked, bumping into a lord and lady twirling past.

"No, of course I wish you here. *Want* you here. I didn't know about my participation until moments ago and was near to despair until I saw you." Heat flooded her cheeks so completely her ears grew hot. Oh, why couldn't she be aloof like Princess Victoria?

"I am glad I eased your worry," he said, and she wondered whether his face was flushed from dancing or the conversation. "I thought you might have invited another of your admirers to compete for you."

Compete for her? The idea caused a shiver of terror. "I invited no one and I fear I am not prepared at all to be a bride. It is all very disconcerting." At his stricken expression she said, "Oh, I am muddling this entirely." She blew a loose lock of hair off her forehead. "It is so much easier speaking with you on parchment."

His warm chuckle, although hushed, brought her attention back to his face.

"I am equally out of sorts," he said, his voice low. "You have grown even lovelier and your nearness has hampered my brain and feet." As if to prove it, he stepped on her toe and collided with another couple. It had the glorious effect of putting her at ease.

"Perhaps we shall have to continue our correspondence," she said, giggling.

"I should like nothing more."

Although they had only met the one time, two years of letters had created a bond of sorts. A familiarity she could not deny. And as he grinned down at her, she hoped he did win the competition, for no one else would ever be as dear to her. He gave her hand a gentle squeeze before stepping on her toe again. As his eyes apologized for the misstep, something sweet and wonderful filled her heart. No, no other would ever be as dear.

* * *

Kate ducked behind a pillar as Bregovi and Victoria drew closer. She had managed to dodge the bandit prince since their arrival and intended to do so until the festival's dying breath—a day that couldn't come quickly enough. She would never have agreed to help Victoria had she realized how many would be in attendance. Of course, if her uncle had ever allowed her to go to a festival, she would have known.

Unfortunately, Victoria held little sympathy about the numbers. Kate couldn't very well tell her that Zafarians might be in their midst, for that would involve admitting she had knowledge of and was fleeing from said Zafarians, and nothing shy of that would convince the princess that Kate was in danger. Her cousin wouldn't even let her skip the ball to stay out of sight, but insisted Kate be there in case she needed something.

While waiting for Victoria and the prince to pass, Kate decided monitoring the princess from a position far behind the crowd would do better. As she glanced about for a more secluded area, she caught sight of Wolfe, Bregovi's blond comrade in the woods. The man was staring straight at her, a wicked grin on his face. Glancing away, he gestured toward her with a tilt of his head.

Taking that as her cue to move, she pushed through the thick crowd in the opposite direction. It was like swimming against the tide.

Just as she found an opening, someone caught her arm.

"Kate."

It was *him*.

"My name is Hildegard," she said, still trying to wrap her tongue around the alias.

"I was told your intimates call you Kate." Bregovi winked.

"Of which you are not." Kate pulled her arm from his grasp and noticed Victoria alone at the edge of the dance floor.

"Join me?" Bregovi said.

"You already have a partner."

As the prince glanced toward Victoria, Wolfe whisked her off among the others.

"She appears to be paired again, and now I am the one without. Come, show me if you can dance as well as you duel."

While she would love to show the man many things she was good at, including some magikal abilities that would land him on his backside, she could not afford to entertain him or herself. Staying out of sight was imperative.

"It would not be appropriate," Kate said.

"Since when do we do what is appropriate?"

Gasps echoed behind her, spreading a blush to Kate's cheeks and anger to her brain.

Determined not to let him make a fool of her twice, she said, "I am sure one or two maidens here would melt at your invitation. I suggest you bestow the honor upon one of them."

"Ah, perhaps you could steer me in the direction of such a maiden. Until then, my invitation stands."

She remembered his similar response in the woods and wished she could erase the knowing smirk from his chiseled face.

If he drew her onto the floor she would stand out in all forms—position (untitled), favor (his), and dress (hers). Perhaps the last would deter him.

"Milord, as you see, my gown is too plain for such an event."

His gaze roamed down her figure, leaving her mutinous skin tingling in its wake.

"On the contrary." He smiled. "Your gown is anything but plain due to the maiden wearing it."

Caught off-guard by the compliment, and before she could voice a third objection, she found herself tugged to the center of the room. Was it all part of his game? Despite his praise, her gown was not nearly as lovely as those worn by the others spinning about the hall. Others who were now darting angry glances her way.

"I looked for you after your arrival," he said, guiding her in the dance.

Her heart hammered as she scanned the room—the onlookers—readying to bolt at any moment. But no one lunged from the crowd to claim her. The gazes she caught held curiosity more than anything else. Perhaps if she showed them what they expected to see, a lady-in-waiting, no one of note, she would survive the dance without anyone realizing who she really was.

"You disappeared," Bregovi said.

"Disappeared? Hardly. I have been helping Princess Victoria prepare for the festival."

"Ah. I was certain you were hiding, leaving me to search everywhere. Desperately. I have been on expeditions less difficult."

"Desperately?" she said, quirking a brow.

"Yes, my conscience would not let me rest until I apologized for the jest."

The twinkle in his eyes told her he was toying with her still. Just one long prank by one spoiled prince with her at the center. Unfortunately for him, a jest could only carry on if the victim stayed the victim, and Kate had never been good at playing that part.

"Oh, there is no need for apologies. Princess Rachel explained about your bandit charades as children," she said. "I'm just sorry I ruined the surprise."

"Yes, well, there is also the other issue." He leaned into her so that his lips hovered over her ear. "The kiss."

His warm breath tickled her neck, distracting her in sensation for a moment. He was good at the whole jest-seduction thing, she'd give him that. But she'd not give him the satisfaction of snaring her again. She cleared her throat and summoned a smile Victoria would have been proud of.

"Kiss? Oh, of course! I had forgotten."

"Forgotten?"

"It was certainly unusual, but nothing spectacular. Perhaps that is what you should apologize for. It is not every day a maiden gets to duel and kiss a *real* bandit. If I had known who you were, I would never have risked it."

"Risked what?" he asked, in a stoic tone.

"Stealing your blade and attacking you. I am truly grateful I didn't harm you in the duel. I would have ended up in the dungeon and you'd be meeting your future bride a wounded man."

For a moment he actually looked injured. As she sought a final remark, a slight bump and a sharp elbow to her back pulled her attention away. A quick glance to her right revealed the sapphire princess whirling off with her partner.

"You could not have harmed me, milady," he said, sounding slightly surly.

"Of course not," she said with a wink. "I'm sure your guardsmen would have protected you."

Her merriment lasted but a moment, for he drew her close, spinning her tightly.

"Dear Kate," he whispered, his lips brushing her ear, "had I wanted to best you in those first few seconds, you would have been helpless. At my mercy. Mine."

Mine. The word hung there, like a musician's last lingering note. He stared at her, as if distracted from his lecture.

It had certainly distracted her from *her* point. Instead, she became keenly aware of the heart beating hard against her breasts. *His* heart. She affected him in some way.

Suddenly, she could not get enough air. And as she concentrated on filling her lungs, she caught his scent again—minty and masculine. It stirred a mesmerizing hunger in her, and her attention shifted to his wicked lips. A slow grin formed before her. She looked up and gazed into the devil's own glinting eyes.

"Perhaps not completely forgotten," he said.

She squirmed in his arms, forcing him to loosen his hold. "Perhaps not when you seem so determined to remind me."

"My intention was not to remind you, but to assure you I did not—"

"I am not some silly maid you need to assure of anything," she snapped. "Let me assure *you*, I am not fantasizing about having your babes, so you have no need to concern yourself."

He studied her for a moment and chuckled. "I was going to assure you I had not intended to let the jest go so far. But discussing your fantasies sounds much more interesting."

Her jaw dropped open, then she snapped it shut. Time for a discrete exit before she said anything else or looked at those lips again.

She pulled away while his mocking dimples taunted her.

"Milord Bandit Bregovi, I fear this matter has occupied too much of your time, and you have others desiring to dance with you. Please excuse me—"

"Your royal highnesses and honored guests," Randolph boomed out. "Please give your ear to the King's choices for this year's special entrants."

As everyone turned toward the man, Kate tried to slip away.

Bregovi gently took hold of her arm. "Not quite yet."

Gracious gods, did he intend to torture her all night?

A hush fell over the hall as the elderly crier raised a parchment. It was a generous custom of many kingdoms to invite a man or woman who did not qualify by title or property to participate with the royals. A commoner was usually chosen and the laypeople loved the idea that one of their own could win the games, even if they rarely did. When Randolph announced the blacksmith Brock White, buxom maids and weathered townspeople cheered. Smiling, the smithy stepped from the crowd—a tall, brawny specimen of a man. He crossed the room proudly and bowed before the king.

The young maidens in the room chattered in excitement before they hushed to hear which one Randolph would name.

"King Thomas Winston Tennerelli of Florian now formally invites…Hildegard Katela Fishbeck of Cragmont to participate in the competition for the hand of Prince Edmund."

Kate glanced around for the lucky maiden before recognizing the name.

"Congratulations, milady," Bregovi said, sounding far too delighted.

"No. It's a mistake," she cried out. "I didn't ask to be entered." But as the words rushed past her lips, she knew she had, by drawing the eye of the man beside her. "You have outdone yourself, your highness. I would have let you find me and conceded the point if it would have prevented yet another prank."

"It's considered an honor," she heard him say as a cloud of angry feelings encompassed her.

Emotions of rage and jealousy flew through her weakened defenses, sinking like daggers into her soul. As a child, she had been just as overwhelmed by the feelings of others, but it had been years since she'd been barraged by such an onslaught.

She closed her eyes and struggled to concentrate on something, anything, that would stop the deluge. Through the thick haze of emotion, she heard an echo of her mother's voice reminding her of what to do.

Trying to slow her breathing, Kate imagined a clear stream of clean energy flowing from the heavens, swirling around and through her, cleansing her, carrying away the unwelcome feelings. And as she imagined the stream emptying into the sea, releasing the emotions to the earth, her heart steadied and slowed.

Taking another long breath, once again feeling only her own fretful emotions, she opened her eyes.

Bregovi stared at her for an uncomfortable moment and extended his arm.

Laying her hand upon it, she let him escort her to the throne, moving past the angry glares of her competitors and the furious looks of the townspeople.

She felt as exposed as a naked woman in the stocks. She had fled to Florian to hide and instead had been thrust on stage before a kingdom. The false name gave her a sliver of protection, but she'd never be able to shrink into the shadows now. And if any of the Zafarians recognized her, they would send word to her uncle.

Alone and powerless, it took all her will to appear calm as they neared the throne. She wasn't sure if she managed to keep her hand from trembling on his arm, but her voice wavered as she said, "May I request you involve another unwitting participant for your next prank? I fear I have taken up too much of your attention of late."

She curtsied before the king.

"My apologies once again, milady."

Was that a hint of regret in his voice? She turned to see his face, but only caught the back of his head as the crowd parted to let him pass.

As Randolph recited the competition events, each one seemed a heavier blow.

Dance. Music. Trivia. Gemology. Poetry. Croquet.

Even if she had been prepared to compete, she did not dare for risk of discovery. And refusing a king's invitation was unheard of.

The only solution was to break her promise to Victoria and run again.

This time with fewer options than when she had fled Cragmont. None actually. As she fought to steady her fears, a hand slipped into hers.

Princess Rachel offered a sympathetic smile. "I thought you could use a friend."

With a squeeze of Rachel's hand, Kate whispered, "Thank you."

As she grappled with what to do next, Randolph continued announcing the men's events. Dancing, jousting, archery, racing, kingdom treaties, and an obstacle course.

"Just as the maiden who wins the most games will be bride to Prince Edmund, he who triumphs in the men's tournament will take Princess Rachel to wife."

Rachel's grip tightened.

"Now for the winners of the Opening Ball's dance event," Randolph said. "King Thomas."

All eyes turned to the king who appeared less than pleased about the job at hand.

"Yes, I suppose this task falls upon me this night. In years past, my lovely Queen Amelia would have chosen. It was her favorite of the games." The king quieted as a hush fell over the hall.

Rachel sniffed next to her, and tears misted the princess's eyes as she moved to her father.

"Papa, may I help you decide?"

As the princess knelt before him in quiet discussion, Kate recalled days long before, when she had knelt before her own father to hear accounts of distant lands. The stories he brought back from his adventures were always better than the trinkets. She had sat mesmerized for hours on tales of mystical places where the animals were as large as carriages and the sun never sets. So much had changed since those days.

King Thomas arose from his throne and took Rachel's hand. "With my dear daughter to guide me as her sweet mother would have, I have selected tonight's winners."

The crowd responded with enthusiastic cries before quieting for the pronouncement.

"The young beauty who displayed grace and skill on the dance floor and who will be rewarded with a seat next to my son at the breakfast banquet—" The king looked around. "Edmund, where is Edmund?"

Bregovi slipped from the crowd and took his place next to his father.

"As I was saying, the winner is Princess Victoria of Cragmont."

As the guests heralded his choice, a dashing count escorted Victoria to the throne where she curtsied before the king and his family. At least the princess had won the first event. Perhaps that would ease her anger after she discovered Kate had left.

"Congratulations, child," King Thomas said. "And for the young nobleman who displayed stately charm and a fine lead according to my daughter..." He winked at Rachel, who turned crimson. "Lord Sebastian of Brandish."

Cheers again rose up from all as Sebastian stepped forward.

"You shall sit next to my Rachel for the morning feast."

Sebastian bowed, stole a glance at Rachel, and stepped back onto Princess Sophia's foot. She squealed, he fumbled with apologies, and Kate slipped out of the hall, determined to flee before anyone noticed she was missing.

Bursting into her bedchamber, Kate scrambled to gather her things—not that she had many. She grabbed her satchel from the bedstand, tossed in her lavender soap, and added a chemise and stockings provided by Victoria. Lastly, she snatched up her cloak, threw it over her shoulders, turned toward the door—and screamed.

CHAPTER SIX

"We have an agreement," Victoria said barely inside the room.

"That was before the whole kingdom saw me." Hugging the satchel to her chest, Kate watched in dismay as Victoria locked the door.

"Who could possibly recognize you?" the princess said, pocketing the key.

"Everyone."

"Did Rachel's guards recognize you?"

"No."

"Anyone on the journey?"

"No, but—"

"Or here in the castle?"

"Not yet," Kate said, a minuscule measure of hope arising.

"Not yet and possibly not ever. You have been sequestered up at the north cove so long, *I* hardly knew you."

Victoria might have pinpointed the one benefit of Lord Morten's controlling nature—Kate's face was unknown to most of the kingdoms. The only ones who could identify her were servants in her village who sympathized with her and a band of clever gypsies who would not betray her.

And, her nervous heart reminded, three dozen high-level Zafarians who would turn on one another for the honor of delivering her to their revered Order Master.

She must leave.

Kate darted into Victoria's room through their adjoining door. Unfortunately, the exit there was equally uncooperative.

Following on Kate's heels, the princess said, "I gave you clothes, an alias, *and* I took you to Florian. I have done my part, now you need to do yours."

"How can I help you win if I am competing? It will be better for you if I leave."

"If you leave, I won't have anyone to aid me. And you needn't worry about the contest. You aren't prepared for the events, so you have no chance of winning. See, you've increased my advantage already. I have one less competitor."

"What about the prince? His interest in me won't aid your cause."

Victoria's jaw twitched. "His interest in you is for sport, nothing more. We can use that to our advantage. You will distract him from pursuing my competitors, and you can gush about my assets at every opportunity."

Brilliant. For Victoria, not Kate.

"I can't risk it. You must see that. If any of Lord Morten's supporters are here, he will find me and I won't be able to tend to anyone." Kate tried the door handle again, this time with more force, but no better result.

Victoria stepped closer. "What you must see is if you desert me, word will likely reach your uncle of how my new lady-in-waiting abandoned me." Victoria's gaze pinned Kate in place.

"You wouldn't do that."

"We're both a bit desperate, Kate."

"When he comes he'll find out you helped me. He'll retaliate."

"*If* he comes, he will think you manipulated me to help you. I do not fear him."

Mighty gods, she should. Victoria had no idea who—what—they were dealing with. Kate was fortunate the gypsies even spoke to her after the curses he'd cast upon them. She sank back on the bed. Trapped.

"If he comes for you, I will help you as I did the first time. Until then you will help me win. Agreed?"

Either help Victoria and hope Morten would not find her, or flee and guarantee he would. No choice at all really.

"Agreed, but if we hear so much as a rumor that I've been discovered or that Morten or his men have entered Florian, you must promise to help me escape, regardless of where events stand in the competition."

"Fine," Victoria said. "I think you're overly paranoid, but you have my word."

If only it was just paranoia.

* * *

As Bregovi swallowed a bit of ale and sized up Rachel's latest dance partner, he felt a familiar slap on the back.

"I see you ran her off again," Wolfe said, raising a goblet in salute.

"I appear to have a talent for it," Bregovi said.

"It's your idiotic jests. Although amusing among friends, they are not the best strategy for winning a maiden's affection."

"The forest prank was intended for Rachel, and tonight I did her a favor. The maidens consider it an honor to be invited to participate."

"From the look on her face, Kate didn't consider it an honor."

That much he knew. Her dismay had pained him, but not enough to let her out of the competition.

"Either way, you know what this means," Wolfe said.

Bregovi nodded. "Madora."

Wolfe grinned and took a long pull from his goblet. "Did you make any progress with your father?"

"Yes." Bregovi motioned for Wolfe to step away from the crowd.

They moved to a spot near the wall where pillars secluded them from others. "I convinced him to release me from the contest if I locate and deliver to him the leader of the Zafarians."

"Zafarians?" Wolfe said. "They're active again?"

"Unfortunately."

"Where is this man?"

"We don't know."

"Who is he?"

"We don't know."

Bregovi watched as realization registered in Wolfe's eyes.

"It will cost you another boon," Wolfe said.

"I expected nothing less."

"This one will be a challenge. The reward must be equally great."

Bregovi waited. He suspected Wolfe enjoyed devising his price nearly as much as locating whatever needed finding.

"We take Angelina on a voyage."

"Around her islands?"

"Anywhere she wants to go."

"Anywhere? What if she chooses the north cap? Or the south?!"

"How badly do you want out of this marriage contest?"

"Fine. But you start tomorrow."

"I start tonight," Wolfe said, grinning. "Any clue where to begin?"

"Father told me sorcerers were spotted in Westmont last week."

"Westmont it is."

"You've heard the legends, so you know to be careful."

"Yes."

"The Zafarians are collecting Order artifacts. Having a few of the objects may help you infiltrate their ranks. Take what you need from my library."

Wolfe nodded. "I'll send word to you through Isabel."

"Good. Once you determine the man's identity and whereabouts, don't try to take him alone. I'll gather the men and we'll go after him together."

* * *

Much later that night, after checking to ensure Victoria was deep asleep, Kate knelt by the hearth in her bedchamber with her satchel and a pitcher of water. As she had done each night since her escape, she pulled out the items needed to renew the spell blocking her Gifts.

She broke off a small piece of blackberry vine and laid it on a clean portion of stone. Next, she added a tiny sprig of dried lavender, a strand of her hair, and a drop of primrose oil. Using a sewing needle to prick her finger, she pressed a drop of blood onto the nest. As she reached for the final ingredient, the bed linens rustled in Victoria's room.

Praying the princess had not awakened, Kate quickly continued, sprinkling a pinch of salt over the top as she whispered the spell and lit the offering with the candle.

"Kate?" Victoria's voice carried in to her. "Are you up?"

Kate's heart pounded as she hurried to finish. If she didn't perform the spell by morning, her powers would be unleashed and Lord Morten would be able to track her. But if the princess caught her using sorcery, she'd face an inquisition.

The goblet shook in Kate's hands as she waited for the flame to turn to blue, indicating the spell had taken. As Victoria's footsteps grew louder, Kate readied the water to complete the ritual.

Please, please, please.

"Kate?" Victoria said again, just as the flame turned and Kate doused it out.

The princess appeared in the doorway between their rooms as Kate shoved the spent remains into the ashes in the hearth.

"What are you doing?" Victoria asked, her hair wild and her chemise in disarray. "It smells smoky in here."

Kate glanced at the dwindling embers. "I was trying to stir the fire."

Victoria took a long look at the hearth. "It's nearly dead."

"So it appears," Kate said, rising. "I'm sorry if I woke you. Do you need something?"

"No, but you do," Victoria said resolutely. "I have thought more about your predicament and have the perfect solution."

"Does it involve a horse and a sack of coins?"

"We are going to find you a husband."

"A husband?" Kate gulped.

"Once you marry, Lord Morten won't have any claim over you. A husband trumps an uncle."

Unfortunately, a genie master trumped a husband, and an Order Master trumped both.

"There are plenty of men on the hunt for a wife. I am sure we can convince one to take you."

Her pride balked at *convince*, but it didn't matter. Marriage was too much of a risk unless she wedded someone who could disappear into the woodwork. Or the woods. Like a hermit. She doubted Victoria would arrange such a match.

"I am not going to marry."

"Nonsense. You can't work as a servant the rest of your days."

A princess like Victoria could never understand, but Kate's plan was to do exactly that. She had the education necessary to become a governess, but she had also spent the past year persuading discrete townspeople to teach her to sew and cook and do all manner of tasks given to household staff.

"I am fine being a servant if it will keep me safe." Kate stashed the satchel by her bed.

"It won't. It will simply keep you poor. You need a husband and this festival is the perfect place to find one for you."

"Victoria—"

"There is no need to thank me. I have already set my mind to it. There were some widowers at the ball who do not need the dowry. I will make inquiries tomorrow."

"Please, that isn't necessary."

"Unfortunately, it is. We need to get moving on it before the good ones are snatched up." As Kate watched her disappear back into her lair, the princess called back. "You will see, by the end of the festival, I will have you matched!"

Matched? Matched! Was she cursed?

* * *

The next morning, as Kate helped Victoria prepare for breakfast with the prince, Holly, a blond, curly-haired maid, arrived with an arrangement of congratulatory pink roses. Delighted with the flowers and wishing to win further goodwill from the monarchy, Victoria sent Kate back with Holly. Her mission, to deliver a message of thanks to Rachel and to offer any assistance the princess might need.

Kate trailed Holly through a maze of hallways while the castle buzzed with activity—royal guests, attendants and servants all with some purpose at hand.

"Aren't you just thrilled, miss, at being entered?" Holly asked.

Mortified was a more apt description.

"I hadn't expected it," Kate offered.

"Don't let no one tell you commoners don't win," the girl said as they continued through another labyrinth of corridors. "Mia, the baker's daughter, won two festivals ago." Holly looked back either to emphasize the point or to make sure she hadn't lost her charge. "But a prince wasn't up that year. She won a dairy cow. Her family couldn't speak for joy."

Kate couldn't imagine Victoria being anything resembling joyful with a dairy cow.

"Her pa wanted to keep it when she married the tanner's son, but she won out in the end and he gave it as part of her dowry."

"How fortunate for them."

"Mighty fortunate." They passed through a circular room and took the corridor to the right. "No one can believe Prince Edmund agreed to the contest this year."

"Oh?" Kate dodged a maid with a heavy pitcher.

"No, a princess refused him many years back and he's not loved a woman since."

"That's surprising." The man's kiss wasn't that of a monk.

"'Tis true. But now he's finally to have a bride. Who knows, maybe it'll be you."

Unless the stars and demons aligned in the most unfortunate of ways, his bride would certainly *not* be her.

"I thank you for the encouragement, but it's doubtful I'll win any of the events. He has a dozen royal maidens battling for the honor."

"Even so, I'll be cheering for you," Holly said as they turned down a long wood-paneled hall. They passed heavy oak doors engraved with vines and stopped in front of one outlined in carved rosebuds overlaid with gold. The maid knocked, paused briefly and opened the door for Kate.

The room was far more beautiful than the chambers she and Victoria occupied. The windows curved in a semi-circle, showering in the morning light, and furniture made of all sorts of woods carried on the rose theme, as did several vases of fresh violets. A bed sat to one side, its brocade canopy embroidered with white roses, which is where Kate discovered the princess and a petite maid sifting through a mound of gowns.

"Your highness, Princess Victoria asked me to deliver Miss Hildegard to you," Holly said.

When Rachel looked up, Kate said, "Victoria sends her thanks for the flowers and offers my assistance if you have need of me."

"You must return my thanks to her, because I do have need," Rachel said, desperation in her eyes. "Lydia hasn't arrived from Cragmont yet and I can't decide which would be best."

It's the same all over the castle. Maidens and their finery.

"Flora," Rachel said to the maid at her side, "you and Holly may see to your other duties."

"Yes, your highness," they said with matching curtsies before slipping out.

77

"The gowns are all splendid," Kate said, inspecting the choices. The vibrant colors and silky fabric were even more luxurious than Victoria's collection, and hers was extensive.

"It shouldn't be formal for morning, should it? The mulberry fits well, but I fear it's too dark, and I love the lime, but the decorations are green today and I don't want to look like a table covering."

Kate laughed. "I don't think anyone would mistake you for a table covering. You're lovelier by far."

Rachel grinned. "These decisions are just so important and Mother always helped me."

"It must be difficult to go through this without her," Kate said, lifting a pale yellow gown off the bed.

"I miss her terribly." Rachel glanced at Kate. "It's been nearly two years, but feels much shorter. And longer."

"I understand. I remember moments with my parents as if they happened hours ago." Yet it seemed like she'd lived another lifetime since she last saw them.

"How old were you when you lost them?"

"They were both gone by the time I was twelve."

"I'm sorry. Is that when your *mysterious* uncle became your guardian?"

"Yes," Kate said. "Truly, he's not a kind man, your highness. If he catches word I'm here, he'll cause terrible problems—"

"Please call me Rachel. And you needn't worry, I won't speak of it again."

"Thank you."

"I may not have a scary uncle, but I do know something about secrets."

"Now, that sounds mysterious."

"It isn't." Rachel stared at the mound of dresses on her bed. "But I'm still not sharing." She added a wink, and Kate couldn't help but grin back.

"Very well."

A bit of periwinkle fabric peeked from under the stack, and Kate pulled it from the pile. "This one would look striking on you."

"That's the one I started with," Rachel said with a sigh. "It's one of my favorites."

Kate helped her to put it on. As was the style among the wealthy, the bodice hugged Rachel's figure with side ties, and the sleeves hung open at the elbow and dipped to the floor.

"I don't know how you pick favorites, they're all exquisite."

"I have many more. Mother had scores and they're all mine now." Rachel flipped through the gowns. "You're slightly taller than I am, but I think they will fit you as well. Why don't you select one to wear to the breakfast?"

"Thank you, but I'm not attending the banquet."

Rachel looked up. "But you must."

"No one wants to see me there, especially the other maidens in the competition. I'm more than happy to oblige them."

"I want you there, and I'm sure Victoria will want you there. And since you are going, you must wear one of my gowns. This one will look lovely on you." Rachel held up a lavender gown as fine as any Kate had seen at the ball.

Kate resisted and Rachel persisted. In the end, Kate tried it on.

She'd never worn anything so beautiful in her life.

Kate couldn't help but run her fingers over the smooth cloth as Rachel adjusted the ties on each side. The scooped neckline was trimmed in ruffled silk the color of cream, and the open sleeves, which dipped to the floor like Rachel's, were lined with the same.

"It's a good color for you. Come. Look."

The princess led her to a looking glass, beaming proudly as Kate took it in. The fabric lay perfectly over her slender frame, and Rachel was right, the color contrasted well with her hair and even brightened her gray eyes.

"Edmund will be speechless."

"Speechless would be wonderful, but I'd prefer not to draw any more of his attention. It always ends badly."

"Should I scold him again?" Rachel asked, her face stern.

Kate choked back laughter. "Again?"

Rachel nodded. "He was quite wrong in not revealing himself to you in the forest. I told him he should apologize."

Kate could hardly believe the petite princess had lectured her older, larger, princely brother.

"Did he apologize?"

Remembering his attempt on the dance floor, Kate said, "Somewhat."

"Good," Rachel said.

"Then he had me entered in the competition."

"Yes, well, that wasn't his best idea, but I don't believe he meant harm. Most are thrilled with the honor."

Yet one more way Kate was different.

"I wish he would have extended the opportunity to another, more deserving maiden. Just as there are others more deserving of this gown. It's far too lovely. I'm afraid I cannot—"

"It is yours."

Kate's breath caught. The dress was worth more than her entire wardrobe in Cragmont. "You are much too kind, I really cannot—"

"Of course you can." Rachel dismissed her protest with a wave.

Kate began to object again when someone rapped solidly on the door.

Rachel called out, "Come," and the door opened before the word had settled.

"Ready to meet your suitors?" Bregovi playfully asked.

Blessed gods, was the man everywhere?

"Edmund. Yes, I'm quite ready, but Kate isn't."

Bregovi glanced her way and halted. As Rachel predicted, the man was speechless at the sight of her. But Kate suspected that was because his brain was devising his next prank.

Unfortunately, she had no such excuse. At the sight of him, words escaped her as well and, in troubling fashion, her eyes seemed fixated on his fitted brown tunic.

As his gaze roamed over her dress, her heart forgot a beat, snapping her back to reality. It was as if she had been cursed by a spell rendering a maiden's brains to mush. Perhaps the sword was tainted or his lips bewitched.

"I've given her the gown, but she won't have it," Rachel said. "I think it's lovely on her. How do you think she looks?"

"Stunning," he said.

Stunning. No one had ever described her as stunning. The majority of the population had honey blond locks, and Kate's dark hair and strange eyes made her stand out in an unfortunate way. She'd been called *gypsy daughter* so many times, it was no wonder she felt at home with the wanderers. While they weren't her people, they understood her. Bregovi clearly did not and only sought another way to torment.

"An ox would look stunning in this dress," Kate said.

"I don't think it would fit an ox the way it does you," he said, his gaze openly dancing over her figure.

Kate's blood warmed unpleasantly.

"Edmund." Rachel waited until he looked at her. "You must stop teasing Kate. She doesn't like it, and it isn't aiding my cause."

"And what is your cause, dear sister?"

"To persuade her to wear the gown."

He nodded with great seriousness, then turned and studied Kate's attire. *Again.*

"If I'm not mistaken, she's already wearing it," he said, his eyes lingering on her bosom. "Perhaps my role should be to lead her out the door."

"I do not need an escort or a gown so fine. I'll wear mine." Kate lifted her dress from the bed. It looked like a rag in comparison.

"If you insist," Bregovi made himself comfortable in a heavy oak chair. "I'll wait right here."

"Oh Edmund, you are no help at all," Rachel said.

As Kate noticed the room lacked a changing screen of any sort, she let out an exasperated breath.

"On the contrary. I think I've helped quite a bit."

In frustration, Kate tossed her dress back on Rachel's bed.

"Wonderful," Rachel cried.

"Come," Bregovi said, hopping from the chair. "Now is the time for graceful acceptance and a delicious meal." He smiled, taunting her further with his annoying dimples.

"Your highness." Kate curtsied to Bregovi. "While I will gracefully accept this gown and look forward to a delicious meal, I refuse to be subject to any more of your pranks. Maidens are not yours to toy with as you wish, and I suggest you learn to amuse yourself in a manner that doesn't involve other people. Especially me."

With his right brow quirked and his grin broadening, she fled the room and started down the passage before he formulated a retort. She took a turn to the right, then wove around a wood-paneled corridor to the left, went up some stairs, then down, and found herself facing a circular room with three corridors forking off of it. Choosing the one in the middle, she crossed another and followed the passage as it curved around to bring her to the same circular room once again.

As she weighed her choices, a hand firmly gripped her elbow from behind.

CHAPTER SEVEN

"If I promise not to be amused, will you allow me to show you the way?" Bregovi whispered in her ear.

His breath tickled her neck, sending a vexing sensation to her toes.

"You followed me," she said, more accusation than question.

"Rachel wanted to make sure the gown made it to the feast," he teased. "I know you would have found it eventually, but I didn't want you to miss this afternoon's joust."

"I believe my instructions were to apologize for driving her off," Rachel said from behind him.

"Ah, so you've caught me. I'm the one who was concerned for your welfare," Bregovi said, holding a hand over his heart.

"The apology," Rachel prompted.

"My dear sister, I apologize with all sincerity for driving your breathtaking companion from your presence."

Warmth spread to Kate's cheeks. She wished she really could take his breath away. And his speech.

"Edmund," Rachel said in a tone she must have picked up from a governess. "Kate's apology." To emphasize her point, she even shook a finger at him.

Kate bit back laughter.

Bregovi didn't bite back anything, as a rumbling laugh burst from him. He took Rachel's hand and kissed the top of it.

"Kate's apology will flow from my lips in a more private moment," he said with a wink at Kate.

Oh, no, it would not. "I'll forgo the apology if it includes forgoing the private moment."

"But you should never have to forgo anything," Bregovi whispered, sending an unpleasant tingle up her back. "Beginning with the banquet."

Those green eyes bore into hers, and she realized the banquet would be the safest place to be, at least when it came to Bregovi. The sooner they got there, the sooner she could slip away among the others.

"Shall we be on our way then?" she said brightly.

He grinned at her a moment longer than she'd have liked, then tucked her hand at his elbow and led her through the corridor to their right. Rachel followed.

"I *would* have found it," Kate said.

He only chuckled as they passed by a stateroom and a gallery, then moved through the king's study and sitting room. He announced each as they passed or entered.

Stepping through the armory, Kate took in the arsenal on display and memories of her uncle's familiar weapons chamber surfaced.

She didn't realize she was clutching Bregovi's arm until he patted her hand and said, "We rarely use these, but the sight intimidates our enemies."

"I don't doubt it," she said.

"This is my least favorite room," Rachel said. "It's eerie."

As they continued on, passing through a billiard room and another called the swan room with no discernable purpose, she realized the prince was toying with her once more.

"Princess Rachel, is this the route you usually take to the banquet hall?"

"It's a shortcut," Bregovi said.

"How could it be shorter? We're meandering all over the castle."

"It's a scenic cut," he said. "Much better than a series of long corridors."

"You can't seem to resist provoking me, can you?"

He chuckled. "Music Hall, milady."

As Kate glanced about the room, a tall instrument on the far wall caught her eye.

"You have a harp," she cried. It had occurred to her that blending in during the games—neither doing too well, nor too poorly—would give her the best chance at going undiscovered. The harp provided that opportunity for the first event. On any other instrument she'd be laughed out of the hall.

"Do you play?" Rachel asked.

"I did years ago. May I use yours for the competition?"

"Of course," the royal siblings said as one.

She'd find her way back later to practice. After several more halls, two sets of stairs and a textile gallery, Kate said, "We must be nearly there, for I can't imagine you've left any rooms out of the tour, save the dungeon and your bedchamber."

"My bedchamber?" Bregovi said. "Is that a request?"

"Absolutely not."

"A complaint then. My apologies. Unfortunately, we will have to rectify that another time," he said, guiding her into the very full banquet hall.

Whispers spread among the occupants as all eyes turned to them.

"Thank you for the escort, your highness," Kate said, releasing his arm. Not waiting for his reply, she hurried toward the end of the banquet table. Unfortunately, Rachel caught her before she'd reached safety.

"You cannot run off now. You must dine at the head table," the princess said. "It will compensate for some of my brother's pranks."

Her brother's pranks seemed to be sprouting offspring.

"Of course," Kate said, with a sigh.

"Oh, don't fret. I won't force you to sit next to him."

She followed Rachel to the head of the table, where the princess kept her word, placing Kate between Lord Sebastian and Brock, the handsome blacksmith. While Rachel was distracted with the nobleman, the smithy proved to be an entertaining companion for Kate. He was even more handsome up close and kept whispering witty observations about their rivals in her ear.

As the meal stretched on, she realized that for the first time in a long while she felt beautiful, desirable and happy. For a few short moments she even allowed herself to imagine what her life would have been like had her parents lived.

As Lady Katherine Durant, she would have attended balls and banquets. She would have entertained royalty from all the kingdoms. She would have participated in festivals if she wished to, not as part of foolish jests. And she would *not* have been on the run from sorcerers or avoiding a troublesome prince. Or if she had been trying to avoid such a prince, she would have had the family backing and the power to deter him.

* * *

Of course, family backing and power were moot if the gods had other plans, and Kate was beginning to think the latter were finding particular amusement with her plight.

While trumpets sounded loudly and spectators crammed the stands overlooking the jousting field, she hurried behind Rachel into the royal box where Bregovi took up half a plush bench on the front row.

Scanning the seats, Kate looked for a place as far from him as possible. There wasn't an extra chair to be had. Maidens fanned out three tiers deep behind him, with a few more on each side. Sophia, the sapphire heiress, had managed to procure the spot to his immediate right, and Victoria sat to her right.

"Oh, dear. We should have arrived sooner, " Rachel said. "It appears all the maidens in the kingdom have joined you today. Can we bring in another chair, for Kate?"

"Oh, no, don't trouble anyone. I'll find a place in the stands." Kate had no qualms about watching with the masses and was sure she would enjoy the event more without Bregovi nearby tormenting her.

"No, it's my fault we're late and I'll feel horrible if you have to sit with strangers." Rachel surveyed the bench again. "It will have to do. We can all sit here."

"What?" Kate cried.

"Yes, this will work beautifully. Edmund will sit on that side, Kate in the middle, and I'll sit to the right."

Kate's stomach dove for the dirt. She had wished to see Bregovi as little as possible, and Rachel was practically putting her in his lap.

"It'll be awfully tight, Rachel," Bregovi said. "Kate may not be comfortable with that."

Definitely not comfortable with that.

"The stands are just as crowded and this way she can sit with us." Rachel got that stubborn look on her face—the same one Kate had witnessed earlier when the princess insisted she wear the gown.

"I fear we shall not win this battle," Bregovi said.

Kate glanced up and caught him watching her, heat simmering in his eyes. Her wicked mind immediately called up a memory of lips and hands and, worse yet, *sensations.*

Bregovi motioned toward the cozy accommodations. "Ladies?"

Rachel happily took her place while Kate hesitated.

"What are you thinking, fair Kate?" he asked.

"That I can't seem to escape you."

He chuckled and took his seat, throwing his arm across the back of the bench as if it had been his plan all along.

As Kate reluctantly squeezed between the royal siblings, she ordered her body not to react to the very solid man pressed tightly against her right shoulder, hip and thigh.

It blatantly ignored her demand.

Trying another tactic, she directed her mind to dwell upon the appalling pranks he instigated, rather than the unwelcome sensations he stirred. Finally, after intense concentration, irritation replaced desire. Her spirits soared in triumph and no small measure of relief, but then Bregovi turned.

With his lips hovering at her ear and his knee nudging hers, the bewitching bandit sent ripples of heat through her with one soft whisper.

"Perhaps you should just let me catch you."

* * *

Somewhere off in the distance, Bregovi heard Randolph announce the jousting event. A round against the quintain. Followed immediately by a round at the hanging rings. Further rounds would break any ties. And all he could think about was the round curve of Kate's hip pressed against his.

He couldn't remember the last time he'd been so pleased with one of Rachel's suggestions. The look on Kate's face alone merited a new string of pearls for his sister.

Kate squirmed next to him, no doubt attempting to scoot away. But he had no intention of cooperating. Each time she eased her knee off his leg, he couldn't resist sliding the latter closer to hers.

While he found her plight intensely amusing, her frustrated huff told him he needed to distract her before she bolted.

"Now that we've satisfied decorum—" he began.

"Satisfied?" Kate said with an unladylike snort. "Decorum is mortified."

"Very well, now that we've mortified decorum, I believe we should move on to other pleasantries."

Her gray eyes quickly found his, one lovely eyebrow quirked up.

"Polite conversation," he said, in case she wasn't familiar with the order of things.

"Polite with a teasing undercurrent?" Kate said.

"If you wish." He winked, thinking of all the polite things he'd like to whisper in her ear.

Her cheeks turned the color of a tropical sunset as she looked away, muttering something unintelligible.

"What was that?" he asked.

"Aren't we here to watch the joust?" she asked, gesturing toward the field.

"Ah, yes," he said taking note of the first rider—a lanky duke in green.

The man positioned his steed and lance for his run at the quintain.

"You know, this is my favorite event."

"Truly?" Princess Sophia asked. "I couldn't help but overhear and would love to learn what you enjoy most about it."

Others echoed the request.

"Would you like to know why as well, Kate?"

"Of course," she said with batting eyelashes and a honey-sweet tone. "Please pontificate."

He couldn't help but grin and mentally added a ruby to Rachel's reward. "As you wish." Clearing his throat dramatically, he raised his voice so his audience could hear. "To start, each challenger tests his skill at the quintain, as this duke is preparing to do. The only way to pass it safely is to accurately hit the shield on the wooden figure." He gestured to said figure on the course. "Kate, would you like to share what happens when the rider misses the mark?"

"They wish to hear you speak, your magnificence, not me."

A maiden to his right coughed loudly. After which Kate said, "Perhaps Princess Victoria would care to provide the answer."

He glanced to his right.

With a smile, Victoria said, "Missing the mark causes the counter arm to swing around and knock the challenger off his horse."

"Correct. Thank you, Princess Victoria," Bregovi said. "It's a worthy challenge for knight and nobleman alike, and I expect a few young rivals will lose their seats this afternoon."

"Has the quintain ever knocked you off your horse, your highness?" a feminine voice asked behind him.

"What do you think?" he whispered to Kate.

"I dearly hope to all the gods it has," Kate said.

"I'm always delighted to fulfill your dearest hopes." He nudged her knee again, then said to all, "Yes, I've lost my seat a time or two."

"A time or two?" Rachel said. "I witnessed at least three when I was eight."

"That's hardly old enough to remember clearly," Bregovi said.

"You were besotted with a dark-haired maiden," Rachel said.

"She was a redhead."

"Perhaps there were two," Rachel said.

Images of both a brunette and a redhead came to mind, and he realized he'd forgotten about both. Later that festival he'd met Camilla and that had been the end of any infatuation with the others.

"If I recall correctly, his trousers didn't survive the third landing," Rachel said as giggles and gasps echoed around them. "It didn't bother Edmund, but I laughed until I had a stitch in my side," Rachel said with a giggle of her own.

He had played off the fall well at the time, but it had more than bothered him. He had dedicated the three months following the tournament to mastering the task. Since then the quintain had rarely bested him.

Kate turned, beaming. "I so wish I could have seen it, your eminence," she said, her voice thick with enthusiasm. She gasped and continued, batting her eyelashes ridiculously. "Might you re-enact the wondrous scene for us today? It's my dearest hope."

Laughter burst from him and a tiny grin hinted at her lips, leading him to believe the maiden was enjoying herself despite her discomfort. The small sign spread warmth through him like a heady pint of ale.

"What matters at present is which of Rachel's suitors will keep *his* seat," he said gesturing toward the field and the first rider.

On cue, the duke rode hard and straight, marking the wooden figure well and continuing past in safety. Cheers cried out as he raised his lance in acknowledgment, then all hushed as he readied himself for the rings.

Again the man charged forward, expertly catching the first cable-suspended ring. Unfortunately, his lance lowered a fraction as he approached the second. He was close enough to send it swinging wildly, but didn't capture it. Possibly distracted by the error, he missed the third entirely. Three points for the quintain and two for the ring. A fair showing, but Bregovi suspected one or two would do better.

"Which do you enjoy more, your grace? The quintain or the rings?" Princess Sophia asked.

"The rings," he said. "Riding at the dummy takes skill, but the target is stationary and one only has to keep steed and lance steady. With the rings, a rider not only has to control mount and weapon, but adjust quickly if even a slight breeze sets the rings in motion."

"How many riders can capture all three?" Sophia asked.

"Usually one manages it if the day isn't blustery," he said.

Next up was Alden, a portly earl. He started off well, but lost his grip on the lance halfway to the wooden target. As he struggled to correct, the horse veered off course. He hit the quintain off mark, but due to his wayward ride was able to avoid the punishing arm when it swung around. The crowd went wild. Although he had not scored, the earl appeared delighted with maintaining his seat.

Alden again took position and began his run at the rings. He snagged the first, then the second, and just when it looked like he had the third, a breeze sent it swirling and he missed. Four points.

As Kate clapped for the earl, Bregovi's senses reeled. Every time she moved, a whisper of lavender teased the air *and him*.

The tournament continued in that same pattern. A scrawny or

gallant or portly contender giving it his all and Kate cheering them on, pressed against him, smelling tantalizing.

As Lord Sebastian readied himself, Rachel whispered something to Kate before standing to extend her handkerchief over the rail.

When the man rode over and took the lucky token from Rachel, her face turned a pale pink and Sebastian's went crimson. Sebastian dipped his head and trotted back, tucking the handkerchief in his sleeve. All seemed well until he turned to take his starting position.

The young suitor's face had turned as pale as sand. Rachel had just cost her favorite the event.

Charging his mount forward, Sebastian took aim and hit the figure slightly left of mark. The unforgiving quintain whipped around in an instant, slamming him off his horse.

The lord crashed to the ground still clinging to the lance.

Rachel and Kate cried out, as did most everyone present. The nobleman dusted himself off and trudged toward his horse.

Pull it together, Bregovi willed the young lord.

CHAPTER EIGHT

"Does it hurt?" Kate whispered. Bregovi turned and she looked up at him, soft eyes heavy with worry. "Does that thing hurt when it slams into you like that?"

"It isn't pleasant, but the only thing it'll injure is his pride."

She turned her attention back to Sebastian, but she held Bregovi's. She had scoffed when he'd told her she looked stunning, but she truly was. Rich dark hair, fair skin, a delicate nose, misty gray eyes he could get lost in, and rosy lips he'd like to get reacquainted with. As she'd looked over at him time after time, he repeatedly fought the urge to taste them again. Right there. In front of everyone.

Imagine her reaction. A slap. Or a fiery rebuke.

He realized either would be nearly as fun as the kiss and chuckled at the thought.

When a collective groan echoed from the stands, he quickly ascertained Sebastian had missed every ring.

"Laughter is unkind, milord," Kate said. "It is not amusing."

"I laugh at my own folly, not his."

Her gaze bore into his.

"You shall find only truth in my eyes. But look as long as you like. I'm enjoying the view."

She blushed and opened her mouth to speak as gasps echoed around them. Both turned to the field to discover Brock positioning himself for the quintain. The smithy was outfitted in chain mail head to steed.

"Now that's stunning," Kate said, and in one moment all the heat she had stirred up turned to ice.

Brock charged the figure and struck a perfect blow. The crowd cheered and all the maidens jumped up. At the rings, the smithy caught the first and the second, but fortunately sent the last flying rather than capturing it on his lance.

Brock and Lord Preston had tied with seven points each. Another round yielded another tie. The crowd cheered louder, and Kate seemed awestruck by the chain mail show off.

To Bregovi's grave disappointment, the last run proved to be the undoing of Brock's rival. Much too full of himself, Preston waved to the crowd on his way to the quintain and misjudged the mark. He slammed to the ground, landing on his back, legs splayed. On his final pass, he only managed to snare one ring.

The blacksmith needed only the figure to win.

Brock nodded to their box. Rachel and Kate waved back.

"Oh, mighty gods, just ride," Bregovi muttered.

And he did. To the screams of all but Bregovi, the smithy nailed the quintain, caught another two rings, and would have had the third had it not spun off the tip of his spear.

"He truly is amazing," Kate whispered to Rachel.

* * *

The rear view of Bregovi as he rushed from the booth was a most welcome sight. Not for the picture of his form, becoming as it was, but because Kate could breathe again. Perhaps now that he had gone, her heart would set course on a steady rhythm—something it had been reluctant to do for much of the joust. Taunting him had been a new high point of the day and she didn't need high points to include this or any other prince.

A roar from the crowd drew Kate's attention to the field.

As she strained to see what had caused the cry, men scrambled to reset the rings. Then she saw him. Tall, masculine and magnificent. Bareback on a stallion as black as night, Bregovi looked as keyed up for battle as the horse did.

Brock offered his lance. Bregovi rode by without a word. Without as much as a nod. *Brock*. He had won the hearts of all, including the maidens in their box. Was Bregovi so prideful a blacksmith couldn't be admired?

A lord handed a lance to the prince and the crowd hushed in anticipation. Bregovi gave a quick command to the steed, followed by a slight kick, and they were off, barreling toward the target.

With a graceful deftness unlike the others, he struck the wooden figure perfectly, sailed past, then turned without halting and rode hard at the rings. One, two, three. He captured them all.

The place erupted, crowd roaring, all on their feet. Including Kate. Pride or not, he had done what no one else had. The maidens in their box chattered in awe about the dashing prince and his magnificent ride.

Mission accomplished.

Bregovi faced his mount to the stands, raising the lance and the three rings. The masses cheered louder.

He then turned toward the royal box and locked eyes with Kate.

All the air whooshed out of her lungs. He held her gaze. Determined. Intense. Her heart ricocheted off her ribs, forgetting all about steady rhythms.

He nodded to her, turned this steed toward the end of the field and only looked away when he charged off.

Kate turned to Rachel to confirm she hadn't imagined it, but didn't need to ask. The angry glares from the maidens around them said it all.

After Randolph pronounced Brock the winner of the event and

recipient of a chaperoned garden walk with the young princess, a posse of royal maidens followed Kate and Rachel onto the field where riders milled about commiserating.

Kate glanced around for Bregovi and was relieved to find he had disappeared.

The smithy had not. Surrounded by a harem of village girls clamoring for his attention, the chain mail god charmed with the same ease he'd shown with the lance. Bestowing a dazzling smile here, kissing a hand there, he set them abuzz with giggles and excited chatter.

"Well done," Rachel said as they neared.

"Congratulations, you're a wonderful rider," Kate said.

"Thank you, milady. I did my best." Brock nodded over her shoulder. "I know others tried their best as well."

They turned to find Sebastian approaching, looking slightly ill. With a bow, the lord held out Rachel's handkerchief. "Thank you for the honor."

More than a few maidens snickered as the princess quietly took the token.

"Many a good man has lost a match distracted by a pair of fine eyes," Brock said. "And having a sweet bit of lace teasing him with her scent could undermine the finest rider."

Sebastian flushed.

"Oh, but," Rachel stammered. "It was for luck." She took a quick whiff of the cloth and dropped her hand to her side. "I only meant it for luck."

"I shall do my best not to disappoint you in the next event," Sebastian said.

"Disappoint?" Brock boomed. "Man, we do not talk of disappointment. We talk of winning the battle. Conquering the tyrant. Slaying the dragon."

"Dragons are extinct," Rachel said with a giggle.

"There are always dragons, your highness," Brock said. "Just different sorts."

So true.

* * *

Kate spent the remainder of the afternoon and evening doing the princess's bidding—selecting and airing out Victoria's gown for the next day, polishing the viola the princess would play for the competition in the morning, and listening to her rehearse.

Victoria had decided they needed to forego the evening banquet to properly prepare for the day to come, but Kate suspected the princess also wanted to keep Kate away from Bregovi.

It wasn't until Victoria emerged from her bath that her cousin finally spoke her mind.

"Interesting day, wasn't it?" Victoria said as Kate helped her on with a fresh chemise.

"How do you mean?" Kate replied, unsure which moment Victoria referred to. The exquisite gown. Nearly sitting in Bregovi's lap. The prince's ride *and unnerving gaze* at the joust. All had been on Kate's mind, but she wasn't eager to discuss any of them. "Brock was impressive," Kate said.

"I was thinking of Prince Edmund."

"Prince Edmund?" Kate said, keeping her voice light. "What of him?"

"You should take care with him."

"I hadn't planned on doing anything with him." Kate gathered the wet bath linens.

"Perhaps, but he may have plans for you."

"I haven't encouraged him."

"That kiss in the woods may have been enough."

Kate snuffed out a few extra candles in Victoria's room, searching for the words to end the conversation. Thanks to Victoria, the memory of the kiss sent warmth to her cheeks despite herself.

"Don't let him toy with you, Kate."

"No one toys with me." Yet he had, hadn't he?

"After the banquet this morning, I mentioned you to a baron and lesser lord. Both thought you were Prince Edmund's mistress—or soon to be," Victoria said in an accusatory tone.

"You know I'm not," Kate said.

"I assured each that wasn't the case, but they didn't want to stake a claim if you were drawing Edmund's favor."

"But I'm—"

"And after the joust...now *everyone* thinks you're drawing his favor."

Kate struggled to formulate a response that wouldn't throw timber on the fire. "No one is more alarmed by that than I am." And wasn't that the truth? She couldn't have him, yet she couldn't deny that a part of her soul she hadn't known existed had started to come alive with him. He made her feel desirable. Worse, he made her desire.

"It's understandable if you like him," Victoria said. "He has good hair, good teeth, a title and he can be quite charming."

"Good teeth?"

"Unfortunately, his notice of you puts us in an awkward place." Victoria patted Kate's arm. "To avoid uncomfortable questions from suitors, I think we should worry about your prospects after we ensure I win at the games. By then, I'll be in a better position to help you."

"You may be right—"

"Of course I'm right," Victoria said. "It would have been better to make a match during the games, but you muddled up the plan. Now you'll have to make do with whoever is left."

Somehow, Victoria's tone made it sound as if *she* would have to make do as well.

A short while later, after the princess dismissed her, Kate returned to her adjoining bedchamber in her chemise. The princess had insisted on hanging the lavender gown among her own so it wouldn't wrinkle, and Kate hoped it wouldn't disappear into Victoria's collection.

After shutting the door separating their rooms, Kate tested the water in the tub. Still warm! When Victoria had ordered that the bath be brought to Kate's room so it wouldn't clutter her own, Kate had gladly agreed, hoping for this very opportunity.

Quickly pinning her hair atop her head, Kate slipped off the shift and sank into the tub to ease the day away. The combination of warm water and lilac scent had her resting her head and her eyes.

Her mind wasn't so cooperative, taunting her with images of the joust. Touching the prince had been intoxicating, but so was the heat in his eyes. And his display on the field, and his determined look at its conclusion, had unusual parts of her in knots.

Perhaps Victoria was right. Perhaps he viewed her as a conquest. A woman to bed and toss aside. But she wouldn't allow that to happen. She'd prevented Morten from using her and Bregovi wouldn't fare any better.

At the thought of Morten, she realized she'd made it through another day undiscovered.

Fifteen days. More than a fortnight since she had fled, since she had been bound as a genie.

A clock chimed from somewhere in the castle and the notes echoed in the night. The musical tones drew her mind to the competition on the morrow and she wondered what others would play. Then, as the tolls reached twelve, she leapt from the tub.

Amidst the events of the day, she'd forgotten all about practicing. She quickly dried off and threw on the chemise. Her dresses were still in the trunk, save one in Rachel's room and the gown in Victoria's. The heavy lid groaned loudly, but didn't yield.

When she heard Victoria stir in the adjoining room, Kate decided not to risk drawing her attention. She threw on a cloak to cover the shift and grabbed a candle. Stepping into the dark corridor, she hoped the castle was still enough for her to find her way to the music hall unnoticed.

* * *

Bregovi lay back in the tub trying to wash away Kate's scent and the memory of his foolish display. He'd been so jealous of the smithy that he'd had to show her he was the better rider. But why? She was merely an amusement. A maiden to distract him from the competition for *his* name. Yet he had felt an overwhelming need to compete for *her* against the man.

Perhaps the compulsion stemmed from a desire to ensure he wouldn't lose his favorite new toy until he chose to. For Kate certainly was his newest enjoyment. Battling her with blades and words was more fun than he'd had since exploring the jungles of Balmar.

His blood heated to sizzling at the thought of dueling with her naked on a soft mattress. But would she do the same with the smithy?

Somewhere deep inside, he ached for her to want him. Perhaps that had been the issue with Brock. She sure looked like she wanted him.

With a grunt, he leaned back against the tub. The sound of water splashing on the floor reminded him of the sea, and he wished he were there at the helm of a tall ship.

Closing his eyes, he imagined the spray on his face, the rocking under his feet, the thrill of spying a new land and the pleasure of lovely native maidens. Maidens who welcomed his affection. Another grunt.

The vixen had toyed with him, insisting she'd forgotten the kiss, but no one forgets a kiss like that. He grinned as a new goal came to light. Before the tournament was through, Kate would want him and admit it readily.

A rap on the door interrupted his musings.

"Yes?"

The door cracked open and a flurry of amber silk swirled in. When the fabric settled, a flaxen-haired maiden locked her eyes on his chest and gasped.

So it begins. The year his brother's head was on the altar, Stephan had reported three such visitors hoping to compromise themselves into a crown.

"Oh, excuse me, your highness," she said as she eagerly looked over his bare torso.

When she didn't retrace her steps, he said, "As you can see, I am not prepared to accept guests at the moment."

"Of course," her eyes flitted to his chest again and to the open water covering the rest of him. "But since I am here, do you need anything? I, um, I could wash your back for you," she said, her voice wavering slightly.

"Already done."

She nodded, but continued staring, forming another plan of attack. As he considered standing to escort her to the door, another head peeked in.

"Milord?" It was Alice, the now elderly maid who had tended him since birth. She took one look at the intruder and shooed her out. "Dear child, this is not how you win a prince. Off to bed with you."

"But—," the maiden protested.

"And make sure it's your own bed," she added, shutting the door behind the girl.

"I did nothing to encourage her," he said.

"Except look like you do and ride like you did today." She turned as he got out of the tub, dried and put his breeches on.

"You heard about that?"

"What heard? I *saw.*"

He handed over the wet linens.

"It's been a long while since I've seen you so intent over a woman." Alice's familiar blue eyes danced with amusement.

"Who said it was over a woman?"

"Why you did, child. Very clearly. Out on that field."

"Made a fool of myself is what I did. Wolfe would be laughing still."

"She looked a bit undone by it herself."

Undone. That pleased him more than he cared to acknowledge.

"Lord Wolfe's bird delivered this note," Alice said, handing him a tiny scroll. "She's on the perch in your library if you wish to reply."

"Thank you."

"Will you be needing anything else this eve? A guard perhaps?"

"No." He laughed as she left. "Sleep well, Alice."

"And you, child," she said, shutting the door.

He rolled open the note.

> *Prince Bregovi,*
> *Hope you found Kate without me this time.*
> *Haven't located sorcerer yet, but encountered four bandits*
> *when leaving Florian. They were on western border, heading south.*
> *May want to watch for them. Caught a lead on Zafarians to the north.*
> *Am heading that way. Will keep you apprised. Return Isabel.*
> *Your servant, D.W.*

* * *

After more than thirty minutes of searching for the music hall, ducking around corners to avoid being seen, Kate finally stumbled upon the latter part of the route Bregovi had led her on that morning.

Holding her breath as she entered the hall, Kate discovered a candelabra on a table near the door. Placing it and her candle on opposite sides of the harp, she looked over the instrument.

Engraved vines entwined over the dark wood from the base to its full height. And it stood three or four hands taller than her mother's had been. As she gently brushed her fingers across the strings, the beauty of the notes sent ripples of peace through her.

Pulling over a stool, she tucked her body under the curve of the instrument. Leaning in, she reached for the strings, but her cloak pulled uncomfortably. If she were to gain any benefit from practicing, she needed to move freely. She wanted to shed the garment, but the thought of being caught in only the chemise sent its own ripple through her. Fear.

Could she risk it? She reasoned she'd hardly crossed a soul on her route to the room, and that wing of the castle seemed deserted.

After careful glances out each doorway and several moments spent listening for any signs of company, she determined it safe enough. Although the glass panes at their center would provide little concealment, she shut both doors as well.

Laying the cloak over her chair, she once again settled herself against the harp. First, she tested it with some rolling strokes, sending sound vibrating through her. It was perfectly tuned. Tucking in closer, she pressed her right shoulder to the wood and closed her eyes. Playing had always brought her comfort, and she hoped it would again that night.

She began with a tune her mother had loved. As if by magik, the anxiety she'd felt about playing again slipped away as her fingers danced over the strings. With the beautiful notes ringing out in the night, her mind took her back to a happier time—days when she and her mother had played for her father. She had been so innocent then. So full of hope. So unaware of the tragedies to come.

As her thoughts drifted to the horror of her mother's death, a melancholy tune flowed from her hands. Memories of her own helplessness welled up like a flood. Although she fought them back, the regret felt fresh and raw.

Following on the tide of sorrow, the events of her father's death crept out of hiding. She had refused to believe he was gone and had snuck out to the docks everyday for months. Finally, a ship returned bearing some of his crew. While none would give her details, she had overheard enough whispers to piece it together.

An ambush at night after they had picked up a load of fabrics and pottery. Fare that didn't usually interest pirates. A few men had survived by jumping into the ocean and clinging to debris.

For a long time, she had hoped her father had done the same. A man with Gifts such as his certainly could escape a handful of pirates. But it wasn't to be. Her heart shattered the day his first mate returned and took her aside to tell her how her noble father had put his men first. Rather than flee, he and the first mate had fought their attackers, allowing others time to escape. At first the man wouldn't reveal what had happened in her father's last minutes, but ultimately he couldn't refuse her hysterical pleas.

After being stabbed by two pirates, the first mate watched them corner her father and run him through with their swords. The man explained through his own tears that they dropped the body into the flooded hold before setting the ship on fire. He'd only survived himself because a shipman had hauled him over the side.

She still couldn't fathom why her father hadn't saved himself using his Gifts, and for years she had wondered if Morten had played a part. Had her uncle tracked him? Had he commissioned the pirates? Morten had gained the dukedom and considerable wealth with his brother's death, and he had murdered others for far less.

As her heart wrestled with the terrible events, she poured her pain into the harp, and the instrument responded by comforting her in an ethereal musical embrace.

* * *

Bregovi escorted three more wayward maidens from his room after Alice left. One said she was looking for Rachel, and another that she was worried about his health because he hadn't appeared for dinner. The third, sapphire Sophia, professed she was lost and insisted she needed a guide back or she'd never find her room. He had finally consented when it looked as if she'd stay 'till morning if he didn't go with her.

After depositing the princess within sight of her door and dispatching Wolfe's falcon Isabel with a note for her master, he took his time heading back to his bedchamber. He'd forgotten how much he loved the castle after the bustle died down. He felt the same about the ship at night too. With most of the crew asleep, it was just him and two mesmerizing seas—ocean and stars.

As he neared the banquet hall, candlelight flickered from the door to the music room. A soft melody rose and dipped on invisible currents. Delicate and hauntingly sad.

Curious to discover who would play with such feeling, he quietly slipped into the room to listen. He should have known.

Kate sat not ten feet from him. The chemise and her fair complexion gave her a phantom-like appearance, but the dark hair spilling down around her hinted more at enchantress. As she reached for the strings, the fabric slipped from her left shoulder and solidified the point.

As he fixed his gaze on the curve of a breast peeking above the fabric, a perfect droplet landed on her creamy skin.

Tears. She was weeping.

Had the music moved her or did something trouble her? Did he? Hoping he wasn't the cause, he debated whether he should let her be or comfort her.

Perhaps he was just reaching for an excuse to hold her again. Hell, there was no *perhaps* about it. As he stood there contemplating his choices, she finished the melody and opened her eyes.

CHAPTER NINE

At first, Kate thought it was a trick of the light, but as she stared, the shape in the shadows became clearer. As if materializing from the mist, broad shoulders emerged, followed by glistening hair and those enticing eyes that taunted her mercilessly.

Bregovi.

Bregovi!

She gasped and jumped up, scrambling for her cloak.

Unfortunately, jumping in any direction wasn't wise when wedged under a harp. She slammed her right shoulder into the instrument, tipping it over and clipping her head. She grabbed for it, but it was too heavy.

Her chair toppled. She was destined to follow. Seconds before the harp crushed her, Bregovi did the deed instead, smashing her to his chest with one arm while steadying the instrument with the other.

She wished the harp had prevailed.

She would much rather have been plastered to the floor than squished against Bregovi's very solid, very warm body. Worse than the duel, and certainly worse than the joust, only two layers of thin linen separated her left breast from the skin of his chest. Not nearly enough.

"Are you hurt?" He ran his fingers over a tender spot on her head.

Although his touch was gentle, she winced at the pain. Not eager for further inspection, she brushed his hand away and wiggled out of his grip.

"I'm fine."

In the commotion, her cloak had slipped to the floor. Snatching it up, she clutched it in front of her ill-concealed breasts.

His eyes followed her hands, then flicked up to meet her gaze.

"I assure you, I'm well. Nothing to be concerned about," she said.

"I'm glad you're well, but I see plenty to be concerned about."

Was he referring to the tears? She turned to right the overturned chair and quickly wiped her face. As she struggled to lift the heavy piece of furniture, she said, "I'm sure I don't know what you mean."

"Don't you?" he said, taking over the task and returning the chair to its feet.

"No," she said, growing frustrated with his hazy statements and his ability to repeatedly throw her off-balance. She needed to leave. Retreat. Not stand about in the dark conversing with the man. "I assure you, nothing is amiss."

His jaw tightened, and a muscle twitched on his cheek. But rather than respond, his gaze wandered over her frame. No, not wandered, *explored*, as if he could see through the cloak and was memorizing every inch underneath.

Her cheeks blazed. "As I said—"

"Is this part of your plan to ensnare a husband?"

Her chin nearly hit her chest.

"Like a siren, you lure in your man with the music, and then seduce him in that scrap of cloth?"

Glancing down, she discovered the chemise had slipped dangerously low and the cloak didn't conceal nearly as much as she'd thought. Mortified, she hastily turned her back, adjusted the shift, and pulled the cloak securely around her. When she spun back to face him, he had an arm draped lazily over the harp.

"Too late. I've already seen what's under there. It's burned into my memory," he said, tapping his temple.

Exasperating man. "You have certainly *not* seen what's under here."

"Well, I've felt it, and that's nearly the same thing."

Could one blush everywhere? If so, she was sure she had. It irked her immensely that he could cause such a reaction in her. He was the one who was constantly up to ill.

"In regard to your, your, accusation—"

"My observation."

"First, I've no plans to *ensnare* anyone. I was merely practicing for the event tomorrow."

"Truly?" he said, his voice thick with doubt.

"Second, seduction is your game, not mine."

"Kate," he said a bit too condescendingly. "Any man with eyes would conclude you're using your wiles to some romantic end."

"I am not," she huffed. "And I don't have wiles."

"Oh, but I assure you, you do," he whispered, slowly closing the distance between them. "And I just might succumb."

"Nonsense." Kate quickly darted around the harp, her insides swirling uncomfortably. "And I suggest you resist whatever urge has taken hold of you."

After a lingering gaze, he said, "As you wish, milady."

He conceded so quickly she almost felt insulted.

"You realize most men would not be so easily diverted," he said. "The castle is full of visitors. Strangers. Anyone could have come upon you. One could have taken quick advantage."

"Oh? You mean as you have?"

"I've never taken advantage of you," he said, looking offended.

"Bregovi the Bandit?"

"I may have misled you with a ruse, but you initiated that kiss."

"Only to get it over with. You're the one who seized the opportunity to, to—"

"You were irresistible. I'm not made of stone."

Irresistible?

"And if I recall correctly, you participated rather enthusiastically."

"I was trying to appease you. So you'd let me go."

"You were doing no such thing. If anything you stoked the fire."

She wanted to protest. To cry her innocence from the tower. Unfortunately, he was right. She had stoked like a dockside harlot.

One dark eyebrow quirked up, as he awaited her reply. He knew he was right. It was written all over his smug face. But he'd wait decades if he expected her to agree with him.

"I made sure no one was about," she said, running a hand over the harp.

"Not sure enough, for I am about."

"Yes, well, you are everywhere," she grumbled.

"Please promise me you'll not wander the castle again dressed in so little. While I'll be forever grateful for the sight, I would hate for you to suffer harm."

Concern had replaced his teasing tone, and she felt the full impact of his words. She really had been foolish. She didn't have use of her abilities, and anyone could have overpowered her.

"Of course," she said, pulling the cloak tighter.

"Good."

"I assure you, I wouldn't have worn this tonight if I'd been able to get my trunk open."

"Send for me next time, and I'll open it for you."

Send for a prince? This prince? Victoria would skin her.

"I suspect you could have gone on without the practice," he said, plucking a few strings. "You play beautifully."

"Embarrassing myself seems to come naturally of late, so my aim is merely to avoid that tomorrow."

"I don't think that will be an issue for one as gifted as you."

The compliment struck her at the heart, vibrating through her as if he'd plucked the perfect chord.

"That's kind of you. I hope you're right."

"How long have you been playing?"

"My mother taught me when I was seven. I was so small, I couldn't even reach all the strings. But I loved it," Kate said, touching the instrument. "Her harp was equally beautiful. Where yours has vines, hers had angels. As a child, I pretended they were playing with me. It was so breathtaking."

"Was? You no longer have it?"

"When my parents died, our fortune went to my uncle."

"He wouldn't allow you the harp?"

"He did for a time, but I'm afraid I wasn't as agreeable as he wanted and he destroyed it."

"That sounds cruel."

Cruel, but not nearly the worst punishment she'd received.

"What did he ask of you?"

"Obedience," she said. Remembering the incident brought chills yet again. When she was fifteen, he had been thrown from his horse and had injured his leg. She had refused to heal him. "I disobeyed and he chopped up the harp and tossed it into the hearth." The memory of the angels being engulfed by fire still haunted her dreams on occasion.

"I'm sorry," Bregovi said. "He sounds heartless."

"He is, but I'm free of him now." Even to her own ears, she sounded falsely insistent.

"I'm glad," he said. Then his voice softened as he added, "I'm sorry about your parents too. It's tough losing those we love."

"Yes, it is. I'm sorry about your mother's passing as well."

"I wish you'd met her. I think she'd have enjoyed you. She particularly loved plucky souls."

"Plucky? I may swoon at the compliment."

"Swooning is good." He grinned and casually stepped around to her side of the harp like a wolf on the prowl.

She retreated a few paces, preferring to keep a safe measure of breathing room between them in case she wanted to bolt…or touch him.

"Do you never cease teasing? I bet you tormented Rachel endlessly when you were children."

"I don't think she'd classify it as torment, but I did find countless ways to make her squeal." He laughed at some remembered moment, and his eyes shimmered with amusement. "What about you? Did you have any sisters to teach your bewitching ways to?"

"No. And I don't bewitch."

He grinned. "What about brothers who spent their afternoons looking for ways to spark your temper?"

"No, you seem to be uniquely skilled at that."

"No siblings and your parents are gone?" he said, softer than before. "So, you're all alone? I really am sorry."

The tenderness in his voice washed away the lighthearted mood, and the bothersome tears welled up again.

She turned her back, so he wouldn't see. "Has the hour reached one already? I think I'd best get back to my chamber before I'm missed."

"Forgive me." He stepped around to face her. "I didn't mean to upset you." His fingers brushed her arm as gently as his words had her heart. "Please, if you give me a moment, I'm sure I'll do something to vex you again."

An unbidden laugh burst from her as she struggled to shake off the emotion *and* his touch. She didn't need his kindness. It only confused her. It made her want things she couldn't have—someone to hold, someone to make her heart dance and her blood sizzle. It made her think things she couldn't afford to believe—that there might be more to him than the prankster he'd proven himself to be.

"I'm not upset. And I'm not alone. The castle is full of people, isn't it?"

"I find the castle can be quite lonely." He picked up a lute from a nearby table.

She laughed again. "Is this how you seduce women? Convince them you're lonely?"

Mischief sparked in his eyes. "No, there are far more effective ways to seduce a woman." He then produced a horrible sound with the lute.

"That's clearly not one of them."

"No." Dimples winked as he set down the instrument.

She had no doubt he did know a multitude of ways, and since she felt far too intrigued by what they might be and knew he'd gladly demonstrate, she thought it better to steer clear.

"I don't see how you can feel lonely with a family who loves you, servants who dote on you, and maidens clamoring for your favor."

"I agree, my family is a blessing, but the servants are here because they have to be, and the maidens love the illusion, not the man."

"Do you let them know the man?"

"Most giggle incessantly and prattle on about the most inane subjects. Neither inspires any interest in me."

"They're probably nervous," she said.

"Do you suggest I entertain them regardless of how mindless the talk or how unbearably dull I find their company? I wouldn't subject prisoners to such torture."

Although she suspected he was right about many of them, his arrogant tone spurred her on. "If you didn't judge them so hastily, you might be surprised at what you'd find."

"Why are you so concerned with defending the silly maidens of the land?" His voice rose to match hers.

"Why shouldn't I be? Since I'm likely to be one of them," she snapped, daring him to reply.

He stared at her a moment, then shook his head and chuckled, "There's nothing silly about you, Kate."

That stumped her. Took all the fire out of the fight. What did he mean by that? While she didn't want to be considered silly, she also didn't want people to think she was somber. Did he think she was too serious? She looked back at the harp.

"Was I playing the funeral melody when you walked in?"

"I don't know, but it was enchanting. Will you play it for me again? Or anything else you wish?"

Perhaps he did consider her too somber. "I'll play for you tomorrow at the competition."

"I'd really love to hear something tonight."

She should refuse. She should end the conversation and run back to her chamber where she should have been all along. Alone.

"Please?" he asked again, his eyes melting and earnest. "I promise I'll talk with more of the mindless maidens."

"You'd subject yourself to such torture for a song?"

"A small price, I assure you." As she considered, he added, "Three maidens for every song you play."

If he'd agree to such a sacrifice, how could she refuse? For the good of the maidens, she told herself, nothing more. "It'll have to be more than a simple hello, mind you."

"I'll let them bore me as long as they wish."

Not exactly chivalrous, but his dimples told her the sentiment was housed in fun. Either way, if they occupied more of his time, she would occupy less. And that was her aim, wasn't it?

"Very well," she said. "But I'll hold you to your promise."

His face lit up, and he quickly pulled over another chair. She tried to ignore the warm feeling his delight gave her. Loosening the cloak around her shoulders, she positioned herself against the instrument, then took a deep breath to clear him from her senses. As usual, it didn't work.

She began with a light cheerful melody to show him she wasn't always sour.

As she continued, she not only lost herself in the music, but in the deep green eyes gazing at her. He looked so open and handsome watching her. His white tunic gaping open at the neck. His skin glowing golden in the flickering candlelight.

113

She knew she should look away. With her eyes and her heart, she should look away. But she couldn't. He held her captive. The music seemed to wrap around them both, and while she couldn't touch him physically, she reached out to him through the harp. With every stroke, the chords vibrated through her and she hoped through him.

She transitioned to a slower melody. Quiet. Deeper.

He leaned nearer.

When his eyes grew heavy, his gaze roaming over her body, her skin tingled magikally as if his touch had followed the same path.

Closing her eyes, she questioned whatever addled portion of her brain had thought this was a good idea.

Beginning one last selection, she struggled to bring her thoughts back to the music. To her disappointment, while her hands carried on, her mind swam with memories of Bregovi's lips. Finally, she played the last note and let the music drift off into the night.

She may as well have seduced herself on his behalf.

When she opened her eyes, she found him standing before her. Inches away. He took her hand. As her mind cried out not to move, her wicked body arose without hesitation. She let him pull her close and rested her forehead on his chest.

"That's nine maidens," she said into his open shirt.

His laugh rumbled through her. When she glanced up his blessed lips lowered to hers.

This time his kiss seared her. His mouth hot and demanding. He stole away her sanity and her breath, but she didn't care. Her fickle soul wanted him.

As his arms tightened around her, she gave herself over to the delicious sensations he stirred.

He appeared to recognize her acquiescence—or rather eager participation—for at that moment, his devilish tongue snuck inside to tease hers.

Taking his time, he enticed her into a new dance that she decided must be one of his most effective methods of seduction. After tormenting her until her knees were quaking, he commenced a private expedition to other blissful horizons.

His lips brushed a pulsing spot on her neck. Then he nibbled gently on her shoulder, nudging her chemise ever so slightly out of the way. Shamelessly, she wove her fingers through his thick, lovely hair, holding him there, urging him on.

As his hand began the slow climb from her waist, her nipples went taut in anticipation and her mind came alert. *Finally.*

Her eyes whipped open, and she caught a glimmer of light shining through the far door. Was someone watching? By instinct, she reached out to try to read the intruder, but sensed nothing, of course. Whether the visitor was illusion or reality, it broke the spell and she grabbed Bregovi's roaming hand before it reached her breast.

"Wait. I can't." She stared up into eyes dark with desire. "Please. We can't," she whispered.

"I'm sorry," he said, sounding as breathless as she felt. "I shouldn't have taken advantage." A portion of her hair had cascaded over his arm and he ran his fingers through it. "Perhaps it doesn't matter, though. You'll probably forget this kiss too."

She couldn't think straight. He was too close. Too intoxicating.

"I don't think anyone could forget your kisses." *Tell me I didn't say that aloud.* She dipped her head forward.

He gently tilted her chin back up, his eyes sparkling, then bent and kissed her again. Deep and lingering. Tender torture. His wicked tongue tasting, teasing, taunting.

Although her traitorous body longed for more of him, she mustered all her willpower—which wasn't much by that point—and managed to separate their lips.

"Please," she said, sounding embarrassingly breathy. "You must stop doing that."

"I wanted to thank you for the performance."

She laughed in all her nervousness as he gently wrapped her in his arms. He felt so good. So right. So dangerous.

"Come, we'd best get you back to your room before I think of something else to thank you for."

* * *

On the way to her bedchamber with Bregovi's warm hand low on her back, Kate considered the man by her side. Despite his arrogance there was a tenderness in him, which she feared would lead to her undoing. *As could the rest of him.* Merely thinking about his lips on hers sent her senses reeling.

She shook the image from her mind, reminding her foolish heart that the man and his kisses would soon belong to another. If she let her feelings grow in the interim, she'd not only be running from sorcerers but a broken heart.

As they passed through the final stretch of passageways, she began a short mantra—*You don't care for him. He doesn't care for you. He will marry another and you and he will be through.* She repeated it nearly a dozen times and as they reached her door, her head finally felt clear and her blood cool.

Quite proud she'd regained control of her senses, she turned to say goodnight. But the unhelpful man pulled her close and the foolishness started anew.

With a feather-light kiss across her lips, he set her knees shaking. His mouth made her shiver, as it tickled her ear when he whispered, "Sleep well, fair Kate."

As she watched him disappear into the night, her body ached in assorted places.

Being alone with him was a mistake she wouldn't make again.

* * *

Except in her dreams…

Under the veil of a misty fog, Kate followed Bregovi through a maze of rooms, each lovelier than the last. Tapestries, paintings, swans—all dazzled her mind as much as being near Bregovi dazzled her senses.

They paused in a weapons hall identical to her uncle's. Her mother's harp at its center was the only thing out of place.

"Play for me?" he whispered.

In seconds, her fingers danced over the strings. Music swirled around them, embracing them, seducing them. Craving another of his kisses, Kate opened her eyes.

And all the warmth she'd felt dissipated in a heartbeat.

Her balding, brutish uncle held Bregovi captive with knives to the prince's throat and belly.

As terror seized her, Kate leapt up, sending the harp crashing to the floor.

"Now that wasn't very graceful, Bluebell," Lord Morten said.

"Let him go," she demanded, glancing around for a weapon she could use.

"Not quite yet, dear one. Why don't you right your lovely harp with your Gifts? I'm sure your beau would like to see how talented you are," he said, angling the blade at Bregovi's throat. "Unless you're tiring of your prince."

Kate immediately waved a hand toward the harp. The heavy instrument responded immediately, righting itself.

The prince's eyes drew wide as his gaze darted between her and the harp.

"Lovely, Bluebell," Morten said.

Suddenly, she sensed someone behind her. A man. Devious, arrogant and *pleased*. Turning to see who stood there, she found only empty space.

"Something wrong?" her uncle said.

Warm air fanned across her neck. A breath. She spun toward the source, but saw only Morten and Bregovi across the room. Then she distinctly felt a hand creep down her back. Jerking away from the touch, she threw out an arm. In obedience, a large dagger flew from its mount on the wall. The handle landed soundly in her palm as her fingers caught hold.

"Magnificent," a hollow voice breathed beside her.

"Show yourself," she said, whirling toward the sound, dagger at the ready.

An invisible hand clamped onto her, inches above her wrist.

"Show yourself," she demanded again, struggling to break free.

Slowly a shape took form. Broad shoulders. Fiery red hair tied back at the neck. Eyes as dark as night staring coldly down at her.

"You're going to make a formidable genie," the man said.

"Genie?" Kate cried. The same word she'd uttered every night since she'd fled.

"Meet your new master," Morten said from behind her.

As she struggled to escape Sylvan's hold, he twisted her arm sharply, breaking her grip on the blade. It crashed to the floor.

"Release her," Bregovi yelled.

She glanced up to find her uncle at his potions table and Bregovi charging for them. She called for the knife, but Sylvan caught it before it reached her hand and he plunged it into Bregovi's belly. The prince crumbled to the ground.

"No," she cried, dropping to Bregovi's side. Peeling back his tunic she found a deep gash. Whispering to him to hold on, she gently covered the bloody wound with her hands, then closed her eyes to let her spirit join with his.

Instead of feeling his injuries, as she should have, she felt nothing. Something was wrong.

Looking around, she soon discovered the sorcerers had created a large salt ring around her. Around them all. Morten chanted in the ancient tongue, and both men wore Zafarian Order robes. Her uncle's was crimson, representing his position as Order Master, and Sylvan's shimmered an emerald green.

She tried for the knife again. Nothing. She called for a sword on the wall, a spear, anything. Nothing budged.

Lord Sylvan hauled her up from the floor, forcing her to release Bregovi.

"No!" she shouted. "I do not consent."

"Consent is not required," her uncle said.

Sylvan stretched out his free hand, and her uncle cut a deep gash across the man's palm. Then Morten turned toward her, the stale scent of unnatural potions hanging about him.

While Sylvan held her arm, Morten peeled open her fingers and sliced her palm to match Sylvan's.

Before she regained her breath, Morten bound their bloody hands together with a cord and continued chanting the ancient spell.

Kate tried to break the salt ring with her mind. With her foot. Nothing worked.

Bregovi lay dying on the floor, she was being bound to another as a genie, and she was powerless to stop either. A scream of rage exploded from her. If her Gifts weren't blocked, the air would have been swirling with weapons. None of them would have walked away unscathed.

Morten chuckled while he touched a candle flame to the salt, transforming the latter into a blue ring of fire around them. The smoky air smelled of sulfur and damp wood, setting her coughing as it filled her lungs.

As Morten chanted louder, raising his arms to the ceiling, her hand burned as if on fire. Finishing the final stanza with a shout, Morten doused the candle. The fire ring went dark in the same instant. The pain ceased and Sylvan whipped off the tie to examine their palms.

The cuts were gone.

Her hand was whole.

The Binding had taken.

CHAPTER TEN

Kate awoke with a start. Shaking. The result of both the dream and Victoria's intervention.

The princess released Kate's shoulders as she sat up.

"You had that nightmare again," Victoria said, handing her a glass of water.

"I'm sorry I woke you," Kate said, hands trembling around the cup. "I'm fine now. Thank you."

Victoria yawned and headed back to her chamber.

Too tense to sleep, Kate scooted out of bed and paced her bedchamber. Rubbing her aching palm, she wished she had sensed what her uncle had been up to. She had always thought the worst he could do was marry her off to one of his allies. He'd made no secret of his obsession with how her parents had gained one another's Gifts when they married, and she had always been certain he would want her to pass her powers on to a husband who would further his ambitions.

Perhaps the gaining of powers was the problem with that plan. While her husband would have acquired her abilities, she also would have gained his. If she had wed Lord Sylvan, she'd now have the gift of invisibility.

She'd wager that was exactly why Morten had forced her to be the man's genie rather than his bride. An invisible niece would be difficult to control. A genie would not.

Once again she wondered why Lord Sylvan hadn't summoned her back. For days she feared he'd rub a lamp or a wand or some device, and she'd be called to his side.

One thing was certain, her understanding of genies was dismally inadequate. Prior to the horrific ceremony, she'd thought they were mythical spirit slaves, passed from one master to another. Unfortunately, she now knew they all had started out much differently. Much more alive.

Growing chilled in the cool night air, Kate climbed back into bed with lingering thoughts of her latest nightmare. She'd had horrible dreams about the Binding nearly every night since her escape, but this was the first to involve Bregovi—or anyone—in place of her maid.

While she'd never had the ability to see the future, it didn't take a Gift to know she endangered those around her. Yet one more reason to stay away from the prince.

* * *

Castle Cragmont

Splashing the chilly basin water over his face and torso did little to refresh Sylvan's spirits. Once again, they had been deterred. The more people they encountered, the more Sylvan realized Morten was either despised or feared by all but the Zafarians, and even they kept a wary eye on the man.

King Alexander—Morten's cousin—hadn't granted them even a brief audience, only rooms for the night. And by the lengthy journey through the castle, Sylvan suspected they were sequestered as far as possible from the royal family without depositing them in the stables.

Taking a washing cloth, he dried himself before one of the weather-paned windows. Like his chambers in Viridia, the view overlooked a large cove that opened to the sea.

Rocky shores. A vessel anchored in the bay. Night stars reflected on the water. So like home and so different.

Missing were the green streaks shimmering in the sky and the hint of honeysuckle floating on the ocean breeze.

Silent were his father's rumbling chuckle that could infect an entire assembly and his mother's joyful laugh that had made the darkest of hearts grin. But even they couldn't reach him now.

It wasn't as it should be. Nothing was as it should be.

Right was right.

The man who had stolen his kingdom should be made to pay. The man who had taken his sister should suffer for it. The man who had slaughtered his family should be punished.

Right was right. Zee should die.

Behind him, a feminine throat cleared. "Pardon, my lord. I've been sent to—" A little gasp interrupted her speech when he turned.

He doubted he was the first bare-chested man she'd seen, but the maid looked him over slowly, as if she planned to sketch him later.

And since she was looking, he did too. Blond hair, commonly braided, framed a plump face of creamy skin, wide eyes and ripe lips. Bosom and waist were magnified nicely by a snug house gown.

When he brought his gaze back to hers, her cheeks colored the soft rose of sunset and opportunity.

"I'm blessed to receive such a delightful messenger," he said slow and wicked. "I can't wait to learn what you've been sent to provide."

His manner was intended to fluster or arouse, either equally advantageous. Because, in his experience, when flustered or aroused, the feminine sex had a tendency toward speech, and this maid might be the closest he'd get to the answers he sought.

"Oh, my," the maid said on a half-laugh. Upon closing the door, she turned and added, "Gretch said Lord Morten brought a heart-stopper with him, but she has a tendency to exaggeration."

"Does she?" he said, adding the devilish wink Elliana frequently blushed over.

The maid wasn't immune either.

"Oh, my, indeed," she said, blotting her face and bosom with a dust rag. "You're not from here, are you?"

Not remotely.

"Do you hail from the wetlands? Or Brandish?" she asked. "Their kind don't come to Cragmont much."

"That's their loss, when they'd find a lovely lass like you to tend to them," he said with another sly grin.

"You'd best stop that before I forget why I'm here," she said with a giggle that indicated she did *not* want him to stop.

"Of course," he said with insincere penitence. "And what service are you here to supply?"

"I, I...am to light the wicks, stoke the fire—"

"You've accomplished that already," he said in a husky tone. "Anything else?"

Her gaze darted to his breeches.

"Turn down the bed linens and see if you need a meal." With the last declaration aired, she quickly stabbed the wood in the hearth to flame and lit enough candles to guide ships to port.

Next, she circled to the opposite side of the bed. Leaning forward, so that she provided him with a prime view of her ample bosom, she pulled down the bedding. Glancing toward him, she drew a hand over the fabric, caressing it as she would a lover's body.

Sauntering back to his side, she positioned herself near the foot of the bed, her back to him. "Would you like the bed curtains loosed or tied back?" she asked, glancing invitingly over her shoulder, one hand clutching a panel at the foot of the bed.

"Which do you prefer?" he asked, stepping close enough to press his breeches against the back of her skirt and the plump flesh hiding underneath.

She drew in a quick breath and teetered. He caught her in an instant with a hand to her breast. Her hip would have been more efficient, but the breast sent the better message.

"I like them loosed," she whispered, leaning into his palm. "The fabric—" A gasp escaped her as he gently squeezed. "The...the fabric is lovely loosed."

"I can't imagine it's lovelier than you are," he whispered. "Even Princess Victoria, the famed beauty of Cragmont, would pale in your company." He pressed his lips to her neck, where her pulse beat a staccato rhythm, rapid and hard.

Of course, he'd no idea if Victoria were beautiful or not, but it served the perfect means to pull the princess into the conversation.

As the maid responded, he continued caressing to better keep her senses off-balance and her mouth engaged.

"Oh, no," she said, breathy.

His hand slid lower.

"She's, she's very beautiful."

Another gentle squeeze.

"I suppose I'll have to be the judge when I meet her." He nipped her ear. "Tomorrow."

"But you can't," she said, one hand gripping the bed curtains and the other his left leg behind her.

"Why can't I?" he asked, trailing his fingers over the skin swelling above her bodice.

"Because…"

He dipped his thumb under the fabric to taunt one pert nipple. Her head lolled back against his shoulder.

"Because what?" He said, giving the nub a gentle pinch.

The maid let out a long slow breath. "She's…she's away."

"Away where?" Dragging his other hand lower, he cupped it between her legs.

"Holy gods." A moan escaped his unsuspecting informant. "To Florian."

Florian? Home of the Portal? Could it be that ideal? Still, the issue was whether Kate was with her.

"Such a long journey."

"Yes. Three days." Pressing her hips back against him, she released his leg to drag up her skirts.

Taking the unspoken hint, he reached under the hem, slowly running his fingers over her silky thighs, fondling, tickling, everywhere except the spot she'd want most.

"Why didn't she take you with her?"

Another little moan, this one frustrated. "Didn't need me," she said, wiggling to maneuver his hand to the right place.

"I can't imagine anyone not needing you," he said, probing an especially sensitive area.

She gasped.

"I bet she had to take three maids to replace you."

She shook her head at that. "No. Didn't take any…just…just Princess Rachel."

Two princesses without an attendant didn't sound plausible or likely.

She whipped around and fumbled with his breeches. "Princess Rachel's lady-in-waiting and maid were ill and stayed behind."

Flipping open the fabric, she swiftly grabbed hold of his shaft, squeezing and cajoling in expert fashion.

"What about Lady Katherine?" He quickly lifted her onto the edge of the bed.

"What of her?" Still holding fast, she tugged him between her thighs then wrapped her legs around him.

Within the space of a grunt and a squeal, he was inside her. "I heard she was here, visiting her cousin."

The maid's eyes locked on his, hesitation confirming what she wouldn't say.

Rewarding her for the unspoken answer, he gave her what she wanted. Pumping. Rapid. Hard. And then he stopped.

"Is she still here?"

Her chest rose and fell with quick breaths, but she held her secrets.

Perhaps a bit of torture would yield results. Slowly he slid his hands up to her shoulders and her bodice down to her waist until two flushed breasts spilled out.

Leaning low, blowing a hot breath on the right, he asked again. "Is she still here?"

"Wh-who?"

"Lady Katherine," he said, forming the words over the nub. When she didn't answer, he stoked the flames of persuasion higher, flicked the flesh with his tongue, toying with her for long minutes until her breath came fast and shallow again. "Is she still here? Or did she go with Victoria?"

The maid grabbing his hips, but he caught her hands and pinned them to the bed.

"I'll give you everything you need…"

Her eyes found his again.

He took another drawn out turn at her left nipple, then tried again, "Did Kate travel to Florian with Victoria?"

"We're not to speak of Lady Kate," she pleaded low and breathy.

"I know," he said gliding out and in. Once. Twice. "I want to help her."

"But, Lord Morten…" She gasped, rocking against him.

"If I find her, I'll take her where he can't harm her. Tell me, did she go with Victoria?"

The maid's eyes gazed into his. Probably trying to read his soul, little of it that remained.

To provide the last measure of encouragement she needed, he pulled out and started to step away from her.

"Yes!" She growled, clamping her legs about him. "Bloody yes. Milady Kate went with them! Now do not taunt me further, milord."

And he didn't.

Within moments they were sweating, coiling and rising toward release.

As Sylvan neared the peak, a slight breeze fanned his back.

"It's good to see you know what to do with a woman," Morten's amused voice came from behind him.

As if she thought the intrusion might halt their festivities, the maid locked her ankles. She needn't have worried. While he detested both the insinuation and the intrusion, he needed the release and the maid deserved hers. He wasn't about to let Morten cheat either of them.

"Unlike you, it hasn't been long," Sylvan said, not skipping a thrust.

She threw back her head as shudders shook her body. Moments later, he found equal satisfaction.

"Nicely done," Morten said as Sylvan left the maid to wash at the basin. "Such a lovely welcome," Morten said, his eyes fixed on the breasts the maid was now shoving into her bodice. "I look forward to your visit to my chamber as well."

If Morten noticed her understandably repulsed reaction, he didn't show it or care.

"I have duties, milord," she said, edging past the man.

The sorcerer must have caught her intent, for he blocked the way. While running his fingers over her breasts, he said, "You have an hour to tend to your duties, then you're spreading your legs to tend to mine. Understood?"

As Sylvan watched Morten bully the maid, two thoughts roiled in his mind. An image of his sister facing another lustful sorcerer, and the idea that the maid ought to be rewarded, not punished, for the information she'd shared.

"Her duties are with me," Sylvan said, throwing on a tunic.

"What?" the maid and Morten said in unison.

"I've secured her for the night." Sylvan tilted her head in the direction of the basin, and she shot him a grateful look as she ran to it. "You'll have to procure your own bed partners, rather than steal mine."

The only indication of Morten's irritation was a slight tightening of his mouth. Then it was gone. "I'm sure there's plenty of ripe fruit where this one came from. I'll merely wait in the corridor until one comes my way."

Like a spider. "I'm sure you'll catch someone." While the maid washed at the basin, Sylvan guided Morten toward the hearth beyond the bed. Lowering his voice, he said, "The maid had information. Kate is on her way to Florian with Victoria and another princess."

"The gypsy vision," Morten said in the same hushed tone.

"It appears so," Sylvan said. "I'll leave at dawn."

"She may not remain there," Morten said, staring into the flames. "It's best we send a runner to confirm."

"That will take too long," Sylvan said.

"You can't take her on alone," Morten said, jabbing the wood with the poker. "And while I'm happy to hunt for her in Cragmont, I'm not suffering endless journeys chasing each lead."

While Sylvan didn't much care for the journeys either, he'd prefer them over waiting with the sorcerer.

"When I find her, I'll command her to use her Gifts, and then you can travel by your preferred means."

Morten nodded. "Take the men with you. They'll help if you aren't as persuasive as you hope."

The maid shrieked across the room.

Both men turned as she rubbed her arm. Another scream rent the chamber as she clamped a hand over her breast.

"Something pinched me!" she said, a red welt on the now uncovered arm confirming her claim.

"She looks touched," Morten said.

With a yelp, she whirled around.

"Maybe she's not so keen on staying with you," Morten said with a wink.

Or Elliana isn't so keen on her staying with me.

With one last screech, followed by a hearty curse, the maid fled the room.

As Morten sauntered out the door behind her, he said, "I know the perfect method to console a hysterical wench."

A moment after the door latched in its frame, Sylvan shifted to his invisible form.

"I thought you weren't permitted to interfere," he said to the very beautiful, very jealous faerie maiden before him.

"She is not your path," Elliana said, hair and shimmery fabric whipping about her like flames.

"She knew where Kate was," Sylvan said. "Certainly, that deserved a reward, not an attack from the fae realm."

"I did not attack her."

"She might argue otherwise. She isn't going to sleep tonight for fear of another pinch."

Her gentle laughter filled the room like sunshine. Stepping closer, she rested a hand on his chest, her essence flowing into him. Faster than at the gypsy camp, she seemed to restore pieces of his soul from wherever they'd been banished to.

"You're getting better." He covered her hand with his. "At crossing into the physical realm."

"Not really. It's just easier when I'm agitated," she said as an accusatory brow quirked up.

It was his turn to laugh.

When her lips parted to say something most likely profound, confusing or sassy, he had but one thought.

His mouth came down on hers—a touch more desperate than he'd have liked. It didn't signify, though, for the desperation wasn't his alone. She mirrored all he felt…and did.

As their lips played, teased and demanded, the familiar touch of her, the familiar warmth of her, the familiar taste of her, filled him like a golden elixir.

Once, behind a waterfall, their kissing had sent streaks of light pinging off the walls. Now the light was dancing behind his eyes, every color, shimmering, joyous. And when he opened them, he discovered the light filled the bedchamber as well, surrounding them in a swirling play of rainbows.

For a moment, finding Kate didn't matter. Defeating Zee didn't matter. *She* was all that mattered.

"Stay with me," he said, shuffling backward toward the bed.

"Oh," she said against his lips. "Now that your strumpet has run off—"

He silenced her again, and she laughed into his mouth, nipping his tongue for good measure.

"Stay," he whispered. "Give me more than a few moments to feel whole again."

She glanced at their hands still layered over his heart and rested her forehead on his chin, her soft breath tickling his chest.

"I dream of you every night," he whispered. "It's as if you visit me in my sleep."

Shifting slightly, she glanced up through thick lashes. "Sometimes I do."

"Which times?" His heart thudded in a hopeful rhythm.

A warm blush painted her cheeks. A wicked grin lifted his.

"I hope you've been enjoying yourself as much as I have," he said.

When her blush deepened, he couldn't help but laugh.

"It isn't only then," she said, defensively. "I try to bring you happy dreams...about your family."

"And you."

"Yes."

"I wish you'd visit every night," he said, depositing another kiss on his favorite lips.

"I do too. But I can't. The Council is watching me. It was easier to get away before."

"Before you broke all the rules and saved my life."

Lavender eyes met his. "Yes."

"Did I ever thank you properly for that?" he asked, pulling her closer still.

"Yes," she said again, pressing her perfect mouth to a spot on his neck she'd always seemed fond of. "And you can continue to properly thank me by avoiding dim-witted strumpets and sticking to your quest."

"Noted."

Another kiss. Long and deep.

"Thank you for visiting my dreams."

"I won't let you forget…"

His faerie goddess truly was wise beyond her years…or maybe just his. Those dreams reminded him of better days. They gave him hope he didn't feel in his waking hours.

"Thank you," he said, repositioning a whirling strand of hair behind her ear. "You may save my soul yet."

"That is my plan. Unless you muck it up." The eyes looked fierce, but a grin danced on her lips. "Do *not* muck it up."

"I won't," he said, inching her toward the bed. "You *are* staying with me, aren't you?" The hope in his voice made his heart ache.

Hers too, thankfully. For her gentle eyes gazed up at him as she mercifully said, "Only for tonight."

Lifting his glowing love from the floor, he carried her to the bed and gently set her on the downturned linens.

As he climbed up next to her, his hand slipped, letting go for the space of a breath, and bleakness rushed back in as if eager to claim him.

Wisely, Elliana slipped her hand in his, restoring him yet again.

Settling in next to her, he pulled his fae goddess into his arms, where their limbs and hearts entwined as they were meant to.

With her warm hand tucked in his, her lovely head resting upon his chest, and brilliant colors swirling about them, he fell into a deep, contented sleep.

CHAPTER ELEVEN

Kingdom of Florian, the Next Morning

The full contingent of the festival entrants had once again gathered in the banquet hall for the morning meal. Bregovi, spurned on by Kate's chastisement and in accordance with his promise, moved among them, making a point to speak to the more flighty maidens, wishing them luck in the music event and asking about their interests and kingdoms.

Unfortunately, asking the petite duchess from Highbridge what she would play set off a litany of every instrument she'd ever touched and a detailed explanation of why it wasn't what she'd perform for him.

Fortunately, the litany didn't require much participation on his part and the occasional nod seemed sufficient to keep the diatribe going. Although he wasn't much interested in her tale, what did intrigue him was how she managed to say so much of it in one breath. As he wondered if she'd ever fainted mid-sentence, Kate arrived with Victoria.

Like the rest of his anatomy, his eyes sensed her presence and instinctively sought her out. She wore her hair down, but pulled back with a few braids around her face, and her pale yellow gown suited her. She looked weary though and he surmised it was due to the late night practice.

He'd have liked to keep her awake longer, if she had let him. Just the mere thought of touching her again sent fresh heat racing through his veins.

He waited for her to look over and exchange a smile. Instead, she said a quick word to Victoria and joined Brock at the far end of the table. *Still the blacksmith? Perhaps she's not above silly maiden games.* He'd spent much of his sleepless night tormented by her scent and eyes, and it irked him that she could dismiss him so easily.

She'd felt something too. Maybe she just needed a subtle reminder.

He tuned back in to the girl before him.

"…and the viola is so easy to play. Not that anyone could do it, but it's so fun and enjoyable and such a happy thing to spend one's time doing, you see."

"It sounds as if you've much experience with music. I wish you the best of luck in the event," he said nodding to her for what he hoped was the last time.

"Thank you," she said, nearly giddy. "I shall play only for you."

He smiled, excused himself and started toward Kate. But before he'd gone three steps, Princess Sophia intercepted him. He politely greeted her, and the moment he managed to move on another stepped in, then another, and then Victoria. It seemed the line of ladies would never end.

* * *

Hurrying into the hall behind Victoria, Kate immediately saw Bregovi talking to a tiny animated maiden. Kate excused herself to sit far from the royal family, and Victoria seemed delighted to let her go. Relief settled in when she discovered her old friend Brock joking with his runner-up in the joust at the end of a long table.

"Not sitting with the royal siblings today?" Brock asked.

"I thought I'd give the other maidens an opportunity."

"And it's our good fortune you have," the lord of Larchmont said with a bow.

"Kate, this is Lord Preston, a good man despite how he handles a lance," Brock teased.

She curtsied. "You ride splendidly, milord, no matter what the smithy says."

"I thank you for noticing. I've won many an event and hope you'll be congratulating me on a win before the festival is through."

Lord Preston offered a chair between them, which Kate gladly accepted. She had avoided Bregovi, found Brock and met a nobleman. The day was looking up.

As a few maidens greeted Brock and Preston, she noticed Bregovi moving through the room speaking with nearly every woman there. She wondered if he was searching for his next conquest. *That would save you, Kate. Let him go seduce another.* She was careful not to catch his eye, looking elsewhere whenever he glanced in her direction. The last thing she wished to do was give him a reason to come over.

"Good morning, milady," a husky voice loomed over her.

No.

"Did you sleep well?" Bregovi teased looking a bit weary himself.

She felt a blush creep to her cheeks.

"Well enough, thank you."

"I'm glad to hear it." All eyes were on the prince as he smiled down at her. "Aren't you going to ask how I slept?"

"How a man sleeps is not a lady's concern."

"Yes, I suppose she'd be more concerned with how he does other things." His bold gaze mocked her.

She stood, not sure what that would accomplish, but needing more equal footing with the man.

"Of course I'm referring to things like hunting, and riding, and swordplay," he said.

"Of course you are." Brock chuckled.

Bregovi's smile disappeared as he took in the blacksmith.

Ah, a diversion. "Have you met Brock, your highness?"

"Yes," he said, turning his attention back to her. "Is it your memory or your heart that falters, milady?"

Her breath caught in her throat. *He wouldn't say anything. He couldn't. In front of so many?*

"I hope neither, your highness," she said cautiously.

"I hope not as well. For a moment, I thought you'd forgotten."

Her stomach did an uneasy flip as she looked between Bregovi and her companions.

"Did you have another engagement, milady?" Lord Preston asked.

"I, uh, no, I didn't, and I assure you my memory is sound."

"I disagree," Bregovi said. "I could mention several things that appear to have slipped your mind."

Merciful gods, why does he persist? As she fretted over how to divert the direction of the conversation, her memory came to her rescue.

"Several things you say? Let me think, could it be the jest in the woods, where you posed as a bandit and made a fool of me in front of all your guard?"

His grin faltered and he shook his head *no*.

"I agree," she continued, "For I remember that quite clearly. Or could you be thinking of the ball, where you threw me into a competition for your own entertainment?"

Again his head jerked back and forth, his amused expression erased.

"Right, that memory is quite clear too," she continued. "Perhaps you're referring to the joust—"

His eyes narrowed. "I was referring to my sister. It seems she is far from your thoughts."

Rachel. In her haste to escape Bregovi, she had forgotten her entirely. Kate hoped the princess hadn't tried to draw her over. She scanned the room and spotted Rachel chatting happily with Sebastian at the head table.

Letting out a relieved breath, she said, "My apologies, but she looks well and without need at the moment."

"None of us are without need, Kate." His eyes bore into hers with all the heat that had been there the night before.

She caught his full meaning and her face burned. *A warm body is what he needs. I am merely convenient.* But memories overwhelmed her—his delight when she'd agreed to play for him, how tenderly he'd touched her, his kind words as they'd discussed the loss of her parents. *Could he really care?*

Confusion, fear and desire swirled about in her heart and she didn't know which one to latch onto. She searched his eyes, desperate for some clue as to his intent, and as she looked, his smile faded and his gaze softened.

"Forgive me, milady. I am sure Rachel is well. I stopped to offer you luck with the harp this morning. I look forward to hearing you play."

"Thank you," she replied.

"Enjoy your meal," he said to all.

Kate curtsied, the men nodded, and Bregovi headed back to the royal table.

"Impressive," Preston said.

"I'm sure he wished luck to everyone this morning," she said, sinking back onto her chair.

"I think he's referring to you," Brock added. "To tame a prince with a gaze is no small feat."

Preston nodded in agreement, but Kate doubted anyone could tame Bregovi.

"You seemed to be of special interest to the man at the joust as well," Preston said. "Is there something between you?"

"What could there be between an untitled maiden and a prince?"

"A great deal has gone on between all sorts of maidens and princes," Brock offered.

"Well, a great deal has not gone on between Bregovi and me."

"Bregovi?" Preston said, one aristocratic eyebrow raised.

"Prince Edmund. Sometimes he calls himself..." she realized the argument wasn't supporting her point.

"I see," Brock teased.

"I know his sister."

"Of course." Preston nodded.

"May we talk about something else?"

"What would you like to talk about?" Preston asked, refilling her glass of mead.

She considered for a moment, and thought the question presented a perfect opening for her quest for employment.

She took a sip of her drink, then said, "Are there many children in Larchmont?"

"Children? I suppose as many as in any other kingdom. Why the curiosity? I should think you'd ask about our horse breeding," Preston said.

"I would like to secure a position as a governess after the festival and wish to determine possible opportunities in Larchmont."

"You're not here to win the prince?"

"Certainly not," she said, drawing laughter from both men.

"And you don't wish to continue on as lady-in-waiting to Princess Victoria?"

"Our arrangement is temporary."

He nodded. "I have no knowledge of such a position, but I can send posts to my sisters. They both have growing broods and may have a need."

"That would be wonderful."

He patted her hand and said, "It would be great to have you in Larchmont."

"You are so kind, and now, if you'd humor me, I would love to hear about those horses. Is it true Larchmont is home to a thousand wild herds?"

"Hundreds, yes." He sat taller. "And aside from our king's

holdings, my family has the largest stock in all Astonia."

As he waxed on about the various breeds his family owned—only the finest—their superb manner of taming, and his immense wealth, she thought many ladies would find him fascinating and handsome. He was shorter than Bregovi by a half foot and his eyes were the color of the sky after a storm. A deep, fresh blue. A slight tan warmed his skin and his lips curved up on each side, giving the impression he was constantly pleased about something, but they were thin and didn't look much good for kissing. *Not like Bregovi's lips.* Preston's lips turned up even more and she caught herself staring. Apparently so had he.

"Milady?"

"Yes?"

"Do you ride?"

"I'm sorry?"

"Horses?"

"Oh, yes, I enjoy riding immensely. I assume you do as well with such impressive mounts at your disposal."

"Yes, of course. I rode before I walked and have spent my life on horseback. While I didn't prevail in the joust yesterday, I've been champion too many times to count. I plan on making up for it in the race tomorrow. I've never lost."

"Never? How is that possible?"

"Skill and the best mount in the kingdoms."

"And perhaps a bit of luck?"

"Luck plays no part. I've been raised to excel at all events involving a horse and we keep the fastest mounts for our family—and the king, of course."

"Of course. I suppose we shall see the results of all that training and breeding tomorrow."

He nodded and chomped on a chunk of ham.

"I'd love to see you ride as well."

He said it as if he were considering a purchase and she wondered if he would choose a bride based on how well she handled a horse. She smiled, glad she wasn't in the running. A life on horseback in the beautiful Larchmont valley would be exciting, but she was growing weary of the lord's bragging.

The thought brought guilt to her mind both because of Preston's recent kindness and the chiding she gave Bregovi over his boredom with some of the maidens.

She glanced over to the prince and her stomach knotted. He certainly wasn't bored now. Sophia sat next to him as they laughed at some shared amusement. Kate realized she hadn't seen him laugh much. Their conversations were more heated. In all sorts of ways.

Sophia touched his arm and leaned in to whisper something, to which he laughed again and nodded. The princess made a perfect match for him with her title and wealth, and for the first time in her life, Kate wished she'd been born a princess. But she needed to be practical. Bregovi certainly would be. Wasn't that why they selected brides through the festival? Only those with dowry, title, and alliance could enter.

Yes, she needed to be practical as well. She needed to think about finding work. A position somewhere safe. She tore her eyes away and fixed them back on Lord Preston who had moved on to recounting his family's holdings to a buxom maiden to his left.

A glance to her other companion brought her eye to chin with Brock, who'd been watching her.

"Weighing your options, milady?"

"Situations, sire, not options."

"And what sort of situation do you desire?"

"Desire has little to do with it. I seek security. Safety."

"Safety from what?" His eyes peered into hers as if he knew the answer.

"Safety from the rain and famine and those who would harm me."

Brock shook his head in disapproval and tasted a bite of roast.

"What sort of situation should I desire?"

"Love."

He said it without hesitation and her breath hitched. She had expected a practical theory.

"A man to laugh with, to tumble with, to have babes with, to love 'till the stars fall from the heavens. A love to make all of the toil worthwhile."

"Why, Brock, with all of your talk of wenches, you're a romantic?"

"Cannot a smithy and a wench find love?"

"Perhaps, but it is so rare," she said. "My parents found love with each other. And our cook and her husband. But I've not met many others. Have you?"

He rested his mug of mead on the table. "Yes. I've known many who've loved. Maybe it is more difficult for those in the manor than those in the cottage."

"You may be right," she said. "So, why haven't you fallen in love with one of those young maids clamoring for your eye? Hasn't anyone tugged at your heart?" She couldn't imagine the brazen blacksmith settling for one with so many offering their attentions.

He thought for a long moment and took another drink before answering. "One stole it."

"Stole it?" The man kept surprising her. "And what of her heart?"

"It was mine and none other's."

"Was?"

"She died of the fever two winters back."

"Oh, I'm so sorry, Brock," she said, resting her hand on his arm as emotion stabbed at her.

He took another swig.

"Had you married?"

He shook his head. "She wanted to wait until the spring, when the flowers bloomed."

Kate felt such a need to give him solace. It made no sense. She didn't much believe in love herself, but she wanted him to.

"Perhaps you'll find love again someday."

"No man could be so blessed."

"A good man could."

A slow grin crept across his strong face.

"So now milady believes in love?"

"For a blacksmith."

"If I again hope for love, you must do the same."

As impossible as it seemed with the genie binding and her uncle and the uncertainty of her future, some small part of her wanted to hope.

"Very well. I'll believe if you will," she said.

"I expect an invitation to your wedding," he said.

"Only if I may attend yours."

"I would be honored. Come, Kate, let us toast." He raised his mug.

"To hope," she said lifting her goblet.

"To love," he said.

As she drank, her eyes couldn't help but drift back to Bregovi.

* * *

Brock and Preston insisted on escorting Kate into the music room for the next event. To her dismay, they also insisted on greeting each smiling woman they encountered, most of whom offered Kate insincere wishes of luck with her performance.

After one particularly unpleasant exchange, she steered them toward Rachel and Sebastian.

Rachel smiled as they approached. "Kate, I'm looking forward to listening to your piece. I hear you've a true talent."

Kate's stomach knotted. Rachel could have only heard from one source, and she hoped Bregovi hadn't shared much.

"What instrument are you performing?" Sebastian asked.

"The harp," she replied.

"How ambitious," Sophia commented behind her, the tone dripping with condescension.

Kate turned to discover Bregovi with Sophia and Victoria on opposite arms. It shouldn't have bothered her that the two princesses flanked him, but she was secretly glad she had the elbows of two handsome men. Touché.

"How so?" she asked.

"It's such a difficult instrument, isn't it? And you couldn't have brought your own. If you even own one."

"I'm sure Kate will do fine on our harp," Bregovi said.

"Yes, it is fortunate for her you have one," Victoria said.

"And what will you play?" Brock asked, his eyes fixed on Victoria. The princess replied, "The viola."

"We should sit," Preston encouraged as the room started to fill.

"Best of luck to you, once again," Bregovi said.

Kate curtsied and nodded her thanks.

"Yes, best of luck," Sophia interrupted. "Honestly, I wish I were you right now. You're under no pressure because you aren't royal and everyone expects you to fare horribly."

Kate quickly composed several biting responses. She was of higher birth than all of the entrants save Victoria and Sophia and, as Lady Katherine Durant, had as much right to be there as any of the competitors. Had her parents lived or her uncle been honorable, her dowry would have been ample enough to please even the king.

"And what will you be playing, Sophia?" Preston asked.

"Preston," she nodded. "You know I'm accomplished at the viola."

"Of course, like Princess Victoria," Preston said. "How original."

"The viola is a popular instrument among royalty," Sophia said.

"As well as commoners, I've heard," Preston said.

Sophia's face reddened. "If it is popular among the lesser classes it is only because they wish to emulate their superiors."

"And not the ease with which one can learn the instrument?" Preston said.

"The viola is not easy to learn," Sophia said.

"Yes," Preston said, "as you'll likely demonstrate for us today."

As Kate coughed to cover her laughter, she caught Bregovi's mischievous gaze.

"If we're to witness the battle, I mean *event*, we should claim seats now before the best are taken," Bregovi said. They all came to agreement on that point and parted.

"Thank you," Kate whispered to Preston.

"My pleasure," he said. "Sophia's kingdom borders ours and I've known her family since we were children. They're exactly like her. Rich, spoiled, conniving. Despite their wealth, they often short us on horse deals. It's nice to jab back now and then."

The chairs were arrayed in the shape of a horseshoe and Brock and Preston selected seats on one end. They assured her it was the best location to be seen, but she suspected their motive was to have an ideal position from which to view the maidens in attendance.

Uninterested in either seeing or being seen, Kate turned her attention to the instruments at the center of the room. As Sophia had indicated, the viola was popular and several lay on a table awaiting use. A lute, recorder and the harp rounded out the collection.

As they watched lady after princess perform, Kate was secretly pleased that Bregovi—still flanked by Victoria and Sophia—didn't appear nearly as interested in the performances as he'd been in hers the night before. She glanced at the harp and her mind flickered to their conversation, the music and the kisses they'd shared. As her blood warmed at the thought, her gaze went immediately back to Bregovi. She sucked in a breath. He was staring right at her.

The room had gone eerily silent and all eyes were on her. Holy gods, had she said something?

She turned to Brock, who whispered, "You're next, milady."

With relief sweeping through her, she arose and hurried to the harp. She didn't expect to win—although boring, many of the viola pieces were flawless—but she did want to show she could hold her own against the royal vixens.

She tucked in under the instrument, resting it on her right shoulder, took a breath and started the first chords of the cheerier tune from the prior evening. She had nearly finished the first few measures when she hit a wrong note. She quickly reset her hands and tried again, but the same sour note rang out. A string was off. It grated against every nerve and she heard a few groans from the crowd.

Pressing onward with the next refrain, she built to higher keys. She avoided the problem string, but hit another worse than the first. As she finished the first stanza another few bad notes rang out and she knew someone had tampered with the instrument.

Pride battled humiliation and she decided to quit before they laughed her out of the room. As Sophia had said, they didn't expect much from her and she thought it better to retake her seat than to look like a fool crying sabotage.

Her face grew hot at the snickers and whispers around her, but she fought the urge to defend herself.

Encouraging smiles from Brock and Preston greeted her as she sat between them.

"Interesting choice," Brock nodded.

"At least it wasn't the viola," Preston added.

"I think I'd have fared better at the joust," she said, hoping she sounded indifferent about it.

She spent the remainder of the event wondering who might have tampered with the harp. As had occurred at each gathering, surges of emotion—mostly anger and jealousy—hit her in waves, but with her powers bound, she couldn't determine their source. Even using reason, there were too many possibilities to pinpoint a short list of suspects. When a prince was on the line, a desperate maiden was likely to do anything to eliminate a rival.

Finally, Randolph announced the last entrant and stated Bregovi would declare the best musician. Excited whispers spread when he added that the winner would accompany the prince to the men's archery competition that afternoon.

The royal hopefuls held a collective breath as Bregovi arose and approached the center of the floor. However, rather than pausing to address them, he continued straight to the harp, where he looked over the instrument carefully, running his fingers across each string. When he hit the problem ones, the room cringed yet again at the unpleasant sound.

"It appears someone has tampered with our harp," he said. "I had been looking forward to hearing you all play your best so I could make a fair decision. Unfortunately, it seems a competitor or one of her supporters lacked faith in her abilities. Fortunately, I had the opportunity to hear Kate play last night and know exactly what she's capable of."

Kate sank deeper into her beautifully upholstered chair.

"And considering that performance against the others heard today, I must award the win to Hildegard Katela Fishbeck of Cragmont."

The weak applause from the ladies was drowned out by that of Brock, Preston, Rachel and Sebastian.

"Must have been some performance," Sophia griped loudly.

Kate tried to smile, but wasn't sure she pulled it off.

"Milady?" Preston nudged.

She looked over and Preston tilted his head toward Bregovi, who stood in the center of the room expectantly. She arose and moved toward him. His eyes held hers the entire time.

Easy, Kate. Don't forget to breathe. And don't tear his twinkling eyes out.

She stopped barely out of reach and curtsied.

"Thank you, your highness."

"You earned it." He grinned as gasps and murmurs spread through the crowd.

"That's debatable," she grumbled.

"Wonderful. I look forward to debating it at the archery event this afternoon."

Blessed gods, there is no escape.

CHAPTER TWELVE

Amidst errands for Victoria, Kate warded off comments from envious maidens all afternoon.

"Just what did you perform on, I mean *for*, the prince to deserve such high praise?"

"How far do you plan to go to win the next event?"

"That must have been quite exceptional playing, Miss Fish*beak*."

Then there were those who suggested that to generate sympathy she had sabotaged the harp herself, as it was the only way she could possibly win.

So, with her last task accomplished—delivery of a post to the courier—she nearly sprinted to the archery field. Her eagerness due in no part to the idea of being with Bregovi and in large part to the thought of seeing the faces of the spiteful royals as she sat, talked and laughed with the prince under their haughty noses.

Slightly breathless, she stepped into the royal family's box and found her plan off to a poor start. Although the seats overflowed with maidens, they lacked one specific prince. Perhaps he had grown wise and ran from the brood.

On the field, the competition had begun and archers positioned themselves to take one of several shots at wooden targets. A prominent X on each figure indicated where to hit for maximum points and she couldn't help but note the comparison to herself. The targets, not the men. Bregovi had certainly struck the maximum point blow with her, even if she didn't have a bold X painted on her gown.

"The prince must have found another servant to tend to his needs," Princess Sophia said. "It appears your performance wasn't memorable enough after all."

"Nor yours, it appears," Kate replied. Although she didn't expect much of a reaction from Sophia, the princess blushed, and Kate felt a bit of satisfaction. As other maidens eyed her, likely formulating barbs of their own, Kate decided if Bregovi was elsewhere, she could be too.

As she turned to escape, a young squire intercepted her. His freckles and curly blond hair were of the same mold as Rachel's chatty maid, Holly.

"Miss Kate?" he asked with practiced formality.

"Yes?"

"Prince Edmund would like you to join him. Will you please come with me?"

She didn't miss Sophia's frosty glare. Or Victoria's.

"He isn't watching from here?" a duchess cried.

The squire's eyes drew wide as he took in the numerous gazes turned in his direction. "I'm sorry, milady, but he's sitting elsewhere."

"Is there room for me?" another asked.

"I'm sorry, mum, uh, milady, but I have specific instructions to deliver only Miss Kate."

Relieved to be free of the glaring harem, Kate followed the young man across the field. On the way, she learned her escort was named Foster and was indeed Holly's brother.

As she arrived at a small box at field level, Bregovi stood, eyes and dimples out in full glory. Weapons of conquest.

She felt like the promised land.

"Thank you for joining me, Kate." He held a chair for her. The wood was a deep mahogany, and the burgundy upholstery was finer than her gown.

She sank into the cushion and took in the refreshments on the table before them. A pitcher and two goblets. Cheeses. An array of fruit, some of which she couldn't identify. The scene had been set for courting.

The box with the hostile maidens would have been safer.

Bregovi settled on a matching chair next to hers.

"I thought this might be more comfortable than sharing a bench," he said.

"You've succeeded with the chair."

"Not the rest?" He looked at the tray and goblets, a hint of disappointment in his voice. "It's simply a friendly meal. Please try something. Have you tasted kiwi?" He held up a piece of green fruit on a fork.

"I lost my appetite after the competition." It was true. She'd felt queasy all afternoon, but that strange fruit was tempting her.

"Because the harp had been compromised?" He popped the kiwi in his mouth.

"Because the entire kingdom thinks I performed more than the harp for you."

"That's not what I told them," he said, helping himself to the yellow cubed fruit.

"It doesn't matter what you said. It's what they think."

"What they think shouldn't matter to you."

As he prepared a slice of apple with cheese, her mouth watered.

"Unlike you, I do not have the luxury of laughing off gossip."

He studied the platter, then selected and ate a tiny cluster of grapes.

"I need to secure a future, and no one will want me if they think I'm the prince's—"

His head snapped around at that.

"Mistress." She had intended to say whore, but caught herself at his reaction.

"Who are you concerned about?" he asked. "That smithy? Or the horseman from Larchmont? Neither seems much of a find."

"That doesn't matter. What matters is I'm merely a bit of folly to you. The whole party knows it. Even you. Isn't that why you spent the morning flirting with every maiden capable of blushing?"

He stared at her with that one, not rising to the bait, and when a smile played at the corners of his mouth, she turned her attention to the buffet. He would not draw her in, at least not any further in.

Her stomach growled at her to take some action, so she stabbed a slice of kiwi. It melted as she chewed. Tangy and sweet. A perfect diversion and a safer topic.

"This is delicious."

"Last night you chided me for not speaking to them enough. And, if I recall correctly, you made me promise to speak to nine of them."

He'd actually taken that seriously?

"Are you never pleased?"

"It didn't look as painful as you described," she said, taking another slice.

He filled their goblets and took a long drink.

"Looks can be deceiving."

"You seemed delighted with Sophia."

That brought a grin and those dimples again. She almost forgot why she was angry with him. Almost.

"Should I not enjoy Sophia's company?"

"What you should not do is seduce maidens you will not marry."

"You were the one doing the seducing."

"No, I was merely playing the harp."

"In nothing but a chemise."

"I had a cloak."

"Not on you. What man can resist a near naked woman?"

Her jaw dropped and her face warmed. "I was not nearly—"

"Then to finish me off, you lured me in with that mesmerizing fire."

"Now you're confusing me with some other unwitting conquest. There was no fire, just a few candles."

"Ah, but there was fire, milady. It burned in your eyes and on your lips."

She cleared her throat. Although clearing her mind seemed a better idea, because his mention of fire and lips brought back a vivid recollection of *his* lips on hers.

"You have a poetic imagination, your highness. Misguided and delusional, but poetic."

"I thank you for the poetic part. As for the other," he leaned in and whispered, "there was fire and you know it." His glittering eyes stared into hers, causing another sort of fire to race through her veins. The man saw too much. Knew too much.

She let out an exasperated breath and distracted herself from the fire, and his eyes, and merciless thoughts of lips by stabbing a chunk of the yellow fruit. It burst with flavor in her mouth.

"What is this?" she asked, losing her manners and speaking before she'd swallowed.

"Pineapple."

She took another. And another. And after a few moments of silent chewing, she hoped he'd finally let the matter go. Foolish thought.

"Is this so painful, Kate?"

She dabbed her mouth with a napkin. "Not at present, but it will be."

His steady gaze demanded further explanation.

"I know you. You live in a castle, born with a crown and responsibilities and privilege beyond what most can imagine. You will marry an equally privileged bride with wealth or alliance or assets necessary to strengthen your kingdom and to perpetuate your life of entitlement. And, unbelievable as it is, you are bored. You play bandit for fun and seek amusement to pass your days. I have no illusions. I am one of those amusements. When you finish with me—when you grow bored again—you will move on faster than I can blink."

He sat back in his chair, hearing the truth of her words, she supposed. His gaze lingered over the playing field and on the stands, and while he contemplated, she snatched another bite of the pineapple before he called an end to their afternoon.

"Perhaps we've discovered the true problem."

Right. Prince. Servant. Wealthy. Penniless. Boredom. Amusement.

"Come," he stood and extended a hand. "I will show you who I am."

An unbidden image of him naked flashed through her mind.

"Don't worry, it is not my bed," he said with a devilish grin.

She'd swear she heard *yet* whispered on the breeze.

"No. You can show me here. Or tell me here. We don't need to go anywhere."

"The showing and telling cannot happen here." He took her hand and gently pulled her to her feet. "Please, Kate, you presume to know me, but you are wrong. There is more to me than what you see. Let me show you." His soft eyes awaited her answer.

She glanced back at the castle. It would be empty except for servants.

"Come," he said, his hand tugging hers. "You've nothing to fear with me."

A nervous energy brewed within her. She'd not admit it to him, but she was intrigued.

"We can take the fruit," he said lifting the tray, a smile playing at his lips.

He was disarmingly persuasive without even trying. And she was, after all, a foolish, brain-addled maiden. At least around him.

"Very well, but if you make any attempt at seduction—if this isn't truly something legitimate—you'll be eating that fruit in one bite."

He chuckled, handed her the pitcher and snatched up the cheese tray as well.

"I assure you, milady, any seduction will be of your doing, not mine."

"Then we're both safe." At least she hoped as much.

As he led her inside, she prayed to all the gods that whatever he showed her wouldn't make her love him.

By the time they arrived at the family wing, curiosity had banished caution.

"Is it a family heirloom?" she asked. "Perhaps a humble challis, sure to enlighten me about your origins?"

"Better. You'll see." He turned a corner and led her past Rachel's bedchamber.

"Is it something you created in your youth? A drawing or a statue?"

"I'm not artistic, but you've quite the imagination," he said as they moved through a long portrait-lined corridor.

Painting after painting displayed a remarkable resemblance in eyes and chin.

"Are you taking me to your namesake's portrait? Perhaps a saint of a man?"

"I'm afraid, while my ancestors were honorable, none were saintly. Any other guesses?" He grinned back at her as he nudged a door open with his foot.

He indicated she should enter and she stepped into a very ordinary *bedchamber*.

"Bregovi. You promised—"

"The promise stands," he said, passing into an adjacent room. "This way,"

She followed him into a large nursery. Everything a child could wish for adorned its interior. Toys, easels, dolls, a globe, a miniature horse figure and more. All clean, well kept and ready for use. She couldn't help but imagine him there as a child. He'd have been full of mischief, leaping off furniture, acting the part of bandit from behind the drapes.

"Is this supposed to demonstrate your longing to populate this room with children?"

"Holy gods, no," he said.

The walls displayed bright tapestries and murals, one of which took her by surprise. The mountains jutting to the ceiling, the desolation to the right, and the collection of the children to the left meant one thing.

"This isn't your usual nursery artwork," she said, glancing his way.

"When the Ten were parceled out to the various kingdoms, Florian took in Diana." He set his two trays on a low table and stepped over. "She was the oldest," he said, pointing at a tall young woman. A girl half her size held one hand while Diana pushed back flowing copper curls with the other. "She had a talent for painting."

"She did this?" Kate asked, incredulous. "The detail is so fine, I almost expect the figures to come to life."

"I know. When I was a child I spent long afternoons watching it, thinking it might."

"I bet you did," she said with a laugh. "Did she paint happier scenes of Zafaria as well?"

"No, just this one. Apparently, she did it so she wouldn't forget the faces of the others."

"Wasn't she the one who insisted they follow the tunnels through the mountain?"

He nodded. "The spell sealing them in the cave didn't disperse when Zafaria turned to dust. She said Felix, the little one, panicked and tried to run out after the guards died outside, but the entrance threw him back into the others. Felix and Diana are both in my ancestral line." He pointed at a dark-eyed boy, not more than two or three, in the arms of an auburn-haired girl—an auburn-haired girl with blue eyes and a face Kate had known all her life.

"Who's carrying him?"

"Athena. I can't recall who took her in." He paused and peered closer. "I'd bet on Cragmont."

"Yes, the resemblance is remarkable," Kate said.

"You'll have to tell Princess Victoria we found her ancestor in the nursery."

Kate's too. She was looking at an image of her great-great something grandmother. And with her bloodlines tracing back to seven of the Zafarian Ten, six other great grandparents were staring back at her as well.

"So, this is all very interesting," she said, meaning it. "But what am I to glean about your true nature from this? That you enjoy art and are an expert on The Ten?"

"This isn't our destination," he said, sliding the fruit onto the platter with the cheese. "Come, we're almost there."

Picking up the one full tray, he pulled aside a tapestry to reveal a hidden panel and an even more hidden passage. She took a breath and followed.

The secret corridor was lit by small windows of cut glass and, unlike its counterpart in Cragmont, Bregovi's passage appeared to be on the cleaning roster. Cobwebs and rats were nowhere in sight.

"This was designed as an escape route for the royal children should the castle fall under attack," Bregovi said from ahead.

"Was it ever used for that?"

"Centuries ago. Before the alliance between the kingdoms."

They came to a fork and took a narrow spiraled staircase up one flight. He halted at a landing barely large enough for both of them. Feeling out of sorts in the dark and too close to Bregovi, Kate edged toward the wall for support. Her heart hammered in her breast, a result of his nearness, the climb up the stairs and the excitement of the adventure.

"Now for the big revelation," he said, his breath warm on her ear.

He pulled a lever behind her, and the wall she'd been leaning against slowly slid away to reveal an enchanted land. Or, more accurately, an enchanted library.

She crossed the threshold and let out a choked laugh. Something legitimate indeed. So many treasures clamored for her attention, she didn't know what to inspect first.

The ceiling stretched two levels high in the center and, to her left, sunshine poured in through an enormous wall of windows, illuminating objects like jewels. A second floor balcony overlooked the room from above. Under it, she noted a second door, likely the usual, less enchanting entrance. Books in enclosed cases lined the walls, and exotic treasures gleamed everywhere.

She ached to see and touch it all.

Bregovi took the pitcher from her and set it with the fruit on a table near the window. It didn't miss her attention that his eyes were fixed on her the whole time. This mattered to him.

The table closest to her displayed a hand-painted globe of the world. She reached out to turn it, but hesitated.

"Go ahead," he said. "You may touch anything."

So she did. Gently spinning the globe, she noted its detail and the odd names written on various lands. Then, still under his gaze, she explored the room. Her father had often brought back treasures from his travels, but the prince's collection dwarfed his. She inspected delightful carved figures of unusual animals, with Bregovi naming each for her. She opened giant books with exotic flowers and leaves pressed between their heavy pages. The pinks, oranges and yellows were brighter than any she'd seen.

"Where did you find these?"

"Various islands. The names are written there on the pages."

So they were. He'd cataloged everything.

A cabinet near the windows held jars of all sizes. Plants grew from some and others held dry specimens.

"What are these?"

"Medicinal herbs."

They too were labeled with the date, location obtained, name and remedy. Arnica flower applied for pain. Hydrastis Canadenis root for stomach. Echinacea herb for fever. The dates were as recent as three months and went back a year or so.

Everywhere she looked she found a new discovery. There were unusual costumes of silk and straw. Intricate painted masks. And unique jewelry carved from ivory. Exquisite goblets of rose-colored glass and luxurious blankets woven with shimmering thread. Colorful crystals in an array of sizes and shapes. Even the floors were covered in carpets of elaborate designs that should have been hanging on the walls.

She didn't try to hide her delight. The man could seduce her if he wanted to, solely for letting her play with his treasures.

A shallow glass box atop a mahogany trunk drew her eye and inside she discovered a turtle barely larger than her hand. She reached in to stroke its back and it quickly ducked its head inside its shell.

"She's gentle, Galileo," he said, picking it up. "Try offering him the greens."

She pulled a fresh leaf from the pen. "Come on, Galileo. Just a nibble?" she coaxed. With Bregovi holding it, she ran her fingers over its back and its rough legs. "I've seen baby turtles on the shore, but none this size."

"I found him on an island in the far seas."

"Galileo? Galileo, I have some fresh lettuce for you," she crooned, trying the leafy food again. A green beak slowly poked out. Soon his eyes and neck followed and he took a bite. She nearly squealed.

"I thought there wasn't going to be any seducing today," he said.

She laughed. "Can I hold him?"

He laid the creature in her palm, sending a tingle up her arm when his hand brushed hers.

"Do you have any pets?" he asked.

"When I was young, I had a cat named Bluebell. She was a dark gray tabby with a bell on her collar."

"Hence the name?"

"I was a very literal child." She had loved the tabby, but thinking of her also brought back painful memories of her demise. Memories she didn't wish to revisit.

She set the turtle back in the pen within easy access to the lettuce leaf.

"Any other surprises?" she asked.

"Of course," he said, his eyes sparkling. "I have many."

Too many, I fear. His room of treasures reminded her of her father. The two men were much alike with their love of adventure and exotic lands. A love she shared as well.

She wandered over to another case where a sphere, a wooden box, daggers, and more all bore the familiar Zafarian symbol—a serpent encircling the image of a dragon perched upon a mountain with a crystal clutched in one claw.

Panic flooded her at the thought that Bregovi's family could be part of the brotherhood. Had he been playing with her while he sent word to Morten? Or was he unaware of who she was? She slowed her breathing, trying not to tip him off that anything was amiss.

She must have paused too long, for Bregovi stepped over to look at the items as well. As she scrambled to piece together any clues she'd missed, he picked up a hand mirror.

The handle and backing were black tourmaline, the face polished black obsidian, and delicate quartz points circled the glassy surface like jewels around a crown. The Mirror of Regret had captured her imagination when studying Morten's books on dark magik. Infamous among sorcerers, the object had sent many a man to his death or worse.

Turning it to show her the back, he said, "This is the mark of the Zafarians. I'm sure you've heard the legends."

"Yes," she said as thoughts tumbled through her mind. Was he showing it to her to instill fear or was it merely another collectible to him? Did he know what the items could do? Was he testing her?

"I studied their history for a time and, until recently, thought they were extinct," he said.

"You think they still exist?"

"Groups claiming to be Zafarians have been attacking the

kingdoms to collect objects such as these. They must be more than trinkets."

More indeed. Zafarian objects held powerful magikal properties. Although most lacked the skill or Gift to use them, those who could were formidable opponents. The mirror in Bregovi's hand had and could reverse any spell back onto he who cast it. Her uncle would slaughter kingdoms to obtain it and the rest of Bregovi's collection.

"Do you believe in magik?" she asked.

"I've never seen evidence of this sort of magik, but accounts of the past testify to it. And the objects are unusual."

"How so?" She felt energy emanating from them and wondered if he could as well.

"They're hot."

He handed the mirror to her. It felt slightly warm where he had been holding it, but not unusually so.

"It doesn't feel hot to me."

His brows hitched in puzzlement as he took it again.

"But it is. And the longer you hold it the hotter it gets. Here, try again," he said, handing it back.

Same result. She shook her head.

"Here, compare it to this." He gave her a small silver box from another shelf. He smiled, appearing confident she'd see it now. She didn't.

"They feel the same to me." As shaky as she felt, she couldn't help but grin. Partly at his perplexed expression and partly from relief. If he were a Zafarian, he'd not try to convince her there was anything unusual about the objects, and he wouldn't keep them on open display. And he certainly wouldn't hand her one of the most powerful weapons ever created.

She let out a breath she hadn't known she'd been holding and drew in a few more to steady her nerves. Finally, her hands stopped trembling and her legs grew steady again.

As the befuddled prince tried other items in the case, Kate glanced more closely at the box he'd handed her and discovered the image her mother had drawn for her years earlier—the silhouette of an island surrounded by the sun, moon and stars. The symbol of her mother's people.

Quickly glancing to the shelf he'd retrieved the box from, she discovered silver daggers, rings and more all bearing the same symbol.

Caligo? How could it be?

"Where did you find this?"

"In the Outer Isles. It bears the marking of Caligo." He ran his fingers over the image. "It's a mythical island cloaked by mist so men can't find it. Stories tell of inhabitants who have the Gift of healing and never die."

"Do you know anything about its location?" She didn't think he would, since the secret was so well guarded, but he'd traveled so much, perhaps he'd heard a tale.

"Again, it's mostly myth, but it's said to be where the great oceans meet." He looked over an adjoining case of books then pulled a heavy volume from it. "I've always been intrigued by legends— Zafaria, Caligo and more. I paid a fair sum for this, but unfortunately it's in another tongue. I've learned bits of five languages, but none compares. I've not been able to decipher it."

"On Caligo? I didn't think there were... Where did you? How?"

Chuckling at her response, he handed it over.

She opened it with shaky hands. Her mind couldn't take in what her eyes saw. The cover shimmered like her mother's locket. It looked to be made of an iridescent shell that changed colors with the light.

The familiar symbol covered the entire page. At its larger size she noticed figures of people and animals, along with other shapes she couldn't identify. The next page contained a map of the island with unusual markings around it. Nothing indicated its location. She knew from her childhood that her mother had come from the island and had given up her life there to be with Kate's father. After her parents' death, Kate had desperately wanted to find it. Her mother had told her the locket was a gift from her grandfather and held the key to returning, but Kate hadn't been able to learn its secrets. She turned the pages with reverence, skimming the verse. She recognized some of the words, but many were lost to her. It had been a long time since her mother had taught her.

"Don't tell me you can you read it."

"Hardly," Kate said. "My father was an explorer, and as a child, I studied the tales of Caligo. I know a few things, but most of it is beyond me."

She didn't wish to lie, but telling him the truth wasn't an option. Turning another page, she caught her breath. On it was a pastel etching of a dark haired woman with gray eyes. Just like her mother's.

"You're welcome to the book—"

"You'd give it to me?" Her hands trembled along with the rest of her limbs. She'd never expected to find any clues about Caligo, let alone a chronicle.

"It's yours on one condition."

"Fine," she said, closing her prize.

"Fine?" A mischievous brow lifted. "You don't yet know the condition."

"Right." She laughed. "I suppose I agreed a bit premature. What's the condition?"

Her stomach fluttered with excitement. It didn't matter what it was, she would consent. Another kiss? Done. More? She couldn't believe she was considering it. He'd lured her close with the room, the treasures, and completed his seduction with the book.

"It's too late to back out," he said, eyes glinting. "You already agreed."

"I'm not backing out." She clutched the book to her breast.

His gaze followed and lingered there for a moment.

"Name your condition."

CHAPTER THIRTEEN

"Checkmate," Bregovi shouted.

"What? It can't be." Kate's eyes darted to the board.

She had once again flipped open the book on Caligo while he contemplated his next play, and she'd been so focused on the page, she hadn't heard his two attempts to get her to make her move.

He watched as realization hit her.

"Nice try, bandit boy," she said, turning her attention back to the game.

"I could have rearranged all your pieces while you weren't looking," he said. "The board was mine for the taking."

"No, you couldn't. I know where my men are at all times. And nothing here is yours for the taking." She hadn't looked up, but her voice danced with amusement.

She twirled loose strands of hair around her fingers as she studied the board. She did that when concentrating. He had learned as much as he watched her play chess and as she lost herself in that book over and over again.

When he had complained to her he might as well be playing alone, she had put it away for a time. But eventually it was open before her again. Truth be told, he didn't mind. Watching her study it had become a favorite pastime.

She seemed to recognize words or symbols on the pages, although he had never met anyone who could identify the language. It fascinated him. *She* fascinated him. She held her own with a sword, played the harp with eloquence, and challenged him in a tough chess match. While she'd agreed to the game as payment for the book, he suspected he could have asked for a far more intimate favor from her.

But he'd promised no seduction and she'd no doubt insist that included favors. He'd not push his good fortune.

As he waited for her to make a move, he selected a wedge of cheese and took a swallow of wine.

"The rook to pawn looks to be your best option," he offered.

"And then you take the rook with your knight? I don't think so."

She acted angry, but a grin played at her lips. She seemed happy. *He* had made her happy and his heart lifted as if he were the one receiving the gift. Wolfe would dub him a sappy fool, but he didn't care. She'd lowered her guard that afternoon, asking him question after question about his travels while her eyes sparkled like frosty stars. He had described the lands to her in as much detail as he could remember, and still she pried more out of him.

She'd told him of her love of the ocean. How she'd sit on the beach for hours watching the waves and gulls, playing with crabs, looking for shells, walking with her feet in the surf or atop the cliffs where the view went on forever. And she'd confided she'd always wanted to see the distant shores beyond the horizon.

As she contemplated her move, he picked up the book that held her so enthralled. She eyed him warily.

"Easy, Kate. I won't lose your place."

She forced an unconvincing smile. "Please take care with it."

"I take great care with all my things," he said, gazing into her eyes. He had hoped she would catch his meaning—that he'd take great care with her too—but she only grew alarmed.

"I thought you gave it to me."

"It is yours," he said. "I meant I take care with those things in my possession. And while possession may indicate ownership, in this case it indicates what's in my hands at the moment." He added softly, "I take great care with what's in my hands at the moment, or arms, too, for that matter."

Her eyes met his, searching, then challenging.

"No seduction."

"Do you find that seductive, Kate? I was merely discussing this fine book."

"So read it and let me think."

"As you wish, but you know I can't make out the words." Still, he let her concentrate while he flipped through the heavy tome. It had been several years since he'd studied it. For a time he had been so intent on deciphering its contents that he'd taken samples of the script to scholars on his travels. But no one could identify the lettering, making his efforts fruitless.

He sucked in a breath. Kate's eyes stared back from the page. The sketch was of a woman with long dark hair swirling about her face. The nose was longer than Kate's, and the chin sharper, but the eyes were hers. Almond shaped and gray like the morning mist. He looked up and discovered those same eyes staring intently into his.

The room grew still. It seemed important, but he didn't understand how. The Isle of Caligo was myth. Sailors had tried and failed to find it for centuries. Longer. But why did she seem to recognize some of the words? Were her people from there? Is that why she'd wanted the book so desperately?

He had so many questions he didn't know where to start, but his gut told him not to press just yet. So did her eyes. She wasn't ready to share what Caligo meant to her. And while he craved to know what it all meant, he craved time with her more.

"Did you move one of those men you're so aware of?" he asked, his gaze still locked on hers. He could almost sense her considering, weighing, then slowly relax.

"Yes," she said. "You've one less bishop."

"No, not the bishop," he cried, delivering the book to her open arms.

Kate set the book aside and didn't open it again for a long while, to keep him from looking as well, Bregovi surmised.

As the match went on, Holly brought in meats, bread and a pitcher of cider, then candles as the sun set beyond the hills.

A handful of figures remained on the board for each. Kate sat watching him with her feet on her chair, her knees tucked under her chin, and her arms around her legs. He could see the young girl she must have been. Relaxed. Playful. Sharp.

He toyed with her by touching this man or that, as if about to move it.

"What does sacrifice mean to you, Kate?"

"How would I define it?" She raised her head to consider.

He nodded.

"I suppose it is giving up something you cherish."

"Giving up that cherished thing for something you want more?"

"Or to avoid peril."

That sent her into hidden thoughts and he wondered what secrets she kept locked away.

"Are you thinking of a particular sacrifice?" she asked.

"Actually, yes, I am. There is something I've long cherished. It has brought me through many a tight situation, but it's time to part with it for the greater good."

"Truly," she said with a hint of skepticism. "What is this beloved item to be sacrificed to all that is holy?"

"A warrior of noble character and unquestionable honor. Courageous. Valiant."

"I see," she said, eyeing his last knight. "And what would make you give up such a faithful servant?"

"A loftier aim. A woman of courage and charm. Intelligence.

Cunning wits. A woman of beauty from skin to soul."

Their eyes met and color seeped into her cheeks.

"An impossible combination. No woman could be all you say."

"Nay, I know of one." *Two.*

"You cannot."

"I say I do and she sits here before me." Holding her gaze, he moved his knight check with her king.

Eyes darting over the board, she sank back in her chair.

"You want my queen."

And you.

She would have to use the queen to protect her king and his remaining bishop would take her as soon as she did so. The moves played out as he had anticipated and left them with six pieces on the board between them.

As he chided himself for pushing them so close to the end of the game, his father entered and blew an icy quell over them both.

Kate dropped her feet to the floor and shifted to a more formal position.

"We missed you at the archery event, son. I should have suspected you'd be here. With a maiden," he said, eyeing Kate. "Take care, child, my son plays to win."

He caught his father's full meaning and wouldn't have it.

"Kate presents a worthy opponent and needs no words of caution."

"Aren't you this year's commoner?"

Muscles throughout Bregovi's body tensed as he watched some of the afternoon's joy leave her.

"Not by my own doing."

"Where are you from?"

"Cragmont."

"Ah, the kingdom with the fleet," his father said, inspecting a relic from a nearby case. "Tell me, dear, has your family ships?"

"My father had his own, but both he and the ship were lost at sea."

"At sea?" Bregovi asked. "I thought he succumbed to illness."

She shook her head. How had he missed that?

"As I've said, son, the sea is unpredictable. Tempests can bring down even the strongest ship."

"Yes, it's true, but pirates took my father, not a storm," she said, fidgeting with a captured rook on the table.

"I'm sorry." Bregovi covered her hand with his. He had heard of pirate attacks—all seamen had—but they'd been fortunate.

"Thank you." She gently pulled her hand from his and rested it in her lap.

"Something to consider if you continue exploring, Edmund."

"Agreed."

"As is your purse," he said, turning to Kate. "How large is your dowry, child?"

"Father," Bregovi cautioned.

"I have no brothers and a greedy uncle who had his own designs on my dowry."

"It is unfortunate your parents didn't see better to your future."

She stiffened, and Bregovi hoped the maiden who had battled him with the sword would soon make an appearance.

"Do you hold any alliances to benefit our kingdom?" his father asked.

She thought on that. "None that would likely interest you."

"And no title either," the king said condescendingly. "Nothing to offer."

Bregovi stood as his father turned to him, but she cut them both off.

"Although I have no designs on your son, I assure you I offer other assets of worth to a husband."

"Indeed," his father said. "However, it is wise you do not seek that which is beyond you."

He lifted the Caligo volume from the table and thumbed through it.

Kate's face went white, her gaze fixed upon the book before turning her attention back to the chessboard.

"Kate won the harp event and thus some of my time," Bregovi said, taking the tome from his father. "There is no need to interrogate her."

"If you focus too intently on this one, you will only offend the maiden who will become your bride. Might I suggest you conclude this dalliance and rejoin our other guests?"

"Checkmate," Kate declared, her voice flat.

Both men studied the board. She'd cornered his king with a knight. His only move gave the figure to her rook.

"Nicely played," his father said. "Edmund rarely loses."

Kate stood. Bregovi tried to catch her eye, but she didn't look his way.

"Thank you for the game, your highness," Kate said. "Please excuse me. I fear I'm neglecting a princess or two myself."

Bregovi caught her arm as she started toward the door. "Kate."

She forced a smile. "I must go. I need to tend to my duties." She curtsied to his father, turned and disappeared out the door.

* * *

Kate hurried down the hall, rounded a corner and paused against a rose-carved post for a moment. She needed to catch her breath. She needed to steel her emotions. She needed to forget the unforgettable day with Bregovi.

He had told her of his adventures in such detail she felt like she was there—wanted to be there—with him. He had given her the book of her mother's people. And more dangerous by far, he had made her hope.

By the time the king had arrived, she had imagined a life with him, traveling on the seas to exotic lands, talking for long hours, making love from sunset to dawn, bearing him children with midnight hair and green eyes. Fantasies she had no business entertaining.

A door creaked behind her, and she moved on with Bregovi's likeness watching her from the family portraits on the walls. Turning a corner, she found herself face to face with the living version.

"I want a rematch," Bregovi said with the earnest expression he used when persuading her to play the harp and see his library.

It wouldn't work this time.

"You should challenge one of the other maidens." Remembering her promise to Victoria, she added, "Princess Victoria would be a worthy opponent."

"I'm not looking for an opponent."

"I'm not looking to be your entertainment." She stepped back a foot or two. He was too close and it seemed as if he was sucking up all the air in the corridor.

"You can't deny you enjoyed yourself today." He closed the distance, touching her arm.

"What I can't deny is your father is correct," she said, brushing his hand away.

"I wish you'd forget what he said."

"I am grateful for what he said. I was too caught up in tales of your adventures to see what was happening."

"What was happening?"

"You were distracting me from reality. From my life. And that life will never involve you, so I wish you'd let me alone."

"Why don't we let another chess match decide it?" he said, grinning. "If I win—"

"I do not wish to be your plaything—" she shouted.

"I doubt you're anyone's plaything," he said, growing surly.

"And I can't be anything else to you," she finished.

"Not even a friend?" he said, sounding markedly *unfriendly*.

"We were never friends. I was an amusement, remember?" she said, equally frustrated.

"So, you learned nothing about me today. You continue to think of me as a spoiled prince."

"I learned a great deal about you, but none if it matters. It doesn't change the facts. You are using me as a diversion from this archaic competition. What you should do is spend time with the other maidens. You should court *them*. You should show *them* your treasures. You should—"

"Enough," his icy voice interrupted. "Now that you've reminded me of my place, I suggest you remember yours."

Her cheeks stung as if he'd slapped her. Then he turned his back and disappeared down the corridor.

"That's the problem," she whispered to no one. "I do remember."

She was a genie on the run, living under a false name. She was a maiden with no home, no refuge and an unknown future. She was a sorceress hiding what she could do for fear of the burning stake.

She was in no position to play fairy princess with a beautiful, adventurous prince that made her want things she could never have.

"Kate?" Rachel said from behind her.

Padding through the hall, the princess wore a peach dressing robe, her hair plaited and hanging down her back.

"I thought I heard Edmund. Were you two arguing?"

"As usual, yes." Kate forced a smile. "I am sorry if we disturbed you."

Rachel waved a hand in the air. "I'm too alarmed to be disturbed."

"Alarmed about what?" Kate asked.

"This horrible competition," Rachel said, leading the way to her bedchamber. "At first I thought it would all work out perfectly, but now…" Stepping into the room, Rachel spun around and said, "I may have to marry one of those strangers!"

Kate shut the door. "I gather Sebastian didn't fare well at archery today."

"Didn't fare well?" Rachel said, flopping back onto her bed. "He was a disaster."

"Oh, no."

"Oh, yes. The only thing he hit was the post on the deer figure."

"Did you give him another token?" Kate asked, sitting beside her.

"No. Nothing," Rachel said, abruptly sitting up. "All I did was smile at him."

"Perhaps that was enough to do him in." Bregovi's upturned lips regularly undermined her. She had lost her concentration a couple of times that afternoon because of his dimples.

"I think he's trying to lose," Rachel said, now taking a turn at pacing the floor.

"I don't believe that," Kate said.

"How could anyone do so poorly unless they were trying to?" Rachel said pacing faster. "He's an archery champion all over the kingdoms, and I shoot better than he does."

"Perhaps his competitors weren't very good," Kate suggested.

"Perhaps, but—"

"I'm certain he cares for you," Kate said, blocking Rachel's route to slow the pacing and the fretful thoughts.

"Do you think so?" the princess asked, her poor heart in her eyes.

Kate knew heartache herself and rested a gentle hand on Rachel's shoulder. "I'm sure of it. He blushes every time you look at him."

"Soon it won't matter how much he cares. If he keeps losing, I'll have to marry another."

"I hope it won't come to that," Kate said. Someone deserved a happy life.

"I do too," Rachel said, resting again on the bed, but with less desperation this time. "Why didn't you and Edmund watch the tournament? I thought that was your reward for winning."

"He showed me his library instead."

The princess's eyes pulled wide. "He must favor you. He doesn't share it with many."

Her forgetful heart leapt. But he didn't favor her. He wished favors *from* her. The sentiment was completely different.

She just wished she didn't favor him so much.

* * *

It was well past nine by the time Kate returned to her bedchamber. Her aim was to renew the spell and crawl into bed. The earlier the better.

She needed to stop thinking about Bregovi's library. She needed to stop thinking about his adventures. She needed to stop thinking about the book and the chess and how the gold flecks in his eyes shimmered when he grinned at her. She needed to stop thinking about *him*.

The only way to do that was to stop thinking at all. Sleep provided the perfect escape, or it would if she could persuade her brain to rest as well. She wished she knew a spell to stop a person from dreaming.

"Kate, is that you?" Victoria called.

"Yes, do you need something?" Kate stepped into the princess's bedchamber.

Victoria had relocated the bathtub to her room and, from the looks of the water on the floor, had recently emerged from it. The rug was slightly wet, as were Victoria's long curls as she sat at a dressing table.

"I need you to braid my hair," Victoria stated.

"Of course." Kate moved over to the princess and began weaving the mass of ringlets into braids. She avoided Victoria's gaze in the mirror, knowing an inquisition was on the horizon and not wishing to encourage its commencement.

"I couldn't find the lilac for the bath," Victoria said.

"It's on the bureau in my bedchamber where you instructed me to leave it."

"Nevertheless, I couldn't find it."

"Would you like me to fetch it for you? We can keep it in here if you'd like."

"Later."

Kate nodded, nearly finished with the last braid.

"I used your herbs instead."

Kate's fingers froze as her eyes quickly darted to the tub. The sack that held the items for the spell lay on the floor, and lavender and blackberry twigs floated in the bathwater.

"The combination made a wonderful scent. What were the sticks? Mulberry?"

The princess could have no idea what the items had been for, but she'd be an idiot not to suspect they were important to Kate. The satchel and its contents were all Kate had taken when she'd run.

A shiver crept the length of her. If she didn't renew the spell by dawn, Lord Morten would find her. *Tomorrow.* She'd have to find the missing ingredients tonight.

"The herbs weren't sentimental, were they?"

Kate forced her hands to finish the braid and her eyes to meet Victoria's.

"No, not sentimental."

"Good. I should hate to ruin something dear to you."

Of course, her cousin had intended to do precisely that. As it had been with Morten, Victoria's punishment had been meant to bite.

"I'll clean up now and get the lilac for you." Kate grabbed the sack and nearby satchel and hurried to her bedchamber. As soon as she'd crossed the threshold, she pulled open the smaller of the two.

The vial of primrose oil was missing. The pouch of salt gone. All that remained of the lavender and blackberry was a tiny piece of the latter hooked in the fabric. The piece was barely large enough for one spell. She would need more for tomorrow, but for tonight that was one less ingredient to track down.

Moving on to the satchel, she discovered her knife, coins and soap were untouched. Victoria certainly had chosen correctly, selecting the items that would do the most harm.

Returning to Victoria's chamber, Kate delivered the lilac as promised, but her primary intent was to look for the primrose bottle and the salt pouch. Both were sitting atop a table near the tub. She quickly replaced them with the lilac and tucked the two items in her bodice. Perhaps they weren't empty after all.

"What did you and Edmund do today?"

"We played chess," Kate said, turning down Victoria's bedding.

"Did you speak of me?" Victoria asked, settling against the pillows and pulling the blanket over her lap.

"I suggested he challenge you at the game."

"That's good. I'm a fair player. Anything else?"

"There wasn't much opportunity."

"For talking?" Victoria said, her mouth a tight line.

"No, he spoke a lot about his travels, but I didn't know how to work you in."

"You could have mentioned Cragmont's ships."

"Of course. I'm sorry, milady. I'll do that if I've another opportunity."

To steer Victoria off of the prince, Kate said, "Rachel told me Sebastian did poorly today."

"Poorly? He was painful to watch. Only one other did worse, and that's merely because Sebastian hit the base of the target. The two were tied with nothing, but the hit elevated him a hair."

"How did Brock do?"

"Well, but he didn't win. I think he's more comfortable with heavier weapons."

"Did you speak with him?"

"He came over to the box and asked if one of us would touch his bow for luck."

"Did you?"

"Of course not. But the midget from Highbridge did. She nearly knocked Princess Sophia from her chair to get to him."

"What did Brock do?"

"Kissed her hand. A few others called out good wishes, and he sauntered back to the shooting range like a rooster with too many hens."

"It's unfortunate Sebastian doesn't have his confidence."

"None of the men have the confidence of that smithy," Victoria said, a tinge of admiration in her voice.

After several more topics of discussion, which Kate was sure were intended to torture her further, she finally escaped to her bedchamber.

A quick inspection of the damage revealed a dry primrose vial and a salt bag that couldn't have been cleaner if it were laundered. All she had was a speck of blackberry vine. Panic tried to grab hold, but she kicked it back. Losing hope wouldn't help her find the items. Throwing on her cloak, she slipped into the hall, certain—or at least moderately confident—the kitchen stores would hold what she needed.

An hour later, Kate still hadn't found her destination and was growing to believe the halls were enchanted, with shifting, maze-like walls.

Rounding a corner she'd tried before, Kate heard female voices, low and bickering. From the huffs and grumbles, it sounded as if the parties were exerting themselves.

Thinking they might help her find the kitchen, she followed and became uneasy with the topic of discussion.

"Did you smell that room? That wasn't ordinary smoke. I tell you it's magik," the first voice said.

"You're being fanciful," the second said. "No one believes in magik anymore."

"Yes they do. Old Quent says Zafarians are rising again."

"Old Quent isn't right in the head."

"How does someone light a carpet afire if they aren't doing magik?"

"By dropping a candle."

"I didn't see any candle wax, did you? And what would they be doing in an empty chamber?"

"Maybe it was a lovers' tryst and they got scared away."

Caught up in what they were saying and concerned about who

might be performing magik, Kate turned a corner and nearly toppled the two maids.

Holly shrieked and the other dropped her cargo—one end of a thick rolled carpet.

CHAPTER FOURTEEN

"Milady, you startled us," Holly said. "Are you lost? Do you need something?"

"I'm sorry I frightened you," Kate said. "And, yes, to both your questions. I'm lost and need a few things."

Holly's petite companion looked dubious.

"Princess Victoria used the last of some of our herbs in her bath, and I was hoping to find more in the kitchen," Kate said. "Would one of you show me the way?"

"Of course, milady," Holly said. "I'll take you as soon as Flora and I deliver this below stairs."

Flora's small build belied her strength as she hefted up her end with no more than a grunt.

"I'd appreciate that," Kate said as the girls continued down the corridor.

After several turns, they arrived at the top of a narrow staircase. Despite Flora's strength and Holly's determination, Kate felt certain the two maids would end up in a heap at the bottom if she didn't help. She took up the rear and the three managed the descent with one slip and no tumbles.

To Kate's relief, the maid's destination was the laundry. At

Morten's home in Cragmont, the staff kept the lavender in the laundry. Perhaps Florian's maids stored it there as well.

"Might you have lavender here? It's one of the items I'm looking for," Kate said.

"We do, milady," Holly said as they dropped the carpet near a workbench.

"Your princess puts lavender in her bath?" Flora asked. "Jasmine is the favorite here."

"I'm afraid she does, and she used the last of it tonight," Kate said, brushing dust off her cloak. "But if you have a bit of jasmine to spare, I could take that to her as well."

Holly moved to a cupboard and looked among its contents. "That's odd. Usually, it's here."

Kate and Flora peered in as well.

"The jasmine is gone too," Flora said.

"We can ask Alice about it tomorrow and bring it to your bedchamber," Holly said.

"I need it tonight."

Both nodded, but she could almost hear the questions bubbling in their heads.

"Tomorrow will be very busy and the princess is very particular. I'd rather deal with this tonight if it's possible," Kate said. "Don't you keep lavender anywhere else? Perhaps in the kitchen?"

"We can check," Holly said, starting off across the room.

Kate quickly followed.

In the kitchen, Holly helped Kate find a small bushel of lavender drying on a wall along with roses and jasmine. Unfortunately, they didn't have blackberry vine.

"I've not heard of anyone keeping dried blackberry," Holly said, causing some distress in Kate. Without it, the remaining ingredients were useless.

"Don't blackberries grow in your land?" Kate asked…hoped.

"Sure, in the forest, but we don't use them for much outside of jams and pies," Holly said, helping Kate refill her sack with salt.

The last item, primrose oil, presented more of a challenge, and they were off again, this time to the apothecary.

"These are strange ingredients for a bath, milady," Holly said.

"I agree," Kate said, wishing Victoria hadn't used them for hers.

After they rounded several corners and took a few long corridors, Kate said, "I heard a bit of your conversation with Flora. Do you really think someone is doing magik in the castle?"

"I can't say for certain, but odd things have happened," Holly said.

"What sort of odd things?"

"The harp. The instruments were tested in the morning and servants were with them until the event. No one could have meddled with it unless by magik."

"Indeed," Kate said. If Zafarians were about, why had no one turned her in? Were others there using Astonian Gifts? "Could someone have bribed one of the servants to do it?"

"Not here," Holly said, aghast. "We're all loyal. To the royal family and the kingdom."

Kate didn't think loyalty had much sway when coins were involved.

As they climbed a spiral staircase, they crossed paths with an elderly maid with white hair and a wiry build.

"I thought I heard you, Holly," the maid said. "Did you take care of the carpet?"

"Yes, Miss Alice," Holly said with a curtsey. "Flora is tending to it in the laundry."

"Very well," Alice said with a smile at Kate. "Hello, child."

The familiar term was odd coming from a maid, but the fondness in her voice counteracted any offense.

"Is Holly aiding you?"

"Yes," Kate said.

"She needs primrose oil, so I was taking her to the apothecary,"

Holly said.

"I'll take her," Alice said. "You and Flora are both dismissed for the night. We've much to do tomorrow."

"Yes, mum," Holly said with another dip before scurrying off.

One flight up, Alice stopped at a thick door and took out a heavy ring of keys to let them in.

"Primrose oil isn't a common remedy is it?" Alice said, looking over vials on a shelf.

"It is in Cragmont," Kate said.

"Might I say, it's lovely having you here?" Alice moved to a cabinet full of green bottles. "I haven't seen my master so taken with a maiden in a very long time."

"Thank you, but I don't think he's taken."

"I do." Alice smiled as she handed over a small bottle.

Kate carefully filled her vial and handed it back.

"I appreciate your help."

After Alice had deposited Kate back at her bedchamber, Kate couldn't help but think about what the maid had said. Alice might think he was taken with her. Bregovi might even think as much. But how could he be?

Kate sank to the floor to renew the spell once again.

Caring for someone, being *taken* with them, involved actually knowing them. Bregovi didn't know who she really was. What she really was. And he never would.

* * *

The next day, maidens and spectators gathered in the Grand Hall once again. This time for the trivia event. Twelve high back chairs upholstered in blue brocade stretched in a long row across the center of the room. The competitors already seated studied notes and exchanged nods with those about the room. Across from them, the throne awaited the monarch and his family. The remainder of the hall held chairs and benches filled with spectators.

"Miss Fishbeak," a haughty voice came from behind.

"Good morning, Sophia," Kate said, turning to find the princess flanked by the maidens from Highbridge, Sydmore and Meltzer.

"Are you feeling prepared for today's challenge?" Lady Quinn from Sydmore asked.

"I hope so," Kate said.

"Don't expect a pity win this time," Sophia said.

"Unless someone tampers with her answer slate," Lady Emma from Meltzer said with a laugh-snort.

"Yes, I'm afraid you'll have to win this one on your own," Sophia said. "Regardless of how well you performed yesterday."

Kate didn't miss the emphasis on *performed*, nor did she miss the moment Sophia's mouth tightened to a scowl. Following the princess's gaze, Kate discovered Bregovi near the door with Victoria chatting easily on his arm.

"At least you got one win in," said Lady Anne from Highbridge. "That's more than most commoners."

"And you're even poor for a commoner, no?" Sophia added. "From what I've heard, the dairy maid has more of a dowry than you do."

The royal snobs made the gossips in Cragmont seem like dear friends, and Kate longed to inform the catty maidens she had a rightful place with them.

Randolph announced the beginning of the event as Foster, the squire who had escorted her to Bregovi the day before, gave each maiden chalk, a cloth and a lap-sized slate.

"Good luck, Fishbeak. Try not to embarrass yourself too much in front of the prince," Sophia whispered before sauntering over to a seat.

As Kate took to her own chair, she wished she had studied that morning. Because suddenly she had a monstrous need to win the event.

* * *

"As you all know," Randolph began, "Florian traditionally holds a trivia contest to test knowledge of the kingdoms of Astonia. As you also likely know, this contest has resulted in many ties, due to an extensive education on the subject. Therefore, this year, we will instead test knowledge of the prince."

The room exploded into excited chatter. Bregovi's head pounded and he turned to his father and Rachel.

"Did you two know about this?"

Rachel smiled mischievously. "This will be more fun than the stuffy trivia contest."

"I approved," his father said.

"Are you sure this isn't your way of giving your pick an advantage?" he asked Rachel.

"Of course not!" she said, looking offended.

"You didn't feed answers to anyone?"

"Only Randolph," she said.

"Father?" Bregovi said.

"Of course not," his father said. "But I may have provided a few interesting facts to your admirers."

"Why, Edmund?" Rachel's eyes narrowed. "Who do you fear we colluded with?"

Fear wasn't the emotion at play. No, it was something more uncomfortable. Something he couldn't quite identify. A strange mix of hope, anticipation and dread.

Inevitable. Kate had said he was pervasive and that she couldn't avoid him. But he could say the same about her. The maiden was like a storm in the tropics. As soon as you'd thought it had passed, another cloud drenched you.

"Your attention, if you please," Randolph said. "I shall announce each of twelve questions and give the competitors one minute to write their answers. After that minute and on my mark they shall show their answers together. We shall determine who is correct and keep a tally here." He indicated a large slate board on an easel, with each of their names listed on the left side. The princesses Victoria and Sophia were listed first and second, Kate's name finished the list at the bottom.

"First question," the man's voice boomed. The room grew silent. "What is Prince Edmund's eye color?"

Chalk flew across boards. All the maidens should know that. If the remainder of the questions were as simple, Kate may not take the day after all.

Randolph called time and they revealed their answers. Every maiden had responded correctly with green. Foster put a tick mark by each name and they continued.

"What is the prince's favorite tournament event?"

Again, they answered alike. Jousting. Another tick for each.

"His full name."

Bregovi doubted many would prevail, but the maidens surprised him. All but Sophia, Anne and Margaret got the answer correct with *Edmund Oliver Bregovi Tennerelli.*

Next, Randolph asked Bregovi's age. All were correct except Lady Harriett. The answer was six and twenty. She had shaved off a year.

Favorite game? Seven answered correctly with chess. He wondered how many were answering from knowledge and how many were guessing.

Four maidens were tied with five points each, Kate included.

After chess came favorite pet. While others bent to their boards to answer, Kate looked to the mural on the ceiling. Rachel knew Galileo held the favorite title, as his mascot on his travels, and Kate was the only other maiden in the room who knew of the creature. If she named him, she'd take the lead.

Ten of the twelve had listed the horse. Jillian opted for hound. Kate, of course, wrote *Galileo.*

Instead of awarding her the point, Randolph declared, "All are incorrect. The prince's favorite pet is a turtle he found abroad."

As whispers of *Galileo* floated over to him, Kate glanced to the others with a ready-to-battle gleam in her eye. Rather than give her the opportunity to explain how she had learned the name, Bregovi motioned for Foster. He quickly gave his instructions to the squire and sent the lad to Randolph.

As Kate raised her slate to gain Randolph's attention, Foster delivered the message.

Unaware of Kate's indication, the elderly gent said, "It appears the turtle's name is Galileo. Miss Hildegard wins a point."

A few of the maidens groaned, and Kate shot a look of pure triumph toward Sophia.

His fiery lady-in-waiting was in the lead, with Victoria, Laila and Whitney behind her by one point, and Princess Sophia and a slew of others behind by two.

"Seventh question. Where is Prince Edmund's scar?"

All eyes turned to him as if they'd find one marring his forehead. He flashed them a toothy grin, and a few giggled before writing their answers. Kate thought on it the longest. It wasn't until Randolph announced the final ten seconds that she finally wrote something on her slate.

Five had noted the scar on his shoulder—the four maidens who had visited his room, and Kate. She hadn't seen him shirtless, but it didn't surprise him she knew about it. Two maidens listed his left hand, which was the answer Randolph was looking for. The late-night visitors mumbled amongst themselves and it was Lady Quinn's turn to raise her slate to get Randolph's attention.

"Yes, Lady Quinn?" he said.

"Might I request you verify the locations of Prince Edmund's scars?"

Randolph spoke to Foster, who hurried over to Bregovi, who sent the lad back with his answer.

Upon learning the truth, Randolph said, "Lady Quinn is correct. The prince has scars on both his hand and shoulder."

That brought murmurs from the crowd and a steely glance from

Princess Victoria toward Sophia and the other maidens who had listed his shoulder. He'd love to hear how they would explain their knowledge when challenged later.

Next up was languages. How many does he speak? Kate and Margaret, to her right, got it correct with five.

Ninth, favorite food. Kate answered with *keywee*.

Randolph proclaimed her answer correct and advised her of the accurate spelling.

He loved many traditional dishes more, but since he had mentioned to Rachel that kiwi was his new favorite fruit, he couldn't change the answer without appearing to be favoring someone in the game…or sabotaging Kate.

Three questions remained and Kate hadn't missed one yet. Her closest competitors were behind by four. Even if she missed the remainder, she had the win.

Randolph continued. "Ten. Which was the first land Prince Edmund traveled to over the sea?"

Kate knew that too. She had milked every detail out of him about his journey to the Palasian Islands. She added another point to her lead.

"Eleven. What did he collect on his last expedition?"

A tough question. They had not discussed the purpose of his recent trip and there was no way she could know he had collected medicinal herbs on his last voyage.

Kate turned her slate over and revealed *medicinal herbs*.

Unbelievable.

Before they concluded, Randolph announced that the event winner would receive a castle tour given by Bregovi before the men's race that afternoon. For the first time during the event, Kate's eyes found his.

"Last question. What would the prince say is his most memorable animal encounter?"

While Bregovi had loved riding elephants and camels, and

watching cheetahs run, the lion cub topped them. He'd come across it as his party trekked across a plain. Its mother lay dead nearby, a victim of an attack by another animal. Although the group insisted they leave the cub, he wouldn't abandon it. Corralling the feisty creature had been difficult, but he'd managed to trap it in a blanket. He'd cared for it for days before delivering it to a guide who had promised to watch over it. Rachel knew of the adventure, as did Kate.

The maiden answered the last question as she had the prior— correctly—and won in an unsettling clean sweep.

* * *

The maidens could no longer use the pity argument against her. While that brought Kate immense satisfaction, the thought of spending another afternoon with Bregovi sent her stomach to the floor. The plan to vindicate herself hadn't been well thought out or prudent.

With no intention of collecting her prize, and with Bregovi busy commending and consoling her competitors, Kate slipped out to find the kitchen before she began her hunt for blackberry vine.

A short while later, Kate headed for the stables, armed with cheese, fruits, as well as dubious and, unfortunately, conflicting directions to various blackberry brambles in the forest. Holly had insisted she try the Kissing Bridge, but the spark in the maid's eye mixed with Flora's insistence that the lake patch was half the distance had Kate opting for the latter.

At the stables, she began to wonder if the gods were on Morten's side. Although she counted more than two dozen horses in residence and only half that were competing for the princess, it seemed every animal with legs was reserved for the race.

She moved from stall to stall with the same result each time. Reserved for count this or saved for lord that. They wouldn't even let her take a workhorse. Finally, she reached the last stall and discovered the black stallion Bregovi had ridden in the joust. Its glossy mane shimmered as he danced around the enclosure.

Scooping a handful of oats from a bucket, she held out the offering. After eyeing her for a moment, he trotted over and eagerly ate from her hand. When the treat was gone, he nudged her chest with a snort.

"Can't have that one either, miss," a wiry stable hand hollered. "No one rides Odyssey but the prince."

"Odyssey, is it?" she whispered, scratching the steed between his coal-black eyes. "Are you interested in a little adventure?"

He nuzzled her arm.

She took that as a yes.

"Why don't ye come back after the race," the stable hand said. "We'll have plenty o' horses then."

But she didn't want to come back. She wanted to ride.

Spotting a side saddle nearby, she thought she'd be able to strap it onto Odyssey if she could manage to sneak it into the stall. Fortunately, a commotion started at the other end of the stable—a temperamental creature destroying his enclosure, from the sound of it. Exactly what she'd be doing if she couldn't get out of there soon.

Not one to squander rare good-fortune, she quickly looped the satchel across her body, then gathered the saddle, bridle and a blanket and slipped in with Odyssey. The horse minded his manners while she placed the gear on him, but started dancing again as soon as she cinched the saddle. Pressing a hand against his right flank to keep him from knocking her over, she glanced around for a way to mount. The stall didn't supply.

Peeking out, with the steed snorting in her ear, she spotted a stool next to the opposite stall. With the men distracted trying to calm the anxious horse, she hastily led Odyssey to the step and climbed up. As a burly stable hand came running, Kate and her accomplice charged out to freedom.

The steed was surefooted *and fast*. As he pulled at the reins, she hoped they hadn't intended him for Sebastian, for the lord could have ridden the animal backward and still won the race. Catching a glimpse of two stable hands giving chase, Kate leaned forward, anchored a hand in the steed's mane and gave the horse its head.

As if released from a trap, Odyssey ate up the trail. By the time they'd cleared the castle grounds, they'd lost the stable hands and Kate's hair had tumbled free along with her spirits.

Slowing the steed to a walk, she caught her breath and took in her surroundings. The noonday sun illuminated leaves in varied colors of green while a breeze whispered through the forest.

Following the route Flora had laid out, Kate took each fork to the right, eventually trading the wide trial for a walking path, where she spied the lake through the trees.

Finally, she came to the clearing near the water that the maid had described. To her right, towering elms extended over boulders piled up as if they'd been tossed in place by giants. To her left, bees swarmed around overgrown berry bushes drinking in the sun.

In the distance, boulders jutting from the lake's surface looked like miniatures of the distant mountains reaching for the heavens. The size of the frosted peaks indicated she was at the base of the divide separating Astonia from Zafaria.

Birds dancing on the wind drew her gaze to the sky. Bright. Brilliant. Azure blue. As the cool breeze stirred her skirts, she filled her lungs with the crisp air.

A chipmunk scampered past, leaving tiny marks in the mud underfoot. It wasn't the only creature to have ventured that way. Dirt and mud extending from the lake to the woods perfectly preserved an adult bear's prints as well as the wolf tracks inside them. Both urged her to get to her task before their owners returned.

She slid off Odyssey and led him to the water while eying the forest for animals. With nothing in sight, she turned her focus on the bushes. The outer berries had been picked clean, making it difficult to tell what type of fruit they'd been.

When the horse tugged her toward greenery near the water, indicating he'd had his fill, she led him to a patch of grass near the trail, looped his reins around a low tree branch and left him to it.

Shifting the satchel to her back, she took a closer look at the berry bushes, pushing her way into the prickly patch until she found ripe fruit. The color was right—a rich, deep black. But when she broke off a piece of the vine, she realized Flora's mistake. The stems were wrong. Too short. Too thorny.

She pulled off one of the fat berries, sending juice dripping and bees swirling. It tasted tart and sweet, but not as sweet at blackberries. The maid likely hadn't known the difference. Scanning the patch, she searched for any sign of another type, but they were all the same.

Black raspberries.

* * *

Kate had dodged him. They hadn't set a specific time for the tour, but she knew it was to be before the race. While Bregovi had hoped one of the other maidens would win the event, Kate's triumph earned her the prize, and he wouldn't default. He'd planned to show her more of the public rooms, giving her the formal treatment, and then escort her to the race where they would sit with the others. Separately. But the issue turned out to be moot. The maiden had disappeared again.

After the futile search, he decided to join the race instead. The route around the lake was one of his favorites, and a fast ride was just what he needed to clear his brain of her. At the stables, he discovered why he hadn't been able to find Kate. A good hour beforehand, the minx had ridden off on his steed.

Bregovi considered going after her, but pride bit at honor. If she wanted to hide, why should he deprive her?

As he wouldn't race on anything but Odyssey, he decided to watch the finish with Rachel and check on her progress with her beaux.

* * *

Sebastian charged his mount near the head of the pack. It nagged at him that Rachel hadn't wished him luck before he'd left. After his dismal performance in the other events, he was certain if he lost the race he would lose her too.

The path ahead was clear, but not wide enough for two horses, making it impossible to pass. The route would take over half an hour more at full speed and they were nearly halfway there. He needed to take the lead.

Others—likely with the same goal—broke away to cut through the forest. Within moments protruding tree limbs downed a rider.

Sebastian veered onto a narrow path to the right, near the lake, and charged onward, hoping to cut off the pack when the two routes met again. A handful of riders followed.

* * *

As Kate picked her way out of the berry bushes, she heard rumbling from the trees. Then shouts of "ha" and "I have you!" At first she feared it was bandits, but then remembered the race.

Odyssey heard them as well and danced around, tugging at his reins as the noise grew louder. A rider shot through the woods not far from them. From the bright hair she concluded it was Sebastian.

The horse jerked back, fighting his tether to the branch.

"Whoa," she cried, breaking free of the bushes and running through the mud to reach him. She dodged a squirrel darting for safety as two wolf cubs scampered from the woods just beyond the horse.

Shouting at one another and their mounts, several riders followed Sebastian's course.

Odyssey reared up and snapped the branch like a twig. Trampling one of the cubs, he bolted. In a heartbeat he was gone.

With instinct overruling sense, Kate scooped up the limp cub. It was no bigger than bluebell had been, a few months old at most. She spoke softly to the creature, as she'd done to dozens before, and reached out to its soul.

Of course, nothing happened. Thank the gods nothing happened. Had she lost her mind?

An unexpected breeze of sorrow swirled through her. She was a healer. She was good. She helped, not hindered, with her Gifts. And her uncle had taken that away from her.

"I'm sorry, little one," she whispered as she carefully set it down.

It was only then that she noticed the others. A third cub and their mother, frozen, hard eyes fixed on Kate.

"It's all right," Kate said in a soothing voice. "I haven't hurt your babe."

The wolf began growling, baring sharp white teeth. Two pups mimicked their mother, while the injured one yelped and struggled to stand.

Kate backed slowly toward the boulders as the pack crept closer, lower. The fur on the mother's back ridged up and it looked like she was coiling up to spring.

Pulling the satchel off her back, Kate swung it before her as she worked her way up the boulders. Unfortunately, the rocks weren't high enough. The animals would reach her the moment they gathered their courage.

A low-hanging branch on one of the elms brushed her shoulders, urging her to move. With a scream, she hurled the satchel at the mother as it jumped onto the boulder. Whirling about, Kate hauled herself onto the branch, scrambling upward as quickly as she could while the wolf snarled and jumped at her from below.

* * *

As Bregovi sat with Rachel at the finish line, a shout of "Horses approaching!" came from the woods.

The rumble of heavy riding grew louder as Rachel latched onto his hand.

"Come on Sebastian," she whispered.

Bregovi gently squeezed back, and they both cheered when they spotted his carrot hair toward the front of the pack.

"Rider down," someone shouted.

When Bregovi looked to see who had lost his seat, all the air left his lungs. The riderless Odyssey finished first, followed by Lords Preston and Sebastian.

"I didn't even look at him this time," Rachel cried, dropping his hand.

Whistling for Odyssey, Bregovi hurdled the wall of their box. The steed galloped over, sweaty and snorting.

Bregovi dropped the side saddle to the ground, jumped on bareback, and charged off in the direction the riders had come.

Images flashed through his mind. Of Kate lying in the forest. Wounded. Bleeding. Impaled by a branch. Or worse. His hands clenched the reins.

Prideful fool. I should have gone after her. The forest is no place for a woman alone. The thought set off another wave of fears. Of bandits far less kind than he had been. Of men who would take what they wanted from her.

A scream rent the air. Toward the lake.

He veered in that direction until he found a single set of tracks. Urging the steed faster, he followed their course.

CHAPTER FIFTEEN

After what seemed like an eternity, the wolf finally ceased growling and laid down on the rock to watch her cubs. The injured one had started limping about as the others chased each other around the clearing.

If Kate could get her to move. If she could startle her enough to get her to join the others...

Sitting on a high branch, Kate leaned against the trunk and removed her boots.

Shimmying lower, where she had a clear shot, she hurled a boot, grazing the mother wolf's back. The animal merely jumped to her feet, but Kate followed with a fierce scream that would have sent anyone within earshot running.

The wolf shot off the boulder in an instant. When the animal turned to look for her, Kate scrambled lower and threw the other boot, adding another scream and waving her arms like a crazy maiden.

The wolf edged back as her cubs headed for the forest. Picking up the wounded one by the scruff, the wolf gave Kate a last look and followed her cubs.

Having experienced a trap or ten in her life, Kate stayed on her perch a bit longer, just to be sure they didn't return. And it was while she was waiting that she heard a steady rhythm in the forest. A rider.

Quickly, she scrambled out of the tree, jumped off the boulder into the gooey mud and ran toward the sound.

"Kate!" Bregovi's familiar voice echoed through the trees.

Her stomach pitched. She debated for a half-second if the wolves would be the easier of the two options. Reason said the contest might be close, but she wasn't daft.

"Here!" she shouted. "I'm here!"

He burst from the trees.

"Holy gods," she whispered. While the sight of Bregovi at the joust had turned her insides to mush, seeing him charge from the woods bareback on the powerful steed snatched her breath.

Both animal and man were fired up, glinting sweat and adrenaline. Bregovi jumped from Odyssey mid-stride and sprinted to her.

"Are you hurt? Are you injured?" he shouted as breathless as the animal.

"No."

His big hands grabbed her shoulders. "Did he throw you? Are you—"

"No, he didn't throw me. I'm all right."

Releasing her, he began pacing. "What in the three hells are you doing out here alone?"

"I was...I needed to...I was looking for blackberry vines."

"Blackberry vines?" he muttered. Then he stopped and faced her again, his expression close to a snarl.

She took a prudent step back.

"You came here for fruit? Are you without sense? Rational maidens would ask the kitchen servants. Don't you know what could happen to you out here?" His arms gestured about wildly. "You could have been thrown. Killed. And did it occur to you there are wild animals in the woods? A hungry wolf would certainly love to make a meal of you."

"I—"

"And bandits," he said, stalking across the clearing. "There are real bandits in the world, milady—some reportedly nearby—who would take more than a mere kiss from a maiden like you. And believe me, you'd never fend *them* off!"

* * *

Kate had scared him senseless and the maiden needed someone to scare sense into her. He felt a tinge of guilt for lecturing her so harshly, but it had worked. She'd realized her mistake. He could tell by her flushed cheeks and the deep breaths she was taking. If he knew anything about women, she was struggling not to weep.

Perhaps he should hold her for a moment to let her calm. Perhaps that would help him to calm as well.

"I'm very aware of the dangers," she shouted, fists clenched at her sides.

Apparently, she wasn't ready to be calmed.

"The animals, the bandits, getting lost and having to sleep out here alone. In the dark. With both. And I've already fended off those wolves you lovingly mentioned, so maybe I'm not as helpless as you think."

Wolves? He scanned the forest for any signs that they were still about. "You were fortunate, Kate, but stupid too," he said. Not his most comforting moment, but he couldn't think right while his brain was wrestling with jarring images of Kate fighting off wolves.

It was then that he noticed a boot embedded in the mud. He picked it up.

"You really are horrible at rescuing maidens," she bit out, snatching the boot from him. "Could you go back and send someone else? Brock for instance? I'm sure he wouldn't berate me as you are."

"A man rides at breakneck speed to save a woman, with horrors as to what's happened to her terrorizing his mind, and she asks for another? *You* are horrible at being rescued, milady."

Grumbling something he didn't catch, she swiped her other boot from atop Croley's rock, then sat on a low boulder near the water and hiked up her skirts.

"What are you doing?" he asked, throat dry, eyes fixed on the long muddy stocking she was peeling off her long muddy leg.

Brows raised, she met his eye, telling him expeditiously what an imbecilic question that was.

He let her gaze go and returned his focus to her mud-caked flesh.

"I don't have any other boots and am not going to ruin these by putting muddy feet into them." She dipped the stocking in the lake and rinsed it out, then wiped the mud from her leg with the clean fabric.

Yes, that sounded reasonable, he thought, hoping to the gods that the other leg was just as muddy.

Odyssey nudged his shoulder and Bregovi remembered him and led him to the water, all the while watching Kate tease him with all that creamy skin. He knew what she was doing. Luring him in like the siren that she was. He just didn't care.

Rather than let his mind play out ways to relieve her of her remaining garments, he opted for a safer course, a safer topic.

"Did you realize you selected one of our landmarks for your blackberry hunt?" he asked.

"Here?" she asked, slowly peeling off the other muddy stocking. "What's so notable about this spot?"

"Have you heard of the lake monster?"

She immediately leapt to her feet. "Why would you let me sit here if—"

"No one has seen it in decades," he said.

Shooting him a reproachful glance, she retook her seat and hiked her skirts once again.

"So tell me about your lake monster, then," the temptress said, running wet hands down her wet leg.

Turning his back to circle the clearing, he kept his eyes off her and

196

his mind on the tale.

"It was festival time a century back, and Prince Croley was up to marry the victor of the events."

"A familiar tale thus far."

"He fell in love with one of the maidens, Princess Aularia of Gochland. And although she loved him as well and competed valiantly, she didn't win. He was set to marry another. The Council ruled that if he spent a full night on the lake and survived the monster, he could have the bride of his choosing. No one had ever withstood such a challenge."

"The Council thought the task would deter him. That he'd marry the other princess?" she said, drawing his gaze before he could stop it.

She'd started on her toes.

He swallowed as Odyssey tugged him to a grassy patch.

"Yes, and Aularia didn't want him to try. She preferred him alive and married to another, rather than a victim of the monster."

"A wise maiden." Kate slipped one of the boots on to a very naked foot.

"Croley didn't think so. He opted for the lake."

As Kate looked out over the water, Bregovi's gaze followed hers. He would have done the same for Camilla. Hell, he *had* tried to slay dragons for her, but that was then. He hadn't felt that strongly about a woman since. He pulled his eyes back from the lake and settled them on Kate as she donned the second boot.

"How did he manage it?"

"He crafted a light boat that looked more like a log than a vessel and made it through to dawn. He exited the lake there." He nodded toward the shore. "Right into Aularia's arms."

She stood and glanced about them.

"The monster followed. Stories state Aularia's scream alerted him, but others say it was her maid, as the couple was too busy kissing to notice. The monster reached out of the lake, grabbed Aularia's ankle, and pulled her out of Croley's arms and toward the water."

"Oh, dear."

"Croley attacked. With a swift blow of the sword, he severed the monster's limb and freed her. It went after him next. Croley wouldn't be taken. While he fought, Aularia and the maid hurled stones. The creature kept grabbing, and Croley kept chopping. Legend has it he struck the final blow over this boulder right next to you there. You can still see the chinks where his blade hit."

"Hmm." She ran her fingers over the marks in the stone. "I suspect the account is embellished, but it's a sweet story. Unfortunately, love like that just isn't real."

"You don't think anyone would slay a monster for you?"

Her soft, bitter laugh floated on the breeze.

"Not for a moment," she said with a pat on his chest as she headed across the clearing, her wet stockings in-hand. Her voice was light as sunrise, but the seriousness of her gaze unsettled him.

"Do you need someone to?"

Gathering her satchel from the dirt, she brushed it off and stashed the stockings inside. "Shouldn't we go?"

"Are you hiding from someone other than me?"

"I'm not hiding from you." She slipped the satchel on over her head.

"But you are hiding from someone."

A sick feeling stirred his belly. Many a maid had run from an unwanted marriage.

"Is it your husband?"

"No." Kate rubbed her right palm. "I am unwed."

"Your uncle then?"

She met his gaze for a moment.

"I'll not believe a lie, Kate. Who are you hiding from?"

Blowing out a long breath, she said, "My uncle made an arrangement with one of his confidants. He gave me to him."

"Gave you?"

"Yes."

Yes? That's all? "Did this man abuse you? Did he…"

She rubbed her hand again, making him worry that she'd injured it. He took the hand to check, but found nothing.

"Did he rape you?" He should have couched the question more gently, but his insides roiled like a cyclone.

Her hesitation in answering increased the turmoil.

"He tried." She pulled her hand away.

Comforting was probably in order, but sweet words escaped him. All he itched to do was pummel something, preferably the man's face…and nether region.

With an oddly amused expression, Kate said, "He didn't succeed. I outmaneuvered him and ran."

Of course she did. Thank the gods she did.

"And now he's searching for you?"

"I'm sure they both are."

"We'll protect you here."

"No one can protect me from them. Not if they find me."

She was wrong about that. He'd do whatever was necessary to keep her safe.

"I really do need to locate blackberry vines," she said, taking Odyssey's reins and heading toward Bregovi. "Will you help me find them before we go back?"

He didn't miss her obvious attempt to change the subject.

"The kitchen staff—"

"Doesn't have any," she said as he lifted her onto the steed. "Please? I will take it as a great favor?"

Bregovi led Odyssey toward the boulder and climbed on behind her. "I suspect you could ask for anything," he whispered into her ear. "And I'd try to get it for you."

"Blackberry vines are all I need," she said, but her voice had a little waver in it.

He may have a chance yet. She wanted blackberries and he wanted her. Suddenly a new goal solidified. While he helped her with her quest, he'd charm the maiden into wanting him too. Before the day was out, *she'd* be the one making moves. And they'd be of a *physical* nature.

* * *

A short ride from the lake, they picked up a trail snaking along next to a creek. The water rushed over smooth rocks and under rich brush flourishing along its shores. As they rounded a cluster of pine trees and entered a clearing, the rushing water grew louder. From a rocky overhang some thirty feet above, ice-blue water cascaded into a shimmering pool. The air felt fresh and crisp in Kate's lungs as she drew in a deep breath.

Bregovi stopped Odyssey near a blanket of moss glistening in the afternoon sun.

"Klug Falls," he announced and hopped off.

Instead of lowering her from the steed in a quick movement, the man took his time, as if he wanted to be sure she slid over every solid inch of him.

When her feet finally touched down, she hurried off toward the water to prevent him from seeing the color he'd brought to her cheeks.

"Careful, the moss is slippery near the edge."

Heeding his warning, she walked as close to the pool as she dared. He was right, she nearly lost her footing twice. The water was so clear she could see to the bottom, which looked to be a fair distance below. Bright flowers and shrubs grew along both sides of the falls in perfect symmetry, and she'd never seen so many colors. Off to the left, a small mound covered in tiny white buds rose up between a cluster of trees. The crash of the falls reminded her of the sound of the surf. It was spectacular.

"Klug?" She turned to him. "Another ancestor?"

"Yes," he said, joining her. "He had a *Bregovi* in his name as well, his second name, but went by his given name. The story has it that he was passing through en route to meet a potential bride. The princess of Larchmont. The day was stifling hot, so his party stopped here to cool off. But Florian's royal family had the same plan. The eldest daughter, Nicolene was the first to arrive. She discovered Klug swimming in the pool. *Naked.*"

Kate glanced at the water, imagining Bregovi instead of Klug. If the water was as clear then as it was now, Nicolene would have seen *everything.*

"He never made it to Larchmont, did he?"

"No."

At his wolfish grin, Kate laughed despite herself.

"It's breathtaking," she said, glancing everywhere but at his dimples.

"It's been a favorite place among the family for centuries. Mother especially loved it here."

"I can see why."

"When I was a child, we came for picnics and afternoon swims on hot days. The pool is so deep, one can jump from the top of the falls and still not touch the bottom."

The distance to the crest made her stomach pitch.

"Your mother let you jump from there?"

"She didn't know." He laughed. "My brother and I would dare each other. I'd be the bandit and he the knight. We'd chase each other right off the edge."

She could imagine the two of them racing around the falls and sensed the appeal to a prince anxious for adventure.

"It's beautiful."

"If you want those blackberries, you're going to have to take a ride with me," he said, emerging from behind an ancient tree that spanned over much of the pond. The thick rope clutched in his hand extended heavenward into the treetops.

"You're not serious."

"It's the only way across to your precious blackberries."

"Where are they?" she asked, surveying the landscape.

"Now, I'm not making promises, but there used to be berry bushes up near the cave behind the falls."

She didn't see a cave, let alone bushes, but he had her. The alternative was not checking at all.

"Come on, put your foot in the loop above mine," he said, indicating the footholds low on the rope. "I won't let you fall."

Something light and warm fluttered in her stomach. The enormous tree extended out over the pool, but they'd be heavy. "Are you sure the branch will hold?"

"Fairly sure. It's held wrestling brothers much heavier than you. You and I aren't going to cripple it."

She looked at the rope, Bregovi, the water, back at him.

"You'll be safe, Kate. You won't leave my arms."

As her muddled heart leapt at the thought, she put one foot in the loop, testing it, keeping the other firmly on the ground.

"And your arms will go nowhere near—" The sentence caught in her throat as he pulled her up and pushed off.

CHAPTER SIXTEEN

Letting out a scream, Kate wrapped her arms tightly around him as they swung out and back over the water. After a couple of passes with both tree and Bregovi holding strong, she began to relax.

"Rachel used to be able to get to the other side in two swings," he said.

"She did not ride on this," Kate said, laughing.

"Oh, but she did, milady. And I assure you, my young sister plays an excellent damsel in distress."

The thought of the delicate, proper princess swinging over the water while her brothers fought battles made Kate long for siblings she'd never had.

"She never fell in?"

"Oh, yes, she did. Soaked to the bone." He laughed. "After the first time, she brought a spare gown."

"And your mother—"

"Didn't know." He chuckled again.

"I can see you were a wicked influence on her," she said, enjoying the flight, the freedom.

She closed her eyes, breathing it in. Yes, this is what freedom would feel like when she finally found it. Weightless. Carefree.

Thrilling.

Tipping her head to enjoy the soaring sensation, she became fully aware of Bregovi's body pressed snug against hers. His muscles flexed, graceful and solid, as he controlled the swing of the rope. His legs rubbed against hers as he shifted, and the hand on her back spread warmth from his fingertips.

And on some of the broader swings, when her hips slid against him just right, something zinged through her, making her hot and trembly all at once.

Breathe. Breathe. Thinking it wiser to pull her thoughts off of Bregovi and their intimately pressed bodies, she glanced around at their surroundings. But then everything began to spin, for the mischievous man had them moving in quick circles as he let out a loud *whoop* that vibrated through her.

"Stop. Please. I'm getting dizzy."

"Yeah, Rachel didn't care much for spinning either."

"You swung with her like this?" she asked, trying to focus on something still.

"Not exactly like this," he said, humor tainting his words.

"Well, I hope not." She managed to laugh, thinking of how intimate it was to be pressed against him like that.

She rested her forehead against him as the spinning slowed, suspecting part of her dizziness came from merely being near him. She snuck a glance at his face to see if he was as affected as she was, but he too was looking up.

She followed his gaze and saw only leaves and branches far above them.

"Take your foot out of the stirrup," he said in a rush as they swung back toward where they'd started.

"What? I'll fall—"

"I've got you," he said, tightening his grip as they sailed across once again.

"But—"

"Now, Kate!" he commanded as they neared the far bank.

As soon as her foot came loose, he hurled her onto a patch of pink wildflowers. She rolled and hauled herself upright in time to watch him ride the rope into the water. A short section dangled from the tree, but the rest had disappeared with the prince.

She hopped to her feet, searching the pool for him.

Then he broke the surface, scanning around until he saw her.

"Are you all right?" he shouted.

Not remotely. The man looked glorious wet, his hair dripping, his tunic clinging.

"I'm fine," she said, brushing invisible petals off her gown to distract herself from the view.

He kicked out backward, eyeing the piece of rope dangling above.

"Father and his brother hung that rope when they were boys. It's weathered a generation. One encounter with you and it topples."

"Let that be a lesson to you," she said.

Their eyes caught, a wicked gleam shining in his. "Of what? That you'll topple me as well?" He didn't wait for a reply, but disappeared under the surface, swimming toward the falls with smooth strokes. Moments later, he climbed up the bank to her right.

She shouldn't look. The action was dangerous to her resolve. But what reasonable maiden would *not* look when such a sight presented itself? The only bits of clothing not clinging to the man's body were his boots.

"Any chance you've got a change of clothes in the satchel?" he asked, dripping her way.

"No."

He peeled his tunic over his head and shook out his hair. Muscles. A smattering of dark hair on his chest and trailing down his belly. Breeches that clung, well, everywhere. And it all came closer as he sat next to her and pulled off his boots.

He dumped out the water, then removed the socks and wrung those out much as she had done earlier.

"The breeches stay on or you're going back in," she warned.

Dimples popped. "Trying to get me to reenact Klug's fateful swim?"

Heat crept to several places on her anatomy.

"Not today."

"Another day then," he said, far too sure of himself.

"While you're basking in the sun, why don't I go look for those blackberries?" she said, gesturing up the hill. She didn't like—or, more accurately, liked entirely too much—the feelings stirring within her. Distance or a dip in the pool would curb them. She'd opt for the first.

"I'll join you."

"No, you should stay and dry off." She gave him a friendly pat on his shoulder as she passed. The feeling of warm skin over solid muscle made her wish she hadn't. A primitive reaction, she told herself as she picked a path up the hill. Humans shared that with animals, didn't they?

The gods had gleefully implanted instinct, need, urges, so that humans would mate and procreate. She did not have to succumb to the pull just because he was covered in muscle and smelled like cinnamon and a strange earthy scent that made her want to burrow her nose in his neck.

He'd probably bought the potion abroad for the specific purpose of seducing maidens. She would not be controlled by urges or potions, no matter how strong.

At a level spot halfway up the falls, she stopped to check a neat cluster of berry bushes that were also host to bees and a fair number of white-spotted butterflies. Unfortunately, like the other patch, they did not appear to be blackberries.

The leaves were too round.

To be certain, she broke off a small section to inspect it closer and, in the process, caught her thumb on a sharp thorn.

"Damn it all," she grumbled.

"I take it they aren't the sought after blackberries," a deep voice said.

She spun to discover Bregovi not two feet behind her. He'd put the wet tunic back on.

"I thought you were drying off. You'll catch a chill."

"I've spent many a summer day here in wet clothing."

"But it's still Spring and the water must be freezing."

"I'll be fine," he said, eyeing her thumb, which she'd been holding up as if she was testing the wind.

"Thorn," she said.

"Hmm." He inspected the wound and pinched the flesh, making it bleed.

"Hey—"

Then he pulled her hand up and drew the wounded thumb into his mouth. As his tongue gently swirled over her helpless finger, Kate blushed *everywhere*.

"You're wicked," she said, sliding her thumb out.

"Just a little," he replied, wiping his lip.

"More than a little," she grumbled, checking the cut. The bleeding had stopped.

"There's another patch toward the bottom," he said. "We can check that too."

Kate didn't ask why he hadn't pointed that out at the beginning.

She should feel flattered he enjoyed teasing her. She should feel a lot of things and *not* others.

"Is there really a cave?" she asked, needing to focus on something—anything—else.

"Of course," he said, acting far too wounded. Grabbing her hand, he tugged her farther up the falls, past patches of crimson and yellow roses growing against the rocks. She recognized some from his expedition books.

"Did you bring these back from your travels?"

"Yes. They were mother's favorites."

She'd been about to ask him more about them, but they'd reached an opening in the rock, and the rushing water was deafening.

"Be careful," he shouted. "It's slick."

His grip tightened as he led her in. She ducked to get through the low entrance, but it opened up to cavern height behind the falls. It reminded her of a favorite cave in Cragmont, except where soft blue calcite covered the walls of hers, rose quartz glistened from the walls of his.

She ran her fingers over the pink stones. "This is beautiful," she said, her voice echoing.

"Look up," he said.

She obeyed. Once her eyes adjusted to the dim light, she sucked in a breath. Radiant amethyst stalactites stretched from the ceiling. Some of the purple formations were clustered so densely together, she had trouble finding a patch without the crystal.

"Our boulders may be bigger, but your caves are better," Kate said, wrapping an arm around the lowest—and largest—stalactite. "I thought Cragmont's cliffs were beautiful, but now…" She laughed. "You win."

"Would you like one?" he asked.

"One what?" she asked, thinking he couldn't possibly mean a stalactite. It'd take several brawny men to break off one.

Instead of answering, Bregovi ran his hands over the crystals hanging near the mouth of the cave. Fixing his attention on one area, he wiggled one of the stones, as if working a tooth loose. Within minutes he produced a deep purple point the size of her palm.

"It's lovely," she said, marveling at both the beauty of the crystal and the sweet gesture. "Thank you."

"That should make up for the duel," he said.

"A whole stalactite *might* make up for the duel," she said.

"Hmm," he said, looking far too pensive. "Something smaller then. How about the kiss the night you played the harp?"

"That kiss was definitely not smaller." The mention of that night sent heat to her cheeks, and she hoped the filtered light coming through the falls didn't illuminate that.

"No?" He inched closer. "Perhaps not."

Was his voice growing deeper? Was the cave getting warmer?

"Why don't we consider it a deposit until I can do something that will satisfy you," he said, throwing in a wink and the dimples.

Blessed gods, was he *trying* to taunt her or did it simply come naturally?

"Fine," she said, suddenly growing parched. "So, does the water taste as fresh as it looks?"

"Better."

When she moved toward the edge and reached out a hand to touch the falls, Bregovi quickly grabbed her hips. Not the distance she had been trying for.

"I'm being careful," she stammered.

"Just making sure," he said. "It looks gentle enough, but it carries some force and I wouldn't want it to snatch you along with it."

His hands didn't move, so she thought she'd best get on with it. After quickly tucking the amethyst in her bodice, she cupped both hands to catch a bit of the liquid. The cold water tasted fresh and delicious.

After enjoying her fill, she stepped away and shook out her hands. "How could you swim in that? It's so cold my fingers are numb."

"It's the snow melt. We don't usually swim until the summer months. Here," he said, taking one of her hands between his big palms.

She realized why heat rippled through her whenever he touched her. His hands were toasty like bread fresh from the oven. As he finished with the first and took her other hand between his, her demented brain wondered if the rest of him was equally warm.

Venturing a glance to his face, it looked for a moment like he might be contemplating warming her elsewhere too. Perhaps it was the location, or the gift, or the rush of the water drowning out the voice of her good sense, but she wished he would try.

If she told him her lips were equally cold, would he attend to them as well?

He seemed to read her thoughts, for he leaned toward her. With an invisible current pulling at her, she leaned closer, toward his ready, willing, tantalizing mouth. His warm breath caressed her cheek. Shutting her eyes, she waited for him to close the distance.

Moving his hand to her back, he pulled her tighter.

Her heart stuttered in anticipation.

His lips brushed her ear.

Her legs grew unsteady.

"It's time to leave the cave," he shouted.

Jerking back, she found him grinning and motioning toward the entrance.

Embarrassed by her own thoughts, she started toward the opening on the opposite side.

"It's best to go back the way we came," he said.

"We broke the rope, remember?"

"There's a footbridge farther downstream."

Which he'd failed to mention earlier, so he could get her up on that rope. Blasted man.

"I'd like to see the flowers over here," she said.

She did want to see the flowers, but more than that, she needed to put distance between his warm self and her scandalous ideas. As his enticing body blocked the other exit, the only route to avert humiliation was on her side.

"It's too slippery."

"I'll be careful," she said, frustration making her disagreeable. He seemed overly concerned about her safety and comfort, touching her in subtle ways that drove her mad, yet he couldn't manage a small kiss. How inconsiderate.

"You go your way. I'll go mine," she said, ducking through the opening.

"No," he said, grabbing her arm.

"No?" she snapped back, turning to face him. "Is it forbidden?"

"No," he said again, looking far too amused. "But if you insist on your route, I'll lead."

She pulled her arm away. "I'm capable of finding my way without you."

"Just like you found the dining hall? Sometimes a guide can be helpful."

Starting out the opening again, she hollered back, "I can be my own guide."

Emerging from the cave, she stepped onto a narrow moss-covered ledge extending over the pool. Up the hill to her right, yellow flowers flourished to the top of the falls. Ahead, beyond the ledge, looked to be steps cut in stone. They too were covered in glistening moss and extended to the pool and the base of a flower-covered mound.

As she moved across the ledge, she quickly realized why he'd wanted to lead. The route was more dangerous than the entrance on the opposite side.

Her heart pounded its caution, but pride wouldn't let her retreat. After a moment to study the terrain, she hung onto a tree root on the hillside and gingerly stepped onto a rough patch of moss. So far so good. She carefully moved forward, step by step, using a root or plant for support.

Occasionally she pretended to stop to take in the scenery, but was really trying to calm her shaky legs. Bregovi hadn't appeared at the bottom yet, and she didn't want to turn back to see if he was watching.

Another step. And another. Another breath. And another. Finally, she reached the edge of the ledge. Bushes exploding with fuchsia buds grew alongside the steps and up the steep climb to her right. She pretended to inspect one, but was really testing its strength. It seemed sure. Unfortunately, her footing wasn't.

As she stepped from the ledge her lower foot slipped the moment it made contact with the moss-covered step. Her hand flailed back over her head, still clinging to the plant, and slammed into something hard. *Bregovi.*

With a vice-tight grip on her arm, he pulled her upright.

"It's best not to use the greenery for balance," he said, as if consulting on the care of the plants. While his left hand held her steady, his right disappeared under a bush. She noticed a fair amount of dirt and a few pink petals in his hair. She wanted to stay angry with him—it made it easier to keep her emotions in check—but she couldn't suppress a grin. She turned so he wouldn't see, but wasn't fast enough.

"You're going to let me stand here with soil in my hair?" he said without bite.

"I doubt it's the first time."

"Quite true." He chuckled as a mixture of dirt and petals scattered about. "While I know you are in no need of a guide or assistance of any kind, may a bandit point out the footholds cut into the steps?"

She looked down and noticed that, indeed, grooves had been cut next to the hillside on the far right of each step.

"And that at approximately eye level, camouflaged by those flowers you discovered, you'll find iron rings?" He showed her the one he held under the bush.

Since her right arm was still trapped by his grip, she felt along the soil with her left hand and found a ring.

"I suppose bandits can be helpful," she conceded.

He released her arm as she took hold of a ring.

"Glad to be of service, milady."

She continued down the steps using the footholds and rings. "This doesn't mean I wouldn't have made it down on my own."

"Of course not. In fact, had I not stopped you, I'm fairly certain you would have made it down in a matter of seconds."

He was vexingly right. Had he not caught her, she would have fallen straight into the pool, likely hitting a bone-breaking rock or two on the way.

When she finally reached the bottom, she almost cried out in triumph. Almost. But she refused to acknowledge how scared she had been.

"I should call you Jones," he teased. "You're a natural expedition leader."

Jones? The man who lost his men on a voyage to the north cap?

"I'd say I'm a lot better than Captain Jones. We're both still alive," she said, glancing over her shoulder. His smirk annoyed her. So did the fact that he looked as steady as ever, while her legs felt like noodles. He needed a flaw. She was sure anyone as smug as he was had plenty.

"During our long and treacherous climb down the mountain, I gained an appetite."

"It wasn't *that* long and treacherous," she said.

"I'll collect those berries. I bet they're good and ripe." He stepped past her, heading swiftly toward a far cluster of ferns, a proud leaf stuck in his hair.

She grinned and glanced away before he caught her watching.

Vibrant violets and daffodils burst with color everywhere, and honeysuckle grew over a short hill between the trees, covering a low slab like a floral blanket. Careful not to damage the blossoms, she found a narrow path and started toward the mound, suspecting she knew who was buried there.

The marble, extending the full length of the grave, was etched with roses in various stages of bloom. Crystals of rose quartz and amethyst served as the petals. The pattern circled the name of the occupant and confirmed her assumption. The late queen of Florian rested at her favorite place, covered in beautiful flowers brought back from distant lands by a son who loved her.

Bregovi reached Kate's side, holding an enormous leaf overflowing with raspberries. "Sorry, they aren't blackberries either."

Their eyes held for a moment.

"How did she die?" she asked.

"A fever," he said, brushing a few errant twigs from the stone. "They tried everything, but it was too strong for her. I arrived home five days later."

Words escaped her. She knew what it was to love and lose a mother. And she knew how it felt to be too late.

She slipped a hand into his, and he gently curled his fingers around hers.

"Is that why you started collecting herbs?"

"Yes," he said, his voice heavy. "I'd discovered all sorts of remedies abroad, but I'd been more interested in silly trinkets than medicines that would benefit my family and people."

"You couldn't have known."

"Illness sweeps our land every few years, taking life at will. I should have been more aware. She might be alive today if I had been less foolish."

The pain in his voice pierced deep.

"It's not your fault she died." Kate truly believed he wasn't to blame, but she understood guilt all too well.

"What took your mother?" he asked.

"Childbirth. She died trying to deliver my brother. Her time came early while my father was at sea." A combination that had proved deadly. Had he been home, he could have healed both her mother and the baby.

"I'm sorry." He squeezed her hand.

"I could hear her," *and feel her,* "through the door. Something was terribly wrong. She was in so much pain."

"That must have been horrible."

"The midwife didn't care about her. She was from the village, and they all whispered tales about her because she looked different and wasn't from Astonia. The woman wouldn't let me help."

"You were a child, Kate." Releasing her hand, he gently brushed a loose lock of hair from her face. "What could you have done?"

"I could have been with her. Comforted her." *Healed her.* She hadn't wanted to talk about it, but his tender concern uncorked the dam and the tale flooded out—at least the parts she could share with him.

"I kept sneaking in," *unlocking the door with my Gift.* "But the midwife kept forcing me to leave. Finally, they locked me up with my governess far from my mother's chamber."

Kate had been torn between the desire to break down every door and evict the meddling woman, and the need to conceal her powers. Her parents had warned her never to use them in front of others, so she'd been afraid and hadn't done what instinct told her she should. If only she had realized her mother was more than hurt—that she was dying. If only she had read her better. If only...

"Were you able to see her before she passed on?"

"No," she whispered. "Hours later they told me she was gone. I had to beg them to let me see her," Kate said, her voice catching. As she struggled to push against the unwanted emotion, Bregovi pulled her into his arms, soothing, encouraging. "She looked fine, as if she were merely asleep. But when I tried to wake her, when I shook her, her skin felt cold. The baby's too. They were both so cold."

She must have shivered, for he rubbed her back the same way her parents had. Comforting. Sweet.

She wished she could tell him how she had placed her hands as she'd done with little animals, channeling life energy from the gods—and when that didn't work, her own energy—trying with all of her might to heal her mother. Kate hadn't been able to sense her mother's essence, but she'd refused to stop trying. She'd begged the gods to help. Promised the angels anything they desired. But the heavens were silent.

A long while later, her governess had found her lying over her mother's body too weak to move. Someone had carried her to her room. They had thought she'd been overcome with grief, but much later, her father told her she had nearly exhausted all of her life energy. Although empaths were only supposed to use the energy of the cosmos to heal, Kate had never been able to hold back her own energy when the outcome mattered to her heart. With her mother, Kate had given nearly everything she had and would have died as well if she'd kept on much longer. He had not blamed her for her mother's death, but Kate knew if she'd been stronger, if she'd used her abilities to throw the midwife out, her mother would have lived.

"I'm sorry, Kate."

She nodded, wondering for a moment what he would do if she told him everything about that day. About her life. Her Gifts. But to be accepted for who she was and what she could do was too sweet a dream to imagine and fear snuffed out the notion in seconds.

"Time doesn't erase all pain," he said, searching her eyes. "Although I wish it could."

He led her down the path and over to a grassy spot where they sat and ate berries and watched the falls. Although they only touched when he handed her more of the fruit, the intimacy felt palpable. It had the mysterious effect of making her more at ease with him. With herself too.

"Your maid Holly mentioned another place we might find blackberries."

"Which was?"

She felt foolish just saying it. "The Kissing Bridge."

"If you want to kiss me, Kate—"

"I do *not* want to kiss you," she lied. "Is there or isn't there a Kissing Bridge?"

* * *

"Oh, there's a Kissing Bridge," he said, hauling her to her feet. "And it's time you saw it."

"Did your bandit boy adventures take you there as well?" she asked, as he lifted her onto Odyssey.

216

"Bandit boy!" he cried, climbing on behind her. "For this mistreatment, I shall not entertain you with another story until I hear one of your childhood misadventures."

"What makes you think my adventures were anything but proper?"

"A maiden doesn't take on a man with his own sword unless she's already gotten into and out of a scrape or two."

Still, he couldn't have been more surprised when she finally relented.

"When I was eight, I stowed away on my father's ship."

"You did not."

"I hid behind barrels of ale at first, but I got cold and decided Papa's cabin was better. I'm afraid my next hiding spot wasn't well thought out."

He waited.

"Beneath the dining table."

"Did he step on you?" he asked.

She shook her head. "Rats had already staked out the accommodations and didn't appreciate the competition. I screamed when one ran up my skirt, and that was the end of the adventure."

"Damned rats."

"I know," she said with a quick laugh. "Despite tears and my solemn assurance that I'd left a note for my mother, Papa turned the ship around."

"No."

"Until the death of my parents, I think that was the biggest disappointment of my life."

Bregovi laughed at the thought of the young Kate pleading to sail the oceans with all of those brawny men.

"Father took me on my first voyage when I was a couple of years older than that," he said. "I fell in love with all of it. The sea. The lands. The ship. The stars."

"Holy god the stars are amazing, aren't they?" she said, leaning into him.

"Mmm," he murmured. "I became fascinated with pirates on that voyage and practiced pirate moves on the maids."

"You didn't."

"I targeted those with the best screams." He directed the steed onto a trail toward yet another full brook.

"Poor things," she said sternly, but he thought he detected amusement too.

"I switched to bandits later," he said. "Yours was not the first carriage I'd held up, which was why I was certain Rachel would recognize the prank. What real bandit would ask for a kiss?"

"I believe that was my argument at the time."

"Yes it was, but I'm grateful to the gods you didn't catch on. The duel was an unexpected treat." Pure enjoyment from start to finish.

"I don't think we're of much interest to the gods."

"You never know. Perhaps they're keenly interested," he said, kicking the horse to a gallop.

Bregovi followed the dirt road as it snaked along next to the water. The forest had always seemed especially enchanted in that area, with fingers of light reaching down through the trees, illuminating the plant life below.

The Kissing Bridge only added to the mystery. It was wide enough for a carriage, but the road ended at the bridge, not beyond. And other than the legend, there was no explanation for its origin. All fuel for an imaginative mind, which he knew Kate had in ample measure.

He halted Odyssey at the base of the bridge.

CHAPTER SEVENTEEN

"It's beautiful," Kate said, a hint of surprise in her voice.

"You expected something different?" Bregovi asked.

"Well, yes," she said as they dismounted. "I pictured a wooden footbridge with hearts carved all over it. But this..." she said, approaching the stone bridge. "It really looks like something out of a fairytale."

As if on cue, a thick ray of sunlight broke free from the clouds and set the structure shimmering in blues, greens and purples. Kate jogged right past the sought-after blackberry bushes and up onto the bridge. Halfway across, she turned to call to him over the waist-high side wall.

"The floor shimmers too!"

Bregovi led Odyssey behind her, grinning. Seeing Kate excited about the place, set off all sorts of sappy emotions.

"And it looks like one solid piece," she said before disappearing behind the wall.

Snagging a few berry twigs adorned with the fruit, he started across the bridge and discovered why she'd dipped low.

"They're similar to the Zafarian symbol," she said as he caught up with her. "But different."

"Yes." Bregovi squatted next to her to inspect the carvings. "These don't have serpents."

"And instead of the mountain in the middle, these have an island."

He nodded. "The Zafarians may have developed their symbol from this one. The bridge is ancient."

He handed the berry twigs to her as they stood, watching her carefully look them over.

"Are they blackberries?" he asked as she tasted one.

"Yes." She grinned, popping a berry into his mouth. "They're perfect!" As she carefully wrapped the twigs in cloth and set them in her satchel, she said, "I still can't reason out the age of the bridge. The masonry in Cragmont wears within decades, and this looks as if it was carved yesterday."

"All that effort and you just tuck them in your satchel? Shouldn't we celebrate? Offer thanks to the gods?"

"I'll do that later," she said. "For now, I'd rather talk about the bridge. Just how old is it?"

"It's been mentioned in wedding records for centuries," he said, as Odyssey sidled up to nudge Kate's cheek.

"Trying to make up now, are you?" she said, petting the steed's face. "Why wedding records?"

"That's where the Kissing Bridge part comes into play. It's said if a couple kisses on the bridge on their wedding day, they will be blessed with joyful days, long nights and plenty of babes."

"I don't think Flora or Holly are wed, and I got the impression that they'd both been up here a lot."

"Some come to practice for the special event," he said with a wink.

"I see," she said, a knowing glimmer in her eye. "If not for the records, it would be difficult to believe couples have been kissing on this bridge more than a year."

"It's one of the mysteries of the place."

"There are others?" She glanced about, as if one would emerge from behind the horse.

Why not show her the rest, he thought. If she was as curious as she seemed, she wouldn't be able to resist the adventure and he'd have a little more time to entice a kiss out of her.

"There's a curious rhyme that explains one of them."

"About kissing?" she said, stepping to look at the carvings on the opposite side, Odyssey on her heels.

"Not according to my interpretation. It begins, 'Bridge and brook mark the spot, where the road begins that leads to not.'"

She slowly swiveled to face him. Odyssey followed her lead and turned as well.

"For travelers true to lands unseen, the path delivers where towers lean."

He leaned back against the bridge, enjoying her reaction. She'd heard it. She knew the tale.

Her gaze met his and held. "This is not *that* bridge."

"Through crystal rings above and below, nature baptizes where one must go," Bregovi continued.

"With a final word and a leap of faith, Viridia welcomes and Florian fades?" she said.

"Impressive."

"Are the other elements here as well?" she asked. "Did you find the portal?"

"No one ever ventures much beyond the bridge, but after some investigation on my part, I found a path on the other side."

She darted ahead as he and Odyssey followed her off the bridge.

The brush that usually concealed the entrance to the trail had been broken away.

"Someone has been here recently," he said, catching up. "Normally it's completely overgrown."

"Perhaps one of those couples decided to venture beyond." She brushed past him onto the path.

Perhaps.

The maiden proved to be quick on her feet and an excellent tracker. He watched her follow the trail despite tricky and unexpected turns and wondered if she would handle the turns in life the same way.

"How long ago did you run?" he asked. "Was it recently?"

"Yes," she said, as they rounded a cluster of boulders.

"What do you intend to do?"

"I have been inquiring about governess and maid positions. Ideally, something beyond our shores or on a ship would be safest, but the logistics in accomplishing that are a challenge. Do you know of any explorers in need of a cabin maid?" she asked.

The question didn't fly lightly from her lips and the mention of her tending to cabin needs quickly diverted his thoughts to his bed. Greedy parts of Bregovi's anatomy cried *Yes!* But she hadn't offered that. And even if she had, she deserved more. She should want more.

"You don't see yourself finding love? Marrying?"

"The two don't frequently pair up."

"They can," he said. "My parents loved each other to an embarrassing degree. And I've never seen a man so stupefied in love as my brother Stephen is with his wife."

"They're fortunate," she said. "It doesn't usually unfold as well. Just consider you and your princess."

"I have a princess?"

"One of the servants mentioned you wanted to marry a princess, but she refused."

"Ah." *Camilla.* "That was merely boyish love."

"Isn't love just love?" she said, sifting her fingers through the tall grass as they passed through a meadow.

"Regardless of what measure of love it was, Camilla certainly didn't think it was real," he said, tugging Odyssey, who had helped himself to a mouthful of greens.

"Do you still care for her?"

"No. I'd be a fool to pine for her after she gutted me like a mackerel."

"Oh, my, that sounds ugly. What happened?"

"You want to hear all the humiliating details?"

She spun around on the trail, walking backward, her brows high. "There are humiliating details? For Bregovi the Bandit?" Her eyes danced with amusement.

"You don't need to look so pleased about it."

"I don't think pleased captures the sentiment I feel. But perhaps I'll have more sympathy for you after I hear the embarrassing account. And, yes." She stepped closer. "You must tell me all." One slender finger poked him in the chest for emphasis. "Every." Poke. "Last." Poke. "Detail." Poke. Then she twirled around to continue along the path. "Don't keep me in suspense, now," she hollered back. "I don't think I've been so eager to hear a tale since my father returned from the Third Continent."

He chuckled. Life certainly would be an adventure if he could take the journey with Kate. Despite her lack of sympathy for his downfall, he actually found himself looking forward to telling her. Next to Wolfe, no one else would find it as amusing. Pulling Odyssey behind, he caught up with her in a few long strides and launched into the account.

"Princess Camilla of Darberton was the love of my young life."

Kate let out an exaggerated sigh.

"We had met when her sister competed at the festival that determined my brother's bride. We were both smitten and began corresponding afterward. After hundreds of letters declaring undying love—from both parties," he assured, "I received a letter from her stating she was to be wed."

"She'd never hinted at others before then?"

"No. I was certain her parents had forced the match and immediately charged off to save her. It took me four days to reach her. I arrived as the wedding was taking place and ran straight to the chapel."

Kate stopped mid-stride. "You interrupted the ceremony?"

"Oh, yes. She was at the altar with a rotund, balding man twice her age. I shouted at the ogre to unhand her."

"With as much finesse, I'm sure," Kate said as they continued on again.

"Less, I'm afraid. In front of royalty from all thirteen kingdoms, I drew my sword and demanded he release her."

"He didn't take it well?"

"No, and neither did Camilla. She stepped in front of the oaf to protect *him* and told me it was her choice. She *wanted* to marry him. I, of course, full of youthful candor, pointed out the man was ancient and looked like a toad."

Kate choked on a laugh, and Bregovi couldn't help but grin.

"The man grabbed the clergyman's staff. Camilla didn't need a weapon. She moved toward me, teeth clenched, and said, 'He is going to be a king.' To make sure I understood, she explained this meant she would therefore be a queen. When I replied I could be a king one day, she pointed out my father was healthy and my brother was already producing heirs."

"Oh, no."

"Then she finished me off. She said what we shared was childhood infatuation and she was sorry I *misunderstood*."

"You didn't misunderstand," Kate said. "She just changed her mind."

"I suppose I was an amusement," he said, giving Kate a gentle bump.

"I suppose, but what a set down," Kate said more forcefully than he'd expected. "She didn't have to be so brutal about it."

"I'm afraid she did. I was ready to throw her over my shoulder and fight my way out to save her."

"Well, if a prince came to my rescue, I wouldn't toss him over for a balding ogre. I'd reward him well."

"I do believe a prince did come to your rescue. A short while ago."

She rewarded him with a cheeky grin.

"I'm sorry you faced such a disappointment. And in front of so many."

"It may have been a blessing in the end. I fled to the sea to escape the humiliation and would never have had so many adventures otherwise."

She glanced his way, studying his face a long moment. "Perhaps I should try to view my disappointments that way," Kate said as they arrived at a small meadow.

Exactly as they'd been on his earlier visits, two enormous slabs leaned against one another, curved where they met, creating an archway tall enough for a carriage to pass through. A third slab formed the floor, and beyond the whole of it, the ground dipped as if the Portal were a launch point.

"The towers?" she asked, moving through sprays of bright buttercups and dusty violets flourishing in the clearing. "They look like the stone from the bridge."

"Yes, they're the same. From what I can tell, it's called labradorite."

He watched her circle the Portal, trailing her fingers along the shimmering surface.

"It's covered in the same symbols too," she said.

"Yes."

"And it's dripping from where they meet, but I see no water source."

"I couldn't find one either."

Stepping into the opening, she closed her eyes and tilted her head up, letting a drop of water land on her forehead. "Baptized by nature."

A strange bliss filled him at her reaction. She believed. Just as he did.

"You're going to get *bathed* by nature if you look for the crystals."

Catching the hint immediately, she looked up and squealed. She turned to him, her eyes sparkling, fresh droplets running down her face.

He joined her as she studied the shimmering crystals above their heads. Embedded in the stone, a perfect ring of green crystals glowed in the darkness as water dripped from the center.

"And the ring below?" Kate's eyes fixed on the puddle at her feet.

Squatting, Bregovi scooped out water until the glow of an identical ring of stones shone through.

"This is amazing and all so clear," she said. "Why did it take you so long to find it?"

"You were taken right to the location!" he said, mocking offense. "I had to search a thousand acres of forest."

It surprised him how much he enjoyed sharing his find with her. Wolfe had always been an excellent travel comrade, but even he didn't match Bregovi when it came to the thrill of discovery.

Kate did. She exuded the same excitement at finding it that he had felt.

"One could jump through the opening as the leap of faith, but what is the final word?" she asked.

"I have no idea."

"You've tried, though, haven't you?"

He thought she was teasing at first, but her expression told him she hoped he had.

"I'd be embarrassed to tell you how many hours I spent out here trying every word in my vocabulary."

"Imagine if you discovered the right one and passed over to Viridia. What an adventure that would be."

"Would you go with me?" he asked.

"In a heartbeat," she said as his own heart thudded in response.

Kate had the soul of an explorer, just as he did. She was thrilled about the find, and he sensed she'd be the same at sea. Enjoying each new discovery. Reveling in meeting people from different lands. Learning about different cultures. Making love to him in their stateroom night after night.

As the full image of the two of them traveling the world filled his mind, a great sense of peace washed over him.

"You don't believe me?" she said.

"I believe you. I've just never met a maiden as adventurous as you are." *Or like you in any way.*

"My father said the same thing," she said, her eyes lighting up. "Could there be something about the word in one of your books?" she asked, running her hand over the crystals.

"That was my hope too, and why I purchased many of them, but they all stop short with the rhyme and bits about people from another realm."

"It's frustrating isn't it? Knowing there's an answer somewhere, but not being able to find it."

"Extremely."

He stepped through the opening. "I only wish I knew the magik word to carry us to the other side." He would snatch her up and take her on the adventure of a lifetime.

"Me too," she said, grinning at him. Then she leapt in the air, crying "Freedom," and landed solidly in his arms.

"I guess that wasn't the word," he said, not letting her go quite yet.

"Should I try again?"

"Only if I may catch you."

Her cheeks flushed, and for a moment he feared she'd squirm out of his embrace. Instead, she shifted slightly, wrapping her arms over his shoulders.

"Thank you for sharing your special places with me," she whispered.

"You're welcome."

Was it his imagination or had she drawn closer? And were her crafty fingers weaving into his hair?

"And thank you for rescuing me."

"You're welcome," he said again, on the verge of taking her mouth.

Then her lips quirked up at the corners and, with sunshine glowing about her and eyes sparkling like morning mist, she lowered those sweet lips to his.

She tasted like raspberries, and he suddenly had a new favorite fruit. Slowly, carefully, she dusted perfect kisses over his lips. It was as if he were dying of thirst and she were rationing a drop at a time. Still, each drop was heaven, and he reveled in every one.

"That's what Camilla should have done," she said softly.

"Who's Camilla?"

He caught her throaty laugh in his mouth. Teasing her lips with his, he caressed and nibbled until they were both breathless. When her lips parted, the dance grew intoxicating. Their tongues stroked and played and explored until his legs shook like a green sailor on his first voyage. Never releasing her mouth, he shifted to lean back on one of the towers.

"Am I too heavy?" she asked, her husky voice making his blood sizzle hotter.

"No." He kissed a tender spot at her ear.

"Would you tell me if I was?" she asked on a gasp as he nipped at her neck.

"No," he whispered, trailing slow kisses over her silky skin.

As a quiet "Oh" escaped her, his lips fixed a course down the smooth column of her neck to the delicate dip at her collarbone. Her quickened breath fueled his desire like an east wind on a ship's sails.

With a slight hitch, he moved her higher so his hands cupped her sweet bottom and, equally important, so the ripe flesh rising from her bodice now lay within reach.

He pressed one gentle kiss to the swell of her right breast before moving back to her neck.

She brushed her lips over his forehead before gently steering his mouth back on its previous course.

He needed no further invitation. As a quick thank you, he squeezed her bottom, then explored those twin mounds as he would any important expedition. Each curve, each beauty mark, needed special attention, which he provided with lips and teeth and tongue.

All the while, Kate's exploring hands drew the flames hotter. Over his neck. In his hair. Around his shoulders. When he lingered over her left breast, her hand slipped down his back. *Under his tunic.* If his shaft had been throbbing before, it growled at him now.

He wanted—no craved—to touch her. *Really* touch her. To traverse every delicate inch in meticulous detail, exactly as she was doing to the helpless muscles of his back.

Holding one hand firm under her soft backside, he drew the other up to aid in his quest.

She gasped as he trailed his fingers up over her waist, brushed them along the side of her bosom, and brought them to the juicy pink flesh above her left breast.

Her adventurous hand paused, but her breath hitched faster.

Dark eyes rimmed with gray drew up from watching his fingers. A squeeze of her hand enticed him to venture on.

Holding her gaze, he ran his thumb across the skin at the edge of her bodice, then slowly, carefully, he dipped that lucky thumb under the fabric and found the nub nestled there.

Kate's cheeks bloomed rosier as he took his time teasing her nipple.

"Oh, dear," blew from her lips. "Oh, dear. That's. Very. Unexpected…"

Always the thorough explorer, he shifted his attention to the lovely peak he'd been neglecting. While his thumb stroked and teased, his lips tasted the lush flesh rising from her bodice.

As Kate responded with tiny gasps, her wicked hand continued to glide across his back. And as her fingers quested further, he craved to

229

touch more as well.

Eager, determined, he coaxed the edge of her bodice lower and that perfect nipple higher, until it hid barely below the edge of the fabric.

With gasps echoing from her lips, he lowered his mouth to her breast, letting his tongue enjoy the spoils.

As he pulled the delicate nub into his mouth, she let out a hiss.

Flicking, caressing, suckling, he teased that tender bit of flesh until a deep, soul-satisfying moan escaped her.

"I didn't know anything could feel so, so, lovely," she said with dazed eyes.

Taking her mouth again, he tasted wonder on her warm tongue. Moving his lips over the soft skin of her neck and chest, he built up her anticipation once more, until *he* couldn't wait any longer. The moment he returned to that perfect nipple, a low groan rumbled from her.

A wave of a thousand emotions welled up. Crested. Overflowed.

Desire.

Joy.

He ached to make love to her.

Want.

Need.

On the grass. Against a tree. Anywhere.

Excitement.

Pleasure.

Then she whispered, "Bregovi," into his hair.

Tenderness entered the mix. And on its heels, *protectiveness.*

His feisty maiden wasn't an island native or a street wench aiming to bed a sailor. She was sharp. Beautiful. Brave. She deserved more.

He couldn't take her there.

Moving his hand to her waist, he gave the tender nipple one last tug.

In a whisper, he said, "We should—"

But she caught his lips before he could finish, her hands cradling his head in place as she had her devilish way with his mouth.

Who was he to refuse the lady's needs? He repositioned his hands so both were now happily cupping her backside as he returned her heady kisses.

Seconds later. Minutes. An hour. He couldn't say when, his enticing maiden whispered, "We should what?"

His loins screamed that they should drop to the ground and make love under the Portal. But the fog of desire thinned and reason returned. In a gravelly voice that hardly sounded like his own, he said, "Stop. We should stop."

"Now?" she asked, cheeks blooming, eyes dark, lips ripe.

Absolutely not. "Definitely."

She nodded, but looked unconvinced.

"Don't you recall your no seduction rule?"

"Apparently not," she said with a throaty laugh that heated him up again.

He lowered her slowly until her feet touched the ground. Resting her forehead against his chest, she drew a slow breath.

After a long moment, she shook her head and grinned at him, mischief sparkling in her eyes. "I only meant to thank you."

Laughing, he pulled her close. "I consider myself thoroughly thanked."

"Me too," she said.

"For what?"

"I don't know, but you should tell me so I can do it again."

Taking her mouth one last time, he lavished her lips with a tender caress he hoped would linger in her thoughts, and the wave of desire swept him off again. Just as his carnal needs were beginning to quiet his honorable senses, a familiar whistle reached him on the breeze.

Wolfe.

CHAPTER EIGHTEEN

Bregovi's lips left hers to whisper, "Wolfe is here."

It took a full moment for her lust-muddled brain to register what he'd said. Then a second moment to realize she might not be presentable. A quick glance down confirmed that indeed she was *not* presentable unless she planned to seduce Wolfe as well.

Rushing into the Portal, she stuffed her breasts back where they belonged, and pulled her bodice and shift back in place. She caught a few drops from overhead and patted them on her face, hoping the cool water would tone down the heat in her cheeks.

Stepping out into the sunshine again, she noticed Bregovi combing his hands through the hair she had so thoroughly disheveled. His tunic had been straightened as well, but nothing could dim those rosy lips or the wicked gleam in his eyes.

"Shall we thank him or flog him?" Bregovi asked.

"I haven't decided," she said, still dazed from it all. "Imagine if he'd found us earlier, when you were...when I was...when your mouth was..." As marvelous memories raced through her mind, heat flooded everywhere else.

"When indeed," he said, looking as if he'd like to reenact the scene.

As her heart beat a furious rhythm, their ill-timed visitor emerged from the trees.

"I see you didn't run her off this time," Wolfe shouted, moving with a purposeful stride, a chestnut mare in tow, and a white and gray falcon on his arm.

"Not yet, but you're not helping" Bregovi responded. "What are you doing here? I thought you were on the hunt."

"Still am," Wolfe said, giving the bird a graceful toss, to which it took leave to soar overhead. "I stopped at the castle for a meal and to update you before heading out again."

"You didn't think to wait for me there?" Bregovi asked.

"You gave me a deadline," Wolfe said. "And the sooner I find the man, the sooner I'll be reunited with Angelina."

"Angelina?" Kate said.

"My lady," Wolfe said with a wink.

"He hopes," Bregovi said with a wink of his own.

"So, you're no longer a bandit then?" she asked.

"Nor usually. I'm owner and captain of a galleon."

"A galleon? As in a ship?" she asked. Perhaps he was her answer. "When is your next voyage?"

"Oh, no," Bregovi said. "He doesn't need a cabin maid."

"Says who?" Wolfe said.

"I can cook as well," she said.

"The men would eat *you*," Bregovi said. "You are not cooking for the crew."

"But—"

"Wolfe," Bregovi said with a pointed look in her direction before turning his attention to his friend. "You have some news for me?"

She curbed her tongue, but would resurrect the discussion with Wolfe later...or sneak onto his ship when the time came.

Wolfe inclined his head toward the trail.

Bregovi collected Odyssey and walked a few paces with the man before Wolfe said, "There was another Zafarian sighting in

Kingsbury."

Kingsbury bordered Florian to the north, and Kate's heart kicked her ribs to make sure she took note. So close? Had someone tipped off the Zafarians? As if she'd been inflicted with a spell, panic immediately replaced all the good feelings Bregovi had stirred that afternoon. Kate quickly glanced around as if she expected the sorcerers to jump from the bushes to grab her.

"Zafarians?" She forced her shaky legs faster as she ran to catch up. "So near?"

"They're getting closer by the day," Bregovi said.

"What are they after?" she asked, not sure her voice was steady.

"Until a week ago, they were seeking artifacts," Wolfe said. "I came across a village that had been raided. The townsfolk said the sorcerers had demanded all of their Zafarian possessions. Apparently, the smithy had a sword he didn't want to part with, and they chanted a spell that crushed his hand."

"How long have these attacks been occurring?" she asked, darting around shrubs to step alongside them.

"Just shy of two months," Bregovi said. "They've been growing more frequent."

"And more bold," Wolfe added. "They're now striking when the sun is high."

Suddenly the genie binding made sense. If she wouldn't help Morten willingly, he'd have her master force her to do his bidding.

"Now they seek a dangerous sorceress," Wolfe said.

Sorceress? Had he learned they were searching for *her?* Kate's mind scrambled too fast and her feet too slow, and before she realized what had happened, her knees slammed into the dirt.

"Kate, are you injured?" Bregovi asked, rushing to help her up.

"Fine. I'm fine." She brushed off her skirts and tried to steady her nerves.

"But you're trembling. Wolfe, we need to discuss this later."

"No," she cried. "That isn't necessary. What happened with the sorceress?"

"Sadly, the townspeople didn't know more than that," Wolfe said.

"That's unfortunate," Kate said, letting out an uneasy breath.

"Don't believe that's the end of the tale," Bregovi said as they continued their walk through a grove of trees. "He always saves the best for the end."

"I tracked five Zafarians to a camp in the foothills. I approached as if they were old friends, boasting of how I'd confiscated some artifacts from a woodsman."

"Do you have a death wish?" she said, incredulous.

Wolfe laughed. "They especially loved the chalice and said the Order Master would be pleased. But then another said nothing would please him until they found her. The sorceress."

Kate felt a sudden urge to bolt down the trail, but forced her legs to stay put. If he'd known they sought her, he would have already revealed it.

"I sat back as they discussed her amongst themselves."

"His favorite way to glean information," Bregovi said, clearly not as perceptive as his friend. For if he were, he'd have noticed all the blood had drained from Kate's face.

"From what I gathered, she's the ward of the Order Master. Beautiful. Powerful. With Gifts they were all awed by," Wolfe said. "Although they stopped short of saying what those were. Unfortunately, she's mentally unstable. She killed her maid and possibly others."

Mentally unstable! The blood rushed back to her cheeks. She hadn't killed anyone, and her mind was as sound.

"The Order Master was concerned she might harm others or reveal Zafarian secrets, so he's put a reward on her head. Any man who provides news of her whereabouts will gain one hundred Crown. The man who delivers her will receive a thousand."

A thousand Crown!

Kate felt as if her belly were readying to reject the raspberries.

Bregovi whistled. "No wonder they're hunting for her instead of the objects. A tradesman won't see either amount of coin in a lifetime."

Wolfe nodded. "A thousand Crown would fund us for a few years. You sure we shouldn't look for her instead of the Order Master?"

Her heart stopped. Literally. For at least two beats.

"Did they say who she is?"

Wolfe shook his head. "That's where events went south. I subtly asked how they would identify her, and my new comrades looked dubious. They said everyone in the Order knew her name and what she looked like, if not from personal knowledge, then from the brotherhood. I laughed it off and said I meant how would they find her if she were in disguise."

Bregovi laughed. "You have twelve lives."

"That settled them down and they debated disguises for a time. When one began questioning me about which brotherhood I was from, I deflected answering until I could take a piss in the woods. Then I left."

"Intriguing," Bregovi said. "But no name."

"No. But if we can determine who she is, we can identify her guardian, the Order Master."

"They were heading to Florian next, so I thought I'd get ahead of them to warn you, and maybe scout west or south," Wolfe said.

Kate hadn't realized she'd stopped walking until Bregovi returned to her and gently took her hand.

"You needn't worry, Kate, if she comes here, we'll find her."

Not a comfort.

"It's brilliant, really," Wolfe said.

Bregovi nodded, guiding her along the path. "If we capture her and make it known we've done so..."

"This Order Master will come to us," Wolfe finished.

"Exactly," Bregovi said.

While Kate feared being discovered, she felt equally alarmed that they'd confront Lord Morten.

"What do you plan to do once he's here?" she asked.

"We'll capture him," Bregovi said, as if the man were a common thief.

"Are you mad?" she blurted out. "His little minions crushed a man's hand in a moment. How do you expect to capture him without ending up a pile of dust?"

"The lass has an excellent point," Wolfe said. "This may be one of the few times you should exercise caution, rather than charge in like a rhino in heat."

Rather than look duly concerned, Bregovi broke into a broad grin. "I do believe you both love me."

He lifted Kate's hand and kissed it while she gazed on, dumbfounded. Wolfe got a slap on the back.

"I don't believe I declared anything of the sort," she said dryly.

"I didn't say it either, but he's correct about my camp," Wolfe said. "And to honor that bond, my friend, you ought to think this through."

"Again, I'm honored by the concern and the love," Bregovi said as they crossed the Kissing Bridge. "First, your fears are unnecessary at present, as we don't know who the sorceress or the leader are." Bregovi helped Kate onto Odyssey and climbed on behind her. "Second," he said as Wolfe took his seat on the mare, "have you two forgotten my extensive library on Zafarian magik? There must be something written about how to defeat an Order Master."

From Kate's study of Zafarian lore, the only way to unseat a Zafarian Order Master was through his death. If Bregovi did manage a confrontation with Lord Morten, the Order Master would not be the lifeless one at its conclusion.

"I would like to help with the research," Kate said.

"Excellent," Bregovi said. "And you Wolfe? Will you help with the books as well?"

"I'd like nothing better, but will leave that to you two. My skills are best utilized in pinpointing the man and his unbalanced sorceress."

Unbalanced? The only unbalanced behavior she'd ever shown occurred while kissing Bregovi, and it didn't pose a danger to anyone but herself.

* * *

Later that evening, Kate and Bregovi poured through Zafarian books in Bregovi's library. While the tomes recounted the long history of Zafarian magik and the land itself before its destruction, none provided a way to overpower her uncle.

"I wonder if these accounts were written by Order Masters," Kate said. "In which case, they'd want to leave out the means to their undoing."

"Why don't we use magik against him?" Bregovi said. "This volume contains hundreds of spells."

Kate leaned over to see the page and couldn't help but laugh. "You're going to capture him by rendering him mute?"

"It would prevent him from chanting a curse."

Intrigued at the thought of a speechless uncle, Kate scanned the page. Unfortunately, the ingredients would be a problem. "Where would we get horn of unicorn? Or blood of a fae?"

"Hmm," Bregovi said. "Perhaps this is a collection of Zafarian fairy tales."

"Or dark magik. Aren't unicorns and fae sacred?"

"If they exist at all." Bregovi held up another book. "Some of the spells in this one don't have ingredients, just chants. Like the one that crushed the smithy's hand."

"Hmm," Kate murmured over his shoulder.

"I haven't come across any as destructive, though. These lean toward causing water to boil."

"Might be helpful if we wanted to scald the man."

"Why would some spells require ingredients and others not?" Bregovi asked.

The why of it had been a mystery to Kate as well, but somewhere in her third or fourth year of study she'd discovered that those that didn't require ingredients were accomplished by many sorcerers combining energies, chanting in unison. Only those with profound abilities were able to work the chants alone. It took eons of practice and an innate ability few had. The term Order Master derived from that very principle. Any sorcerer to achieve the rank had a mastery of the elements surpassing all others. Her uncle Morten had no equal.

Even if Bregovi stumbled upon the perfect spell *and his personal talisman*, he'd be like a doe on newborn legs trying to outrun a mountain lion.

"We should try one," Bregovi said.

Kate's stomach dipped. "I don't think so," she said, stepping away.

"A simple one," Bregovi said, flipping back through the pages. "I saw one that didn't look too tough." Landing on a page, he said, "Here."

A glance at the page revealed a love spell.

"No," Kate said, retaking her seat.

"What harm could it do?" Bregovi asked. "You don't think it will work anyway."

"Chose another," Kate said. Aside from her distaste for spells that influenced another's desires, he would have no way of judging its success—or lack thereof—and false confidence was one thing he didn't need.

"How about this one," Bregovi said. "It only extinguishes a candle. It calls for few ingredients and the chant is short."

Despite Kate's protest, the foolish man gathered the ingredients— a candle, salt, a bowl of water and a feather.

Bregovi followed instructions to the comma. Nothing happened.

He repeated the steps again. Putting more feeling into the

incantation. Nothing.

"Maybe a maiden's touch will do it," he said, looking her way.

The spell had been one of the first she'd mastered as a child. With her talisman safe around her neck, she'd accomplish the task in seconds. She neither wished to encourage him nor display her abilities.

"I'm not inclined to try," she said, a bit too vehemently.

"It's the sorcerer that makes magik destructive, not the act itself."

"Perhaps, but I shall forgo your little experiment."

"Very well," he said, flipping back through his book. "But I'll master this yet. You'll see."

Not if the gods have mercy on either of us.

* * *

As surf washed over Kate's bare feet, she lifted the hem of her gown and danced on the shore. Blue sky and fresh air filled her soul. Others danced along with her, all with dark hair and gray eyes. The serenity emanating from them filled her with joy she'd rarely tasted.

Then, through the distant mist, Sylvan materialized. Curly red hair, determined gaze, he charged toward her, a silver dagger clutched in his hand.

Frantic, she tried to will the blade from him.

It didn't respond.

As she looked around for a weapon, Bregovi ran up behind her. Relief filled her, followed immediately by fear.

Sword at the ready, the prince darted past her.

Toward Sylvan.

A flash of steel. Then blood.

Bregovi's blood.

Everywhere.

Her scream jolted her to another place. Heart racing, she took in her surroundings. She was still in the library.

"A bad dream?" Bregovi asked, kneeling next to her.

"Yes," Kate said, shaking it off. "I think I read too much about Zafaria."

As he handed her a goblet of water, she noticed the sun had set.

"I'm sorry if our talk of Zafarians frightened you," he said, leaning against the table. "I shouldn't have involved you."

"No," she said. "I'd worry more if you didn't."

A quiet smile pulled at his lips, which she elected to ignore. No doubt he thought it another sign that she loved him. Which she didn't. Or so she hoped.

"We should leave it for tonight," he said.

"Good idea," she said. "Princess Victoria is going to have my head for being gone so long."

"Should I speak with her?" he asked.

"No!" she said, rising.

He laughed and brushed a soft kiss on her forehead. "Let me know if you change your mind."

"I won't. Imagine how furious she'd be if you *explained* things." Even as she knew she should ease toward the door, her hands went to his arms. Solid. Warm. "You really should play chess with her. It would make her happy."

"Would it make you happy?" he whispered, leaning in.

"No," she whispered back. "But it would make life easier."

Laughter rumbled from him as he drew her against him.

"Thank you for rescuing me today," she said into his smiling eyes. "And for the tour of the forest."

"You're welcome."

Capturing her lips, he sent butterflies dancing about her belly and heat everywhere else.

"Good luck with tomorrow's event," he whispered against her mouth. "I hope you win another adventure with me."

Wise or not, she hoped so as well.

* * *

241

All of them? Kate had been distracted with thoughts of Bregovi and his plans to defeat her uncle, but she was sure she had identified at least half of the gems correctly. The faces on the other maidens mirrored her shock.

Six glass cases lined up near the windows in the ballroom displayed precious gems of all carats. Each maiden had started at one end, identifying the stones on a parchment as she worked her way past.

Sophia had stepped forward to lead the way, and Kate had noticed the princess staring intently at a couple of the stones before noting an answer. It had made Kate worry about the difficulty of the task, for the princess always wore sapphires and probably had extensive knowledge of other coveted jewels as well. If she had run into trouble, so would the others.

As Kate had moved down the row of cases, she heard murmurs ahead and behind. "Where did they find these?" "Mixed stones." But while the gems were unusual, Kate thought she had answered at least half of the dozen correctly.

Wrong. She had missed them all. Everyone had. Except for Sophia, who had identified each perfectly. To be certain the rest of the maidens were as incompetent as it seemed, Randolph and the royal jeweler went back through to check. Their conclusion a resounding affirmation that Sophia's answers were correct and the rest were inept.

Victoria, Lady Anne from Highbridge and two others, likely expecting a different outcome, stormed over to the gem displays.

Victoria spoke first, her voice calm, but as sharp as ice, "This stone has been switched."

"I assure you—" the jeweler began.

"It had flecks in it and now it doesn't."

"Perhaps the light made it appear as such," Randolph offered.

Kate remembered the flecks as well and now the green stone was clear of blemishes. But the cases remained within everyone's view through the entire event. No one could have switched them. Not physically.

Randolph announced Sophia the winner of the event and a tour of the castle and its grounds.

"She cheated," Victoria said, joining Kate.

"Her answers do seem too perfect," Kate said.

"There's nothing perfect about her," Victoria growled, then lowered her voice. "I'd wager my crown she uses magik like your uncle."

Kate whispered, "I never said he—"

"Fine. Like everyone says he does," Victoria said. "Do you agree those aren't the same stones we looked at?"

Kate nodded and noticed an old, wiry man watching her from across the room. A mane of white hair, tied loosely, hung down his back. Although his stance looked unsteady, his gaze was anything but, as it alternated between the gems and Kate.

"Why is that man watching us?" Victoria asked. "He can't think we did it." The princess quickly leaned closer. "You didn't, did you?"

"Of course not," Kate said.

"Because if any miracles occur, they had best be in my favor, not Sophia's."

"I heard you mention miracles," Princess Rachel said, stepping up behind Victoria. "It appears Princess Sophia certainly benefited from one today, doesn't it?"

Victoria whirled around. "Yes, we were just saying as much," she said, her voice sweet as molasses. "What do you make of it?"

"I don't know. I'm too worried about Sebastian's next event to think on it," she said with a forlorn expression. "Do you think he'll benefit from a miracle too?" she asked, her voice wavering a touch.

"I hope so," Kate said.

"As do I," Victoria said. "Would you care to join me for tea and a game of chess to distract your mind until the event?"

"I'm afraid I can't concentrate enough for chess, but the tea sounds lovely," Rachel said.

The old man caught Kate's eye again as Victoria left with Rachel. Bregovi and the man had moved over to the gem case tight in discussion. Then Bregovi looked her way as well, giving Kate the uneasy feeling they were speaking about her.

Bregovi motioned her over.

She obeyed reluctantly, not keen on being pulled into another conversation about the ever-changing gems.

Putting on her most non-magikal smile, she approached the two men.

"Kate, this is Quentin our resident expert on all things mystical," Bregovi said. "We call him Old Quent."

"That's only because there's a younger version back at the inn," Old Quent said with a wink.

"Old Quent suspects magik was afoot here today," Bregovi said.

"What do you think, Kate?" Old Quent asked. "You saw the stones earlier. Did they look the same as now?"

Kate took another look at the gem display. "At the time, I thought they appeared differently, however, the lighting or my nerves may have affected my judgment. I'm clearly not as good at identifying stones as I am at trivia. If you'd like to ask me more about the prince, I'm sure I'll do better."

Rather than take the bait, Old Quent stared at her for a long moment. Then he patted her hand as it rested upon the case. "Now I see," he said. "Do not worry, I'll keep your secrets."

Kate glanced to Bregovi, unsure of how to respond. Was he an empath? Had the man read her? Was he a Zafarian?

Bregovi chuckled. "Old Quent likes to think everyone has the old Astonian Gifts. His favorite pastime is declaring who can do what."

"But Gifts are forbidden," Kate said. "Isn't that like accusing everyone of being a sorcerer?"

"Not in Florian," Bregovi said, giving the man's shoulder a squeeze. "No one believes him, but it's entertaining to hear what sorts of Gifts he invents."

"What does he deem your Gift to be?"

"One day I showed him my collection of Zafarian artifacts and he dubbed me Gifted with magikal objects. Not his most creative."

Perhaps not, she thought, but possibly accurate. A Gift with the items would explain why they felt warm to him and why he was so drawn to them.

"He says the smithy has a Gift with locks."

"Indeed? That would be helpful for a smithy."

"Quent, what's Kate's Gift?" Bregovi asked.

"Oh, no," Kate said. "I'd rather not speculate about things like that. Why don't we simply say I'm Gifted with trivia and leave it there."

The old man grinned and elbowed the prince. "This one is going to keep you on your toes."

"Is that her Gift?" Bregovi asked.

"One of many, I think," Old Quent said, patting her hand again. "But I promised to keep her secrets, and I will."

"That's what he says when he needs more time to think up one," Bregovi said. "He's old, so we'll have to humor him. I'm sure he'll come up with something good. Until then, I have another adventure for you. With Old Quent."

She couldn't imagine what sort of an adventure would involve Old Quent. Her expression must have indicated as much, for Bregovi laughed again.

"He has a collection of Zafarian books. I thought we should look them over to see if they hold anything helpful. Would you care to join me?"

As keeping an eye on the prince and his plan to defeat her uncle had surpassed her other pursuits, she agreed to his new quest.

"Where are we going?"

CHAPTER NINETEEN

The trek to Old Quent's treasure trove took them through a lane of shops outside the castle grounds and to an inn bordering the city's back gate. The afternoon meal called, and it appeared many had gathered there for a bite.

As Kate took in the room, she noticed the castle woodcarver's hand everywhere. Engraved vines curled up the walls, around doorways and overhead, but monsters and dragons bloomed where the roses should have been.

"Hey, Quent, it's Prince Edmund and one of them contest maidens," a red-faced brute hollered toward a stocky bald man filling pints at the bar. *Young Quent*, she presumed, wore a thick apron over a large belly, likely well-fed with what he held in those pints.

They wove around tables and over to Quent. The conversation hadn't quieted at all, but the topic had shifted. She heard *joust* and *prince* and *commoner* and even *harp* flitting off eager tongues.

Quent wiped his hands on his apron as she stepped up to the bar, "Somethin' for ye, your highness? Milady?"

"Cider and soup for the three of us," Bregovi said.

Quent nodded and poured from a jug behind the counter. "Bet, love, fetch three bowls of Fannie's stew." A young freckled maid nodded and disappeared beyond a swinging door.

Kate took the mug from him, thanked him and tasted it. Tart, spicy and delicious.

"Everyone knows Fannie's stew is the best, but I wouldn't expect it to top dinner at the castle," he said.

"So far the cider is better," Kate said with a grin.

Quent studied her face and then a slow smile tugged at his mouth. "Town's placing bets on who'll win and you've got your share of followers, Miss."

"I do?" Kate said, surprised. The thought that anyone would be rooting for her seemed unreal.

Bet returned with the stew and set it on their nicest table, near the hearth.

"Yes, mum," Bet said. "At first some was angry, since we all thought Baker Jim's daughter, Jenna, was going to get picked. She's the most beautiful and she'd been practicing the flute. But then you got it and you seemed so shocked. And then someone set you up on that harp and, well, a lot of us forgave you after that."

"Thank you," Kate said, sitting.

Before she knew it, nearly a dozen townspeople pulled benches over or sat on nearby tables as they ate Fannie's fabulous stew. Bregovi seemed equally at ease with them as he did at the royal table, mocking offense when they asked her more questions about the contest than they did him about his latest adventure.

A few wanted to know if she had a poem ready and offered to listen to her rehearse. She declined. Another asked how she was at croquet. When she said she hadn't played in years, they all threw out tips for the final event. "Strategy." "Stay away from the pack." "Forget manners."

"You make it sound like warfare," she laughed.

"Isn't it?" Quent piped in.

"It's war for the prancing princesses," Bet said. "They look ready to throw you to the wolves every time you win. Especially that sapphire one. I'd expect if Croley's monster was still alive, she'd feed you to him herself."

"Well, if she tried, you can be sure that monster would be coughing up sapphires in the end, because I'd take her right along with me."

The contingent roared at that one. They were likely correct, though. Sophia wanted the prince, and Kate wondered to what lengths the princess would go to get what she desired.

A short while later most had gone back to their seats around the inn, leaving Kate and Bregovi listening to Old Quent's stories about magik and the Portal and the glory days of the Zafaria.

"Do your books have information about how to defeat them?" Bregovi asked.

"Come," Old Quent said, gripping Kate's hand to pull himself up.

As Bregovi led the way to the back of the inn, Old Quent whispered to her, "I may even have something that mentions what you need."

"What do I need?" she asked.

Old Quent only smiled.

After stopping in the kitchen where they each took a candle, Old Quent led their little party through a short narrow hall and into a cluttered storage room. It had no windows and smelled like stale biscuits. Judging from the dust on the trunks and objects, she doubted anyone had been there in years.

"I know I have a few volumes on high magik somewhere," he said, shuffling through the door. "I think those might mention how their enemies overtook them."

"Which trunk would they be in?" Bregovi asked.

He looked around the room for a moment, as if imagining a different scene, then zeroed in on a dark chest in the corner. Setting his candle on a dusty shelf, he removed objects from the old trunk. Kate hurried to help him, and Bregovi tugged at the lid. It groaned open to reveal a stack of ancient books much like Bregovi's.

"These belonged to a former Order Master who was captured and executed for sorcery."

"Was he an ancestor?" Kate asked.

Old Quent nodded, "Centuries ago. Descended from two of The Ten. The family hid all of this away in case they needed it someday."

She lifted a volume from the trunk and carefully opened it. The binding was sewn with thick thread, and inside she found pages filled with hand-scrolled instructions.

"He learned to read with them as a boy," Bregovi said, picking up a heavy tome.

"Drove me mum batty," Old Quent said, chuckling. "She feared someone would discover what they were and think we were Zafarians."

"Did anyone?"

"Nah. I was clever."

"You still are," Bregovi said.

"There's many more clever than me," Quent said.

Her eyes quickly found his.

"Some more clever than most," he said with a wink. "It's easy to hide one Gift, and a minor one at that, but to hide great powers would take a wily spirit."

Her heart raced. "Yes, I'm sure your ancestors were faced with that very challenge." Holding an uneasy breath, she glanced at Bregovi, but the man was too engrossed in the book to catch any underlying meaning.

Old Quent patted her hand and sighed. "Indeed, and those with such power do need to be careful who they trust," he said as he carefully shifted books around in the trunk. "Let us see if we can find those volumes on high magik."

They all thumbed through pages on their own for a long while.

"This may be what we need," Bregovi said, holding up one with an ancient script on the cover. "It's full of hefty spells." Flipping through the pages, he said, "Blindness, plague, death. And here are some for enslavement. There's even a genie spell."

A genie spell? Kate hurried over to see the page, but he had turned it already.

"You must be very careful." The man eyed the volume in Bregovi's hand. "Even the most powerful sorcerers took care with dark magik, and those in your hands are the darkest."

"I don't plan on causing a plague, but being able to conjure any form of magik would be helpful."

"May we trade volumes?" Kate asked. "This one deals with more basic spells. There could be something in here to indicate where we should start." It wasn't a lie, but she didn't think he'd be proficient at magik after reading the thing. What she really wanted was a glimpse at that spell.

Bregovi swapped with her. Trying to mask her eagerness, she took a seat on a low trunk and thumbed through the thick book. After discovering several ghastly spells that made her skin prickle, she found the one she sought. Two full pages detailed exactly how to enslave a genie. A diagram showed the salt ring they'd used and pinpointed the positions of master, genie and the Zafarian elder performing the ritual.

She glanced up to ensure both men were occupied, then read on.

The Genie Binding of the Highest Order unites the souls of the genie and master until the death of the master.

A scribble to the side indicated that the genie would then transfer to another, but didn't indicate how or to whom. Another note in smeared ink advised that binding a genie to a master of the same bloodline would result in the death of both parties, answering the question as to why Morten hadn't bound her to himself.

Her eyes skipped up to read through the details of the spell, all of which Morten had followed precisely. Except the last bit. Consummation or bloodshed. *More like murder.* She'd never imagined

Morten would try to kill her, but what if he had? She'd not even have suspected. Instead of slicing her palm, he and Sylvan could have slit her throat.

The book began trembling in her hands and she fought the urge to dart from the room. Reason told her she wasn't in danger, not with them, but every inch of her body felt like it needed to flee.

Taking in slow, steady breaths, she forced herself to focus back on the words. After the first part of the sealing, the genie could be compelled, but consummation or death of the genie was necessary to force the genie to come when called and to prevent the genie from using magik against his or her master.

That's why Sylvan hadn't been able to call her to him. She had escaped before he consummated the binding. Or more accurately, *while* he was trying to consummate it.

As she absorbed that fraction of good fortune, her eyes caught onto another crippling revelation.

The binding not only enslaves the genie, but his or her spouse and offspring as well. This is especially beneficial when the family members of a sorceress or sorcerer are Gifted. One can enslave the weaker member of the couple and gain the servitude of the more powerful spouse and children without needing to overpower that spouse.

It suddenly became clear. The full, cruel magnitude of what he'd done. Whatever life she built for herself, whatever she did to find a home or love, she'd never be able to marry or have children. While the prospect of either had always been a slim one, the idea that they would now be impossible sucked the air from her lungs. Would she ever be free? As her eyes filled with tears, they moved of their own volition to Bregovi.

With a foot propped on a crate, the book on his knee and his candle high, he seemed engrossed in the text. He was passionate and

251

exciting, curious and intriguing, adventurous and kind. He'd become so much of what she wanted and everything she could never have.

"Something unpleasant there?" Old Quent asked, holding up his candle to take a look at the page.

"Just a spell," she said, swallowing a sob.

When she tried to flip the page, he gently set his wrinkled hand on the parchment.

"Let's take a look."

While he bent to read the text, she wiped her eyes and concentrated on not weeping in front of the two men. Dealing with Morten had taught her how to turn off the tears and she called on that strength now.

"Look here," Old Quent said, drawing her back to the page.

One crooked finger pointed to a short phrase written in a loopy hand near the inside margin.

Spell can be broken in entirety by power greater than Zafarian magik.

Broken?! She didn't believe it. How had she missed that? Was it true?!

She read the line three times, then the other scribbles in the margins. There was no other mention of it, nor the manner in which it could be broken.

"Do you know of such a power?" she asked. "This means there is one, doesn't it?"

"It seems it does," Old Quent said. "But I've never heard tell of anything stronger."

"What are you two whispering about?" Bregovi asked. "Something interesting?"

"A mention of a power greater than Zafarian magik," she said.

"A greater power?" he said, taking the book from her.

She pointed to the line, praying he wouldn't ask why she was reading about genies.

"What is it?" Bregovi asked.

Both Kate and Old Quent shook their heads. Whatever it was, she needed to find it.

"Maybe it's mentioned in one of the other books," Kate said. "May we borrow a few?"

The man hesitated, glancing between the two with worried eyes.

Bregovi rephrased the request. "We need to borrow a few volumes and will return them when we have finished with them."

"As you wish," Old Quent said. "But please take care, your highness. This is dangerous business. Much darker than turning a garnet to a ruby."

"We'll be fine," Bregovi said, handing a volume to Kate and adding another to his stack.

As they left the inn, Old Quent whispered to Kate, "Do not give up, young one. You may break the spell yet."

She smiled at him, neither confirming nor denying his suspicions, but hoping more than anything that he was right.

* * *

Upon returning to the castle, Kate talked Bregovi into lending her the volume with the genie spell and stashed the book in her chamber. She then joined the others for the men's treaty event, currently underway in the grand hall.

Bregovi sat prominently between Princesses Sophia and Victoria, and Kate found a place among the spectators. As the event progressed, Kate's spirits lifted when Sebastian gained an early lead. But then he faltered, missing a question, which allowed Lord Nicholas of Sydmore to tie and pull ahead. Once again, Sebastian came in second. Rachel did little to hide her frustration and left the event without word to him.

Poor Sebastian only had one event left. And it was the most difficult—an obstacle course. Five men were now tied with one win each. If any of them won the final event, they'd take the princess.

As Kate accompanied Victoria back to their chambers, it occurred to her Victoria didn't have much time left either. Only the poetry and croquet events remained. While Victoria practiced her poem for the next event, Kate sat to write one herself. She wasn't trying for anything brilliant, but wished to avoid embarrassing herself. She used the prince as her inspiration, knowing the other maidens couldn't ridicule her for the subject matter.

* * *

Rachel finally broke away from the last of her suitors and escaped to her bedchamber. The rain outside mirrored her emotions—sloppy and overwhelming.

Sebastian had changed his mind. It was the *only* explanation. He'd met her and something in her nature or manner had caused him to reconsider. Or perhaps he had realized he wasn't ready for marriage. That would be the only other logical explanation. Upon further thought, another ill conclusion plagued her—he had fallen for another.

In any case, he had changed his mind. Otherwise, how could he have lost so many events, including archery? Archery! After how many tournament wins? The number eleven came to mind. Could that be correct? Eleven? Suddenly, confirming the figure became exceedingly important.

She unlocked the lid to her favorite mahogany trunk and stared at bundles and bundles of letters from *him*. There would be no more. Blinking back messy tears, she gathered an armful from the past winter. He'd mentioned the latest tally of wins sometime after the Winter Solstice.

Dumping the cache on her bed, she found the collection she sought and pulled loose the carefully tied ribbon. She didn't know the total count, but in two years he'd written her nearly one hundred letters and she'd cherished them all, reading each 'till the words were stored in her heart.

Due to those repeated readings, it took little time to find the epistle. Curling up on her bed, she leaned against the pillows and poured over it once again.

> *My Dearest Rachel,*
> *As always, I hope this letter finds you well*
> *and recovered from your sneezes.*

She recalled the winter draft she'd caught and reported to him. That had been why he'd mentioned the competition. His amusing account of his latest win had had her laughing aloud and improved her spirits. Skimming the verses, she found the sought-after passage.

> *With only a tiny measure of boasting, I humbly report this*
> *makes my eleventh archery win for all classes in six kingdoms.*
> *My brother says I could shoot a bee in flight.*

There it was. Eleven wins. And a *bee. A BEE. And he can't hit a target the size of a carriage wheel.* He probably aimed at the post. No, he probably aimed at and struck a *bee* on the post. She had half a mind to go and check for insect remains.

He no longer wanted her. That was the only explanation. He should have told her, rather than put on the fool charade. At least then she'd have been free to encourage another while there was yet time. She felt a chink in her heart and swallowed a knot in her throat.

If only he hadn't come to Florian at all. If only he hadn't been so sweet. If only she'd never written him. He never should have encouraged her. No gentleman would have if he cared at all. He should have told her!

A knock at the door beckoned. Then another. She tossed a lap blanket over the letters and bid "enter."

Holly delivered a neatly folded parchment and left her to read it in isolation.

The knot in Rachel's throat moved to her stomach as she stared at her name. The dispatch was sister to the dozens on her bed.

Same paper. Same folds. Same hand.

Perhaps he'd written to tell her his heart had changed. That he was withdrawing from the competition. That he'd found another. Her pride told her a note was a coward's way out. A noble man would have the good manners to face her. With shaky hands, she opened his last letter.

All it said was:

Please meet me in the greenhouse. Now.
— S —

No apology. No words of love. Just *meet me* and *now*. He planned to inform her in person. How dreadful. How ungentlemanly. She could think of nothing more horrid than standing before Sebastian and hearing him say he didn't want her.

She didn't have to go. She could send a note stating she was otherwise engaged, but she'd see him eventually, and waiting for the inevitable would be worse. Then her mind saw a path to bypass future humiliation.

She would end it. *She* would tell him she'd transferred her interest elsewhere. If he asked to whom, she could name Lord Preston. Of course, the thought of marrying Preston caused the contents of her stomach to shift unpleasantly, so she decided she didn't have to name a suitor at all, but merely release him from their tenuous friendship.

He would be the one to wonder. *He* would be rejected. Not her.

Tossing the new letter with the old into the trunk, she gathered her wits and her courage and her heart, and marched off to confront the man she had thought she loved.

At the greenhouse, she observed confronting was much easier if the confronted actually appeared for the event.

Sebastian was nowhere to be found. After an agonizingly long seven minutes, according to her timepiece—seven minutes longer than she should have waited—the hurt she had stuffed under her anger clawed its way out.

He didn't care. He was toying with her. He couldn't face her. All thoughts of refusing him fled as hope died heavy and hollow in her belly. Before despair had her in a puddle on the floor, she bolted for the side entry. Better all of Astonia witness her heartache than Lord Sebastian of Brandish.

With her vision hindered by tears, her usual graceless state magnified itself. She stumbled over a watering pot and slammed into a lemon tree, scattering yellow fruit in all directions. She hurdled three in motion, astonished she didn't land on one, and then something unexpected froze her in place. A word.

"Don't!"

CHAPTER TWENTY

Concealed behind a large fern of mutant proportions, Sebastian watched Rachel run into the greenhouse from the rain. She stomped her shoes at the door to clear off the mud and tossed her parasol aside. It occurred to him she'd never looked more beautiful. Of course, he thought that every time he saw her, which was part of the reason he'd written out what he'd planned to say. Looking at her tied his tongue in knots.

He glanced over the words once again. Twice again. Ready. He took a breath, steeling his nerves to begin, and then he caught her expression. If he didn't know her better—and really, when one thought about it, he didn't—he'd think she looked angry. And wooing an angry princess didn't seem an appealing task.

But this was Rachel and she possessed his heart, so if he was ever going to gain trust of hers, he had to speak. Any minute. One more breath. One more minute. Readying nerves, he filled his lungs, and she ran. Straight for the door.

My love!

She tripped over a water pot.

Dearest!

She knocked into a fruit tree, and his arms came out to catch her even though she was out of reach. Then she hurtled toward the door, and "Don't!" burst from his gut and, thankfully, his mouth.

Don't for *Don't go*, but the *go* disappeared on his tongue.

Not terribly romantic.

Nevertheless, she halted.

"Don't go, Rachel. Please," he said to her back.

Her hands fisted at her sides as she stood as rigid as a garden statue.

He wished she'd turn around, but didn't want to tempt the good fortune he had of speaking with her at all.

"I've written you another letter. My one hundred and twenty-third." His face heated, and he wondered if she'd been counting their correspondence as well.

He swallowed.

She didn't move.

"May I read it to you?"

She didn't indicate approval, but also didn't refuse in any manner, so he began.

"My Dearest Princess Rachel. I hope this letter finds you and your family well. For there is nothing I wish more than for your happiness."

Glancing up, he thought her hands moved slightly. Still knotted, but not quite so tight? Taking a step toward her, he continued, "Unfortunately, I fear my actions of late have hindered that happiness—if I dare hope my actions could have any influence upon it."

Another look. Another step. No movement from his love.

"I find I'm in the contest of my life, and my performance disappoints no one more than myself. It is as if all the competitions before now were in readiness for this one, and yet nothing could prepare me for so great a task. You see, while I wanted to win at the others, it didn't much matter if I lost. And so I won. Event after event."

He glanced up again and her hands were no longer fisted. He moved another couple of feet, taking a slow breath, hope growing.

"But this time," he croaked and then groaned. *Merciful gods.* He ordered his voice to cooperate. "This time," he said clearly, "everything dear to me is at stake, and I do nothing but lose."

Her head dipped forward a fraction. He hurried on. Lowering the paper, he gazed at her familiar back. He didn't need to read the next part, for he'd labored over it so long, it was written in his heart.

"For you, Rachel, are dearer to me than any trinket or honor. I cherish every word you've written, and my initial fondness has grown into something much deeper. Much more important. Your compassion for others makes me strive to be more giving. Your humility reminds me to be humble, and your clever observations keep me alert and laughing. Your sweet words reached me from the parchment and wrapped around my heart."

She turned to face him, and that same heart battered his ribs. Her cheeks were pink, and her eyes cautious and wet. He took in air and stepped closer, only a few feet separating them now.

"I did not fall in love with your beauty, but with who you are inside. Yet when I saw you again, I couldn't help but think you were the most breathtaking maiden in all the kingdoms."

She had yet to speak, but one tiny tear escaped. With a slow, shaky hand, he brushed it away.

"Please don't mistake my dismal performance for anything but that of a man completely besotted and overwhelmed by the magnitude of the task before him. If I could bribe all your other suitors to bow out, I would. But I fear there isn't enough coin in Astonia to persuade them to walk away from a chance to love you. I know I couldn't. Not for any price."

Her eyes bore into his as she blinked. Once. Twice. Sending more tears on their way. This time she brushed them off.

He hoped they were tears of joy, but was entirely unsure. Perhaps she feared hurting him. His stomach hurtled toward the floor.

Then the dam broke and through gulps she said, "Oh, S-Sebastian. I thought you were losing intentionally."

As her hands went to her face, he closed the distance and pulled her close. She shook against him as she wrapped her arms around him and cried into his shoulder.

"Never," he said. "I'm sorry I gave you reason to doubt." He turned just a hair and kissed her forehead. It was as if he'd held her so a thousand times. A tiny gasp escaped her, and the beat of her heart sped up against his chest.

She shifted and her nose brushed his chin as she gazed up at him. Crisp blue eyes, inches away. Ripe lips within reach of his. Neither moved. It was right. Foreordained. Inevitable. He tightened his hold, leaned in and tasted heaven.

Her soft mouth and strong embrace told him she was still his. And if he doubted it, the hours they spent talking and kissing later that afternoon cemented it in his soul. She was his as much as he was hers. All he had left to do was win her. And win her he must.

* * *

A summons from his father did not bode well for a peaceful afternoon. Bregovi found the man in his study, papers spread out on the mahogany desk Bregovi had purchased on an expedition years prior.

"Edmund, I'm glad to see you've returned from your errand."

"Father," he said with a nod.

"What's your progress on the hunt for the Zafarian?"

"We have some leads."

His father moved over to the table that diagramed the attacks. "Have you learned the man's name?"

"No."

"Do you have a description of him?"

"No."

"Do you know which kingdom he's from?"

"Not yet, but Wolfe is searching, and I've discovered the sorcerer can be defeated with a power greater than Zafarian magik."

"Indeed?" his father said, finally looking pleased. "What is this greater power?"

Bregovi contemplated how to best answer without discouraging his father's budding enthusiasm.

Too perceptive, the man said, "You don't know."

"We will."

"Not in time," his father said, studying the board. "The competition ends in two days. You cannot identify and capture the man in such a short time."

"Wolfe is—"

"Remarkable, but even he can't work a miracle of this size. I'm sorry, son, but you're going to need to wed. And I want to remind you that your bride needs to bring alliances that will aide Florian."

Bregovi's stomach churned worse than when the ship's seafood chowder had gone foul.

"You've enjoyed a few moments with the girl, but now you need to encourage others."

The girl. She was so much more than that.

"Kate is intelligent—"

"And beautiful, I know, but she's not for us. Princess Victoria or Princess Sophia are who we need. They each have strong armies behind them, ample resources and healthy dowries that can help fund your expeditions."

"I don't need their dowries," Bregovi said. "I can supplement my funding by charging passage to others. Selling medicinal herbs."

"You'll need to do more than supplement if you marry the penniless one. You'll need to fund it all yourself, and you well know you can't do so with a handful of passengers and a few sales."

Land bound with Kate or sail the seas without her. His head pounded as if he'd been struck by a rigging beam.

"I'm not saying you must give her up. Keep her as a mistress, if you wish, or take her abroad with you. But marry her you won't."

He'd not deny taking Kate as his mistress would solve their problems, but he doubted Kate or either princess would embrace the idea. He wasn't confident he could either.

"Princess Sophia won the last event and awaits your escort around the castle. I suggest you get to know her during that time and decide whether you want to give the poetry win to her or Victoria."

"Ten other maidens will be competing as well, Father."

"Not to us," the king said. "I don't care if they stutter while reciting the most dull passage of scripture, Sophia or Victoria will win the next event. Understood?"

Understood, yes. Agreed, no. As he set out to find Sophia, he fished his brain for a better solution. For regardless of which direction he came at the problem, he could not see how he could have both Kate and his adventures. And having both Kate *and* his adventures was fast becoming the only life he wanted.

* * *

Bregovi watched Sophia examine the family collection of swords in the armory. She had insisted on the complete tour, assuring him she was interested in *everything*.

She leaned in to get a closer look at a jeweled hilt and moved over to the sword Kate had used in their duel. "If you reset this with new stones it'd be magnificent. My family not only has endless sapphires, but rubies too, which would look brilliant in this setting."

Stepping to her side, he said, "This sword belonged to my grandfather, a gift from my grandmother. It's set with rose quartz and amethyst from our lands."

"They're beautiful crystals, but they're all wrong for the sword's purpose. Rose quartz and amethyst are loving, docile crystals. You need something more powerful, like rubies or garnets."

"I always thought the sword was perfect as it is."

"Of course, it's sentimental, but you can see how it would be improved, can't you?"

He didn't see it and recalled Kate's pleasure at receiving the small amethyst point. He doubted she would think it needed improvement.

"I've heard you have some lovely items in your library. Is that to be included on the tour as well?" she asked.

"If you wish."

"Oh, I do," she said, taking his arm as he led her onward.

* * *

While Kate put the finishing touches on her poem, the rain slowed, allowing the sun to peek through the clouds. Victoria's spirits had also lifted. The princess had told Kate earlier she was reciting a favorite verse from memory, and Kate suspected the princess had mastered it.

After helping Victoria choose and don a shimmering plum-colored gown for the evening banquet, Kate stashed her poem under her mattress and set out for Bregovi's library. She would dig through every book in the place, if necessary, to discover the power greater than Zafarian magik.

* * *

"Oh, it's beautiful." Sophia gasped as they entered the library. "Look at all these treasures." Weaving around the globe, she went straight to a collection of crystal goblets.

"I brought those back for my mother. The rose pattern etched in the face was designed for her."

"I'm sure she loved them."

Next, she looked over an assortment of wood figurines in the case next to the goblets. "These are so primitive," she said, inspecting a roughly carved elephant. Her tone told him it was not an observation, but a criticism.

He had picked them up on safari. "A native from a remote village carved that using a sharp rock as a tool. The wood is from the marula tree."

After returning the figure, she wiped her hands on her skirt and hurried over to a more ornate figure speckled with jewels.

"I hope you didn't pay him much for it," she said.

He had given the man a knife in trade. The native hadn't wanted to take it, but Bregovi had insisted. He could still see the tears in the man's eyes as the carver showed his family. Bregovi wished he'd been more generous and somehow knew Kate would have been. She had loved the figures. He'd have to go back someday. He'd like to see if the man had changed his style of carving with the more intricate tool.

As Kate had, Sophia gravitated to the Zafarian objects.

"These are interesting," she said, lifting a dish emblazoned with the sorcerers' symbol.

"Yes, I've collected a fair number of their artifacts over the years."

"My family has as well. Are you familiar with their powers?"

"Powers?" he said, suddenly more intrigued with the princess. Perhaps she *had* used magik during the gem competition.

She swapped the dish for a griffin figure carved from green stone. "For example, this one is made of malachite, which can strengthen and heal the bearer."

A gasp drew his attention to her next discovery as she quickly traded the griffin for the mirror. She inspected it as if it were made of precious gems. "This handle is black tourmaline, which is protective to the one holding it. It's an amazing piece."

The praise surprised him, considering it wasn't adorned with rubies.

"The quartz points around the face aren't valuable. Wouldn't you want to replace them with diamonds?"

She looked it over once more. "No. The quartz is perfect. You shouldn't change it. You really shouldn't alter any of the Zafarian objects."

"Indeed," he said as she extended the mirror to him. "How did you come to know so much about their artifacts?"

"My family's mines outnumber any in the kingdoms, and we're interested in anything related to gems and minerals. As the Zafarians used them in many ways," she said, gesturing to the mirror, "they've become a favorite research subject." She picked up a broach with a jewel-embellished star pattern on one side and the sorcerer's symbol on the other. "Legend holds that every artifact bearing the Zafarian seal has been spelled with a magikal purpose. That's why the sorcerers have been stealing them lately."

He really shouldn't have been dumbfounded about her knowledge on the subject, but he couldn't avoid it. The maiden seemed more informed than Old Quent.

"In your family study, did you learn how they worked spells?" he asked as she set the broach back in the case.

"Maybe," she said coyly. "But that sort of knowledge is taboo, isn't it? It isn't wise to speak of it."

Now the minx was teasing him, sauntering over to the window, fondling a Zafarian fan.

"Nothing is taboo here," he said, flashing the smile that had melted foreign maidens across the globe.

"Oh, my," she said, electing to put the fan to use. Any flush she may have felt didn't reach her face, though. She looked as collected as ever. The maiden had her wits about her, and he suddenly felt like a juicy fly being lured into a carefully strewn web.

"Would anything persuade you to share your knowledge with me?" he asked. "I've long been interested in Zafarian lore and would be grateful for an expansion of my understanding."

"Perhaps," she said. "But you mustn't tell anyone it came from me. I don't want witch-hunters after me because I knew too much," she said with more flirt than fear.

"Of course," he said. "Simply a few questions, if you'd oblige a curious prince."

"What would you like to know?"

"First, what makes a spell work, or not work, for the one performing it?"

"I can answer that, but what shall I receive in exchange?"

"My gratitude?"

"For such wisdom? Yes, gratitude would be appropriate, but how about a favor as well?" She ran her hand over the globe, giving it a spin.

"What sort of favor?"

"You elect the winner of the next event. Poetry."

"Yes."

"You could award victory to me."

While that was his father's aim, Bregovi didn't wish to commit to a winner quite yet.

"That wouldn't be fair to the other maidens," he said. "Can't we strike another bargain?"

The moment *bargain* left his lips, hers hitched up at the corners, and a wicked gleam spread to her eyes. He'd never been gifted at reading women's thoughts, but instinct told him she'd heard about his duel with Kate and, more importantly, its wager.

As if he'd already heard the words, she said, "The bargain is a kiss for each answer."

Now, it would seem quite ungentlemanly to argue that a kiss from a maiden was not a good bargain for a valuable answer. And since he did want the information, he had no choice but to concede to her demand.

"Very well," he said. "What's the first answer?"

A grin pulled at her mouth, reminding him of a merchant who had received double his asking price.

"First the kiss, then your answer."

He had to chuckle at that. She was a masterful negotiator. Putting a hand around her waist, he pulled her close.

"I didn't say anything about embracing," she teased, settling her palms on his chest.

Another chuckle rumbled from him as he gazed into eyes as dark as molasses. As he leaned in, she tilted her head and met him halfway.

When his lips touched hers—that moment when his heart should thud and passion should mount—all that filled his thoughts was she was taller than Kate.

Releasing her mouth, he asked, "What makes a spell work for the sorcerer?"

Drawing one hand over his shoulder to the back of his neck, she said, "Seed of the earth…most call it a talisman."

"What is this talisman?"

"That's another question," she said, weaving her fingers into his hair.

Once again he pressed his lips to hers, but this time the clever girl was ready. Instead of releasing him to answer, her fingers held him gently in place, while her tongue darted out to taste his lips.

Affection for Kate be damned, the action sent a message straight to his groin.

When he pulled back, her cheeks bloomed a soft shade of peach.

"The talisman?" he prompted.

Nodding, she said, "Every sorcerer has a talisman unique to him…or her. Without it the spells won't work."

Won't work? Could this be the means to disarm them?

"So, without the talisman, he can't use magik?"

Payment number three brought heat to his ears…and other places. This was not her first voyage.

"Yes," she said. "Without it, a sorcerer is left with only his Astonian Gifts, if he has any."

Was this the answer he sought? "But what is this talisman? A cat? A mouse?"

As she pressed her curves against him in preparation for the next installment, it occurred to him their bargain might not have been prudent.

* * *

The castle appeared quiet as Kate approached the library.

Turning the handle slowly, she gently nudged the door open a fraction and froze.

Bregovi and Sophia stood before her locked in an embrace. Sophia's fingers were lost in his hair and he looked hungry for her. Passionate. But it couldn't be. It had to be in jest.

Kate watched as he released the princess's mouth and rested his head on her forehead. Sweet. Tender. She hastily shut the door, lumps forming in her throat and belly. Had he been courting Sophia at the same time he'd been spending time with her?

As Holly's animated voice echoed down the hall, Kate darted for the servants' stairs, following them to the main floor below.

With every step, her mind replayed all the other times he had humiliated her—the bandit charade, entry in the competition, the harp award. Her cheeks flushed at the thought of her behavior at the Portal. It was all a game. As soon as she threw herself at him he was on to another.

Just when she felt like she'd crumble, pain moved aside for anger, and anger made way for a vow. She might have been the fool before, but now it was his turn.

Darting through corridors, she couldn't get back to her chamber quick enough. She had a new poem to write.

* * *

Their lips parted and Bregovi rested his forehead on Sophia's. He needed to end this. While she was willing and skillful, each kiss reminded him who he wanted, and it wasn't the maiden in his arms.

"Do you truly believe sorcerers who fashion magikal objects would need rodents to perform spells?" Sophia asked.

Not a mouse then. Or an animal. *Seed of the earth.* His gaze swept over the array of artifacts. She'd pointed out the tourmaline and quartz. The mirror, the blade, every item in the collection was decorated with stones. No, not decorated, *empowered.*

269

"It's a stone, isn't it?" he said. "Does he carry it with him?"

The devil grinned and captured his lips again. And while parts of his anatomy were eager to reward her for the valuable information, his heart screamed that this was all wrong. She was wrong. She wasn't Kate.

Slowly, he relaxed his hold and moved away.

"Yes, he carries the talisman with him."

"So, if I take a Zafarian's talisman—"

She laughed. "You'll lose your head."

"Not if I know what I'm dealing with."

"You can't be sane," she said, humor gone, eyes aghast. "I thought you merely wanted to know how they managed spells." Almost as an afterthought, she added, "In theory."

"I'm curious about many things, and your fount of knowledge has given me interesting ideas."

"Yes, well, you're a fount of stupidity if you think you can defeat a sorcerer by any means. Even if you manage to figure out what his talisman is, he'll not allow you to simply pluck it from him."

"What do you mean? It's a stone on his person. How difficult could it be to identify?"

The maiden looked at him like he was a simpleton. "Sorcerers don't carry just one stone," she said, making no attempt to mask her view of his idiocy. "They wear jeweled rings on every finger. Wrist cuffs. Emblems. Charms. Necklaces. They even sew them into their clothes. You'd have to strip them to the skin to make sure you got them all."

"Sounds reasonable," he said, part in truth and part to see her jaw drop.

"Maybe with nobodies without any skill, but if you try that with a, with a…" Her lovely face paled remarkably.

"An Order Master?" he finished for her.

"Well, yes," she said, sounding exasperated. "Forget hypotheticals. You've obviously heard that the Zafarians have been attacking and have some misplaced confidence that you can do something about it."

"Misplaced confidence is a tad harsh, don't you think?" he said, enjoying her concern more than he ought to.

"Reports say the Order Master is ruthless," she said, her voice rising in pitch as she began pacing between the globe and Galileo.

"I'm determined and clever," he said, taking a lazy pose against the case with the Zafarian treasures.

"Determination and cleverness are admirable. Recklessness is not," she said on a pass. "No one wants to mourn a dead prince." Sophia gave the globe a spin before she started back toward the turtle. "I never should have told you," she muttered. "I thought you were curious, not *delusional*. Heavens, does your father know what you're about?"

As amusing as she was, he feared she'd reason herself into action on his behalf. He had to stop the path of her thoughts, so he stopped the path of her feet. Blocking her way, he took gentle hold of her arms.

"I'm sorry I've agitated you."

"I passed agitated ten paces ago," she said, a whisper of humor entering in. "You must be careful."

"I will be," he said, meaning it.

There seemed to be more layers to the princess than he'd originally surmised. If he hadn't met Kate, Sophia might have made an interesting bride. But, he reminded himself, he *had* met Kate, and it would take more than a hundred surprising princesses to forget her.

Reaching into the display at his right, he took out the broach she had admired earlier. "Please accept this with my thanks and my assurance that I'll heed your warning."

He placed the item in her palm.

"You don't need to give me anything," she said, studying the object. "But I thank you. It's a rare piece."

He should have persuaded her to take an artifact for each answer rather than a kiss. It would have prevented the odd sense of guilt now nagging at him.

He guided her to the door. "I'd like to keep this discussion between us."

"As you wish," she said, stepping into the corridor. "But you'd best heed my words and take care."

"I will."

A flirty glint hit her eyes. "If you don't take my advice, at least I'll have this to remember you by."

CHAPTER TWENTY-ONE

As Bregovi flipped open a book on Zafarians to search for anything he could find on talismans, Rachel peeked in.

"I passed Sophia." Rachel plotted her usual course to Galileo. "She seemed delighted about her tour."

"I think she was."

"How did you feel about it?" she asked, lifting the turtle out of his case.

"Not as delighted, I'm afraid."

"No?"

"No, you see, I've seen all of the castle before."

She grinned and settled in a chair at the chess table with Galileo on her lap. "And what of Sophia?"

"Hmm. Well, I've not seen all of her."

Her gasp made him laugh.

"What did you think of her," she said sternly.

He noticed Sophia had left the carved elephant on its side. Picking it up, he took a seat across from Rachel, studying the figure as she waited for his answer.

As he didn't intend to reveal Sophia's expertise of all things Zafarian, he said, "She likes nice things."

"I've noticed that too." Rachel traced Galileo's shell with a finger. "Did she show interest in your expeditions?"

"Those that resulted in valuable collections."

"She's beautiful," she said wistfully. "Nothing is ever out of place."

"You are lovelier, Rachel. And far more kind."

"Thank you, Edmund, but I'm not feeling very kind at the moment."

She was so serious he had to suppress a grin. "You, who give your old gowns to the maids? Who taught the stable boy to read? Who sends hot meals to any family in the kingdom with illness under their roof? Who—"

"Stop," she cried, her face flushed. "You're making me feel awful."

"By citing your good deeds?" He laughed. "Tell me, dear sister, what is this blemish in your charitable disposition?"

"I should hold my tongue," she said, studying the turtle intently.

"Now you know that's impossible, so you might as well tell me."

She squealed in outrage, but her eyes smiled back at him. "Very well," she started, her gaze growing serious. "I don't want her to win, Edmund. I don't want Sophia to win you or marry you."

"I see," he said.

"You must see how wrong she is for you. She— "

"I don't want her to win either."

"Oh, thank the gods," she said nearly before he finished his sentence. "I feared she might win you over. She needs to take three events to beat Kate. Two to tie. If you don't declare her the winner in poetry, she can't win the competition."

He nodded. The thought had occurred to him as well.

"I do like Kate," she said, eyeing him.

"As do I." Although like wasn't adequate, was it? Could he love her? Already? After such a short time?

"Papa won't like it that she's poor," Rachel said.

"No."

"If only Kate had Sophia's dowry. That would be perfect."

"Yes, that might make it easier for him to swallow."

"I could give her my dowry," Rachel said, almost too cheerfully.

"No, you'll be needing that soon enough, although it's a generous gesture."

"I don't want to be needing it soon," Rachel said, collapsing back into her chair. "Who ever came up with this custom?"

"You used to think it was romantic."

"It's only romantic if the one you want wins. Otherwise it's just demeaning. I feel like the prize cow in a kingdom fair."

He chuckled, "Would that make me the prize bull?"

She smirked. "Or rooster."

"Rooster!" he boomed, making her laugh.

When her giggles subsided, he asked, "Is Sebastian the one you want?"

"Yes." She let out a long breath. "Edmund, may I share a secret with you?"

"Of course."

"Well, you see," she began, then blushed three shades brighter before his eyes.

"Rachel, what have you been up to?" he teased.

"It's about Lord Sebastian."

"Yes?"

"Well, he and I. We..."

Bregovi jumped to his feet. "Has he compromised you?"

"No, no!" she said, looking alarmed. "At least I don't think so," she said all too uncertain. "We've been corresponding. We met at the festival in Highbridge two years ago. His cousin was in the competition, you see."

Bregovi wasn't sure why the cousin factored in, but nodded.

"And he and I, Sebastian, that is, began writing to one another after that."

"For two years? Why didn't Father approve a betrothal?"

Bregovi didn't think it was possible, but Rachel's cheeks grew brighter.

"I hadn't told Papa yet. I thought there was time. I didn't think he would do *this*," she said, gesturing wildly around the library. Bregovi assumed she was referring to the festival and not his treasures. "And I didn't know if Sebastian wanted to marry me."

"I think it's clear he does."

"Even so, I fear it will not be. He has one event left, and he hasn't won anything since the ball, which, you must admit, wasn't really a competition."

How he loved her sweet nature and wished there was a way he could ensure her dreams were realized. He wanted her married to a good man that she wanted to be with. A man she loved.

"Are you certain he's deserving of your affection?"

"Yes. Oh, yes. He listens to me. Really listens. He says I'm charming. And he cares about people too. He has wonderful ideas about how to help the poor. And he's clever, but people don't always see that."

Rachel grinned as her thoughts took her elsewhere. Kate was charming and beautiful too. And feisty. And passionate, he thought, remembering their last kiss.

"Has he kissed you?"

Rachel's face went redder yet and her gaze darted to her lap. "Edmund, I—"

"Is he a gentleman? Is he thoughtful?"

Her eyes found his. "He is those things and more. I know he cares for me, and I can't imagine wanting anyone else."

"Then I will speak with him tomorrow. I'll do all I can to help your Sebastian win the prize cow of Florian."

"Edmund!" she mocked offense, then softened. "Thank you."

* * *

Bregovi spent the bulk of the night pouring over all the books in his library in search of anything further on talismans or higher magik. And all through the night, one nagging thought tormented him: If he didn't find the sorcerer in two days' time—which looked less possible by the minute—he'd need to marry the winner. And regardless of how he played out the possibilities, the only winner he'd be satisfied with was Kate.

By morning he knew what he had to do. His father would be furious, but Bregovi would find other means to forge an alliance while he continued to hunt for the sorcerer.

The banquet hall buzzed with chatter as Bregovi entered.

"Edmund," Rachel exclaimed, rising from a chair next to Sebastian. "Are you joining us?"

"If you'll have me."

"Of course," Rachel said, retaking her seat and offering the seat to her right.

But he had hoped to speak with Sebastian, and Kate's chair between the smithy and the lord was vacant, so he took that.

Brock looked over. "We're saving that for—"

"She can sit next to Rachel," Bregovi said.

"Ah," was all Brock said before turning back to the maiden at his left.

As the meal was served, Bregovi focused on his sister's beaux. "So, tell me about your kingdom, Sebastian."

"What would you like to know?" the lord asked.

"What's your most valuable resource? What do you trade?" Bregovi asked, adding ham to his plate.

"Brandish is mountainous, so our resources are timber, ore, and animal pelts. Most of the bearskin rugs and beaver furs come from our lands."

Bregovi nodded. He had a number of the rugs, all acquired from Brandish tradesmen.

"Tell him about the water," Rachel said, to which Sebastian smiled at her.

"I've told Rachel about our efforts to share water with nearby kingdoms. Our heavy snowfall and a natural spring high on the Divide give us more water than we can use."

"Sometimes it floods," Rachel added.

"I spend a great deal of time on the mountain helping with the ore mines."

"They had problems with flooding in the mines and down in the valley, and Sebastian figured out a way to stop it." She said it with such pride, Bregovi couldn't help but grin.

The lord beamed under her praise.

"How did you stop it, Sebastian?" Bregovi asked.

"I studied the paths of the rivers coming off the mountain and proposed we create a new one."

"They made their own river," Rachel emphasized.

Bregovi was becoming more and more intrigued by the skinny nobleman. He came across as somewhat hapless, but perhaps that was only when it came to his heart. His mind was certainly quick.

"It took two years, but we were able to build a manmade river to divert some of the spring water and snow melt to Larchmont, where they needed it for their crops."

"Isn't that brilliant?" Rachel said.

"Indeed," Bregovi said, sincerely impressed. "Tell me, Sebastian, if you can devise and execute a plan to move a river where it had no intention of going, how is it you are not able to triumph in an event to win my sister?"

Rachel sputtered and coughed, nearly choking on a slice of bread. As her face turned red, Bregovi jumped to assist, but Sebastian shifted instantly to pat her back and held his drink out to her. She took it, after which Sebastian offered a napkin and made sure she was well before turning back to him. Bregovi suspected Sebastian would sidestep the issue, but the nobleman surprised him again.

"To answer your question, I wish I knew the answer. I've been trying my damnedest to win. I know much is at stake."

"I can see you care for my sister."

Sebastian blushed. "I do."

"And I know she cares for you."

Rachel blushed and took a shaky sip from her glass.

"I've hoped that's true," Sebastian said.

"It is, man. She wants you."

"Edmund," Rachel pleaded.

"To win," Bregovi finished with a wink. "Do you mind if I offer an opinion on the matter?"

"I'd be most grateful," Sebastian said.

"I think you need to forget you're competing for my sister and instead tell yourself the prize is something less important. I don't know, like maybe a cow."

Rachel groaned.

Both men looked her way, and Bregovi caught her eye. He'd miss teasing her when they were both wed and apart.

"I don't know," Sebastian said. "That would be difficult."

"What was the prize for the archery competitions you've won?"

"Usually a bow. Or quiver of arrows. Once a horse."

"Very well, consider the prize a new bow instead of Rachel."

"I'll still know it's for Rachel. I know what you're trying to do, but a lot is at stake. I can't simply think it's only for a bow."

Although Bregovi had felt their conversation was fairly private, Brock had apparently been listening and chose that moment to join in. "Might it help to practice?" the smithy said. "The obstacle course for the competition is guarded, but running through another couldn't hurt."

Despite his ill regard for the man, Bregovi had to admit he offered a good plan.

"It might help," Sebastian said. "I'm willing to try it if you know where we might find another course."

"We could create one," Bregovi said.

"I'll help," Brock added.

Yes, Bregovi was beginning to like the smithy, especially since Brock wasn't going to win Kate in the end.

"I'll help too," Rachel said.

"No," all three men said in unison.

Her face fell. Bregovi's heart lurched, and he opened his mouth to say something when Sebastian leaned over and whispered to her. A smile tugged at her lips as the two joined hands under the table.

He sure hoped their afternoon practice helped Sebastian, for he truly wanted Rachel to marry whomever she wished. He wanted it nearly as much as he wanted Kate for himself.

Victoria caught his eye across the room and he excused himself to find out why his maiden hadn't joined the banquet.

Victoria greeted her way through the guests. "Why, Prince Edmund, it's lovely to see you this morning," she said with a curtsey. "I'm looking forward to sharing my poem with you and hope you haven't heard it before."

"Even if I've heard it, I'm sure your rendition will be unique."

"I hope so. I wanted to choose something already composed, rather than pen something myself as Kate is doing."

"I didn't know she writes poetry," he said, wondering what other hidden talents she hadn't yet shared with him.

"This might be her first," Victoria said. "She skipped the banquet to work on it, so it isn't coming easy to her."

As he escorted Victoria out of the banquet hall, he wondered what she'd write about. Her family? Her time in Florian? Him?

* * *

While Victoria and Bregovi were distracted with the morning meal, Kate snuck into Bregovi's library. She poured through every magikal book she could find, but was unable to discover any mention of a power greater than that wielded by the Zafarians.

The Caligo volume may have held the answer, but its pages

refused to yield their mysteries. She had recognized the style of words, but couldn't remember what any of them meant. Familiar, yet completely foreign and utterly frustrating

As she looked up to scan for any books she'd missed, her eyes caught on the chess table. Memories of the enchanting afternoon with Bregovi flooded her mind. Then the image of he and Sophia kissing crashed in and washed away the rest.

He had used her. Not as her uncle had, but just as painfully. More. For she'd never let down her guard with Morten as she had with the prince. It didn't matter that she wouldn't have wed him. That she couldn't have him. He hadn't known that.

He had done the pursuing. He had kissed her that evening by the harp. He had courted her in his library, given her a valuable book, showed her his kingdom. And while she couldn't deny she had instigated that kiss at the Portal, he had surely baited her all afternoon with stories of love and touches and raspberries. He'd tasted like raspberries too when she had kissed him and she doubted she would ever eat one again without recalling his betrayal. Not only had he taken liberties, touching her wherever he wished, he'd stirred up longings she'd no business entertaining.

On her way to the library, she had considered skipping the event. She had no particular desire to see the man again, but after her mind replayed all the memories, she once again felt the scorching need to expose him for what he was.

After nearly running to her chamber for the poem, Kate slipped into the Grand Hall and took a chair by a side door. Across the room, Bregovi entered with Victoria on his arm.

Sophia, Lady Quinn and Lady Anne stepped over to intercept them. While he greeted the maidens with a broad smile, his nod to Sophia oozed indifference.

Perhaps he'd used her too.

Although she held no great fondness for Sophia, the maiden's confused countenance was like kindling on the flames. The man needed to be dropped a notch or three. Fortunately, she was more than ready to do the honors.

* * *

Bregovi claimed an open seat next to his sister, Sebastian and his father. As Victoria hadn't left his arm since she'd greeted him in the hall, he offered her the open chair on his opposite side.

He had looked for Kate among the competitors milling about, but didn't see her until then. She sat away from the center of activity, studying a parchment and stunning yet again in lavender.

He willed her to glance his way so they could exchange a smile, but her eyes seemed to be drawn to everyone but him. Deciding on a more direct course, Bregovi arose to speak with her, but Randolph called the first contestant forward before he'd taken a step. He had no choice but to retake his seat, praying to the gods the poems would be short.

Thirty minutes and two maidens later, he realized they should have limited the length of the selections. The first had memorized an eleven minute piece, and the other read her saga from a thick volume.

Sophia went third with an eloquent verse about beauty. He kept hoping for Kate's turn, but Randolph called maiden after maiden before her. Then Victoria was up. Taking her place at the center of the room, the princess recited a poem about adventure and quests and the drama of exploration. The author had captured it well and Victoria delivered it flawlessly.

Finally, Kate's moment arrived. He held his breath as all eyes in the crowded room focused on her. He smiled when she looked his way. She nodded in polite acknowledgment. *Nerves*, he told himself.

"My poem is called, An Admirable and Faithful Prince."

A few chuckles echoed about the room as her gaze dropped to the parchment. "The dashing and brilliant prince gallant; The Bandit, as he likes to be called…"

His heart jolted. She had written about *him*.

"Spends much of his time exploring; buying trinkets with the coffers of all."

Someone gasped. *What was that? Coffers?* He must have heard wrong.

"His love for fair maidens runs deep; as you'll soon see if you cross his way. He'll charm and seduce and flatter; but beware, his sweet attentions last only a day."

He'd heard correctly that time, and whispers fluttered around them. His stomach tightened. She glanced up for a moment, spearing him with a look.

"He's bold and strong and courageous; and enjoys a biting jest. He's obsessed with and devoted; to himself and his silly quests."

The chatter rose in pitch and volume. Rachel rested her hand on his arm and he glanced over at her. Although tears shimmered in her eyes, he'd never seen her look more livid. His father's face was steely.

"Why is she doing this?" Rachel whispered.

"I don't know."

"We must stop her," she said, but Kate was already on the next verse.

"The lucky maiden who wins him; will wonder forever of his love. But she'll be blessed with crown and treasure; which even love cannot rise above."

Her footsteps thundered in the silent hall as she quit the room. He was sure she had ripped his heart out. He hadn't known how completely he loved her until that moment, for if he hadn't, she couldn't have gutted him so thoroughly.

"Edmund?" It was Rachel's voice bringing him back. "Edmund?" her tender face peered up at him. She hadn't moved her hand from his arm. "How could she say those things? You must be furious."

Furious? Yes. *Grasp onto that.*

"You need to declare the winner, son," his father said.

He hadn't been listening to judge. *Damn Kate.* He'd had it all figured out. How could he have been such an idiot for love? Again.

He glanced around the room. Sophia had asked him to award her the win. His eyes landed on the princess. She whispered in conversation with Lady Quinn, a sly smile dancing on her lips. The gears shifted into place. The library. The bargain. The kisses. Kate was Sophia's greatest competition and he'd handed the princess enough ammunition to knock any rival to her knees.

Unfortunately, rather than speak to him about it, Kate launched an unforgivable assault. Not only had she condemned him with her scathing poem, she'd condemned herself. For no maiden worthy of a crown would resort to such a cruel public attack.

He'd been wrong about her. She wasn't what he needed. No, he needed a maiden who knew her place, who would fit with his family, who would support his *silly* quests. Damn, she knew just where to slip the blade.

"Edmund?" Rachel prompted.

Victoria had ships and an obscene dowry, but also an unfortunate connection to Kate.

"Did you know?" he asked her.

"Of course not," Victoria said. "I would have forbid it."

As if anyone could forbid Kate to do anything.

"She's shamed me as well as herself," Victoria continued. "And I promise you, I'll have her apologizing at your feet before the day is out."

"There's no need," he said.

"But surely—"

"I don't wish to see her."

The wound was still too raw. The anger too deep. The disappointment too fresh. It had taken just shy of a year at sea to get over Camilla. Kate might take ten. In one swift blow she'd ruined everything.

"The winner, son?" his father said as the crowd hushed.

He couldn't reward Sophia for the betrayal and, despite her attendant, the Cragmont princess was still his best choice.

"Victoria."

Quiet applause followed as he crossed the room to exit into the gardens. He needed the sea, but fresh air would do for now.

Brock fell in next to him. "Might this be a good time to run a course with Sebastian?"

"Perfect. Bring your sword."

CHAPTER TWENTY-TWO

As Kate followed a path through the gardens, she wondered if she should have written something stronger. During that brief glance, Bregovi's face hadn't appeared remotely distraught. Victoria had shot her daggers and Rachel had looked ready to weep, but the prince wasn't moved at all.

She longed to read him, to know if she'd at least made him pause. Of course, if she'd been able to read him, he would never have been able to use her. Regardless of how green his eyes or thick his charm, he'd never have drawn her in.

How did people live like that? Not knowing others' motives? Their sincerity?

She cut through the greenhouse.

They were constantly deceived is what they were. Sophia and countless others certainly had been. Rachel, with her pained expression, had no idea who her brother was or what he did to vulnerable maidens with a weakness for his touch or his dimples or whatever.

The clanging of swords drew her eye to the field where Brock and Sebastian were sparring. Nearby, Brogovi was hacking a wooden target to splinters. No Gifts needed to glean the man was spitting mad. So he had felt the sting after all.

Although he'd deserved every last word, she cut a wide berth around the area and headed away from the castle toward a pond she'd seen from Rachel's room. Thick wood surrounded it on all sides except the edge nearest to the castle, which to her relief wasn't near at all. Nothing would disturb her there.

"Hiding?" Came a winded shout behind her.

Kate's stomach flipped as she turned to Rachel. Cheeks flushed, eyes angry, the princess trotted up to Kate.

From so many things, but not this. "No."

"You should be," Rachel spit out. "Why would you make such hurtful claims about Edmund? He's kind and noble and—"

"He's not always the kind, noble brother you know."

"Perhaps not, but I can't imagine he deserved what you did to him."

Kate snatched up a rock and threw it far into the pond. The splash leapt for the sky and sent ripples flowing across the surface.

"He used me."

"No he didn't. He cares for you."

"Just as he cares for Sophia?"

"Don't be ridiculous, he doesn't even like her."

"I saw them together."

"Touring the castle? Seriously, if that made you jealous—"

"Kissing her. Passionately."

"What? He couldn't have," Rachel said, finally showing a bit of hesitation.

"He did. And after what he and I did..."

Rachel's face flushed.

"He deserves more than a tongue-lashing. He deserves something horrific. Like boils. Or a fiery rash somewhere incredibly uncomfortable."

"Mighty gods, you mean it. He really kissed her?" Rachel said, sounding a little angry herself. "I don't know why he would do that."

"I do." Kate threw another stone. Farther this time.

"No, you don't. The competition has him on edge."

"He didn't look on edge."

"Then you're not very perceptive," the princess said. "He's been tormented by his need to marry a bride our father approves of and his desire for one Papa does not."

That brought her eyes to Rachel's.

"He's a good man and he cared for you a great deal. Whatever you're thinking, I know there's another explanation and you need to find out what it is."

Kate wasn't as certain. Even if he provided a completely plausible reason for it, which she highly doubted, she couldn't be with him anyway. Perhaps the gods had steered him in Sophia's direction to save Kate from her heart and him from harm.

"I can see you two need my help to mend this." Rachel hurled a stone well past Kate's. "So, while you stand here stewing and tossing rocks, I'll go ask my brother exactly what he was thinking."

"No, Rachel. Wait!" Kate spun to catch the princess.

Fortunately, Rachel hadn't made it far. Unfortunately, the princess's progress had been blocked by four dangerously authentic bandits.

* * *

"Miss Hildegard? Kate?" The one with oily black hair and ebony eyes said to both of them as the others fanned out to block their escape.

Neither Kate nor Rachel responded, and Kate grabbed the princess's arm to keep her from saying anything.

Were they there for the reward? To take her back to Morten and Sylvan? Or were they after Rachel for ransom and trying to rule out Kate?

Whatever the answer, she needed to convince them she was the one they wanted. She could defend herself, but Rachel...

"What do you want with her?"

"Now that's our business, isn't it?" the fat one said. He was the size of a bull, and the grime on his skin testified he'd not bathed in months. The only thing clean on the man were his black boots, even the silver buckles shined.

The third, the one with a scar from eye to ear, said, "I tell ya, they said she has dark hair like a gypsy. This one could be Slate's sister," he said, pointing at Kate with a large blade. "She looks like she's straight from the caravan." They all laughed, nodding to the black-haired one who she assumed was Slate.

The men's horses were close enough that Kate thought she could reach one before they caught her.

"Yep. Black hair." The fourth, with a grungy beard and reeking of sweat, stepped within a foot of Rachel and her. "What are we gonna do with the other one?" he added, leering at Rachel.

"Leave her," Slate said. "Get a rope." He gestured to Black Boots, who started toward their horses.

Good. If they were planning to leave Rachel, she'd go along until they were away from the princess. Then she'd try to escape.

Unfortunately, her plan was short-lived, because Rachel chose that moment to bolt for the castle, screaming for the guards. As Grungy Beard took off after her, Kate darted for the horses. With heavy footfalls and cursing growing louder behind her, she ran harder. She reached a large steed and latched onto its reins at the same moment a large hand latched onto her hair. As the bandit jerked Kate back, pain coursed from her scalp to her fingertips. When he whipped her around, she discovered Scarface holding tight.

Rachel lay on the grass with Grungy Beard laughing on top of her. One of his filthy hands covered her mouth, as Rachel squirmed and kicked fiercely.

"Take them both," Slate said. "Let's go."

Grungy Beard jerked Rachel to her feet.

"No!" Kate cried. "I'm the one you want. Leave her."

"Now ain't that sweet," Grungy Beard said against Rachel's face.

"She's tryin' to protect you."

Rachel jerked her head away, but he just laughed harder and threw her over his shoulder.

"Bless the gods, I love a hellcat," he said, squeezing Rachel's bottom, for which the princess screamed and pummeled his back.

Kate's captor jerked her by the hair to another horse. She didn't know what to do and regretted not memorizing the Zafarian incantations to move objects. Why learn a spell, when you can move anything with a flick of a finger? Her uncle, on the other hand, had a favorite that she'd seen him use many times. Unfortunately, the words evaded her.

Scarface hauled her up in front of him on his horse. Wrapping an arm around her, he pinned her arms to her body and her body to his. Rachel was similarly positioned on Grungy Beard's mount.

They rode hard away from the castle and down back trails around the town. As they passed behind the inn and headed into the forest, Kate looked over her shoulder and thought she saw the side door open.

Glancing over at Rachel, she noticed the princess working a ribbon loose from her bodice. Rachel subtly shook it free and it fell to the ground. Their eyes met. Rachel had fought and screamed and had kept her wits about her. Kate had underestimated her.

* * *

While Bregovi and Brock sparred, Sebastian shot arrows at anything worth aiming for. Bregovi's mood had lightened with the physical exertion, and Sebastian finally seemed ready for the next day's trial.

"Milord, milord," Foster cried, running at full gate. "The princess," he said, gasping for breath, "and Miss Kate."

"What is it?" Bregovi asked.

"What's happened?" Sebastian demanded.

"Taken," Foster said, bending over to breathe. "Into the forest. A maid from the inn saw. She's inside."

Bregovi's heart stopped. At least for a moment, then it raced faster than his legs as he, Brock, Sebastian and Foster ran back to the castle, weapons in-hand.

"Is Wolfe back?" Bregovi asked. If ever they needed the man's Gift, it was now.

"No," Foster said.

"Alert me as soon as he returns," Bregovi ordered. "And round up the guards."

"Stiles went for them," Foster said.

"Where's the maid?" Bregovi asked.

"Receiving hall," Foster said.

Bregovi charged into the castle with Sebastian and Brock on his heels. Within moments they faced Bet, the freckled maid from the inn, and a handful of townspeople.

"What happened?" Bregovi boomed.

"I stepped out the side door to toss a pan of soapy water for Fannie, and I heard horses riding hard," Bet said. "So I looked and saw four men heading into the forest on the trail to the mountain. One had the princess and another Miss Kate."

"You're sure it was them?" Sebastian asked.

"Yes, sir. I've seen the princess all my days, and the maiden was at the inn just yesterday. I know it was them."

"Has anyone searched their chambers?"

"Yes," Alice said. "The servants are scouring the castle. They're not to be found."

"I tell you it was," the maid cried. "The princess wore a green gown and Miss Kate's was purple."

Every muscle in Bregovi's body tensed. Rachel and Kate had been taken.

Just then Holly arrived leading Victoria.

"I haven't seen Kate since the event," Victoria said. "What's happened?"

"Benevolent gods, is it true? They've been taken?" his father asked, barging in. "We need to go after them."

"Bet, have you seen the men before?" Brock asked. "Have they been to the inn?"

"I don't think so. I'd remember them."

"Could it be Kate's uncle?" Victoria asked. "He may be looking for her."

Her uncle? Why hadn't he thought of that? But the man wouldn't take Rachel, would he?

"I don't know, milady, but they looked like thieves," Bet said.

Stiles charged in next. "Your highness, the men are at the stables, ready to go."

He met Sebastian's gaze. The lord's face was ashen, but determined. He stood poised for battle with his bow slung over his shoulder and a full quiver of arrows on his back. Something passed between them. An understanding. They'd get their maidens back or die trying.

Unfathomable. How could he still think of Kate as *his* maiden? But there it was, true as the tide, he did.

"Milord, we should go." It was Brock, standing ready with sword and spirit.

"Yes. Yes," Bregovi said, turning to his father. "Will you stay in case someone asks a ransom?" His father was strong with the sword, but he feared the men would be much younger and more agile. And someone in authority should stay in case there were demands.

The king nodded and Bregovi saw his own torment mirrored in his father's eyes.

"We will find them, Father." He ran out with his men following. They had to find them.

* * *

The men hadn't let up, even when the trail grew rough and muddy.

"Are they going to give us more for delivering the two?" Black Boots asked Slate.

"Don't know," came the reply.

"Who sent you?" Kate asked. "How much is your reward?"

"Reward?" Scarface asked over her shoulder. "You've not been gone an hour and you think there's a reward?"

Morten's men would have known about the reward.

"Ransom then? What are you asking?"

"Why? Are you valuable?"

If not ransom, then what?

"Hey, this one's askin' 'bout ransom," Scarface said. "What are they gonna ask? Maybe we should get a bigger cut."

"The purse is plenty," Slate said. "We don't need to get tangled up with ransoms."

"What about hellcat, here?" Grungy Beard asked, squeezing Rachel to him. "They didn't ask for her."

"We'll decide about her at the transfer," Slate responded.

Kate's heart jolted. There were more.

She took in her surroundings. The forest grew thicker the farther they rode, and brush and trees encroached upon the curving trail. She needed to slow their progress. She could throw herself off the horse and onto a shrub, then run into the woods. She wouldn't escape, but she could cause a delay. Not a brilliant plan, but it was all she had.

As she looked for an ample bush, the trail opened at a clearing where two trails crossed, and the men pulled up their horses.

Slate let out a shrill whistle. A second echoed in the trees.

Kate quickly threw her weight sideways, hoping the momentum would carry them off the steed.

No luck.

Scarface had a healthy command of his seat and, now, a strong grip on her hair.

As she struggled against him, the thunder of pounding hooves grew louder. And closer. With a spider-like touch, fear crept up Kate's neck. Within moments, two dozen men on horseback surrounded them.

She searched for familiar markings on their clothes and weapons, but nothing stood out. What did stand out was their steady gaze. On her. Some looked pleased, others wary.

They knew who she was. Who she *really* was.

"She don't seem dangerous," one said.

"Maybe they got the wrong one," said another.

"The eyes are right, though. Ice gray."

Others nodded in agreement or looked more closely until they were distracted by a blond on a white stallion. The man rode into the circle, clutching a broad sword with a dragon design on the hilt.

Casting a satisfied glance at Kate, he said, "Give me her locket."

Her talisman! Yes, they definitely knew who she was.

"Give us our money, and you can have the maidens and their jewels," Scarface said.

Noticing Rachel for the first time, Dragon Hilt directed his horse over to the princess.

With the man's attention diverted, Kate quickly unclasped her locket, letting it drop into her bodice and under her shift.

A small sack of ingredients for her nightly spell lay concealed between her breasts, and it caught there.

Rachel's steely gaze met Dragon Hilt's. "If you don't return us now, my father will have your head."

"Imbeciles," Dragon Hilt hissed. "I told you the maiden Kate only."

"This one got in the way," Scarface bit back. "When she cried out, we had to take her."

"If you don't want her, I can make use of her," Grungy Beard said.

"You will not touch me," Rachel spat.

"I *am* touching you." He laughed, groping at her breast.

Rachel shrieked and panic stirred in Kate.

"Don't want her?" the blond roared. "Man, you've taken their princess. The entire kingdom will be after her."

"Yes, they will," Kate said. "You'd be wise to leave us here and flee while you can."

Dragon Hilt turned his horse, studying all. "We're taking everyone."

They moved so fast Kate didn't know who drew first, but suddenly the four bandits had daggers at the ready, and the army faced off with swords.

Kate's captor held his blade inches away from her belly. For a moment she considered trying for it, but then what would she do? There were close to thirty men among the army and the bandits.

"The deal was our payment and farewell with delivery of the maid," Slate said.

"The deal changed when you took more than you ought," Dragon Hilt growled. "Now you'll stay with us."

"They'll turn us over first chance they get," Slate said.

"The ladies know we're doing yer bidding," Black Boots barked.

"If they can't find the ladies, it'll be your word against ours."

Rachel's eyes found Kate's, her face pale.

"Who's to say you weren't going to frame us all along?" Slate said.

Scarface pulled another knife from his boot. The other bandits began arming up as well.

"That was never the plan," Dragon Hilt said, nodding to a couple of his men, who moved to block a side trail. "You know we honor our arrangements."

The bandits slowly moved their mounts closer together, watching as their former allies surrounded them.

"I told you we shouldn't take a kidnapping," Black Boots said. "They never end well."

"I ain't dyin' for this," Scarface said.

"My blade's getting itchy," Grungy Beard said, scratching his knife across his chin.

"If you return us, we'll tell the king of these other men," Kate whispered. "I don't know what they're offering, but it's not worth your lives."

None of them acknowledged her.

"I'll tell my father you saved us," Rachel whispered.

No response.

"Well men," Slate broke rank and turned to face his crew. They were lined up side by side, almost in formation. And Kate saw Scarface move his knife forward slightly. His other hand held the horse's reins and another blade. Sensing they would act soon, Kate wove her fingers into the horse's mane and nodded at Rachel, who saw her and did the same.

"It looks like we forgot about old Charlie," Slate said.

Old Charlie?

The men nodded. The horses stirred too, as reins were pulled tighter.

"And it's time we go fetch him. Ha!" He cried the last word so loudly, she jumped.

In an instant he charged between their ranks as the remaining three spun in unison and raced after him back toward Florian.

Blades flew and five of their opposition dropped lifeless from their mounts as the men passed. Others struggled with knives embedded in arms or legs. She shuddered and saw more blades pulled from crevices in their saddles and boots. They wouldn't go down easy.

As shouts and the pounding thunder of hooves followed, the bandits rode faster than she thought possible. Gripping the horse tighter, she fought to stay on.

CHAPTER TWENTY-THREE

At the stables, Bregovi found the guards saddled up and ready. Brock and Sebastian took to mounts while Bregovi strapped on a dagger belt. With the sword and the dagger, and the twenty or so men in their party, he was determined to capture and punish anyone involved in the abduction.

Sebastian tied an extra quiver of arrows to his saddle, and Brock took up Bet on his steed so she could show them where she had last seen the maidens. A short time later, they halted behind the inn, at the old trail to the mountain. Bregovi hadn't been that way in years, not since the seasons he had spent searching for the Portal.

Sebastian jumped off his horse and snatched something off the ground. Upon studying it for a moment, he held it up. "A ribbon from Rachel's gown," he said gravely, as the delicate tie fluttered in the breeze. The lord tucked the ribbon in his glove and remounted.

Brock lowered Bet off his horse, and Bregovi thanked her for her help. She wished them Godspeed, as they charged into the forest.

The last time Bregovi had raced after Kate, he'd been terrified she was injured or at the hands of bandits, but he'd managed to put the latter second, as a remote possibility. This time there was no doubt. She and Rachel were at the mercy of men without scruples. His mind spun with scenarios as he urged Odyssey faster. If they knew who Rachel was, they might honor her virtue for fear of retribution, but an untitled maiden would not hold the same respect.

Fear started to overtake him, but he pushed it back, turning it instead to anger at the men who took them. And the taste of anger led his mind to Kate's poem. He had been prepared to declare her his bride, and she'd flogged him publicly. What a fool. Even a bigger fool, for he still wanted to protect her.

* * *

The race continued longer than Kate had expected, which she attributed to years of experience on the part of the bandits. Arrows whizzed past, falling harmless on the trail, as the four ruffians maneuvered down the mountain. But the shouts behind them were growing louder. Closer.

Some sounded like incantations. *In unison.* Some of their pursuers chanted the spell she'd been trying to recall earlier. Paying close attention, she finally had the wording.

Compelled by the spell, a huge boulder flew past her, barely missing Rachel and Grungy Beard. It slammed into Black Boots at bone-shattering speed, sending both horse and man to their maker.

As Scarface angled around them, Kate locked her focus upon the boulder, reciting the verse with as much intention as she'd ever willed into a spell.

"Bloody sorcerers," Scarface muttered. "That better be a curse you're sayin', cause prayers aren't gonna work against this lot."

As Kate reached the final phrase, she visualized the boulder hurtling back toward their pursuers. As the last word left her lips, she knew the rock had obeyed, for pained shouts and the crash of splintered trees echoed from the trail behind them.

As they raced around a bend, an arrow shot past and sliced through Slate's arm. The bandit continued on unfazed, blood flooding his shirt from the wound.

Scarface whipped their horse with the reins, and miraculously it increased its speed.

A couple of Zafarians rode past, swords striking at Grungy Beard and Slate. Both flicked strategically placed blades in return.

One pursuer lost an eye. The other fell back to pull a knife from his hand.

Another of Dragon Hilt's men raced forward and sliced through the saddle straps on Rachel's mount.

The steed reared, sending the saddle, Grungy Beard and Rachel sliding off in a heap.

As Kate and Scarface hurdled over them, something thumped against Kate's back.

Scarface. Blood gushed from his mouth over her shoulder.

Kate grabbed for the reins, but he latched onto her waist and took her with him as he tumbled off the steed.

Gravel bit into her skin as they slammed into the dirt and rolled to a stop. While rushing to untangle herself from Scarface, she discovered the reason for her captor's demise—a large dagger had found a home in his back. With a quick breath for courage, she pulled out the blade and looked for Rachel.

Grungy Beard was battling three of his opponents, and Rachel was lying across the front of one of the Zafarian's horses. As the princess kicked and squirmed, the horse danced in circles while the man struggled for control of both.

Without plan or thought, Kate charged for them, dodging a fight between Slate and two others. As Rachel's captor spun, Kate took a clean swipe at his leg. Unfortunately, his cry sounded more angered than pained.

When his attention turned to Kate, Rachel scrambled off. Another grabbed the princess by the hair.

Kate bolted for the trees.

The man she'd cut launched himself from his horse and chased her on foot. As her pursuer gained, branches and shrubs blocked her way and grabbed at her gown. Then he tackled her, crushing her beneath his weight and knocking the wind from her lungs.

Gasping for breath, she flipped over and kneed him in the groin.

The man collapsed on top of her, swearing. Struggling to push him off, she managed to roll sideways with him, then squirm away.

The dagger had fallen nearby, and she scrambled for it.

Just as she'd grabbed hold, Dragon Hilt came out of nowhere.

Standing on her gown, he forced her onto her back and brought his sword to her chest. Her breath came so heavy, every intake brought her in contact with the sharp point of the weapon.

"You've cost me good men today," he said.

"Your kidnappers cost you your men, not me," she said, trying to slow her lungs.

"Nevertheless, you are at the heart of it." He slid the tip of the sword down to her belly. "And it would be quite satisfying to make you pay for the brothers I've lost."

"You won't get the reward if you kill me," she said, feeling around for rocks or something she could use.

He slid the blade back and forth across her belly. "On the contrary. The Order Master promised half the purse if you aren't breathing. That sum would keep my men and I fed and bedded for years."

Holy gods. Her eyes met Dragon Hilt's. Surely he was lying.

The malice in his eyes said he wasn't. "You must be quite a nuisance to the man."

Morten wanted her dead? Dropping her head back onto the dirt, tears prickled her eyes. For all the trouble they'd been to one another, she never thought he'd end her life. What chance would she have if every Zafarian in the kingdoms was intent on killing her? They could be anywhere. Anyone.

Her heart stopped. She was sure of it. Then it kicked back in, pounding stronger than before, when she saw a large figure charging through the trees.

* * *

As they raced deeper into the forest, shouts and clashing steel carried through the trees.

"Weapons!" Bregovi cried.

The guards and Brock drew swords. Sebastian gripped his bow in one hand as he directed his horse with the other. A short distance further, they rode hard into the chaos on the trail.

A dozen or so guardsmen battled two rough bandits. Bregovi didn't recognize the guard, but rushed to help until he saw one of them pulling Rachel by the hair.

"Capture everyone!" he ordered.

In one shot, Sebastian put an arrow through the shoulder of the man grappling with Rachel.

The man released her immediately, and the lord and several guards encircled her.

When Bregovi didn't see Kate in their midst, a surge of panic washed through him. Then a glimpse of lavender caught his eye. In the woods. Off the trail.

Kate lay on the ground with a man standing over her, a sword to her belly and her bodice covered in blood.

Bregovi launched himself toward them.

"Release her!"

When the man turned, Bregovi swung hard and fast. The kidnapper blocked with his blade.

Relief flooded him when Kate scrambled to her feet.

* * *

Something twisted in Kate's soul. She'd never expected he would come to rescue her. Not now. A flash of red hair caught her eye, and she saw Lord Sebastian fighting another of Dragon Hilt's men. Brock was there too, and the royal guard, and Rachel.

Sebastian's back was to the princess as he fought off any that approached, and the three other guards flanked her from all sides.

Rachel.

Bregovi was there to save his sister. They were all there to save the princess. Kate was secondary.

Her eyes fixed again on Bregovi as he fought. She saw nothing of the playful bandit she battled at their first meeting. This man was determined and fearless and, she realized, noble. He fought to save a woman who had scorned him. He might not care the way she wanted him to, but he was honorable nevertheless.

* * *

Bregovi's opponent had ruthless skill. The man anticipated his moves, but Bregovi did the same in return. Pressing on, he forced the man back toward a fallen tree, their weapons clashing.

A branch snapped behind him and Kate shouted his name. Spinning, he blocked a sword in full swing. The second man was stout, but strong.

As Bregovi pressed him back, Kate cried out again. He glanced her way as the first man wrenched Kate's dagger from her.

Bregovi ran to help her, but before he reached them, the man spun her, bringing the knife to her throat. Eyes huge with fear, Kate pulled at the man's arm.

Bregovi halted mid-stride, his sword anxious to kill the bastard. "Release her."

"Not just yet," her captor said as he pulled her sideways toward the trail. When Kate stumbled, Bregovi's gut tightened. One fall and the blade would slice her open.

"Take a horse," Bregovi ordered. "Let her go."

"I'll be taking anything I want to," the man said and whispered something in Kate's ear. That set her fighting him again, despite the knife.

As Bregovi inched closer, he saw Sebastian take aim from across the trail. The nobleman nodded to him. They'd both need to be precise. As soon as Sebastian released the arrow, Bregovi would need to act.

"Be careful, Kate," Bregovi cautioned.

She caught his eye and stopped struggling.

"Yes, be careful, Kate," the man said. "Wouldn't want to damage the prize."

They were almost to the trail, where her captor could move faster. They needed to take him. *Now*.

Bregovi nodded to Sebastian. The lord shot without hesitation.

Lunging forward, Bregovi yanked the dagger free a second after the arrow pierced the man's throat.

As the dead man dropped, Bregovi pulled Kate away.

Glancing down at her attacker, she put a shaky hand to her neck.

Rachel knocked her out of his grasp as the maidens embraced. "You're hurt!" Rachel said.

"No," Kate said, looking down. "It's not my blood."

"I thought they were going to kill us," Rachel choked out.

As tears swam in his sister's eyes, Bregovi moved to hold her. But she turned to Sebastian instead.

"You're safe now," Sebastian said, gathering her close, as if it were the most natural thing in the world.

Kate met Bregovi's eyes and began to say something, but he turned away. His actions to save her already said too much. He would not humiliate himself further by looking like a lovesick fool. He would not let the men think he would permit her to abuse him and then go back for more. Nor would he let *her* think it.

Instead, he focused his attention on the battle's aftermath. Brock and the castle guard had corralled the half-dozen kidnappers that hadn't fled or fallen. Some of his own guard had also sustained nasty wounds that would need tending soon.

"Your highness," Brock said quietly. "One of their men started chanting what sounded like a spell. I gave him a blow to the head to knock him out."

Zafarians?

Bregovi studied the dagger he'd grabbed from Kate's captor and discovered the Zafarian crest on the blade. Had they planned to demand his artifacts in exchange for the maidens?

"Strip them," Bregovi ordered.

"Of what?" Brock asked.

"Everything," Bregovi said. "If they are Zafarians, they have objects on them that help them do magik. Take everything."

His men jumped into action.

* * *

The first time Kate had seen a man naked, she'd looked on in fascination. Crew from one of the ships docked near the manor had spent a hot summer eve swimming in the surf. From her perch on the cliffs, Kate had marveled at how different their bodies were.

The second time she'd seen a man naked, she'd looked on in awe and no small measure of desire when she caught the smithy's apprentice and a housemaid enjoying one another's affections in the storage pantry.

The third time—this time—she looked on in horror. Not because their bodies weren't just as intriguing—truth be told a couple of the Zafarians were very well formed. No, her terror grew from the fact that the men were not only being stripped of their clothes, but every gem, trinket and band upon their persons.

Bregovi knew. Sometime since their last meeting, he had learned about the talismans.

Subtly pressing a hand to the front of her gown, Kate confirmed the tiny sack of spell ingredients and her talisman were still wedged in her bodice.

He hadn't yet learned about her though—he couldn't have—or she'd likely be stripped to the skin as well. And while Grungy Beard and the four Zafarian captives were shooting hostile glances her way, none had yet revealed her secret.

Were they still hoping they'd prevail and get the reward? Were they holding their tongues out of Zafarian solidarity? Did they fear she was as unstable as Morten had indicated?

After Bregovi had made certain the men were free of anything they weren't born with, they were each given a pair of pants to don, and not necessarily the ones they'd worn earlier. They hastily threw on the clothes without complaint, except for Grungy Beard, who ended up with a pair too small for his legs. A swap and a few minutes later, his lower half was covered, and the men were corralled to begin the walk to the castle.

Earlier, Sebastian had led Rachel away from the scene, holding her until her tears had ceased. Now, he helped the princess onto his horse. After he climbed on behind her, Kate watched Rachel lean back into his arms, the sweet action bringing back memories of the day with Bregovi. While she wasn't ready to apologize for the poem—not without an explanation—he'd risked his life to save hers and she needed to thank him for that.

As the guards prepared to take everyone back to the castle, Brock brought her the chestnut mare Slate had ridden earlier. While her master had fallen, the horse didn't even look shaken.

"You okay?" the smithy asked.

"Mostly," she said as he helped her onto the animal.

The prince whistled for Odyssey, mounted the steed and fell in line with his sister and Sebastian, who had started down the trail already.

It was now or never. "Bregovi?" she called out, trotting to catch up.

He exchanged a word with Rachel and charged ahead.

Kate slowed next to the couple. "He isn't going to speak to me, is he?"

"I wouldn't," Sebastian said.

"It's done," Brock said, catching up. "Maybe you should let it go."

"She can't let it go. Not yet," Rachel said.

She was right. The reason he'd been able to hurt her was because she cared. And while she was furious with him, the anger was now mixed with gratitude. The strange brew of emotion served as a confusing elixir to her heart, making her want to both shout at him for Sophia and throw her arms around him for saving her.

Whatever the final words or sentiment, she doubted she'd have the opportunity to say them at the castle.

She kicked her horse and raced after him, managing to lessen his lead in little time. Of course, once he noticed her following, the task became more difficult. Just as he had when she'd ridden him to the lake, Odyssey's legs ate up the trail as if Bregovi was weightless.

Fortunately, her mount had bandit stock in her blood and seemed as eager as Kate to catch the pair. After a long stretch of road, where the man and steed gave no ground, Kate finally started gaining.

No. He started slowing. Fear and relief wrestled for dominance as she eased the mare to a trot. But before she had a chance to think of what to say, he turned Odyssey sharply and disappeared into the forest.

Her mount needed little urging to follow, and moments later she and the horse were barreling through the woods as the prince disappeared into the trees ahead.

Kate grew more impressed with her mount by the step. She only wished she was as skilled at pursuit as the mare, which seemed to be taking the barbs and branches in stride.

The animal carried her up hills and down, around bends and over fallen trees. When the path opened up, she'd gain ground. When the forest grew dense, she'd lose him.

She felt like a barn cat chasing a rat—an annoyingly savvy rat.

As sharp branches scraped her face and tore through her gown, sanity finally cleared its throat and suggested speaking with him might not be worth the trouble. Unfortunately, by that time, she was hopelessly lost.

They'd taken so many turns she couldn't find her way back to the last tree, let alone the castle. She had to catch him or spend another cold, fearful night in a forest. And unlike Cragmont's this one had wolves.

She broke off a dangling branch and used it to break away errant limbs as she followed his course toward a roar of water.

Could their ride have led her to Klug Falls? She knew her way back from there. Had her fortune turned?

Pushing aside a leafy tree limb to see, she discovered that instead of arriving at the idyllic pond, they were at a river. One that she and the mare were heading toward at an alarming rate.

A scream escaped her as they plunged in, but she sucked it back when the frigid water drenched her to the thighs.

The mare struggled for footing as the swift current forced them downstream.

"We can do this," Kate shouted to herself as much as to the horse and tried to guide the animal toward the opposite bank.

Unfortunately, they'd missed Bregovi's tracks and were already too far away to get there.

Damn the man. Damn her stupidity.

The bank grew steep where she reached the other side, and along with the realization that her horse couldn't manage it, came the harsh affirmation that Bregovi cared nothing for her. For if he had, in any small measure, he'd never have risked her in such a way.

As her horse tried to climb the impossible riverbank, anger drowned all remnants of remorse and gratitude. The man who'd led her there didn't deserve either.

She turned the mare back toward the opposite side. The terrain didn't look much better, but she wouldn't pursue him any further. She'd rather wander all night in a forest full of wolves and bears and *Zafarians* than seek anything from Bregovi the Bandit.

Feet numb and temper boiling, she started back across the river. But the horse faltered. The large rocks caused the animal to lose its footing, and the mare stumbled forward and crashed into the water.

So did Kate.

Tumbling over the mare's head, she clung to the reins to keep from getting swept away. Gasping for breath, she struggled to stand while the current's icy tendrils wrapped around her skirts and legs. The animal had managed to find its feet, but the river hadn't given up.

The bank was at least four horses away. The water was above her waist and too strong to walk against. She had to get back on the animal.

With numb fingers, she tried to pull her body onto the saddle. Before she'd made any progress, she began shivering so violently she lost her grip, and the merciless river quickly took advantage, dragging her under.

Was this it?

She managed a short gulp of air before she went under again.

Had she survived her uncle, a genie binding, more, all to drown here? Now?

As she fought to reach the surface, a word, a feeling, roared from her soul.

No!

This would not be the end. Not *her* end. With everything she had, she pulled on the horse's reins until she resurfaced. Coughing up water she hadn't known she'd swallowed, she grabbed for the saddle. Unable to focus on anything but breathing, she clung to the animal and tried to work up the strength to pull herself onto the mare.

Suddenly, her world shifted. Something hauled her up. Out. And she found herself on another larger, stronger animal. Odyssey.

As she coughed out the last of the water, Bregovi pried the reins from her hand and led her horse back up the river, close to the bank.

Sitting sideways, her shoulder at his chest, she shivered so violently she doubted if she'd ever be warm again.

"Are you daft?" he said. "Why would you follow me?"

A million retorts scrambled through her frozen brain, but all she could manage through her chattering teeth was, "Daft. For. Chasing. You."

"We agree there," he said, directing Odyssey into the woods.

She was furious with him for her current state. She hated how he'd used her. But what she hated more was how desperately she wanted to crawl inside his shirt. And not for lustful reasons.

Because of the long chase, the man emanated heat like an iron stove. After riding up the hillside toward who knows where, her left side actually grew warm. Wanting the same remedy for her right side, she argued she needed to turn the other way due to an unspecified injury.

After some grumbling, he accommodated and the rest of her began to thaw.

While he might not be loyal, at least he was hot.

CHAPTER TWENTY-FOUR

Bregovi's anger at himself nearly matched his anger at Kate. He didn't know why she wished to speak with him, but he refused to let her press the barb further or discover she had wounded him. So he had tried to lose her, convinced she'd give up and turn back. But the maiden was more stubborn than a mule at a salt lick. The river had been a last resort. Only a fool would follow him across.

Of course, Kate had plunged in without hesitation, revealing they were both fools. His stupidity had ensured much more time together than if he had just let her say her peace and be gone. He had accomplished one thing, though. She no longer seemed eager to speak.

He had been headed back to the castle initially, but changed his mind when she had chased after him. Now, the sun was setting, the temperature was chilling, and the castle sat an arduous hour's ride through the forest.

In her wet gown, Kate would catch a fever long before they reached home. They'd have to stop at one of the hunting cabins to dry off.

Nestled under giant oaks, the cottage looked much as it had years earlier. The wood frame appeared damp from the recent winter, and tall grass and forget-me-nots grew wild up to the only door. Halting Odyssey, he jumped off and tied the mounts to the hitch.

He turned to help Kate from the horse, but she'd already slid off.

Stepping around her to open the door, he hoped the provisions he had left in the past remained untouched. The one-room cabin looked as it had on his last visit. A large hearth, a small shelf with cooking pots and a basin that drained outside, candles, a couple of high back wooden armchairs, and two cots strewn with hay.

As Kate stepped in behind him, he hurried toward the bunk against the far wall. Brushing off the hay, he uncovered the hinged door underneath and opened the storage chest to find the contents just as he'd left them.

"The castle would have been my choice," Kate said.

"It's too far." He set the wool blankets on the cot. Then pulled out a fur. His hands flickered over a cake of soap, then the can he sought. He grabbed the flint and headed for the hearth.

"How long are we staying here?" She stood in the doorway, her dress dripping into a puddle, the sun setting in pinks behind her. She looked horrid. A welt had formed on her cheek, and she was covered in blood. Her gown, hair, arm, all blanketed in the color of death. He should have let her chase him all the way to the castle, not into the forest where she risked further harm. Fool.

"We'll stay until your clothes are dry."

"That could be a while."

"It'll go faster if you get out of that wet gown." He lit a beeswax candle on the mantle and another in a hurricane lamp.

"And stand here naked, I suppose?" she bit out.

"I could give you my shirt if it would placate your modesty."

As he moved toward the door, her gaze flicked from his chest to his face.

"Your shirt is soaked through. It would do nothing to placate my modesty."

"Well, if the shirt off my back won't please you, check the storage bin," he said coolly. "In the past, I kept a change of clothes in there for occasions such as this." Then he stepped out to find wood.

"You frequently dunked maidens in the river, did you?" she shouted after him.

Grunting, he snatched up twigs and branches. When he returned with the wood, he discovered Kate rummaging through the bin.

"One shirt and a pair of breeches are the extent of your stored wardrobe," she said, an edge cutting at her words.

He lit the twigs and blew on the fire to encourage its growth. "Wonderful. Chose whichever you'd like and leave the other for me." Although he had said it to mock her, an image of her wearing only the breeches flashed through his mind, heating his blood quicker than any fire could. "I'll collect more wood while you change." Grabbing the ax, he slipped out the door.

He piled fallen branches near the cottage and chopped the larger pieces into smaller sections until he had a healthy stack. After filling his arms with the wood, he tapped his foot against the door and entered.

She was still fully dressed and spitting angry from the looks of it, although he did see her shoes and stockings by the hearth.

"Holy gods, woman, you'll freeze waiting for another gown," he said, placing the logs on the fire. "Don the shirt and take a blanket."

"I assure you, I'm not daft enough to be awaiting a gown. I just can't remove this one. The bodice strings won't budge, so I can't loosen the fit. I tried to pull it over my head, but soaked with half the river, it weighs more than I do."

He stared at her as the meaning of the situation sank in.

"You need to help me," she pronounced each word slowly, as if *he* were daft.

"Fine," he said, stepping over to take a stab at the ties on each side. She'd spoken the truth. It was as if the threads had been welded together. He drew out a dagger to slit one, and she screamed and scrambled out of reach.

"If you cut them, the gown won't stay on later! You need to pull it over my head."

"Fine," he said again. Setting the blade aside, he stepped in front of her.

"From the back. I only have a shift and corset on underneath, and they're soaked too."

He nodded and thoughts of her in wet undergarments won out over whatever he'd been trying to think of.

"Ready?" he asked.

"Yes."

As she lifted her arms overhead, he took a breath, grabbed handfuls of the skirt and peeled the heavy garment up and off of her.

She might as well have been naked.

Her corset hid her waist, but everywhere else the shift clung to her like a second skin. The wet fabric was so sheer he could even see the color of her flesh underneath.

"Thank you." She reached for the shirt. "I also need help with the corset. It should be easier to untie."

Should be, but wasn't. As his fingers fumbled with the delicate ribbon, his eyes kept straying to the wet shift, or rather the peach skin barely concealed beneath. He managed to get the string untied, but still had trouble loosening the corset.

"Why are you taking so long? Is it stuck too?"

"Yes," he grumbled. Snatching the knife, he slit the tie up the center.

Kate gasped and grabbed the front of the shift as the corset fell to the floor.

Now she *really* looked naked. Despite all that had happened, his fingers and shaft twitched, wanting to touch.

"I need a minute," she said.

He needed much longer than that.

* * *

The door slammed shut behind Bregovi.

Grateful for the privacy, Kate quickly fished out the spell sack and her locket. Both had nearly dropped to the floor with the corset and she shuddered at the idea of explaining them.

Emptying the pouch in a small dish near the hearth, she looked over the items. It appeared everything had survived the river, including a few clumps of salt in the tiny sack. Unfortunately, the blackberry and lavender needed to dry before they'd be of use. She prayed to the gods that would occur by sunrise.

With the dish out of sight, she peeled off the wet chemise, wincing as it brushed the cuts on her arm. Gooey crimson blood dripped from her hair too. Revulsion shivered through her as she recalled Dragon Hilt's threats and his demise. Using the chemise like a wet rag, she wiped off her body where the blood had seeped through the fabric to her skin, then wrapped her hair in the cloth and piled it atop her head. She rolled up the right shirtsleeve and slipped on the tunic, careful not to touch the scrapes on her arm. Considering Scarface's fate, she was lucky that's all she injured in the fall.

How had the kidnappers known where she was? If they'd found her, others probably knew as well. Did Morten? Lord Sylvan? Shooting a nervous glance at the door, she half expected the men to charge in and claim her. She'd be defenseless. Sylvan would be inside her in minutes, and then she'd never escape him.

The hunting cottage lacked useful weaponry, except a thick poker near the hearth, which would do little good against them.

She marveled at her stupidity in chasing after Bregovi. Without any idea where she was, she wouldn't know which way to flee if needed. Shivering in the cold, she moved closer to the fire.

But, she countered to her fretful mind, they were indeed deep in the forest and the Zafarians wouldn't know where to find her. They'd target Florian, not a remote hunting cottage. A wet drop trickled down her check. Brushing it off, she discovered blood on her fingers.

If she didn't rinse her hair soon it would dry in cakes.

She checked the containers at the basin, but they were all empty. Collecting a large wood pitcher, she padded to the door.

She hated asking Bregovi for help and was fairly certain he enjoyed providing it even less, but her desire for blood-free hair prevailed. Outside, darkness had settled in and a cool wind hit her. Resting on a stump, the lantern cast a warm light upon the prince as he wiped down the horses. Odyssey kept butting a nose against Bregovi as the prince brushed the blanket over the mare.

"You're to make do with grass, but I'll find some water just as soon as I'm finished with your friend."

Kate had seen a bucket inside the door, so she grabbed it and returned to the threshold.

"May I have some water too?" she called out.

He looked over.

"I found a pitcher." She held it out. "And a bucket for the horses."

"I'll fill them." He avoided her gaze when she handed them over. As he disappeared into the blackness, he barked, "There's a blanket on the cot."

The man, with his burly tone and hard eyes, was still angry with her. And that was fine with her. She wanted to hold onto her anger as well—anger at him for leading her out there, for not letting her speak to him, for kissing Sophia—as irrational as that might be. Unfortunately, she was too exhausted. And too cold.

She'd let *him* be angry. Let *him* hate her. It's what they both needed, wasn't it? She was never going to be able to stay. Even if he'd been loyal, she'd never have been able to love him. He was always destined to marry someone else. To love someone else.

She found a cake of soap and two blankets on the cot. The thick wool had been boiled, with one dyed blue and the other a deep green, both the finest quality. She wrapped the blue one around her body, careful not to rub it on her injured arm, and took the soap to the basin.

Bregovi returned with the pitcher.

"Thank you," she said, taking the water from him.

His face paled unexpectedly as he gestured at the scrapes on her arm. "How did that happen?"

"Scarface pulled me off his horse."

His gaze met hers with that one. "Scarface?"

"One of the bandits."

Bregovi carefully lifted her arm to look at the wound, his hands at her elbow and wrist.

"He caught a dagger in the back. When he fell off his mount, he took me with him."

Bregovi plucked a bit of gravel from her elbow, and although he was gentle about it, she still winced. So did he. Then he caught her eye again as her confused heart softened.

"I think he got the worst of it," she added with an attempt at a laugh.

Surprisingly, he chuckled and lowered her arm. "Don't use the rainwater on it. I don't know how long it's been in the barrel."

Taking an empty pitcher and the lamp, he headed out into the dark. "I'll get fresh water."

Kate unwrapped her hair, careful to keep it away from the blanket. Tucking in the corner of the wool over her breast to keep it in place, she leaned over the basin. Starting with the ends of her hair, she poured water onto them and worked in a bit of soap, but the blood was sticky and difficult to get out.

She pulled a large bowl from the shelf above the basin and filled it with the clean water. Leaning forward again, she submerged her hair. Unfortunately, she dislodged the blanket in the process and it dropped to her feet.

Tucking her toes in to keep them warm, she hurried to rinse out the blood. After a good measure of swishing, soaping and wringing, she lifted her head to check the bowl. The crimson shade turned her stomach.

Snatching the wet mop of hair from the bloody pool, she emptied the water into the basin. As it drained, she added the last of the rainwater to the bowl and started once more. The water reddened yet again, but not as bright.

As she wrung out her hair, Bregovi returned, bringing in a cool breeze behind him. She heard him set the new pitcher on the shelf near her.

He must have noticed the color of the still-red runoff, for he said, "I'll get more rainwater."

"Thank you," she said as he stepped away.

His footsteps halted, and the blanket stirred at her feet. Without uttering a word, he lifted it from the floor, shifted it so the opening was at the back, pulled it above her breasts and wrapped it snug around her, tucking an end in under her arm. It wasn't at all romantic, but the quiet intimacy of it stirred something in her.

"Thank you," she whispered again as the door closed behind him.

While she waited there, leaning over the basin with blood-soaked hair in her hands, her fickle heart pointed out how kind he was acting. Guilt, she quickly countered. And he enjoys rescuing lost creatures. As soon as she was fine and safely delivered he would go back to tasting the lips of the other maidens at court. *Rich royal maidens.*

Familiar pangs hit her. If only he didn't love to explore as her father had and as she dreamed of. Or tease with the playfulness of a beloved friend. Or bestow generous gifts. Or look at her as if she were beautiful. Or kiss her so that every fiber of her body ignited.

Unfortunately, she reminded herself, she wasn't the only one enjoying those kisses, which is likely how he got so good at them. It had nothing to do with affection. He likely tasted any lips available. He kissed and enticed and touched until a maiden threw herself at him, and then he sought out another.

Well, no more. She would not fall under his spell again. She would finish with her hair, wash her arm and stay as far from him as possible until they returned to the castle.

The door opened and her uncooperative heart skipped.

Grabbing for the bowl, she once again emptied its tainted contents down the drain and set it to her left. He stepped up on her right.

She glanced sideways at him. "Could you please pour it into the bowl?"

"Immersing your hair in bloody water isn't effective."

"It's the same as bathing in a tub."

"Not without hot water and soap. A clear lake or pond would do better. At least you wouldn't be soaking in what you had just washed off."

"Since neither lake nor pond are available at present, this is my only option."

"No it isn't."

He moved away and was back a moment later with her wet shift. He folded it with the cleanest part showing.

"Cover your face with this," he said, handing it to her.

Dumbstruck, she did as he suggested. Was he actually going to wash her hair?

CHAPTER TWENTY-FIVE

No one but her mother and governess had ever done such a thing for Kate. What would he want to wash next?

Just as the thought made her face flush, cold water rained over her head.

Bregovi acted quickly, his fingers expertly working the soap through. He washed and rinsed several times, gently, thoroughly, finally wringing out her hair from scalp to ends.

Removing the chemise from her face, she saw clear water spiraling down the drain.

"Thank you," she said, carefully twisting her hair into one long section, which she draped over her shoulder.

"That needs rinsing too," Bregovi said, gesturing toward her arm.

The gashes ran the full length from wrist to elbow, and she hoped the dirt caked over it wasn't the only thing keeping it from bleeding. As she reached for the fresh water pitcher, her teeth started to chatter again.

"We can take care of it by the fire," he said, gathering the bowl and pitcher.

She followed him to the hearth, where he set the items on a stool. Curling up on the floor, she tucked her legs under the blanket, as he stoked the blaze until the flames danced thick and hot.

Bregovi positioned the bowl on her lap, just under her arm, and poured the icy river water over her cuts.

She jerked her arm away. "That's even colder than the rainwater."

"It's snow-melt from the river. It's cleaner. The cold should numb the wounds some."

Extending her arm again, she watched as he carefully poured a bit more. The flesh was raw in places, with bits of gravel stuck in the cuts.

"I need something to wipe it off with," he said.

"The shift?" she suggested.

He fetched it from the basin and shook it out. Much of the fabric was covered in blood, but the section she'd held to her face was still relatively clean. After rinsing that portion with the fresh water, he repositioned himself on the floor in front of her and gently wiped the edges of her cuts with the cloth. "We need to get the gravel out."

"May I do it?" she asked. "It might hurt less."

He handed over the cloth. She worked at the tiny pebbles until they came free, and he rinsed the fabric each time she paused to breathe. When she had finally cleaned the last of it, he ran the crisp water over her arm again.

"We could wrap it with the chemise," she said, but was hoping there was an alternative, as the garment was now filthy.

Bregovi didn't seem to like that idea either, because he inspected the contents of the storage case again.

Kate gathered up her blanket and went to see if they could use the underlining of the gown. Her heart ached as she approached it. She hadn't realized how badly it had fared. Gory blood, dirt and the huge gash from the branch had ruined it.

He joined her as she flipped the lavender layer back to reveal the lining. Sections were just as bloody as the top layer, but portions of the skirt were still clean. Bregovi fetched a dagger and sliced a thick strip the full width of the gown.

Tears filled her eyes.

"It's only a gown," he said.

"I know, but I've never worn one so lovely." It was the most beautiful one she would ever wear. It was a queen's gown, not a lady maid's or a governess's, she thought, heading back to the fire.

Once she'd settled back in front of the blaze, he used the cloth to wrap her arm from wrist to elbow and back again. He then tore the end and tied it.

Although the cuts stung under the bandage, she finally felt clean.

Bregovi pulled one of the heavy armchairs in front of the hearth and she curled up on it.

"Thank you," she said, pulling the blanket around her as he took the bowl and chemise to the basin.

"You're welcome."

She wondered again at the meaning behind his actions. He had fetched her the water, washed her hair, and built her the fire. Although the fire was for himself as well, she reasoned.

And instead of abandoning her at the river, as she had thought, he had been there in an instant—or nearly an instant—when she'd fallen. He'd been watching.

Had honor motivated him or did he care, as Rachel said? As if in answer to the question, an image of him kissing Sophia came to mind.

Her eyes stung *from the heat of the fire*, she told herself, not emotion. Or perhaps it was exhaustion, because she suddenly felt very weary. Closing her eyes, she rested her head on her good arm atop the chair's armrest. She didn't want to think anymore about Sophia or kisses or a prince that had her brain twisted up like twine.

* * *

Bregovi retrieved the remainder of the bin's contents. Another blanket and a pair of stockings lay on the bottom. He would give them to Kate when she awoke.

321

He fluffed the hay on one of the cots, covered it with the fur and slid it closer to the fire. He would give that to her for a bed as well, taking a place on the floor by the hearth for himself. He would show her she was wrong about him.

The lavender gown caught his eye, and he snatched it up. Moments later, as he stood scrubbing at the fabric at the basin, he chided himself an idiot.

He'd had something rare with her. Something that stirred his soul. And he'd risked it all for something as trivial as information about Zafarians. Could he hope she'd forgive him for kissing the princess?

He and Kate had no agreement, but he knew if the tables were reversed, he'd be a wreck.

While he'd never have publicly condemned her, and she shouldn't have done so to him, she'd led a different life than he had. Where he'd have opted for a long voyage to forget, Kate would pick up her rapier and fight. And wasn't that one of the things he loved about her? Gods, there it was again. He *loved* her.

Bregovi looked at the stained and torn gown in his hands, stunned yet again by the realization. How was it possible? He'd known her mere days. A week at most.

He had known Camilla for years, yet his connection to Kate, with Kate, seemed far stronger. When he was with her, he felt that same wonder he did at sea. The excitement of discovering a new land rivaled the thrill of discovering what intrigued her. And her mind hadn't ceased to intrigue him. Would giving her up be akin to giving up the sea?

He glanced again at the gown in his hands. Bloody. Torn. He could never repair it. Then he took up the soap again and scrubbed harder.

* * *

Warm sun rained down on Kate as she rode through the forest, leaves dancing in brilliant colors all around. Her lavender gown shimmered and fluttered as her mount galloped faster.

"Hah!" a man screamed in her ear.

She turned to see Scarface whipping their horse faster.

Her heart jolted.

Behind him an army pursued with Sylvan at its head.

Then right before her eyes, he and his horse vanished.

Scarface raced on as fear coursed through her. They rounded a bend, then the bandit thudded hard against her back.

He was gone.

Grabbing at the reins, she hung on with all her might.

The trail curved and Scarface tumbled off into the mud.

She didn't look back, but heard the heavy hoof beats gaining.

She charged onward. Determined. Afraid. Alone.

Always alone.

Sylvan materialized ahead of her, holding the reins to Rachel's mount.

When the trail opened into a clearing, he slowed up and Kate followed suit. She had to save Rachel.

Sylvan pulled the princess off her horse, a knife to her throat.

Then Kate saw the others—the king, Bregovi and Wolfe, Sophia and Sebastian, Victoria and Brock—all were there.

And the army surrounded them all.

With her heart racing, Kate told Sylvan she would do what he wished. She pleaded with him to let everyone go.

He laughed.

Bregovi stepped forward, sword at the ready. She warned him back, but he refused to listen.

Sebastian sent an arrow slicing through empty space as Sylvan disappeared, taking Rachel with him.

Kate screamed when he reappeared next to Sebastian, dropping Rachel to the ground, blood gushing from her throat. Kate ran for Rachel. So did Sebastian, but Sylvan stabbed the lord before he reached her.

She tried to cry out, to tell him to stop, to scream she'd go with him, but nothing came out. Her voice was gone.

As the king, Wolfe and Bregovi rushed Sylvan, he disappeared again.

Then, in lightning quick speed, he materialized next to the king, stabbing him from behind. The monarch fell. Kate began to shake.

He was going to kill them all.

"I'll go, I'll go!" she cried, her voice coming that time. "Don't hurt them."

"You shouldn't have run," Sylvan said. "A genie belongs with her master."

"Master?" Bregovi said, confusion and pain in his eyes.

Brock charged, sword at the ready, but Sylvan took him next and the smithy fell.

"No," she cried as Bregovi put himself between her and Sylvan. She grabbed at Bregovi's arm, "Don't! He'll kill you too."

But the prince didn't budge. He just lifted his sword, ready to take on the devil.

She scrambled to get past him, to get to Sylvan first, but Bregovi held her back.

"Ah," Sylvan said. "The knight in tarnished armor."

"More bandit than knight," Bregovi said, swinging the blade.

But Sylvan disappeared again as an invisible knife struck the prince in the gut.

He doubled over.

Kate screamed.

Sylvan reappeared and struck another blow to Bregovi's chest.

His heart.

Clutching at the blade, Bregovi collapsed.

"It seems your knight has fallen."

As Kate rushed to help him, Sylvan's eerily calm voice pierced her. "I command you to halt. I command you *not* to aid him."

Her feet anchored to the soil under her feet, obeying his will, not hers.

"Please, let me help him," she sobbed. "I'll do whatever you wish. Please don't let him die."

Sylvan knew nothing of mercy. As the man's order held her in place, she watched the man she loved take his last breath.

* * *

As Bregovi draped the gown over the remaining chair near the fire, Kate mumbled in her sleep. Stepping away quietly, he retrieved the chemise from the basin as well, overly pleased with himself for getting most of the blood out of both garments. Although some of the lavender hue had washed out as well, the gown looked much improved.

It had taken him longer than he'd thought it would, and the activity had splashed a substantial amount of water on his own clothes, but it felt good. As he had washed the shift, his mind enjoyed replaying the vision of her in it, wet and desirable. He pressed the wet chemise to his forehead, but that wasn't really where he needed it. He wrung out the fabric one more time and, for lack of a better option, draped it on the chair with the gown.

Kate jerked and shifted, and Bregovi moved to change into the dry breeches before she awoke. He had donned the pants, pulled off his wet shirt, and was looking for a place to set them when she cried out.

He wondered if she was dreaming about the kidnapping.

"Kate?" he said to rouse her, then noticed a small table near the remaining cot. Positioning it closer to the fire, he draped his clothes across it.

She cried out again, the anguish in her voice sending chills through him.

"I'll do whatever you want. Please," she said, tears spilling over her cheeks.

"Kate?" he said, kneeling before her.

She continued weeping.

"Kate, wake up. You're dreaming."

She let out a heart-wrenching moan.

"Kate," he said more forcefully, shaking her shoulders. "Wake up."

Her eyes flew open. "Let me save him. Let me help him." She struck at him, pounding her fists into his chest.

"There's no one to save. It was only a dream."

She sucked in a breath, eyes wide, tears streaming. "Bregovi?"

"None other."

She grabbed at him, choking out, "Where are you hurt?"

"I'm not hurt."

Her hands frantically searched for an imaginary wound on his chest, igniting his skin in the process.

"He, he stabbed you," she cried. "I saw, saw him stab you."

"No one stabbed me."

"I, I need to find it," she said more desperately. "Where is it?"

"Kate. I am not injured." He pronounced each word with enough force to finally reach her.

Her tearful eyes flickered up to his. "You're not?"

"You had a bad dream."

"He, he made me watch," she choked out. "I, I couldn't help you and he, he made me watch while you died." She crushed her face to his chest, clutching him as if he really had died.

As sobs wracked her small body, the last of his anger melted away, leaving only a depth of feeling no brutal poem could erase.

He scooped her onto his lap. When she cried that men were coming, he whispered that she was safe. When she talked of his wounds, he assured her he was fine.

Holding her close, he kissed her hair and whispered soothing words in her ear until she relaxed against him, her cheek resting on his chest.

"Better now?" he asked quietly.

"It was so real," she replied, her voice scratchy with emotion.

"Dreams are strange creatures." He remembered years when Camilla haunted his sleep. "I think sometimes our dreams give voice to our deepest longings—"

"I didn't long for your death."

"—and fears."

"I suppose," she said. "But this was different. It was Lord Sylvan, the man my uncle…wanted me to be with. He came after me and murdered everyone. Your sister, Lord Sebastian, your father, Brock and then you." Her voice rose with each name and caught on his.

"Shhhh." He brushed her hair from her face. "The kidnapping stirred up your fears, but you're fine now, sitting safely in the lap of luxury."

"I'm sitting on *your* lap."

He felt her smile against his chest.

That's how they remained for a while longer, both gazing at the fire, lost in their thoughts. Hers a mystery to him. His filled with how to set things right. How to explain. For although she'd done him an injury, he knew his was the greater blow. Somehow he had to explain. As he grappled for the right words, he heard Rachel's frequent admonishment in his mind. *Apologize.* He'd start there.

"I'm sorry."

Gray eyes met his, her lashes still wet.

"I'm sorry," he said again. "I assume you heard about the—" Dear gods, what was it? "The exchange with Sophia."

She slid off his lap. "No. I didn't hear about it," she said, pulling the blanket around herself.

He combed his memory for any other offense.

"I went back to the library to try another book. To see if I could find something more."

His stomach dipped as if he'd dropped from a thirty-foot swell. "Damn the fates."

"Indeed," she said. "I opened the door and you were right there.

Kissing her."

Dragging a hand through his hair, he sought a way to untangle the mess he'd made.

"It was a fool's bargain. She knew things about the Zafarians, and the price was a kiss…or several."

"Several?"

"She knew a lot. Holy gods, that sounds horrid."

"You couldn't barter anything else?"

"She set the terms. I should have offered Zafarian objects, but I wasn't thinking clear. Kate, she knew why the spells hadn't been working. She knew about the talismans."

"You didn't look tortured about it," she said, glancing into the fire again. "In fact, it looked tender, like you really cared for her, like you'd been courting her."

"I assure you neither is the case. It was the first time I'd done anything with her, and that was only because she'd won the tour."

Kate only nodded, staring into the fire. He waited her out.

"Maybe you should have," she said.

"Pardon?"

"I can't give you or your kingdom what you need. Sophia can. She'd be a good match for you."

"Princess Sophia is not a good match and she won't be my bride. Every time I kissed her I compared her to you, and she came up wanting."

"How about Victoria? Although I've done a dismal job of it, I was supposed to help her win you."

"I'm not marrying Victoria. And before you begin listing them, I'm not marrying any of the others, either. In fact, before your unfortunate choice in material, I was going to award you the win in poetry."

She met his gaze, eyes misty. Did she finally believe him?

"Are you mad?" she asked with an incredulous half-laugh. "You can't make me the winner. Your father would be furious. You need to take a princess!"

"One moment you're angry with me for kissing a princess, and now you're thrusting two upon me?"

She dropped her forehead to her knees. "Why couldn't you have been a bandit?"

"But I am a bandit." He took hold of her blanket to tug her closer.

"I'm trying to be rational," she said, not convincingly. "You know you must choose one of them."

"How could I settle for either of them now that I've met you?"

She gazed up at him as if trying to read his mind and he wished she could.

"Trust me, Kate. What happened with Sophia means nothing. She means nothing. I've never kissed anyone the way I've kissed you. You've bewitched me," he whispered, leaning in so his lips were inches from hers. "Body and soul, you've bewitched me."

A tear slipped down her cheek. He brushed it away, slowly closing the distance, giving her time to turn away. Thankfully, she didn't.

Gently taking her mouth, he poured all his emotion into that one sweet kiss, hoping to his soul that she believed him.

CHAPTER TWENTY-SIX

As he sat there in the firelight, his eyes flickering with heat of their own, Kate wanted to believe him. He had been waiting since his kiss, not pressing her, and she had never wanted anything or anyone more.

For if the dream and the anguish she felt at his death showed her anything, it was that she truly loved him. And it was more than she could bear. For despite his sweet declarations, she couldn't have him. Not for long. Not for forever.

Just for tonight.

The thought came unbidden from that place in her soul where secret longings were buried. If she couldn't have him for a lifetime, she wanted one night to remember for the rest of her days.

"I wrote another poem."

"You did?" His gaze held her close as her heart pulsed faster.

"I listed the things I admire about you." She brushed non-existent dust from his leg just to touch him.

"May I hear it?" he whispered, pulling the blanket around her and edging her closer in the process.

"You promise not to mock?"

"I promise."

Gazing into his glimmering green eyes, she began. "The dashing and gallant prince Edmund, Bregovi to some he's called; spends much of his time exploring for remedies to benefit all."

"I already like this one better," he said, taking her hand.

"His love for his family runs deep, as you'll see if you cross his way; It's in his sweet care for his sister and in the garden at his mother's grave."

He brushed a kiss across her knuckles.

"He's bold and strong and courageous, and enjoys a lively jest." Thinking of the bandit charade made her face warm. "He's honorable and devoted to his kingdom and noble quests."

"I like this version *much* better," he whispered.

"Me too," she whispered back. "The lucky maiden who wins him, the one who gains his love, will be truly blessed beyond measure, by standards on earth or in heaven above."

"It's beautiful and much too kind."

"I'm sorry about the other one."

"I'm sorry I gave you reason to write it."

She knew he was waiting, that she would have to initiate if he were to kiss her again, and her heart urged her to move.

It was right. He was right.

She leaned toward him, the slightest movement. He closed the distance in a heartbeat. Warm and tender, his lips brushed over hers. Heady and deep. Slow and complete. More intimate somehow than the passionate kisses they'd shared before.

As she trailed her fingers over his chest, his muscles quivered under her touch, sending a tantalizing quiver through her as well. And when he moved to nuzzle her neck, a delicious heat transferred from his lips to her body.

He was hers. Not Sophia's. Not Victoria's. This man cared for *her* and she needed him to feel how much she cared for him.

Shedding the blanket, she slid onto his lap. As she explored, trying to learn what pleased him, one of his hands roamed slowly up her thigh and rested on her bare hip. Sizzling all over, she longed to touch him everywhere, but had to make do with kissing his cheek, for the marauder had fixated on her neck—kissing, nibbling, enticing her beyond reason.

And while his lips were engaged, his hand moved up and slowly tugged the tunic off her shoulder. Her bared breast brushed against his chest. The sensation felt so splendid she wished he'd removed the tunic entirely.

As she debated encouraging the other side to drop, he continued his journey, taking his time on his way to her breast, stopping to tease her exposed skin until desire made her dizzy.

At last, his warm breath reached her nipple. A soft moan escaped her when his tongue finally tickled the eager flesh, and a bolt of fire shot to where she pulsed below.

Weaving her fingers into his hair, she held him there.

He rewarded her by tugging the nub into his mouth, suckling and stroking with his clever tongue until need made her ache.

* * *

Merciful gods, he loved touching her. With one hand cupping her bottom, another her breast, and his mouth teasing a ripe nipple, he couldn't think clear. *Need* and *naked* mixed in his brain with *wait* and *stop*. If they didn't do the latter soon, the former would win the debate.

With one last swirl of his tongue and a nibble that drew a gasp from his Kate, he pulled back and rested his forehead on her breast. They needed to slow down, he reminded himself again.

He'd just gotten her back and he didn't want to ruin that by seducing her into doing something she'd later regret.

"We need to stop."

She whispered, "I don't want to stop." Then kissed him again, long and deep, putting a chink in his noble intentions.

"We're on course for more than heady kisses," he said, struggling to do the right thing.

"I understand." She took his mouth again as the tunic fell off her other shoulder.

"I don't think you do," he said, eyes fixed on the beautiful breast now exposed before him.

With his face between her hands, her desire-infused eyes bore into his. "I need you to be the mischievous bandit, not the noble prince. I need you inside me."

His privy explorer pulsed at the image it brought to mind, and it bellowed at him to accommodate her.

"Bregovi?" she said, heat flooding her cheeks.

"I want it to be right," he groaned, unable to stop his thumb from toying with her breast.

"It is right," she said with a sweet gasp. "Tonight is right."

She was right. They were right. Tonight was right for them. For if it wasn't, he no longer knew what right was.

He swept her up, taking her mouth again as he carried her to the cot.

* * *

As Kate lowered her feet to the floor, her greedy hands moved over his back and lower, to his bottom, where his muscles flexed under her fingers.

For his part, Bregovi's hands did some roaming of their own under her shirt, leaving a sizzling trail in their wake.

She moved to his chest, sliding her fingers down to where a curly patch of hair disappeared into his breeches. He sucked in a breath when she reached for the tie, and *she* sucked in a breath when the breeches fell to his feet.

The fourth time seeing a naked man bested all the others. Her glorious adventurer stood solid and golden in the firelight. Smooth, taught skin. A patch of curly hair dusted a muscular chest and trailed down to a thick appendage jutting out to meet her. Strong legs held up every glorious inch of him.

"If you get to look, so do I," he said, groaning.

And in one swift move, the tunic flew from her body. As Bregovi did some looking of his own, she understood his angst. For as his gaze lingered over her breasts, her belly, lower, her body tingled as if he were touching those intimate places.

Dizzying thoughts were suddenly replaced by a primal urge to taste and *feel*.

"We should advance to touching," she said, wrapping her fingers around that very hot, very prominent appendage.

Bregovi swayed and scooped her up to deposit her on the cot.

Before she even registered the fur tickling her from beneath, firm muscles and gentle strokes enticed her from above.

How could she have thought he didn't care? His eyes showed it all so clearly.

Bewitched, he'd said. Without her Gifts, she had bewitched this beautiful man. It made her feel powerful and bold and alive.

"You *are* stunning, you know."

Remembering the last time he'd said that, she grinned. "Even without the gown?"

"Especially without the gown," he said, eyes sparkling. Bending, he nuzzled her neck, but only for a moment before kissing a molten path to her breasts, where his naughty lips claimed a nipple and set about enslaving it.

While his mouth continued its marvelous endeavor, his adventurous hands roamed, tickled and enticed every inch of her, turning her into a quivering mess. But before she became a puddle of need at his feet, she wanted a turn at the helm.

Tugging at his arms, she guided him back to her mouth, where their lips and tongues danced another round. And before he could object, she rolled him over so that his warm solid body was under her.

Knowing it would be her only night with him, and possibly the only night she'd have with a man she cared for, she planned to kiss, touch and memorize every last bit of him.

She began with his dimples and nose, then lingered at his neck where stubble roughened her chin. She moved lower and pressed her lips to the scar on his shoulder.

Lifting her eyes, she caught him watching her. She had been about to ask if the scar hurt anymore, but his hands distracted her as they stroked her legs in delightful ways.

Sliding lower, she kissed and trailed her fingers over his chest, thrilling when his muscles jumped under her touch.

She took her sweet time, just as he had, all the while aware of his shaft pulsing between them. Wondering how undone he'd become if she kissed *it*, she slid her lips over his ribs and stomach and lower. Then she brushed slow kisses down that narrow trail of hair below his navel.

"Mercy, Kate," he croaked as he clumsily grabbed at one of her breasts.

* * *

Kate's saucy grin set Bregovi's heart pounding, along with other parts. Her soft lips heated his skin at each brush, and her hair sent shivers through him as it tickled over his chest.

That, combined with her breasts dancing over his body, would soon have him undone if he didn't halt her southern expedition. Taking hold of her arms, he guided her up and back under him. Swallowing her protest, he claimed her mouth. Not easily thwarted, her crafty tongue continued to work its magik.

She seemed to know exactly how to stoke the fires hotter, tricks an untouched maiden wouldn't know. And although the idea of her with another disturbed him, it would make their union easier. If she were still a virgin, he'd take their pleasure more slowly.

As his fractured brain ruminated over how to air the subject, her sneaky hands came to rest upon his bottom, one on each side. When she squeezed, it slipped out with a surprised gasp, "Kate, have you done this before?"

"No," she whispered, relocating her hands to his lower back. "Am I doing it wrong?"

She was obviously not as adept at reading his groans as she was at generating them.

"No. But you know more than you ought."

Her already rosy cheeks grew crimson.

Leaning in, he whispered against her ear, "Just how do you know so much, Kate?"

As he tried to interpret the strange expression on her face, one of her clever hands covered the whole of it.

"Kate?"

"I can't tell you," she said, the words muffled through her hand as he kissed her knuckles. "May we carry on?"

"I'm sorry." He ran a hand up her side to tease one lovely breast. "But this is far too intriguing for me to let it go now."

She shook her head as he wondered if a governess or servant had told her of men and women. But would either have given details? She certainly knew more than the basics.

"I simply must know," he whispered in her ear, then nipped at the lobe, "before we go any further."

A gentle lick. A soft gasp.

"Do you want to go further?" he breathed against her neck.

They would obviously continue whether or not she told him, but he hoped she would. Because her embarrassment made him ache to know. And in that moment he realized he wanted to know everything about her. Her past, her desires, her fears, her secrets. He wanted it all.

As he marveled at the revelation, she came forth with one of her own.

"I watched."

The words were barely audible, and he felt certain he'd misunderstood.

"You what?"

"Watched. I *watched*," she said, sounding annoyed at having to repeat it.

Watched? "Animals?" he offered. "Horses?" For what maiden would watch a man and woman? But she shook her head to indicate the negative. He drew her hand away from her face. "Kate?"

"Our housemaid and the smithy's apprentice," she growled.

Definitely nothing close to what he expected her to say. He'd never even watched, except for a glimpse now and then of a sailor and a wench caught by surprise. His mind spun with a multitude of questions, which also served to increase his desire.

Misreading his stupor, she added, "I didn't intend to see them." She attempted to wiggle sideways from under him.

Of course, under him was exactly where he wanted her to remain, so he quickly halted her progress.

With his arms on either side of her head, and his eyes intent on hers, he lowered his face till they were nose to nose. "I want to hear *all* about it." As he felt her lips smile under his, he added, "Later." Then he tortured her grinning mouth one more time before pulling out every skill he knew to set a woman aflame.

He teased and caressed. Touched and kissed. Listening and watching for what she enjoyed, lingering for a time if she showed particular pleasure. Everywhere, that is, except her most sensitive region. To that area, he paid frequent, fleeting visits, fluttering his fingers over her on his way to other destinations.

The teasing had its intended effect, for on his last touch and pass, she growled, grabbed his hand and redirected him back.

Not wishing to ignore his lady's impassioned request, verbal or not, he spent long minutes discovering exactly how she liked to be touched *there*. She squirmed. She moaned. An occasional *oh* and *my* escaped her lips when he did something especially good, and he took it as a cue to continue.

While he kept to his task, she grew so slick that fantasies of tasting her grew as intense as his need to be inside her. As the first was too intimate for her maiden voyage, he continued with his fingers, preparing her to receive him.

When her breathing grew increasingly quick, he whispered, "Are you ready for me?"

"I don't know," she said with a gasp, squirming under his touch. "Does it feel this good? Because...right now...this feels...splendid." Tightening a small hand on his arm, she added, "Just a little more..."

More? Any other maiden would have seen constellations already. To accommodate her and simultaneously increase her need for release, he decided to give her that more personal touch after all.

She whimpered when he removed his fingers, but a choked *Oh My* escaped her when his mouth replaced them.

As she writhed under his thorough kisses, he held her hips still and tended to his task. Encouraged by the incoherent sounds escaping her, he slowly licked and teased, lazily tasted every tender inch of her, giving her everything she needed, then easing off. Over and over. All the while watching for signs she was nearing her breaking point.

Her hands clenched on his shoulders, "Bre—"

"Ready?" he whispered, kissing her belly.

She nodded, eyes wide and dark. Nudging her knees up, he settled in between. He had never wanted a woman so much, nor cared so much. He needed it to be good for her. To be right.

He teased her with the tip longer than he thought he could take and slid into her a small measure. She gasped and tightened. He nearly came apart, but he'd not be *that* lover.

As he forced himself to hold on, to catch his breath, he felt her relax around him. He edged in further, pausing again. She breathed heavier and pulled at his back. He loved feeling her hands on him, wanting him. And as she hung onto him and he hung onto his sanity, he moved back and forth, inch by glorious inch until, with a final push, he slid in to the hilt.

She closed her eyes, her fingers digging into his skin.

"You all right?" he whispered.

She drew in a long breath and met his gaze. "Yes, it just feels…different."

"Different good?"

"Different good." She smiled. "It's not quite as I imagined."

"There's more."

"More?" her eyes grew wide. "You're not in all the way?"

Unable to suppress a chuckle, he nibbled her ear and whispered, "Perhaps I should check."

And before she could tense, he slowly eased out and just as slowly slid back in.

A slow moan escaped her and something immensely satisfying shivered through him.

As her dreamy gray eyes met his, she breathed, "I think you better check again."

"Anything for you."

She felt perfect around him. Made for him. As he continued gliding in and out, they found a steady rhythm until they were both shaking and sweating and riding the crest of a colossal wave. He fought to hold out until she reached her climax, and after she clenched around him, he let go, clinging to her as he sailed to the stars and back.

CHAPTER TWENTY-SEVEN

Kate had never imagined feeling anything so exquisite. With dazed eyes, Bregovi brushed soft lips over hers as he pulled her close and rolled onto his side. He looked like she felt after an intense healing—completely exhausted.

"Bregovi?"

He opened his eyes. So green. So hers for a few treasured hours.

Words escaped her, so she stared instead, memorizing his face, holding tight to the moment.

His mouth quirked up at the start of a smile, then his eyes closed as he mumbled something about a nap. Unfortunately, Kate wasn't tired in the least, so she watched him slumber for a long while until her blood cooled with the temperature in the cottage.

When the fire in the hearth burned down to embers, she carefully untangled her limbs from his and slid off the cot.

He looked stunning himself lying naked before her, but she covered him with one of the wool blankets before wrapping the other around herself and heading to the hearth.

She had nearly forgotten about the spell and needed to find a way to do it before morning. A quick check on the ingredients revealed all of the items were dry except the blackberry vine. She removed the sprig from the bowl and set it on the mantel to warm.

Adding several logs to the fire, she nursed it until the flames crackled high again. As she turned to deal with her gown, her heart caught in her throat. He had washed it. And the chemise.

Both showed only hints of pink where the blood had been. Repositioning both articles across the two chairs for better drying, she then moved the chairs to the side of the hearth, so the warmth of the fire wasn't hindered on its way to their bed.

Pleased with her work, she glanced over to where Bregovi slept. Sweet peace overwhelmed her. He lay watching her, affection in his eyes. She couldn't suppress a smile as he held up the blanket, inviting her back.

Shedding her blanket, she rejoined him, settling on her side facing him. "You washed my dress."

"I didn't want it to get your hair dirty." He winked. "It takes some effort to get it clean."

"Does it now?"

"Mmm," he murmured, sifting the strands through his fingers. "Although, perhaps other regions would take longer," he said, shifting his hand to stroke her bent knee.

When his wily hand moved up her thigh, she caught it, laughing. "We were talking about the dress."

"I'd rather talk about washing you," he said with that devilish grin she'd come to know.

She couldn't help but kiss his upturned lips. "Thank you. For the dress *and* wanting to wash me."

"Since I am denied the pleasure of the latter at present, I will settle for hearing your big secret."

Secret? Panic quickly replaced the light feelings. Had she uttered something? What had she said?

But before she could deny or inquire, he said, "The housemaid? The smithy's apprentice? An illicit and educational encounter?" His eyes sparked mischief.

Ah, *that*. While sharing the details would be awkward, it was nothing to sharing the secrets surrounding her uncle.

"Should I get you started with a few questions?" he asked, gliding his hand to her hip, where he tormented the skin there.

"If you wish."

He nodded as his fingers dipped to the curve of her waist. "How old were you?"

"Fifteen."

"And the maid?"

"Jenny was nineteen. Luke was the same, or perhaps a year older."

"And how buxom was Jenny?" he asked, moving his hand to her breast.

She slugged him.

He laughed. "Just trying to visualize them."

"Her breasts, or Jenny and Luke?"

"Both."

"Hmph. I don't think I should tell you, if it's going to make you imagine another woman," she teased, forcing his hand away from her breast.

"Now, now, Kate. In my mind, Jenny looks exactly like you, and Luke looks like me." With that, he twined a leg with hers and rested that exploring hand back on her hip, the thumb tracing lazy circles. "So," he began. "Jenny and Luke met for their tumble in the…"

Kate knew she'd have to tell the tale or he'd pester her about it until sunrise. And since she wanted to do other things before sunrise, she decided she'd best give up the details.

"They didn't really meet, but came rushing into the storage pantry in the cellar. I was in the back, where it was dark, sitting on a crate with shelves and kitchen supplies all around. I had a clear view of the door, but couldn't be seen."

His thumb stopped circling. "Were you hiding?"

Always. "Yes, but not from them. When they rushed in, I thought they'd kiss and leave. They didn't. I tried to sneak past them, but they put a crate in front of the door so no one would come in. I considered making myself known, but they progressed so quickly." Kate's face grew hot at the memory. "Before I could speak, her breasts were out and her hand was in his breeches."

"Not their first encounter," Bregovi said, torturing her thigh with gentle strokes.

"Clearly not."

"And you didn't shut your eyes?"

Her face grew warmer still. "Only when I blinked."

That brought a chuckle from him, which eased her embarrassment.

"And then..." he prompted.

"He took one of her nipples into his mouth and pulled up her skirts. She got more active in his pants. Then clothes started flying. In minutes they had everything off but her stockings and shoes. They were *both* buxom."

"They looked good naked?"

"Yes." Especially Luke. His muscular frame was breathtaking. Jenny thought so too, for the maid had thoroughly appreciated it with her hands and mouth.

"And then..."

"It looked like they considered the floor for a second before he sat on a full sack of meal and pulled her on top of him. Straddling him. Honestly, he was so large, I didn't see how he'd fit."

"But I bet he did." The dimpled prince grinned, making her laugh.

"Yes, with some effort. But from the sound of it, they both enjoyed it immensely."

"And did you?"

"Not nearly as much as I enjoyed being with you."

It was true. Watching them had left her warm and tense and throbbing in places she hadn't known existed, but it was nothing to the feeling of relieving that ache with a man she cared for.

"I'm glad to hear it." He pulled her close until all of their most intimate parts touched. "A most interesting introduction to pleasures of the flesh, and all because you were hiding. Did you tell your friend what she missed when she found you?"

"I didn't have friends." Before he could ask about *that* she added, "Not that I played hide and seek with."

"Why were you hiding?"

"I don't remember. I must have defied my uncle once again and hid to delay my punishment." His punishments were always brutal. She shivered as she thought of the kittens and goats he had harmed to torment her. He knew pain to others affected her more deeply than anything he could do to her personally.

"Did he find you?"

"Yes," she whispered. "He always finds me."

"Not this time," he said, drawing the blankets in around them.

As they talked into the night, the unsettling feelings slipped away and Bregovi stole deeper into her heart. He reassured and calmed. He touched and stoked. He teased and enticed. And as they made love again, she forgot about her uncle and Sylvan and her fears and what would come.

She was home and all was right with the world. Nothing bad could happen while she was in Bregovi's arms. And she latched on to every minute, committing every touch, caress and gaze to memory, for she knew it would have to last her a lifetime.

Sometime later, Kate watched as Bregovi settled into a deep slumber. Exhaustion tugged at her too, but the spell had to be done before dawn, and she couldn't risk closing her eyes for fear she'd not awaken in time.

Kate brushed hair from his forehead. No response. Kissing his chin drew the same result. He was out.

After carefully slipping off the cot, she grabbed a blanket to ward off the chill.

Collecting the items from the hearth, she made quick work of arranging them in the necessary manner.

With her back to Bregovi, so he wouldn't see, she added a loose hair, then nipped her finger and squeezed a drop of blood onto the pile. All she needed was a spark to light it.

* * *

With sleep-fogged eyes, Bregovi watched Kate kneeling before the hearth. He should have been the one making sure the cabin was warm enough. Better yet, he should have been warming her so she didn't notice or care that the fire had gone out. Intent on luring her back to bed to do exactly that, he quietly rolled off the cot.

As he drew nearer, he heard her singing a sweet tune. No, *chanting* a sweet tune.

Confused, he peered over her shoulder just as she moved to light a small pile of twigs.

He couldn't conceive what his eyes revealed. Sorcery? It was as if the sea had capsized his ship.

As he floundered in disbelief, some rational part of his brain realized he needed to stop her. When she turned—to make sure he was asleep, he supposed—he snatched the lit wood from her hands.

She jumped to her feet, nearly losing the blanket in the process. Ill-timed, he caught a glimpse of her right breast as she restored the fabric around herself.

"Bregovi." It was more of a statement than anything else. Declaring his name as if he'd forgotten it. But he hadn't. He knew full well who he was and whence he came.

Who she was, on the other hand, was suspect. Was she a Zafarian come to spy? Was he under a spell? Had she truly bewitched him?

But even as the thoughts tried to take root, his heart bellowed to hear her out. And while he had little experience with sorcery, instinct—or misguided love—told him the feelings they shared were much too strong to be from magik.

She needn't know that, though. Not until she explained.

He tossed the shard of wood into the hearth.

"What's this for, Kate?" He scooped the pile into a bowl lying nearby. Herbs and hair anointed with something sweet. "What kind of spell is this?" he asked, glancing up.

An empty cabin was all he found, the open door swinging on its hinges.

Bolting after her, he dropped the bowl on the cot as he passed.

The same thick forest that filtered out the sun by day nearly blackened the moon's rays by night. As he strained to make out her shape, Odyssey snorted and stomped to his left.

Bregovi charged toward the sound bare-assed, barefooted and dangling parts he'd rather not expose to the elements.

As he drew closer, he found Kate half-cloaked in the blanket, struggling to mount Odyssey. Thankfully, the steed wasn't cooperating.

Catching sight of him, she shouted, "Just let me go."

Then she darted toward the trees.

He had her in three bounds. Or rather, he had the blanket. For Kate had slipped out of it as slick as a codfish from a sailor's grasp.

Naked, she ducked behind the mare.

"What's the spell for? Why are you doing magik?"

"I mean you no harm."

"Nor do I." He moved to the horse's opposite flank. "You'll face far more peril naked in the forest than you will with me."

"This isn't how I meant for you to find out."

"Did you mean for me to find out?" he asked as Odyssey's wet nose nudged his back, reminding him of how very naked he was.

After a long pause, she replied, "Of course not."

"I thought as much," he said, slowly loosening the mare's reins from the branch she was tethered to. "Were you doing a love spell?"

"No!" she said, sounding offended.

While she wallowed in righteous outrage, he pulled the reins free and gave the mare's rump a firm slap. The mount responded appropriately. In seconds, nothing stood between Kate and him but a patch of dirt. Before she darted for the trees, he threw the blanket around her and whisked her up.

"Come, let's move this conversation inside before a beast takes a bite out of my ass." He carried her over the threshold, kicking the door shut behind him. "Why don't we start with why you left our bed to do sorcery?"

After tossing her on the cot, he shoved a heavy oak table in front of the door. Confident that it would slow any future attempts at flight, he turned back to confront his witch.

The siren had shed the blanket and lay seductively on the bearskin, her only adornment, the locket nestled between her creamy breasts. As she rested on one elbow, brushing a hand over the fur in invitation and promise, every curve beckoned for his caress. But her eyes betrayed the weight of the moment. Fear motivated her, not desire.

Before his ill-timed arousal became too uncomfortable, he threw the blanket over her once again and scooped her up.

"It's complicated," she said as he deposited her in a chair by the fire.

"I'm excellent at grasping complex issues," he said, donning his breeches to better keep his mind on the more pressing issue— discovering just what and who he was dealing with.

Holy gods, she could have done any of the spells he'd been trying. What a fool he must have looked. Why hadn't she helped him? What was her purpose?

"Tell me why you were doing magik. What was this spell to accomplish?"

"You aren't going to like it."

"What I don't like are evasive answers. I'm sure the truth will only improve my mood."

The concerned look she flashed gave him pause. Whatever it was, *she* didn't like it.

"Does your spell harm me in some way?"

"No!" she cried, aghast.

"Does it harm my family? Wolfe?"

"Of course not."

"My horse?"

"Don't be ridiculous."

"So, if it does no harm to those I love, I see no reason why you can't tell me its purpose."

Her choked laugh told him she disagreed.

Searching around, she snatched up the chemise. The blanket fell to her feet, teasing him with another glorious view before she threw on the garment.

"You can trust me, Kate."

"I'm not accustomed to trusting people."

"It's time you begin to," he said. "Why don't you start with the spell? What is its aim?"

Kate sat back on the chair as stiff as the wood she rested upon. Staring into the fire, she said, "It keeps me from using my Gifts."

"Astonian Gifts?" he said, surprised.

She nodded.

"I thought the Gifts had died out generations ago."

"Most stopped using them to avoid burning. My family did not."

Could her claim be true? Could the kingdoms be full of those possessing the old Gifts like Wolfe's? Maybe Quent wasn't so crazy after all.

"What can you do?" he asked, with something akin to excitement brewing. "Why do you need a spell to control your abilities?"

"They're instinctive and sometimes I use them before I realize it."

"And others grow suspicious?"

"No."

"You do harm?"

"No."

"Then why would you need the spell?"

"You *are* persistent."

"Yes, I am, so you might as well spill the tale and be done with it."

As she wove her hair into a long braid, he sat on the chair opposite her.

"You'll feel better if you tell me."

After several nervous glances, Kate let out a long breath. "I didn't lie when I told you I'd run away from my uncle."

Bregovi nodded.

"He has abilities too."

"Such as?"

"He can sense when others use their Gifts. He can track them and appear at their location within moments."

"Within moments?" he repeated. "Out of the ether?"

She nodded.

"How is that possible?"

"The same way any of the Gifts are possible. Unfortunately, his Gift has enabled him to find me every time I've run away."

"How many times have you fled?"

"This is the ninth."

"Nine?" he said, leaning closer. *Nine?* "Why doesn't he let you go?"

"He wants me to help him." She shifted her attention to her right palm. Rubbing it as if it ached.

"Using your Gifts?"

"Yes."

"What can you do?" he asked, his mind alight with possibilities. "Turn wheat to gold?"

"No."

"Command the tides?"

"Why does it matter?" she asked, standing.

Grabbing her hand, he said, "How will you ever escape him if you're afraid to let anyone help you?"

"No one can help me. He's too powerful."

"I take it your people aren't fishmongers?"

She squeezed his hand, although he didn't know if it was to give him strength or her courage. Settling back on the chair, playing with his hand on her lap, she began. "He's in shipping, like my father was. He holds my father's dukedom in Cragmont."

"So you're royal after all," he said, wondering why he ever doubted.

"My name is Lady Katherine Isolde Durant."

"Lady Kate," he said, raising her hand to his lips.

She smiled weakly. "He's third in line for the throne, but wants to change that."

"How can your Gifts help him?"

"I'm an empath. I can read others' emotions—their intentions— I'd be able to detect deceit in his supporters."

A hefty Gift. He'd love to be able to detect the honesty in the men he encountered at sea. But it wasn't a skill that could win a war.

"That would be helpful, but certainly not enough to turn the tides and steal the throne."

"I also have the Gift of healing. I could restore him or any of his men if they are wounded in battle."

That rocked him for a moment. The only accounts of such an ability were in tales of Caligo. Perhaps that's why she was so fascinated with the island. Imagine the good she could do with a Gift like that. But *good*. Again, it didn't seem like the kind of talent needed to take a throne.

"Healers aren't conquerors. I'd have thought you'd be a secret weapon if he needed you so desperately."

She took special attention with his hand, not denying, not confirming.

An uneasy prickling sensation stirred the skin on his back.

"What else can you do?"

Her gaze met his. Hopeful. Fearful. "I'm telekinetic."

He'd heard of the skill—or read of it—in Astonian lore. Telekinesis neared the top of the ladder when it came to magikal abilities. Only a few had been known to possess it. Powerful indeed.

"What can you move?"

"Anything."

"My chair?"

"Yes," she said, without a glance to assess its size.

"The cot?"

"Yes."

"How large can you go?" he asked, jumping up. "Can you move this cabin?"

"If I concentrate."

"Holy gods," he said. With her powers, they could defeat the Order Master. And as the thought flitted through his mind, he recalled a certain conversation with Wolfe at the Portal. "You're the sorceress, aren't you? The one the Order Master is looking for."

"Yes," she said, her voice flat.

"Your uncle is the Order Master."

"Yes. But he lied. I didn't harm anyone." Now she was up and pacing like a caged tigress.

"Does he have any other natural Gifts?" Bregovi asked. "More than the tracking ability?"

"No."

"His other powers are all Zafarian sorcery?"

"Yes. He can work spells of all levels."

He felt that same heady rush he got whenever he found an elusive port.

"This is brilliant."

Kate halted. "This is *not* brilliant."

"You are the key to defeating him."

"What? No. There is no way to defeat him. His ability to work spells dwarfs all others."

"Your natural Gifts are more powerful than his."

"That doesn't matter. They are no match against his sorcery."

"If we take his talisman—"

The mocking laugh-cry she emitted didn't have a proper name.

"You'll be dead before you're close enough to shake his hand, let alone find and remove his talisman."

"Can't you pin him down?"

"I can *move* things, not freeze them in place."

As he played out other possibilities in his head, she said, "There's one more issue."

The gravity in her voice stopped him mid-stride.

"I told you there was another man. An associate of his..."

"Yes," Bregovi said, with a sinking feeling.

"My uncle used dark magik to bind me to him as a genie."

A *genie*? His first inclination was to laugh, but the bleak expression on her face curbed it.

"I know most think they only exist in legends, but be assured, they're real. Old Quent's dark magik book mentioned them too."

He recalled how she and Quent had spent time on the page. "But genies are spirits."

"If they had killed me, I would be a spirit."

A shudder shook his bones. She said it so matter-of-factly, he knew she'd faced that sort of danger too often. He wished he'd been there to help her. To protect her.

"I escaped before they finished the ritual, so he can't summon me. But they did enough that I'd be compelled to obey Lord Sylvan's— my master's—commands if he were here. If he ordered me to help them—to hurt you—I wouldn't be able to prevent it."

"Can this Sylvan track you as well?"

"I don't think so, but he can turn himself invisible."

Invisible? How could he battle an invisible opponent?

"Then we need to challenge them one at a time. Your uncle first. If Sylvan can't feel your Gifts, then we can lure your uncle in without him."

Her lovely face turned ash white. "You can't be serious."

"It's the best hope we have of capturing him."

"And here I was afraid you'd want to burn me," she said. "You want to use me just like he does."

"No. I want to stop the attacks. To save the kingdoms. To save *you*."

"You won't save anything. You'll only get yourself killed. You'll get everyone killed."

"We can't let him take over," he said. "What would you have us do?"

"I don't know."

"Between your Gifts and your knowledge of spells, there must be a way to stop him."

"There is no *we* here."

"You still don't trust me?"

"This isn't a matter of trust, it's a matter of survival. *Your* survival. I want you to marry a princess and have babies and live a long happy life exploring the world." Her voice cracked. "If we bring him to Florian, if you challenge him with or without my help, you'll be dust before the next sunrise."

Pulling her close, he brushed gentle kisses over her lips to quiet her declarations of doom.

"You underestimate my abilities, my love," he said against her mouth.

"And you underestimate his." She rested her head against his shoulder

"You must realize you are the key to defeating him," Bregovi said. "That's why he wants to capture you—to control you with this genie plan. You are his biggest threat."

* * *

It was one of those moments in life when the world shifted and realigned under her feet. Like when she was five and healed an animal for the first time, or when she discovered she could call objects like her father did.

So much of her life with her uncle became clear.

"I assume the absence of a rebuttal means you know I'm correct."

Pulling back, she met his smug gaze. "It never occurred to me I would be...that I am...a threat to him."

"He didn't want you to see that."

She nodded, wondering how this man could discern truths she had missed for years.

"Will you help me capture him?" he asked. "For your good and the good of the kingdoms?"

"Just because I now realize I may be able to defeat him, doesn't change the fact that it's too dangerous for you. For your men," she said, moving away to gain room to think.

If she was the only one with power that matched Morten's, she would have to face him. Soon. Before the attacks grew in number and casualties.

"We may not have special Gifts, but a sword can inflict a heady amount of damage," he said.

While she loved his confidence, they needed a plan that didn't include Bregovi and his blade.

"It would be best to lure him somewhere isolated. Away from people, including you and your men. Threatening others is his favorite method to keep me in line."

"We'll make sure you *appear* to be alone, but you're bent if you think I won't be nearby to help you."

When she began to protest, he set a soft finger over her lips and said, "How about deep in the mountains? Or Zafaria. You don't get more isolated than that."

It could work. If she lured him to Zafaria, far from anything he could harm, she might stand a chance.

"I'd need a plan of what to do when he arrives," she said, her stomach queasy.

Despite the revelation, thirteen years of fearing the man didn't evaporate in a heartbeat. She'd need to refresh her memory on spells she could use…and on those Morten *would* use.

"We'll make one." He swept her tight in his arms and took her mouth with delicious intensity.

Relief and desire coiled together, stirring wicked sensations in intimate places. His intimate places must have stirred as well, because he began backing toward the cot, pulling her along with him.

"I think a pre-dawn celebration is in order." His enticing grin nearly had her, but *pre-dawn* shook her back to reality.

"I need to do the spell first," she said regretful and slightly breathless. Reversing their course, she added. "Or we're liable to face him here…in the cabin…*naked*."

"I'd rather not invite others to the party just now," he said, claiming her mouth again, the heat reaching her toes this time.

"Me too," she said, eager to get the spell done so they could get back to more enjoyable matters.

"Can I help?" he asked, retrieving the bowl.

"Yes."

Something warm and wonderful filled her as he handed the ingredients to her. She'd never realized how lovely it would be to share this part of herself with someone.

"Bregovi?"

"Hmm? You'll need fire as well, won't you?" he asked, squatting to stir the embers.

"Thank you."

"You're welcome. Shouldn't take me but a few minutes."

"No," she said, touching his broad, strong, golden shoulder. "Thank you for believing me. For believing *in* me."

A quiet smile touched his eyes. "I'll always believe in you."

The lump in her throat prevented speech.

He winked. "Let's get this spell over with so you can thank me properly."

Thinking of nothing she'd enjoy more, Kate once again arranged the ingredients on the hearth.

With Bregovi hovering over her, watching every step, Kate chanted the verse. Taking the lit twig he offered, she touched the flame to the pile.

Nothing.

It didn't catch.

She tried the chant again, then pressed the flaming stick to the blackberry vine.

Nothing.

She added a fresh strand of hair and another drop of blood. After chanting the spell yet again, she set the burning twig in the midst.

Not even a spark.

"Isn't it supposed to burst into flames?" Bregovi asked.

With her heart sounding alarm drums, Kate glanced up at Bregovi. "We need to get back to the castle. Now."

CHAPTER TWENTY-EIGHT

Bregovi had been on more dangerous expeditions across jungles and tumultuous seas, but trekking through the dense forest with only a lantern for light had every nerve on alert for hidden threats to protect Kate from.

Unfortunately, he'd failed to ward off their greatest foe. Pink hues dusted the sky. Dawn had won the race.

He'd had to ride with Kate on Odyssey after chasing off her mare, and was now grateful he'd done so. As the light filtered through the trees, she leaned her tense body against his chest, her eyes closed.

Clutching an arm around her waist, he urged the steed faster.

"If my uncle comes..." she started fretfully.

"He won't. Not until we're ready."

"If he does, you need to leave me."

"He won't come until we're ready," he said again. "We have a plan." Bregovi charged the steed from the last of the trees and onto the road.

"Events never play out as I plan."

"That was before." He kicked Odyssey to a gallop.

As if on cue, a dozen Florian guard intercepted them on the road.

"Excellent. You see, I told you all would be well," Brogovi said.

357

Then he shouted to the men, "We need an escort back to the castle."

Instead of rallying to their aid, the men fanned out, encircling them, blocking Bregovi's movement in any direction. Someone blew an ominous round on an ivory horn—the one used for hunting, when they'd cornered their game.

"What is this? Let us pass," Bregovi ordered.

"We can't, your highness," the bulky Flan said as he and the others eyed Kate with no small measure of suspicion...and fear.

"I demand you to let us pass," Bregovi said, directing Odyssey forward. "Your new home will be the dungeon if you don't stand down."

"Our reward will be the same if we do," Oscar said, holding his place.

"Bregovi transferred the reins to the hand at Kate's waist and drew his sword. With the blade ready for use, he turned the steed in a slow circle and said, "Do you intend to attack your prince?"

The men glanced to one another warily but held strong.

"It's your father," Kate said.

Bregovi followed her gaze to where his father and another dozen guard cut up the dirt as they charged toward them.

"Father," Bregovi said as the guards parted to let their king pass.

"Thank the gods we found you," his father said with a strangely sympathetic smile.

"We're fine," Bregovi said. "Except the men have mistaken me for a bandit."

"We've learned some interesting news about your lady friend," his father said.

Kate stiffened as Bregovi's heart pounded against her back.

"She's a sorceress," his father said, not yet looking at Kate. As if a glance would turn him to stone. "A Zafarian."

"I know, but not a bad one," Bregovi said. "She's going to help us."

"She's bewitched you," his father said with a nod to Stiles to his right.

"I assure you, I have my wits about me," Bregovi said.

"A bewitched man wouldn't know he was bewitched, son," his father said with infuriating patience. Then the man's gaze locked on her.

When Kate whispered what sounded to Bregovi like a prayer, his father shouted, "She's working a spell even now! Seize her!"

His father drew back as the men hurried to obey.

"Stay back," Bregovi shouted, swinging his sword overhead, ready to bring it down on any who touched her.

"No," Kate whispered, pressing something into the hand at her belly. "I'll go with them." She turned, so their eyes met. "If you fight them or get injured, I'll want to help. It will be too difficult to block my Gifts. Just bring the ingredients to me. And this," she said, squeezing his hand.

Everything in him cried out that he couldn't let them take her. But he didn't wish to make her struggle more difficult.

He brushed his lips over her temple. "Anyone with Gifts as powerful as yours must also possess the ability to be their master."

"I've tried."

"Perhaps you can imagine turning them off as one snuffs out a candle or closes a door. Or try to focus on your other senses—sight or smell—instead."

* * *

Before she had a chance to reply, Flan hauled her onto his steed.

"Aren't you going to strip her?" one of the guards shouted.

Blessed gods, no. Horrible thoughts scrambled through her mind. Bregovi looked as outraged as she felt mortified.

"Like hell you are," Bregovi said.

The king motioned Stiles over to consult while the others eyed her with fear, caution and lechery.

With her heart hammering in her ears and Flan's meaty grip under her breasts, Kate waited for the verdict.

"Strip her," the king bellowed.

"No!" Bregovi shouted as several men hopped from their mounts.

Stiles and another older guard blocked the prince with swords and steeds while Flan dropped her to guards far too eager to carry out the order.

Kate struggled as they groped her breasts and thighs, her Gifts charged and pulsing through her veins. Fighting her attackers *and* her Gifts would be impossible. She could do one or the other. Not both.

And while using her Gifts and bringing her uncle to the scene would certainly prevent them from harming her, it would put Bregovi at risk as well as her own future. They weren't ready to face him yet.

With a sickening dread, she realized the only way through was to let the men carry out their task. Drawing on those same skills that had enabled her to survive trials with her uncle time and time again, she distanced herself from the moment. Separating herself from it as if it were happening to another. She could get through it. She would survive it. Nothing they did to her mattered as long as she could control her Gifts and keep her talisman safe.

Following Bregovi's suggestion, she focused on the foul odor of sweaty men to curb her Gifts.

Three of the men held her arms and torso as a fourth brushed rough knuckles over the skin near the neckline and gripped the fabric above her breasts.

A swift yank on the material revealed the noble quality of the gown's making. It didn't budge.

The knife he wielded showed what little he thought of it.

With one swift slice, he rent the garment from breast to waist. Eagerly, the men pulled at the remnants and the damaged gown fell to the dirt at her feet.

As they groped and pawed at her through and under the thin shift, she flushed with fury and humiliation.

Bregovi launched himself from Odyssey.

Although she hadn't wanted him to resist them, she hoped with all of her being he could somehow save her from the moment to come.

He felled one of the guards with a heavy blow of the blade, then turned in a circle to face five more surrounding him. Blades clashed, blood spilled, all while the king bellowed for the prince to stand down.

Hands shaking, heart thudding erratically, it took every bit of concentration to check her Gifts.

A flash of silver caught her eye, then she felt the firm press of a blade at her throat.

"Edmund, cease your attack or she dies!" the king bellowed.

Bregovi spun to face her. He dropped his blade in an instant. One of the men snatched it up and four bloodied guards held him in check at swordpoint.

A clammy hand latched onto the front of the thin fabric and managed to take hold of a good portion of one breast. As he squeezed, she clenched her eyes shut.

When the man at her back ground his hips against her behind, she started to shake.

And when, with his hot breath against her neck, he asked if she was ready for him, the tether on her Gifts unraveled.

She wouldn't be able to do it. To hold back her powers.

In moments, the men would know the full extent of her abilities.

In moments, they would know the full magnitude of her uncle's might.

In moments, they would all be dead.

Including Bregovi.

"Leave her," Bregovi shouted. "I have it! I have it!"

All eyes turned to the prince, including hers.

To her horror, her locket dangled from his outstretched hand.

"No," she cried.

Stiles retrieved the necklace and delivered it to the king.

"Are you certain this is it?" the king asked, her talisman in his grasp.

"Yes, she has no other jewels," Bregovi said.

"Can you be sure, son? She could have something hidden under her garments."

"I've been under her garments," Bregovi said, drawing wicked laughter from the men and a biting pinch that made her jump. "On my honor, this is what you seek. Please. Let her be. There is no need for these men to abuse her."

The king studied her locket, turning it over in his gloved hand.

"Interesting design," the king said. "Looks like a map." Fixing his gaze upon her, he toyed with the item. "My son may be misguided. But from the ghostly look upon your face, I gather this is important to you."

She could only stare.

"What would you do to have it back?" the king asked.

Holy gods, what does he want? Is he bartering?

"Whatever you wish, your majesty," she said.

He nodded. "What I wish is for my son to be free from your spell. Will you grant me that?"

"He's under no spell," she said desperately. "His actions are his own."

"Ah, now you've lied," the king said, with a twisted smile. "I don't bargain with liars."

And with that, he flung the locket deep into the forest, where it landed in a dense patch of forget-me-nots.

A scream tore from her heart...and mouth. The blade at her throat kept her from running after it.

"I suppose that's confirmation enough that you valued the thing," the king said.

Bregovi's eyes were fixed in the direction of her talisman, then he found her face.

Tears of anger and loss fought for release, but she wouldn't let them go.

His fierce gaze told her to hang on. To be strong.

In short order, she was back on Flan's horse, clutching at her ruined dress.

Bregovi followed close behind, surrounded by a dozen of his own men, all guarding him as if *he* were the enemy.

On the long journey down the mountain, she thanked the gods she and Bregovi were still alive. And that she'd managed to keep her Gifts in check, even if by a hair.

Although she'd almost failed, the test had proven to her she had more control over her powers than she'd had in the past or than she thought she could. Not that she didn't feel them. Their energy hummed through her, vibrating on a powerful current of their own, begging to be set loose. But they were also separate from her somehow. Different. As if the fortnight without them had given her a new strength, a new command over them. And while she wasn't yet prepared to test the limits of that strength, she had new hope that she could manage them after all.

As Flan and a dozen guards steered her along the steps leading to the dungeons, the stench grew so pungent her eyes watered. If she needed to focus on her other senses, it certainly wouldn't be difficult.

"Hey, told you they'd get her," shouted a prisoner with eyes the color of soot.

"Not for long," said a gravely voice farther down the row.

"Who's that you say?" said another prisoner as they stopped near his cell. As he peered out the door, she recognized the spiraling tattoo on his right temple. He was one of the Zafarians captured earlier.

"Quiet!" Flan ordered. "In here," he said, motioning her into a dark room across from the tattooed man. Stepping into the small space, she kept a firm hold on the front of her gown, steering clear of a soggy mound of straw near one wall.

As if she needed confirmation she was trapped, the heavy door slammed shut behind her. Straining to peer out the small barred opening in the door, she watched the guards disappear the way they'd come.

Once again, she felt grateful the king had ordered the men to keep Bregovi back when they'd taken her below. For he'd not have stomached the scene and would have tried to do something heroic and rash. Again. And then she might be forced to do something magikal and rash.

Confident that he'd try to find a way to help her from without, Kate glanced around for anything that could aid her from within. Dirt, straw and a stone slab covered with questionable stains formed the contents of her cell. Not much to work with.

"You should have come with us," the tattooed man said. "We'd all be free now."

"You'd be free," she said. "I'd merely be prisoner to another."

"Hey, Dale, did they strip her?" asked the prisoner in the cell next to hers. She recognized the voice as Grungy Beard.

"Yeah, from the looks of her," Dale yelled back. "Dress is all torn."

"Damn, then she won't have her talisman," came a disappointed voice from the cell on her opposite side. Likely the soot-eyed man.

"Don't matter," Gravel Voice said. "She's got the Gifts, remember? She can get us all out before Frank shits again."

Even in the dim light, she could make out the men at the windows of the cells across from hers.

"You gonna save us?" Gravel Voice asked.

"How are *we* suddenly on the same side?" she asked. "You were all going to hand me over to my uncle."

"I wasn't," Grungy Beard said.

"You get me out of this hell, and you're my new Order Master," a blond Zafarian across from her said with a laugh. "I'll swear all my allegiance on this very patch of piss-rich dirt if you open this door before they burn me."

"That's treason, Sheris!" Gravel Voice boomed. "Lord Morten

will peel the skin from your flesh for blasphemy like that."

"Then he better not catch me, hmm?" Sheris said. "How about it, milady? You ready to lead us out of here?"

Unease and a strange hope prickled up her spine.

"She ain't gonna help you," Grungy Beard said.

"You just sealed the executioners warrant," Gravel Voice said.

"Or saved my skin, Kevin," Sheris rebutted. "If the rumors are half true, her powers dwarf ours. Maybe even his. And she's a hell of a lot easier to look at."

Murmurs of agreement spread among the cells and Kate marveled at how quickly her enemies were willing to flip sides. If Bregovi couldn't free her, these men were her best hope of escape. But even so, without their talismans, their usefulness would be limited.

"What Gifts do you hold?" she asked.

"Why does it matter?" Dale asked. "Yours are better."

"Lord Morten can track anyone using a Gift," she said. "He's watching, waiting, for me to use mine."

"I knew there was a reason she didn't toss us all off our mounts," Sheris said. "Didn't I tell you she wasn't using?"

"That's the solution. He'll come and free us."

"His arrival will not mean freedom for me," Kate said.

"Or me," Sheris said, likely regretting his earlier decision.

"We can't draw him here," Kate said.

"If you can't use your Gifts, how are you gonna help us?" Soot Eyes asked.

"Not so eager to follow her now, are ya? She'll get us all killed," Kevin said.

"I've spent half my life sidestepping a cunning sorcerer," she said. "All we need to do here is outsmart a couple of guards."

"We're already as good as dead," Soot Eyes said. "I'd rather throw my lot in with her than wait for the bonfire."

"What's your plan, milady?" Sheris asked.

"Tell me what each of you can do."

* * *

Bregovi went straight to Kate's bedchamber, five guards on his heels. Wisely, his father had assigned new men to him, perhaps sensing how fiercely Bregovi wanted to tear the throats out of the guards who had manhandled Kate.

Watching events unfold had been excruciating. If it hadn't been for Kate's plea not to fight them, he'd have put a sword through the first man who groped her. His gut still roiled.

And guilt and an ache he couldn't identify had tormented him since the moment his father hurled her talisman into the forest. It was his fault she'd lost it. He wasn't strong enough to watch while they tore her clothes from her. Had he to do it over, he would have handed it over before they'd shredded her gown.

Now she was in a filthy cell, barely dressed and fighting her Gifts. With no power to change her location at the moment, he would focus on her comfort. Then the talisman.

He rapped once on the door and entered, expecting the room to be empty.

It was not.

Princess Victoria stood over a large trunk, sloppily folding a gown.

"Prince Edmund," she said, eyes flickering to the guards in the doorway.

Assessing she wanted an audience less than he did, Bregovi slammed the door in the faces of the men.

"Your highness," they shouted. "We have orders!"

"Which you can follow in the corridor."

Victoria tossed stockings and a chemise into another case.

"What are you doing?" he asked.

"I'd think what I'm doing is obvious."

"Where are you going?"

"Home. To Cragmont."

"What about the competition?"

"I'll concede." She moved quickly about the room, gathering a brush, hair ties, and other feminine things.

"What about Kate?"

"I'm sure you can make use of her," Victoria said. "She may stay if she wishes to."

"If she wishes?" Bregovi said. "My father has thrown her in the dungeon."

"Mighty gods, I thought he might," she said, taking another quick look about the chamber.

"We need to help her." He lifted a forest-green gown from the trunk. The fabric was nearly as fine as the lavender gown the men had destroyed.

"That's one of mine." Victoria motioned for him to hand it back.

"Will it fit Kate?"

"Probably, but I can find something more suitable."

"This will do," he said, draping the garment over his shoulder.

"Fine, take it." She slammed a trunk closed with haste.

"You won't stay and help her?"

Without pause, she said, "Anything I do is liable to gain me residence with her."

"Why?" he asked. "Are you a sorceress?"

"No! Of course not," she said. "But she sure was. All along. And right under my nose."

"About that," Bregovi said. "I need the ingredients she was using."

Victoria stopped her mad packing and blinked at him.

"For the spell she was doing."

"I don't know anything about a spell."

"She did it nightly to help keep her uncle from finding her," he said, beginning his own search of the room. On a table near the bed, he discovered a small item, wrapped in white linen. Perhaps a bundle of the ingredients? Inside, he found the amethyst he'd given to her at the waterfall.

"She used herbs and oil," he said, swallowing the knot in his throat. "She must have stashed them here somewhere."

"If that's true, you'll have to unfurl the welcome banners. She'll not stop him now." She gestured to the hearth where flames devoured the last of a satchel. "If the king found that in here, we'd both be burned without trial."

His father wasn't nearly so barbaric, but it needn't matter. What mattered were the items.

"What were they?"

"Some herbs and such, like you said." She tossed a hairbrush atop the mound of clothes in another trunk and slammed the lid. "I advise you to forget her and take Princess Sophia. A dark moon follows Kate's family, and you'd only end up cursed like them."

"I'm afraid I can't do that."

She laughed with an unprincess-like snort. "You should be afraid. Neither her uncle nor your father will let you have her."

"Fortunately," he said with a steely resolution, "the only one who merits a say in the matter is Kate."

Victoria stopped her packing long enough to offer a sympathetic smile. "If you both survive this, I wish you much happiness."

"We will," he said, glancing to the charred satchel. "You sure you don't recall any of the items?"

"Lavender," she said. "Twigs of some sort. Salt, I think. And oil. Maybe primrose."

A rap on the door interrupted the interview.

"Not yet," Bregovi said.

"Your highness," a voice said through the wood. "The king has called for Princess Victoria's presence at the obstacle event. Yours too."

Everyone would be there. Sophia too. And he'd bet Odyssey she knew quite a bit about working spells.

"Very well," he said, throwing open the door. "But first, one of you must take this gown to Kate in the dungeons."

* * *

Bregovi and Victoria, trailed by a handful of guards, joined the king, Rachel and a host of nobles in the Royal box on the tournament field. Princess Sophia sat on the far side, not easily reachable. As he considered how to best speak to her about the spell, the crowd, numbering in the hundreds, roared from the stands as a nobleman attempted the course.

"Oh, Edmund," Rachel said, rushing over. "I'm glad you're back. Is Kate well?"

"She's fine," his father said with a pointed gaze.

"Father had her thrown in the dungeon," Bregovi said, returning the gaze, point and all.

"For what?" Rachel asked. "Surely, her poem doesn't merit imprisonment."

"We'll discuss it later," his father said. "Your Sebastian is up."

As the lord approached their box, Rachel hopped up, pulling a frilly handkerchief from her bodice.

"You're not afraid you'll throw his concentration?" Bregovi asked as she stepped to the rail.

"No, if he can save me from bandits and henchmen, he can maneuver an obstacle course." After pressing her lips to the cloth, she extended it to Sebastian.

The lord took it with a bow, smiling all the while. "If I can't win a simple event for my love, I'll not make much of a husband."

Rachel's cheeks flushed, while Sebastian remained a calm pale shade. The boy had become a man.

As Sebastian approached the starting post, someone whispered to Bregovi that no one had yet passed the course. The lord turned to Rachel, met her gaze and pressed his lips firmly to the kerchief.

Rachel drew in a quick breath. "Hurry and win me," she whispered.

As if he'd heard her, Sebastian bowed and took to his mount.

Gone were all traces of the nervous suitor. Instead, a warrior competed in his place. A skinny redheaded warrior, but skilled and agile nevertheless.

He hit the target with the precision he'd shown against the kidnappers.

He handled the plank with speed and quick reflexes, and he bested the knight, not with strength, but technique. He freed the maiden figure and carried it safely back through the course, just as he'd protected Rachel the day before.

As Sebastian jumped the final hurdle, mounted the horse and crossed the finish—the only man to accomplish the feat—the crowd roared.

Rachel ran to greet him. When she arrived in front of his horse, the lord hopped off, dropped the dummy, and swept Rachel into his arms. Spinning her around, he caught her mouth in a triumphant kiss.

The kingdom roared louder. Then Randolph announced the last competitor—Brock, who could tie the young lord with a win himself.

As Rachel and Sebastian started toward the box, the smithy rode to intercept them, dismounted in one bound and bowed gallantly. They exchanged a few words and Rachel's eyes grew wide. Sebastian shook Brock's hand, and Rachel looked between the two then launched into Brock's arms before bashfully pulling away.

The crowd held its breath, as Brock led his horse off the field waving to all.

Randolph confirmed Sebastian had taken the day and won Rachel's hand, which set off another round of raucous cheering from everyone but Bregovi. He couldn't quite manage a shout considering where Kate was.

* * *

As nobles congratulated Rachel and Sebastian, Wolfe, sweat-soaked from a hard ride, approached Bregovi on the field.

"A group of Zafarians are within your borders," Wolfe said. "They're riding for the castle. And I learned more about the sorceress they're searching for."

The last bit was spoken more softly than Wolfe's usual manner. *He knew.*

"They're after Kate," Bregovi said.

Wolfe nodded. "We knew she feared something, but I'd not have suspected Zafarians."

"The tale is not as dire as they say," Bregovi said. "Not with respect to Kate. She's in danger, though, from within and without," Bregovi said. "How much time do we have before they arrive?"

"Very little," Wolfe said.

"Get to the dungeon," Bregovi said. At Wolfe's quirked brow, Bregovi added, "Father's idea. She'll need help. Free her however you can and take her to my library."

If he had anything that could aid her, it would be there.

CHAPTER TWENTY-NINE

"Sheris, are you set with the animals?" Kate asked.

"They're ready and a wee bit eager," Sheris said, peering out from the cell across from hers.

"Make sure they know the difference between friend and foe," Kevin said.

Kate certainly hoped *she* knew the difference. These men were her best chance, but that didn't mean trust came free of doubt. She'd need to be on alert once they were out, to be sure they didn't turn on her and turn her in to Morten, to boot.

"How about you, Frank?" she asked to her left. "Did you find anyone willing to help?"

"More than we need," Frank said. "These guards ain't gonna sleep 'till winter season."

"*I* may not sleep 'till winter season," Kevin mumbled.

"Quit your whining," Grungy Beard said. "At least you'll be alive." So she hoped.

"Kevin, are you set?" she asked.

"As right as rain," he said.

"Dale?" she said.

"Aye, milady."

"Now, we just need the damned guards," Grungy Beard said.

Banging on the doors didn't draw a glance from above.

"Maybe Kate could scream," Sheris said.

She gave it a try, letting out all of the rage and hurt she'd bottled up for years.

They didn't come.

As they debated about what to try next, footsteps sounded on the stairs.

"She's on the right," a voice shouted.

To Kate's surprise, a stoic guard stopped before her door carrying one of Victoria's best gowns. The green silk one covered in beads. Completely out of place in the filthy dungeon.

"A present from the prince," the guard said.

Although the man seemed annoyed with his assignment, sweet warmth washed through Kate. Securing her release would have been best, but the thought that Bregovi cared enough to send her a gown stirred her heart.

"Stand at the back wall," the guard barked. "No quick moves or magik tricks."

"But there are *rats*," she said.

"Do it or I'll give it to my missus."

Kate positioned herself at the back wall, hoping Sheris had caught the cue.

The key clanked in the lock. A moment later, the guard pushed open the door with his foot and stood on the threshold, the beautiful gown clutched in one hand, the keys to freedom in the other.

He seemed to be considering whether or not to enter.

"May I take it from you?" she asked, inching forward.

"Hold fast there," he said, then glanced to his left. "You hear that?"

"Hear what?" she asked.

"Sounds like squealing," he said, jerking his head to his right. "Like..." His eyes drew wide. "Holy fuck. Rats!" he cried, charging into her cell.

The rodents flowed in behind him as if riding a wave to the shore. There must have been a hundred—more—frenzied and clamoring over each other to get to him, as if they were starving and he was sweet cream.

She pressed her back against the wall in an attempt to create more space between her and the creatures inching up to her feet.

Sheris had outdone himself. The rodents covered the floor and one another like a living blanket. She'd not have thought there were this many rats in the entire kingdom, let alone in the dungeons.

Looking equally unnerved, the guard began whipping the rodents with the gown. When that didn't deter them, he threw the garment over those at his feet. Perhaps to smother them. Perhaps to prevent them from climbing his legs.

Either way, it didn't work. Moving quickly, more scrambled up his body to join those already riding his arms, back and torso.

While he kicked and flailed about to shake them off, Kate waded through the tide of rodents and scooped up the gown.

Securing the keys was another matter.

The iron ring whizzed past her face when he slammed an arm into the wall. She grabbed hold and tried to wrestle the keys from his grasp.

To his credit, the man held it in a death grip as he simultaneously fought off her and the rats.

"Sheris!" she shouted. "He won't release the keys."

"How's he gonna help you?" the guard snarled.

The man must have followed Kate's gaze down to the creatures, because he hollered, "Why aren't they molesting you?"

Then, before she could respond or react, he grabbed hold of her, crushing her body against his and pinning a couple of rats between them in the process.

"Call them off," he ordered.

"Sheris," she cried, struggling to break free. "Now!"

As if they'd understood her, but most likely the result of Sheris skills, the rats paused. *In unison.* Then, in a blink, every animal on the man sunk its teeth into pants, boots and flesh.

Now screaming, the guard shoved her away, shouting, "Get them off! Get them off!"

When a thick, black rat affixed itself with teeth and claws to the man's hand, he smashed his fist against the wall to rid himself of the vermin. Both rat and keys dropped.

While the guard screamed out curses and battled the animals with a newly unsheathed blade, Kate swatted the creatures aside and snatched the ring from the floor.

Scrambling into the corridor, she yanked the door shut behind her and locked it. Rushing past rats who'd been swept from the cell in her escape, Kate quickly unlocked Sheris's cell and handed off the keys.

While he darted about freeing the others, she shed the tattered lavender dress, grateful the shift had survived. After throwing on the new gown, she tied the ribbons on one side, as guards shouted from above for their comrade.

"Make haste," Dale said, cinching the opposite tie.

Dressed for a ball, not battle, Kate ran behind him down the hall.

Joining the others, they ducked into the cell closest to the stairs leading out of the dungeon.

Heavy boots echoed on wood floorboards above, as did the unmistakable sound of sharp weaponry being readied for battle.

"They're on the steps," Dale whispered.

And no small number from the sound of it.

"Kevin, we need that mist now," Kate whispered.

The Zafarian closed his eyes and blew a slow breath. A yellow mist built and spread throughout the tight passage outside the cell.

"Are the ghosts ready?" she asked.

"And waiting for orders, milady," soot-eyed Frank said. "They're rather eager."

"Make sure they know which of us are the enemies," Grungy Beard said. "I don't want no Zafarian ghost haunting me till I'm boots up."

"Shut it," Dale said. "They're near."

Kate held her breath. The men grew still. The guards rushed past.

"What is that foul odor?" a guard asked.

"Smells like piss," another replied.

Kevin grinned beside her and whispered, "Mead is best, but any liquid will do."

Between screams, the rodent-ridden guard shouted, "They've got the keys. They're out! Keep your wits. They can command the rats!"

"And create fog," another grumbled. "The king never should have housed sorcerers."

"Check the cells," a commanding voice boomed.

"This one's empty."

"This one too."

"And locked behind them."

As the guards searched the cells, or tried to, Kate and her band crept out of their hiding place, started up the stairs...and were met by three guards with determined stances and glinting swords.

"We got 'em," one shouted.

"Anytime, Frank," Kevin said.

"On their way," Frank replied. "Best hug the walls now," he added, moving to one side.

Kate and the others followed suit as an eerie prickling sensation crept up her neck.

By the time the guards returned to the stairs below them, a crowd of translucent figures began descending from above.

Men, women and children.

Some quickly. Some calmly. All floating.

Their attire ranged from rags to finery. And more than a few carried remains of an earth-bound injury. Burns on some, a ring circling the necks of others. Victims of witch hunts.

Kate wasn't the only one quaking at the vengeful look about them.

"Holy gods, Frank," Sheris cried. "Tell them we're with you!"

The three guards on the stairs turned and battled together in a tight wall of whirling steel. But their blows passed right through the specters, only serving to make the ghosts more angry.

And their shimmering friends *were* able to move the guards. Quite literally.

One lost his blade and another his footing. As the latter tumbled head over feet down the stairs, the other two scrambled after him.

"Blessed gods, save us!" shouted a guard from below, drawing his sword.

An eerie battle ensued as guards struck out hitting one another, and ghostly figures blasted through the men, moving in from all sides.

By terror or sword, four in their midst fell within moments, and the remaining five or six hastily retreated down the corridor, trying every cell door for haven.

"Can you get them into the last one, Dale?" Kate asked.

With a nod, Dale turned and projected. Within a moment, his voice rang out from a cell far down the passage. "In here!"

The men nearly flew toward it, battling each other to get inside.

Frank snagged the keys from Sheris and darted through the ghostly army to lock them in.

The mass of dead then turned toward Kate and the others. They didn't look any more pleased than when they'd started. In fact they appeared more agitated.

Stepping forward on unsteady legs, she said, "We are grateful for your aid."

"Yes, most thankful," Dale said.

"You have my thanks too," Sheris added.

"A blessed rest to you all," Grungy Beard said.

"Blessed rest?" Kevin said.

"Do you wish them an unpleasant rest?" Grungy Beard asked.

"That's like telling them to go to their graves," Kevin said.

"They're in their graves already, you idiot," Grungy Beard said.

"You have our gratitude and good wishes," Frank said, rejoining Kate and the others. "Go and be well."

With that, all but a handful faded before their eyes. The remaining stood guard over the cells.

Armed with weapons from the fallen men, Kate and her comrades once again climbed the stairs.

"We should have sent the ghosts above, in case there are more," Kevin said.

"Let's have Sheris send the rats instead," Frank said.

All eyes turned to Sheris, who nodded.

Two moments later, they all flattened against the walls once again as a river of squealing rats flowed past them up the stairs.

"Holy gods," a strange voice exclaimed from above. "Did you all chase the guards away?"

"I think it's Wolfe," she whispered.

"Who?" Grungy Beard asked.

"Milady, Kate?" Wolfe bellowed from above. "Did you send this furry welcome party?"

"Friend or foe?" Dale asked.

"Friend," she said.

"You sure?" Kevin asked.

As they crept around a bend in the stairs, the tall figure of Wolfe blocked their path, the last few rats darting past him and on to freedom.

"Milady," Wolfe said, greeting them as if she were at a ball and not on the run in the bowels of a castle. "I was sent to secure your escape, but it appears you've managed it without me."

"Yes, but none too easily," she said. "I suppose you've learned who I am?"

He nodded. "Not much of a surprise though. I knew you were unusual," he said with a wink. Taking in the men, he said, "Whatever your plan is, you'll need to make haste. A band of Zafarians is on the hunt for you."

"How about something fresh?" Kevin said. "Every Zafarian in the kingdoms is on the hunt for her."

"This band may be different. They weren't as welcoming as others I'd met. And their leader had a dark way about him," Wolfe said. "You're in danger from this one, milady."

"Is he wide and balding, with a serpent ring?" she asked, tension coiling in her.

"No, tall and copper-headed," Wolfe said.

"Sylvan," she muttered, her mind racing for a solution.

"Lord Morten's right hand," Frank said solemnly.

"Looks like that skinning could come soon," Kevin said, smacking Sheris on the shoulder.

"No one is getting skinned," she said.

"Damn right," Dale said. "I'll be halfway to the wetlands by the time he rides through the gates."

"I'm on your heels," Grungy Beard said.

"Wait, I need your help," she said.

All but Wolfe looked at her as if she'd grown another head.

"He's going to harm the prince and his family," she said.

"They threw us in here," Kevin said. "Why would we help them?"

"Prince Edmund was trying to free me. He sent the guard with the gown, and then this man to break me out," she said with a thankful glance to Wolfe. "Please?" she said, grasping Sheris's arm. "For your new Order Master?"

Wolfe's brows inched up with that, but he kept silent.

"I heard Lord Sylvan has the gift of the wind," Sheris said.

"Not the wind," Kevin said. "He can turn to mist."

"Worse," Frank said. "He can disappear into air and slit your throat before you feel the blade."

Their gazes held pity, fear and refusal.

"It's a fool's fight, milady," Dale said. "We don't have our talismans."

"Outwitting a few guards is a lot easier than facing a demon," Grungy Beard said.

She understood their reluctance. Self-preservation was a difficult instinct to disobey. But she needed help—magikal help—and these men were all she had.

"What if we can find your talismans?" she said. "Maybe they're in the guardroom."

"I can assist with that," Wolfe said.

"Thank you," she said, nearly hugging him.

Wolfe leaned over and added in a whisper, "I'll do my best to enlist their aid."

"Thank you." She had no choice but to trust and hope he'd accomplish it. "Where will I find the prince?"

"He wants you to go to his library," Wolfe said.

"But where is *he?*" she asked.

Something passed between them. An understanding of sorts.

"On the tournament field," Wolfe said. "Luck be with you."

* * *

"Congratulations, your highness," Princess Victoria said, joining Bregovi and his family on the field. "It's a fine match."

"Thank you," Bregovi's father said. "The young lord will be excellent for the kingdom and my Rachel."

"I'm sure you'll do equally well with Prince Edmund's pairing," she said.

"I hope so," the king said, offering a close second to a smile. "I need to speak with you about your lady-in-waiting. But not here. I'd like to give Rachel her moment."

"Of course," Victoria said. "Shall I meet you inside the castle?"

His father had a reputation as a master negotiator, and Victoria's attempt to escape was easily discerned.

"No," the king said. "You need to remain with us."

As Bregovi glanced around for Sophia, he noticed odd behavior among the commoners in the stands. Instead of the excited chatter that usually followed a victory, they were murmuring and pointing at something on the far end of the field. Near the castle.

Let it be Kate.

Hopping up on a plank used in the obstacle course, Bregovi strained to see what held their interest.

The mass of royals on the grounds parted to allow more than a dozen visitors through, all on horseback and led by the copper-haired man Wolfe had described.

The royals fell back, but not far enough for Bregovi's liking. He quickly waved in the guards, who took up positions around the intruders.

Sensing the danger, Preston, Brock, and the other competitors moved in front of the maidens, hands on their swords.

"It appears we've arrived for a celebration," their leader said.

"Your name, sir?" Bregovi asked, moving between his family and the man.

"You may call me Lord Sylvan."

Bregovi's hand instinctively found the hilt of his sword. The action didn't go unnoticed.

"I see you've heard the name," Sylvan said, gripping his own blade. "All good, I'm sure."

"What is your purpose here?" the king asked.

"I'm searching for someone. She's caused a fair amount of trouble and I'm trying to collect her before she does more harm."

"Her name?" the king asked.

"Lady Katherine Durant."

Bregovi didn't miss the telling look his father shot his way.

"Father," Bregovi said in warning.

"What will you do when you find her?" the king asked.

"Why, take her home to her loving family," he said with insincere sweetness.

Bregovi wanted to send the man back to the gods. He needed to get word to Kate. To keep her away from him.

* * *

"Uncle Morten is anything but loving," Kate said, approaching. She'd not deny her heart pulsed out a warning. *Beware. Run.* But she couldn't. Instead, she tightened her grip on the dagger she'd pilfered from the dungeons.

Guards and Zafarians quickly turned and parted, giving her a clear view of Bregovi and his family mere strides from Sylvan.

She halted outside the gathering, aiming to draw Sylvan and his men in her direction.

"Lovely gown," Sylvan said.

Knowing the garment was already stained and ruined from the battle below, she said, "I wore it just for you."

Laughter came from the stands. Only then did she realize how many eyes were upon them. It appeared every soul within three kingdoms was present.

Sylvan grinned. "A grand effort."

To her dismay, Bregovi ran to her. "At least it's an improvement over the last one," he said with a wink.

"Agreed," she said. "But anything would have been an improvement."

Although the words were light, a heaviness hung in the air.

Bregovi squeezed her hand, giving her a measure of strength and, at the same time, stirring her fears.

"He isn't here?" she asked. "Morten?"

"I don't think so," Bregovi said.

"Not yet," Sylvan said, sauntering his horse in their direction. "You know he enjoys a faster means of travel."

Was he hoping to draw the man? For a moment her intuitive sense thrummed alive, begging for use, but she pushed it back, focusing on the stench from a pile of manure until the pull abated.

"So, my little pet, it looks like you've been busy winning over new friends."

Kate looked at Bregovi, the other royals, the hundreds of people watching from the stands. A handful might have Gifts, but she couldn't count on them to help her. And Sylvan and his Zafarians wouldn't hesitate to harm others if she tried to fight them.

She had one choice. To go with him and search for a way to break free once they were far from Florian.

"I'll go," she said, stepping toward Sylvan, though her stomach turned and her legs wanted to flee. "I'll return with you to Cragmont."

"No, you won't," Bregovi said, pulling his sword.

"How sweet," Sylvan said to Bregovi. "So gallant. I'm wont to agree with you, for I'm enjoying the fine hospitality here and may want to stay awhile."

"If my return is what you wish, there's no reason to involve these people," she said.

He dismounted too near for comfort, but far enough that Bregovi's sword wouldn't reach him.

Kate held her ground as Sylvan stared into her eyes and said, "It seems my wants are a mystery to you. Fortunately, yours aren't as elusive to me." An icy grin slowly appeared, sending a chill to her bones.

"You do not know my wants," she said.

"Perhaps I do. Perhaps I received more than you expected in the Binding."

Was he an empath? Had he obtained her Gifts? Her heart raced. *No, none are so cruel.* He had to be bluffing.

"If you'd received my Gifts you'd have no need to come for me."

His brows shot up.

"You are not welcome here," Bregovi said, raising his sword. "Take your men and leave."

"Not quite yet," Sylvan said. "We need to invite another guest first."

Holy gods, he did intend to draw Morten.

She grabbed Bregovi's arm. "We need to make these people leave. You must dismiss them. Lord Sylvan wants to draw my uncle. And if he does, many will perish."

"Lord Sylvan? So formal," Sylvan said. "Please call me master. No, let me rephrase that—I *command* you to call me Master."

She gasped, as did Victoria, who had not shrunk back as she should have.

"That's barbaric," Victoria said. "She isn't yours to command."

"Oh, but she is," Sylvan said. "She is mine to do anything I wish."

"Slavery is banned in our lands and my brother will have your head on a pike if you take her," Victoria said in a touching but untimely display of solidarity.

"Victoria," Kate said. "Take care."

"Yes, Victoria," Sylvan said. "Take care before I command your cousin to do something equally disturbing."

And he would.

"You must leave," Kate shouted to everyone present. "These men are Zafarians and mean to do harm."

"Stay where you are," Sylvan's voice boomed. "If anyone leaves, one of you will die."

The threat did not go unheeded as cries rang out about them.

"Please," she turned to Bregovi. "You and your family must get to safety."

"You are my family too, Kate," Bregovi said, his eyes catching hers.

If her heart weren't so terrified, it would have melted at the declaration.

"I'm not leaving. Our guards outnumber them three to one."

"But they're *Zafarians*," she said in frustration.

The chatter in the crowd grew louder.

"We conquered the band in the woods didn't we?" Bregovi said.

"They were second or third level at the most. These are Morten's best men!"

She turned to Victoria and the royals lurking nearby. "Lord S—" her tongue stopped short, and she nearly growled as her mouth said, "*Master* can make himself invisible before your eyes. Stand back. Protect yourselves."

"Why warn them to run from me, when *your* Gifts are the greater threat?" Sylvan said.

A sick dread crept through her. He was going to force her to use her Gifts to draw Morten. Likely so the man would help him consummate the ritual.

"You must go now," she cried out again. "All of you."

"Now why do you keep insisting that they leave our delightful party, when I've told you that would displease me?"

Turning to Bregovi, she said, "This is what I dreamed. He'll harm your family. He'll kill you. You won't have a chance."

As royals shifted nervously, a commotion started in the stands. Some had decided to heed her warning, while others tried to prevent them from going.

The king pulled a dagger from his boot and stepped in front of Rachel. Sebastian readied an arrow and moved in front of both of them.

"You've been dreaming about me?" Sylvan said on a whisper. "How romantic."

Then he vanished.

Screams echoed from everywhere.

Sylvan appeared next to the king, holding a knife to the monarch's throat. Rachel cried out, stumbling back as a guard crept up from behind.

Bregovi grabbed Kate's dagger and threw it fast and hard. But Sylvan disappeared again, and it found the guard's shoulder instead.

As he'd done the day of the Binding, Sylvan began flitting about invisibly, taunting them. He flicked Rachel's hair, tousled Victoria's skirts, spun Sophia in a circle, then knocked off the king's crown.

"What will it be, Kate?" Sylvan said in her ear. "A summons from you or the life of one of your new friends," he continued from across the field.

He appeared beside Brock, cutting the smithy's sword belt. Then in front of Preston, striking a heavy blow to the lord's blade before disappearing again.

Each time he grew more forceful. More daring.

Soon, someone would fall.

As the castle staff hurried from the stands, Sylvan grabbed one of the maids. Flora.

Sylvan's long fingers wrapped around her neck to anchor her in place while he dragged the tip of his dagger from her throat to her breast.

Flora whimpered, hands clenched at her sides.

"Don't move now, dear, or I'm liable to knick you," he said. Sliding the blade across her bodice. "So lovely, isn't she Kate?"

Raw hate coursed through Kate. How could anyone use others so mercilessly? She was torn between needing to help the girl and knowing more would die if Morten came.

As he drew the blade back and forth over the girl's breast, Flora began weeping.

It was time to take a stand. Kate looked around for another weapon.

Bregovi shouted, "Only a coward would harm an unarmed woman."

"And what is your view of a woman who would harm a host of unarmed spectators?" Sylvan asked.

"No!" Kate cried.

Sylvan disappeared, leaving Flora stunned and alone.

He reappeared next to Kate. "If you won't dazzle us voluntarily, I'll have to be more direct." Before she could blink, he added, "I *command you* to destroy the commoner stands. Collapse all of it to the ground. *Now.*"

"Run!" Kate screamed as her arm came up of its own accord and, with one sweeping motion, brought the massive structure to the dirt—with everyone on it.

"Holy mother," Bregovi whispered nearby.

Moans and cries assaulted her ears, but she couldn't focus on that now. Morten would arrive soon.

With no reason to hold back any longer, she summoned a blade from one of the Zafarians. It flew to her with ease.

Another wave of her arm sent each sorcerer flying from his horse, landing yards away in the grass. The Florian Guard, Brock, Preston and the others charged toward them, with Wolfe and her dungeon crew coming up from the rear.

Bregovi's astonished gaze held hers a moment, before she twirled around, sensing Sylvan.

The lord whispered in her ear, "Well done, Kate. Our guest should be here soon. How about another trick while we wait?"

She spun, striking the air and heard a grunt when she hit her mark.

"Where are you?" Bregovi asked, sword at the ready. "I challenge you to appear and fight with honor."

"No, no, you can't," Kate said.

"Honor?" Sylvan said from nowhere and everywhere. "How quaint."

"Master, please take me and leave them. As you said, Morten is coming. You've got your wish. There's no further reason to harm them."

"But my dear," Sylvan said, materializing. "I've been challenged."

And in a breath, he thrust a dagger into Bregovi's stomach.

CHAPTER THIRTY

Kate screamed. Bregovi staggered.

Sylvan pulled the bloody knife out and went for another strike, but she summoned the blade and sent it flying from Sylvan's hand in an instant.

Bregovi managed a strong blow with his sword, cutting a gash in Sylvan's arm before the sorcerer vanished again.

Spinning around, Kate tried to sense him, grasping for a way to stop him.

The moment she anchored onto his presence, he reappeared again inches in front of Bregovi. And before either she or the prince could react, Sylvan plunged a dagger into Bregovi's heart.

As he pulled out the knife, Bregovi collapsed to the dirt.

She couldn't catch her breath. Or her thoughts.

"What a heroic beau." Sylvan chuckled. "Shall we check on him," he said, bending toward Bregovi. "He might be breathing, yet."

"Get away from him," she shouted and, with a jerk of her arm, sent him flying thirty strides across the field.

Screams echoed about them and she didn't know if they were at him or her.

Growling, he charged back toward her.

Quickly, she summoned open the door to the gardener's hut and gestured again, sending him air bound another twenty strides and into the shack. The door slammed behind him. One more flick sent debris from the stands flying, pinning a pile of it against the door.

It all happened in seconds, but took much too long.

Bregovi was dying.

She dropped to her knees. Blood oozed from his chest and belly. He wasn't breathing.

Fear choked her as she pulled up his shirt and pressed her shaky hands to his wounds, one on each.

Closing her eyes, she drew in energy from the universe, then poured it all into him. Opening herself, she reached out, reached in. Some of his wounds were healing, but not all. Not enough.

Her father's words of warning echoed in her ears. She would be too weak. She might not recover. But if her life was the price to save his...

As the healing energy continued to pass through her into him, she added her own life force, pushing it through her trembling hands to where it was needed. And as it did so, she reached out for his injuries, seeking to draw their essence away from him and into herself. The second her soul connected with the raw wounds, crippling pain rocked her and a cry tore from her throat.

Then she felt more than the pain. It was the first time she'd sensed him—his goodness, his desire to help his people, his deep bond with his family, and his heartache over his mother's death.

She also felt the love. His love for *her*. Deep and powerful.

As his body healed, her strength waned, as she knew it would. They had only moments before Sylvan was free and Morten arrived. Moments before they would kill her or take her from him.

She needed him to know how much she loved him.

So, as the last of the healing took hold, she reached out to his soul. And somewhere across the chasm she saw him in her mind.

His wounds had healed.

Whole again, he stood surrounded by a silvery mist. She called to him and he turned toward her. She sensed others nearby, but the mist hid them from her view. She tried to reach him, but couldn't move. So she willed her soul to go to him instead, and somehow, without words, she communicated what was in her heart.

"Bregovi, I love you. More than I've ever loved anyone. More than I knew I could. I wish I could spend lifetimes with you, sharing your adventures, your dreams, your love... I give you my heart and soul and all that I am. Regardless of where I go, I am yours 'till the end of the stars."

The mist swirled about him and she began to withdraw, but something caught her.

The haze drifted away to reveal Bregovi holding tight to her hand.

They stood atop a cliff with the ocean stretching to the horizon and raven-haired, gray-eyed people gathered around.

His green eyes sparkled inches from hers.

"Thank you, Kate." He took her other hand in his. "I love you too. Deeper than all the oceans, greater than any treasure and more than my life. You are my ultimate adventure. My heart and soul and life are yours. Forever."

He leaned forward, and when their lips met, fire burned through her to her soul.

* * *

Body aching from the blow to the wall, Sylvan pulled himself to his feet and rushed to the door. Kate had slammed it shut...from more than 50 paces. *Unbelievable.* And from the clatter outside, she'd piled a mountain of wood against the exit.

Spinning about, he discovered no other means of escape. But he did find an ax. Unfortunately, the oak door held strong despite the chunks he removed.

"Surround it!" came an order from without.

Would they burn the hut? Him? A sickening dread coiled in his gut. If he failed, Viridia was lost.

Quickly, he shifted to his invisible form. He'd seen her in the crowd. And knowing her, she was still there.

"Elliana!"

She made him wait.

"I know you're here," he said more quietly.

Stony silence.

"Elliana, they will kill me if you don't help. I need you."

She appeared then, passing through the wall as if it were air, her amethyst eyes slanted in disapproval. "You injured that man."

"It was necessary," he said.

"He may die," she said, sounding more defeated than angry.

"He won't. She loves him."

"One more reason why you shouldn't have—"

"She's an empath," he said. "She will heal him. We *need* her to heal him."

"That's why you did it?" Elliana asked. "So she'd help him?"

"Yes," he said. "We need her weakened when Morten arrives."

Elliana paused. Hesitated. Brows bent, lips tight. Something was wrong.

"What is it?" he asked.

"See with your mind, reason with your eyes," she said in that infuriating manner of her people.

Oh, how he wished he could rewrite the treaty between fae and men.

"That makes no sense. Speak plainly!"

Instead of answering, she rested a hand upon the door and began chanting so forcefully the ground trembled.

* * *

Bregovi opened his eyes to find Wolfe's falcon dancing on invisible currents overhead. He'd had the most unusual dream of he and Kate atop a cliff.

As he grasped for the details, he heard shouting and a steady banging. And he remembered.

He had been stabbed.

He should be dead.

Instead, he was moving and breathing, albeit with a heavy weight upon his chest.

A glance down revealed the reason. Kate lay draped over him, her hands bloody, her body limp.

Panic coursed through him as he sat up, gathering her into his arms. "Kate? Kate, are you hurt?"

As his father barked orders and guards corralled Sylvan's men, Bregovi frantically searched for a wound upon her. A gash on her palm was all he could find. Strangely, at seeing it, his palm burned too.

Then he felt her gentle breath on his neck.

He choked on relief. She was alive.

He pulled at his shirt to tear a strip to bind her hand and discovered that although the fabric was ripped and blood-stained, his wounds were gone. *Unbelievable. Could she have?*

A steady chanting—a woman's voice—grew louder from the gardener's hut as guards fanned out, swords at the ready.

Within seconds the door burst from its hinges, sending planks flying as if from a catapult. Men were either knocked out of the way or dove for cover as debris sailed straight for Bregovi.

With no time to move Kate, he threw up an arm to shield her and watched incredulous as the wood ricocheted off nothing and landed in a heap.

He caught sight of his father then, across the field, staring on dumbfounded.

Scooping her up to take her to safety, Bregovi wondered if she could wield her powers even in her state.

As Bregovi raced for the castle, Sylvan materialized in front of them. "Where are you going with my genie?" the man said, drawing a blade.

Bregovi took a step back, considering his options as his father charged toward them, sword drawn, followed by Wolfe.

"She'll not be going with you," Bregovi said.

Roaring like a child who hadn't gotten his way, Sylvan's eyes fixed on Kate. More specifically on the blood dripping from her hand. Then he brought up his own hand, which showed a matching wound.

"Impossible!" Sylvan growled. "It's unbreakable."

In an instant, he vanished again. As all spun to beware of his reappearance, one of the Zafarian steeds reared up and charged toward the forest, its reins suspended in air.

Clutching Kate tighter, Bregovi continued his race for the castle. He needed to take her somewhere safe. If she was correct, her uncle would be on their heels soon, and she was in no state to face him.

As he entered the main hall, screams drew his attention to the field. Glancing back, he saw a green mist enveloping the area where Kate had healed him.

Morten.

She finally stirred in his arms as he rushed her to his library.

"Kate?"

Her eyes drooped with fatigue. "Bregovi," she whispered. "Your wounds?"

"Gone," he said as she shut her eyes again. "Did you heal me? Are you like this because you healed me?"

"Yes."

Her eyes opened again and the love he saw there humbled him. She had saved him. Knowing the danger it put her in, she had weakened herself to this state for him.

An echo of words they had shared in his dream flitted through his mind.

"Sylvan?"

"I think he's gone."

"Dead?" another whisper.

"No, he rode off," he said, taking another corridor.

"Can't feel him," she whispered. "He's gone."

"Yes," he reassured.

He wished he knew what she needed. He felt helpless as to how to help her. *What does one do to aid a telekinetic empath?*

I need to rest. But Morten is coming. I must prepare.

"The guards will delay him."

As he took a flight of stairs, a strange prickling sensation crept up his back. He looked down at Kate to find her staring up at him in amazement.

She had responded to a question he had not uttered, and although he had heard her, she had not spoken aloud either.

Is it possible? Her mind whispered to his. *Can you hear me?*

He thought the answer in his heart. *Yes, but how can I? You're not speaking?*

She shook her head, *I don't know.*

She gasped and clutched at him. "Morten. He's here."

"Yes. Outside."

Then he heard her in his mind again. *He will kill you for helping me. Leave me. Go.*

I'm not that easy to kill.

Yes, you are, and I can't heal you like this.

I won't leave you.

You must.

Make me. He knew she couldn't, so he grinned to himself despite their circumstances.

An irritated groan escaped her lips.

* * *

As Bregovi carried Kate through his family wing, she tried to make sense of why they could hear each other's thoughts. She had never been able to do that, even after healing, but he had been closer to death than most. Perhaps it was a residual effect of how deep she had gone to heal him. She hoped it would last until her strength came back. She needed to help him fight Morten, and she certainly couldn't do it physically.

"Bluebell?" Morten's taunting voice echoed through the castle as if they were playing hide and seek. "I knew you couldn't hold out forever."

"Bluebell?" Bregovi said.

My cat. A long time ago. He calls me that to remind me of what he did to her.

Glancing back, she tried willing tables to topple and chairs to move, but they only wobbled in place.

Holy mother of the gods, how will we ever fight him? she thought, resting her head against Bregovi's shoulder.

"We'll find a way," he said as they arrived at the library.

He moved quickly to lay her on a cushioned bench far from the main door.

No. In an armchair. He can't know how weak I am.

Bregovi did as she said, then wrapped her cut hand with a clean handkerchief. She hadn't noticed the wound and recognized it from the Binding. She wanted to ask if Sylvan's hand had been bleeding as well, but Bregovi was busy sliding a heavy oak table against the door. She needed to focus on Morten first.

We'll need to use the Zafarian objects.

"I was hoping that might be the case," he said. "Sophia told me they had purposes."

Did she teach you how to use them too?

He chuckled, probably sensing the annoyance behind the question.

"No," he whispered, then brushed a gentle kiss over her lips. "I saved that for you."

Then he was gone again, darting about, gathering up the objects. And as he did so, she felt a surge of power in the room and, strangely, within her.

As Bregovi looked her way, she felt his recognition of it too.

Then she knew. Old Quent was right. Bregovi did have a Gift. It was why he was drawn to the objects and why he had felt their energy, even with his abilities dormant.

He quickly laid items in her lap, his eyes asking a million questions.

Next, he retrieved a Zafarian sword from the wall and unsheathed it. The blade turned from silver to gold and back again before her eyes. He glanced at her as if to ask if she had seen it, then handed it to her and moved to relocate Galileo's case to a shelf.

Turning the weapon in her hands, it glowed once again. If her recollection was sound, she was holding the Sword of Surety, a blade that could fell anything it struck.

"I have a lot more in here." He flipped open the trunk the turtle had been resting upon. "I had a difficult time resisting them," he added sheepishly.

As he slid the chest over to her, her heart thudded with the magnitude of it.

Knives. Daggers. Platters. Goblets and rings. An iridescent fabric—the Cloak of Comfort—if her memory served. A shield. Even an Order Master's scepter, although the post was broken. Morten would be invincible with the cache of items Bregovi had collected.

Then her eye caught on a dome of glass and its base. *Do you have the candle too?*

"Yes," he said, pulling out a thick black candle. "Do you know how to use them?"

"Some," she whispered.

"Tell me. Tell me what to do."

"Bluebell?" came her uncle's amused voice from the corridor. "You know you can't hide from me."

Childhood memories flooded her mind. Years spent hiding, always ending with him discovering her and punishing her for a misdeed, or forcing her to heal some animal or Zafarian he had maimed. Shutting her eyes to block it out, she willed herself to be strong. To have courage.

Bregovi took her hands in his, and she opened her eyes to discover him kneeling before her.

"He won't hurt you anymore, Kate. You *are* strong. You *are* courageous. It is time we defeat him. Together."

In all her years, no one had ever stood with her to face the man. And while she wasn't naïve enough to think the encounter would go well, Bregovi's conviction strengthened her like nothing ever had.

The door began to tremble as Morten chanted a spell outside.

Light the candle.

Bregovi hopped up and immediately dipped the wick to the fire in the hearth and returned, shielding it to keep the flame going.

Put it under the glass.

"It'll go out."

Not this one. It'll protect us, but you have to chant the spell.

"But I don't have a talisman," he said. "It won't work."

You don't need a talisman. You have the Gift to work magikal objects.

"You sure that's not wishful thinking?" he asked, setting the candle in the holder with the dome atop.

"We'll soon find out," she whispered.

But before she could give Bregovi the words, the door shook violently and vanished.

On the other side of the thick table, Morten stood balding, broad-shouldered and bemused.

"A table? How primitive," he said, his manner cheery. With another slew of words, it slid out of his path as if a gentle wind blew it away as easily as a pile of leaves. "My dear, you're looking well."

Before he noticed how unwell she truly was, he took in the Zafarian items in her lap and around the room. Recognition lit up his face brighter than she'd ever seen it.

"My, my, but I feel like I've stumbled upon a treasure cave."

The sword. You will destroy whatever you strike.

Bregovi snatched up the sword, and Morten took a step back, respect hitting his eyes. "I see you have some interesting toys, young man, but do you know what to do with them?"

"You are not welcome here," Bregovi said, raising the weapon.

"Really now," he said in his usual genial tone. "You're actually threatening me?"

Be careful.

"It is time for you to leave her life, either by your own doing or mine. It is your choice."

"But she is my dear niece. How can I let her go? I would miss her desperately." He took a step to Bregovi's right, as if to circle around.

Her heart skipped, but Bregovi saw the move and blocked his way.

"Come, boy, are you going to strike me or merely stand there?" Morten said.

It was too easy. Bregovi raised his arm to swing and she thought, *No!* He tried to pull back, but it was too late. Her uncle had uttered a few quick words—a defense spell—and as Bregovi brought the sword forward, it flew from his hands landing with a clatter near the windows.

The shield!

Bregovi quickly retrieved it from the chest as Morten scrambled for the sword.

Bregovi. He can't get the sword.

The prince lunged for it, reaching, but not close enough.

Suddenly, the sword flew to him, landing solidly in his hand.

"Did you do that, Kate?" Bregovi shouted.

No. She couldn't believe it. She hadn't. *Could it be the sword's power?*

"No?" Bregovi said.

Morten arose, his face red with rage. "You aren't telekinetic?" he asked in an icy tone.

Try to move something else. Will it with your mind.

A second later, Morten lay sprawled on his back along with toppled furniture, for the carpet under his feet had whipped out from under him of its own accord.

"Did you lay with him?" Morten growled as he pulled himself up, his gaze piercing.

She tried to sit tall but failed. He missed nothing.

"Why are you so still, Bluebell?" His cunning gaze roamed over Bregovi, lingering on his torn and bloodied shirt. "Ah. I see Lord Sylvan was here."

"Yes, and he has fled," Bregovi said. "You should join him while you are still able."

Morten ignored him, his focus on her. "You know you will return with me. Now shall we leave your young man breathing or in the grave?"

They had to defeat him, but she couldn't think how, and she hated being so weak when Bregovi needed her. She realized she was more terrified for him than she'd been in all the years she had faced Morten on her own. Her uncle could kill him, and she wouldn't be able to do a thing to stop him.

I'm not going to die at the hand of this man. Not after all you went through to heal me.

She sucked in a breath when Morten moved toward her.

Bregovi threw the sword behind her and, with his free hand, gestured a blow toward Morten that sent the man flying across the room, toppling the globe mid-way to the far wall.

You learn fast.

Bregovi rushed to her, grabbing her hands and dropping to his knees before her. "Quickly, Kate, I need to know what these objects can do. You need to tell me as much as you can."

She had never communicated with anyone telepathically before and wondered if she could pour into him her knowledge the same way she had poured in her energy.

As Morten righted himself across the room, she quickly squeezed

Bregovi's hands and closed her eyes.

She let all she had studied about the Zafarians come to the forefront, calling it forth from her memory.

Then she pushed it all into Bregovi.

When she opened her eyes seconds later, Morten was halfway across the room chanting a spell.

Bregovi snatched from the trunk a rope with a heavy dark crystal anchored to one end. Spinning it overhead, he chanted a verse of his own and let it fly toward her uncle.

The rope twined around the man like a vine and spun him like a top.

Shouting in anger, Morten crashed into a display case, sending goblets and figures to the floor.

With a few snarled words from Morten, the rope loosened and fell to his feet in cinders.

"It appears you do have some skill with your trinkets," Morten said. "It's unfortunate that it won't be enough."

Kate needed to gain strength or she'd be of no use. She recalled something she'd seen in the display case. A griffin carved from malachite, a Zafarian crest on its flank.

As her talisman was malachite, she wondered if the figure could provide extra healing and strength. And the griffin was one of the most powerful symbols. Perhaps…

I need the malachite griffin.

Without questioning why, Bregovi snatched it up and set it in her hand, then looked for something else he could use against the man.

"I hope you don't intend to test out all of your toys today," Morten said. "It could get quite tedious."

"Only for you," Bregovi replied.

Morten's face grew ruddy as he clutched his serpent ring and growled out another curse.

With a swift wave of Bregovi's arm, Morten lost his footing and his place in the verse as he crashed into the back wall, taking three shelves of books to the floor.

He lay motionless, but his fury crackled in the room like lightning.

We need to bind him, Bregovi thought.

I know, she thought back, as she clutched at the tiny griffin. Pulses of energy seemed to flow into her from the object, and she hoped it would be enough—and in time to help.

Throwing open another trunk, Bregovi quickly shifted items and pulled out a gruesome set of shackles. Four Zafarian-crested cuffs linked by chains. With a fleeting glance at Kate, he carefully approached the sorcerer.

Kate held her breath as Bregovi leaned over to cuff one of Morten's ankles. In a moment, that breath came out as a scream when the sorcerer twisted and latched onto Bregovi's wrist.

"Watch out!" she cried. "The ring."

But it was too late. The silver serpent coiled and sunk its fangs into Bregovi's hand.

The prince broke free, looking incredulous as the snake reverted back into a ring again.

As Morten pulled himself off the floor, a black streak began slithering under the skin of Bregovi's hand. She'd seen the work of the snake before. If the creature reached his heart...

It isn't going to, Bregovi thought, holding a tight grip on his arm above the dark mark. *It's a magikal object, isn't it? Can't I control it?*

I don't know, she thought. *I've never seen anyone survive it.*

Then she caught the words Morten was spewing at Bregovi. The blood curse. Terror rippled to her bones. If she didn't stop the man, Bregovi would turn to dust.

Kate fumbled through the items in her lap for the Mirror of Regret, the only object that could reverse his spell. She launched herself between the two men. Holding up the mirror with the quartz points facing her uncle, she chanted the counter spell as fast as her tongue would go.

Morten's eyes drew wide in recognition, but he didn't falter.

Rather than cease the spell to save himself, his voice grew louder, more menacing.

Perhaps Morten didn't think she could wield the object. She was slightly unsure herself.

Without a talisman, the spell could only work for one with the Gift—Bregovi's Gift. But she'd felt the raw energy of the objects since they'd entered the room and prayed to all the gods she'd gained Bregovi's ability as he had hers.

If she hadn't…they'd next meet in the ether realm.

As she and Morten each raced to complete their spells, the globe popped out of its stand, bounced once, then barreled toward Morten's feet.

Her uncle dodged it, exuding rage so raw, the emotion pushed her back several paces and into Bregovi's solid form.

"Whoa, now that's anger," he said, releasing the hold on his arm to rest his hands on her shoulders.

She wanted to tell him not to, to look after himself, but Morten was nearing the end of the curse, and if she didn't complete her spell before him, the snake wouldn't matter.

As she clutched at the mirror, struggling to finish the chant, Bregovi's strength poured into her through his hands.

"You can do it, Kate."

Her tongue flew over the final few words of the counter curse.

Morten's eyes narrowed as he finished a second after her.

The mirror surged, sending a jolt of energy through her body and out her feet. She dropped the griffin and brought up the other hand to steady the mirror as the crystals began to glow.

Morten extended a claw-shaped hand, chanting a spell to summon it from her.

The mirror only glowed brighter—a brilliant orb of white light forming on its surface.

Then Morten dove for her. For the mirror. Probably for his life.

Bregovi pulled her away as the orb flew from the mirror and

dissolved into Morten's chest.

With a roar that shook the room, the sorcerer collapsed to the floor.

Writhing, Morten gritted out another spell, but it was pointless, for there was no cure for the curse he had cast.

Her uncle grew eerily still. Then, laying on the carpet, surrounded by broken furniture and Zafarian treasures, the man who had tormented her half her life turned to a heap of black dust.

"Look." Bregovi held out his arm as the serpent under his skin dissolved, leaving behind a puff of green smoke.

Overwhelmed by relief, joy and exhaustion, Kate spiraled into darkness.

CHAPTER THIRTY-ONE

Bregovi's triumph at defeating Morten evaporated the moment Kate collapsed in his arms.

Lowering her to the carpet, he quickly checked for injuries and found none.

He tried gently shaking her to rouse her. She didn't stir.

Attempts to communicate with her telepathically proved futile.

If she was breathing, it was so faint, he couldn't detect it.

Fear coiled in his throat. He couldn't lose her now.

"Do not leave me, Kate," he choked out as he pressed his ear to her chest.

Finally, hope. The slow, weak beat of her heart whispered she was alive.

As he stood, carefully lifting her from the floor, Wolfe, Rachel and Sebastian rushed across the threshold.

"Edmund," Rachel said, running to him. "We've been searching for you everywhere."

"They're here!" Wolfe shouted out the door.

"Where's the sorcerer?" Sebastian asked.

"Dead," Bregovi said.

"And Kate," Wolfe said. "Is she...?"

"She's alive," Bregovi said. "But I can't tell much else." The falter in his voice gave away what he couldn't admit.

"She'll be all right," Wolfe said, meeting his eye. "She's a strong little witch. She's not going to let you get away now."

He hoped to all the gods Wolfe was right.

His father, Brock and Victoria were next to join the gathering, all with weapons at the ready.

The princess froze and her face blanched when she saw them.

As Brock threw an arm around Victoria, who looked ready to faint, Rachel took the princess's hand and said, "She lives."

His father dropped his sword and wrapped Bregovi—still holding Kate—in a tight embrace.

"I thought I'd lost you," his father said with misty eyes. "He *stabbed* you."

"I know. I would have died if Kate hadn't—" Bregovi's voice cracked with the weight of it.

"She healed you." His father looked at Kate's still form. "She put her hands on you and then you were whole again."

"Yes," Bregovi said. "Now I need to figure out how to heal *her*."

"We will," his father said, his gaze combing the room.

"Is he gone?" Victoria asked.

"Yes," Bregovi said, nodding to Morten's remains. "Turned to dust, exactly like the tales of Zafaria."

"Holy Heaven," Rachel whispered.

"One of the men outside told us he was the Order Master," Sebastian said.

"He spoke the truth," Bregovi said. "She'd been hiding from him."

His father dragged a hand through his graying hair. "Sorcery. Healings. An *Order Master*. In my own castle." He lifted the Zafarian sword from the floor. "Unbelievable."

"It looks like you fought a war in here," Wolfe said, his gaze roaming over the destroyed library.

"We did." Bregovi glanced at Kate's face.

Stepping past the lot of them, Bregovi headed out the door with the only treasure that mattered.

"Where are you taking her?" Rachel asked.

"Where she'll be more comfortable," Bregovi said. "*Not* the dungeon," he said with a pointed glance back at his father.

"If she'd told us the truth..." his father blustered. "Earlier..."

Rachel, Victoria and the men trailed Bregovi into his chamber. His sister pulled back the coverings as he laid Kate on the bed, gingerly placing her head upon a pillow. She didn't stir. Her dark lashes rested upon her cheeks, and he felt as helpless as a child.

As his mind scrambled for a way to help her—to heal her—memories rushed forward. *Her* memories. Of healings. Tiny creatures. A rabbit. A gull on the shore with a broken wing. And Bluebell. Her cat. His stomach turned as he remembered Morten gutting her pet in front of her as punishment for an attempted escape. Her efforts to heal it proved futile.

Then he remembered another she couldn't save. Her mother. He felt her despair and guilt as a nine-year-old Kate had tried desperately to heal her. His heart broke with hers.

And with the healings also came the memories of their aftermath. His were the largest wounds she had healed, and she had poured her own energy into him as well. She should have rested afterward, but because they'd had to fight Morten, she had weakened her strength even further.

No wonder she had collapsed.

He leaned in close, brought his lips to her ear and whispered, "Kate, you need to stay. You need to get well. We have a lot of adventures ahead of us, you and I...sailing the seas, leaping through portals, making love..." His voice caught on the word. Then he pressed a soft kiss to her lips.

"What can we do to help?" Sebastian asked with Rachel's hand clutched tight in his.

"Find Old Quent," Bregovi said. "Tell him to bring his books."

"We will," Rachel said as they rushed from the room.

"What can I do?" Victoria asked.

"Can you find Princess Sophia?" he asked. "I think she might be of some help."

"I think you might be right," she said, and in a swirl of silk, she was off.

"Wolfe."

"What do you need?" Wolfe asked, meeting his eye.

"Her talisman," Bregovi said. "It's in the woods."

His father stiffened, then grew ruddy in the face. "I know where to find it."

Wolfe's brows rose, then he swiftly bowed to the king before they departed.

Brock was the last man standing. At least in the room.

"Will you stay with her while I get some things from my library?" Bregovi asked.

"Of course," Brock said with a tilt of his head. "She's a strong soul, your grace. She'll be awake and wrapping us all around her fingers again soon. You'll see."

A strange warmth crept through Bregovi, certainly not a knowing conviction, but a gentle hope. "Thank you."

And as he rushed off to gather his books and any Zafarian object that might help, he heard Brock say, "Now that you found him, you need to get well so I can dance at your wedding."

"Amen," Bregovi whispered as he ran faster down the corridor.

* * *

Kate awoke in a strange bedchamber with rose patterns carved in the ceiling. Light snuck around curtains, and candles of red, green and lavender flickered throughout the room, along with the black order candle on a bedside table.

Perched on a chair, a bearded and disheveled Bregovi was

engrossed in a book laying open on the bed, Kate's hand tucked in his.

As he turned the page, she recognized it as the volume on Caligo—her mother's people. Then she recognized other things too, objects covering the bed...covering her—amethysts and rubies, violets and buttercups lay atop her in an odd pattern. Like a star.

Or a pentacle...

Once, when Kate had drained her energy healing three kittens trampled in the stables, her mother had done the same with flowers and a salt ring around the bed. The combination had restored her. But no one knew the old ways.

Then cold realization struck her, while they may not know the traditions of her mother's people, everyone now knew what she could do.

She'd demonstrated her Gifts before people from all the kingdoms.

Sorcerers had burned for mere rumors; there'd be no chance to deny what she'd done.

But Bregovi had also wielded a telekinetic power. Or had he? Had it all been a dream?

With a trembling grip, she gently squeezed his hand. His head jerked up and sweet relief gazed back at her.

"Hello," she whispered.

"Hello," he whispered back. "I missed you." He pressed his lips to her fingers.

Emotion swelled in her throat.

"Be right back." He bolted for the door, opened it and tripped over Holly, who sprang from a chair outside. "Kate's awake and needs a meal, can you—"

"Thank the gods. Yes, your grace," she said, rushing away.

As Kate sat up, dislodging flowers, crystals and the malachite griffin tucked at her side, she discovered she was blanketed by the shimmering cloak from the library.

"The Cloak of Comfort?" she asked.

"It's spelled to provide whatever the bearer needs," he said, taking her hand again.

"Amazing." She brushed a hand over the cool fabric.

"I thought about wearing it myself, thinking it would provide me with you," he said, his gaze steady.

"You could have climbed under it with me," she said, grinning through the lump in her throat.

"I thought about it."

"How did you know about the rest of this?" She gestured to the flowers, candles, and crystals, before catching sight of a huge ring of salt and shells around the bed. "It looks as if you resurrected every remedy known to charge, shield and protect energy."

"Your years of study came in handy," he said. "Of course, I also pulled ideas from Old Quent and Sophia."

"Sophia?" she said, suddenly irked. "And what did she require for payment?"

"Nothing," he said with a chuckle. "I suspect she wanted to garner good favor."

"I've no doubt she wanted to garner your favor."

He caught her grumpy mouth in a savory kiss.

When they came up for air, she whispered, "Did we really do it? Is Morten gone?"

"Dust," he said.

"And Sylvan?"

"We haven't seen him."

"He'll be back for me," she said, fear rising all over again. "I need to leave Florian. He'll—"

"First of all, you aren't going anywhere," he said. "At least not without me. And second, Old Quent has some theories about the genie binding."

As Bregovi unwound a bandage on her right hand, a nervous anticipation began to build in her. She'd forgotten about the new wound.

"Lord Sylvan was upset about this cut and had a matching gash of his own. Quent says if the wounds inflicted in the Binding reappear, then the spell is dissolved."

The last of the bandage fell away to reveal a nasty slice across her palm. It had begun to heal, but there was no mistaking the gash Morten had inflicted.

Her heart leapt around in her chest as Bregovi carefully rewrapped her hand. Could she really be free? Then she remembered bringing down the spectator's stands…with everyone on them.

"What about my Gifts?" she said, trying to scoot off the bed. "Holy gods, all of those people fell. They were hurt."

Blocking her way, he sat on the bed linens to keep her still.

"Just scrapes and bruises. No one perished."

"But the whole kingdom saw me do it!"

"They also saw you fight the Zafarians and save me."

"Your father—"

"He's gaining a new understanding about Gifts and sorcery."

He reached toward a water goblet that flew to his outstretched hand. Wiping away a bit that had splashed on his breeches, he handed the glass to her.

"So, I didn't dream that part either," she said.

"Thankfully, no."

"And I received your Gift too, didn't I?" she said, glancing to the Zafarian candle. "How did that happen? My parents acquired each other's Gifts after they married, but we haven't."

He nodded. "Well, I've had some time to ponder this and I think it had something to do with you healing me. Your hand was cut when I awoke and that's when I noticed strange things happening. And we were able to hear each other's thoughts."

"Can you still hear them?"

"I haven't been able to hear you since Morten died. It's been highly unnerving."

"I'm sorry."

"Can you still hear mine?" he asked.

"No, what are you thinking?"

His gaze grew sizzling. "I'm thinking I'd like to spend my life trying to read your mind," he said. "When you were healing me, I had a dream. You came to me on a clifftop. You told me you loved me. You gave yourself to me."

As he spoke, a hazy image came to mind. A memory of her own.

"And then you started to leave me and it felt like someone was ripping out my heart," he said.

"I remember," she said. "You called me back."

His eyes drew wide and something passed between them. She couldn't read his thoughts, but she could feel his love, and she knew he could sense hers as well.

"You said the most beautiful things," she said.

"I meant them. You have captured my heart." Taking her hand, he knelt by the bed and gazed into her eyes. The love she saw there humbled her. "Will you grant me the honor of your hand? Will you be my wife and my friend and my love? Will you marry me?"

"What about the Festival? The contest? I don't want you facing a lake monster."

"The others conceded after they saw you heal me."

"And throw a dozen men from their horses."

"That too." He chuckled, then grew serious. "Let's explore the world, Kate. Let's make love under the stars and raise a few gray-eyed babes of our own. Marry me."

Was she still dreaming? Could fate finally be showing mercy? When she realized he had been waiting for her answer, she half sobbed, half laughed. "Yes!"

A heartbeat later, he drew her into his arms, his lips conveying all the love she felt. As her breasts pressed against his solid chest, she recognized a familiar presence. Pulling back, she discovered her mother's locket and her talisman.

"It took Father and Wolfe two days to find it," he said. "Father insisted on fastening it on you himself." At her teary-eyed response, he added, "I think healing me was a brilliant play."

"It wasn't as if I planned it," she said, still incredulous that she had it back. Pressing trembling lips against his, she whispered, "I meant what I said too. My heart and life are yours. I love you more than I could ever hope to express, but I'll do my best to try." Then she latched onto his rumpled tunic and claimed his mouth as hers.

At some point, in the midst of tangled tongues and whispered promises, she knew what had reversed the Binding.

Drawing back, she said, "It was our pledge to each other on the clifftop. That's what broke the spell. Our love is the greater power."

"Hmm. Could be. Do you think all Caligo natives marry that way?"

"What?"

He brushed a warm finger over her cheek. "Did your parents marry that way? Declaring their love atop the cliffs of Caligo?"

"I don't...how do you...are you telling me you were actually reading that book?" She gestured at the Caligo tomb on the bed.

His mischievous glint had her stomach flipping for conflicting reasons.

"I learned more than Zafarian magik when you poured your knowledge into me."

"How much more?" she asked, feeling exposed in an entirely new way.

"Now that's something we'll have to talk about up at the cabin," he teased.

A knock at the door interrupted them as Holly and Flora entered with trays overflowing with delights. Kate's stomach ached to indulge as the room suddenly filled with Rachel, Sebastian, the king, Wolfe and Victoria all checking on her well-being.

As a slice of juicy kiwi melted in Kate's mouth, Bregovi shared their good news.

* * *

Two weeks later, the Grand Hall overflowed with royals and common folk. Rachel and Sebastian stood hand in hand near the altar, soon to be wed themselves, and Wolfe sat with the king. Brock, Holly and Flora were also among the guests, as were Old Quent and Bet from the inn.

Victoria, Sophia and most of the other competitors had also stayed on to witness the event, although Kate suspected a few had remained in the hope one would be substituted in.

As Kate paused at the top of the grand staircase to await the cue from the harpist, all eyes turned her way. She couldn't help but swallow. Twice. When the notes began to float over the assembly, she began her descent. Joining the music, delicate murmurs rolled through the room like waves.

She couldn't hear the words, but knew the discussions were a mix of speculation about the short engagement and reports of her blatant display of magikal Gifts. Fortunately, the former was the sort of gossip people clamored over. And the latter had become a point of praise. It seemed, healing Florian's prince had garnered so much goodwill that discussions had begun around the issue of permitting Gifts again.

When Kate reached the bottom stair, Bregovi stepped from the altar, swiftly striding down the long aisle to her.

Unplanned.

Looking to his face for a clue, she worried he'd sensed Sylvan, whose unsettling presence had lingered over Florian since he'd fled.

But as Bregovi reached her, instead of feelings of alarm, his excitement flooded her senses, washing away the fear.

"I couldn't wait a moment longer to tell you how stunning you are, milady." With a wink that put her even more at ease, he lifted her hand to his lips.

"As are you, milord," she said, a sudden giddiness rippling through her. They were going to be married. In moments. And he loved her. What more could she desire?

"You're just dazzled by the robe," he said, tucking her hand around his arm. As he escorted her to the altar, he added, "While I am dazzled by *you*."

She couldn't conceal a silly grin. "I am dazzled by you as well." However, she'd readily admit, the robe added to the effect. The purple silk, trimmed in white fur, hung to the floor and dripped royalty. It had adorned his ancestors at ceremonies for centuries, including coronations. However, under it, he wore non-traditional black buckskins, boots and a white silk tunic, all of it perfectly tailored and adding to his striking form.

Had he had his way, she'd have worn a royal robe as well, but she argued it would hide her lovely new gown.

He'd conceded at that point, stating he wanted nothing more than to admire her in her new gown all day…and then out of it all night. Even the lavender dress paled in comparison. The shimmery pink silk of the wedding gown lay over her frame as if it had been designed for her, not altered from one Bregovi had commissioned for Rachel. The lining and sleeve openings matched his tunic, and tiny white embroidered roses outlined the neckline, sleeves and hem.

Rachel had insisted Kate wear pink and white rosebuds in her hair, so Kate felt like a flower from head to toe. Or perhaps a flower bush. She couldn't suppress a grin as Bregovi glanced over at her. His familiar scent of cinnamon and cloves teased her nose as his love flowed through and around her like a sweet, warm whirlwind.

Overwhelmed by the surety of it, she sucked in a breath and tears sprang to her eyes. Before she could blink them back, she saw tears in his as well.

"Is this really happening?" she whispered

"Yes," he said, giving her hand a squeeze "It's really happening." Then, as the holy man uttered something about gods and vows, Bregovi leaned in and kissed her. Not a chaste little reassuring peck, but a soul-searing, heady kiss.

"Not yet," the man said, clearing his throat, while chuckles echoed about the room.

Bregovi released her lips, his gaze holding hers. "Some things cannot wait." Lowering his voice, he added, "And some things have already been said."

While the holy man presented the ordinances and rites, she and Bregovi once again exchanged their own vows in hushed tones.

"I love you."

"I love you."

"I give you my heart and soul and all that I am."

"I love you deeper than all the oceans, greater than any treasure and more than my life."

"I am yours till the end of the stars."

"My heart and soul and life are yours forever."

At the ceremony's conclusion their lips met again to seal their love and commitment, and Kate felt a completely different kind of burning. One in her heart. Of peace, love and joy.

Afterward, they greeted well-wishers and enjoyed a wonderful feast where Wolfe encouraged a honeymoon voyage to Madora, and Brock made a toast to their happiness. Then later, as the afternoon sun sparkled in from the West, Bregovi led her out onto the dance floor. As a beaming Sebastian twirled past with Rachel, and Wolfe spun Victoria until she laughed, Bregovi pulled Kate close to whisper he'd arranged something special for their first night together. Then he stole her away to the sound of warm chuckles in the Hall.

Outside, Odyssey sat saddled and ready for them. The steed's mane had been braided with delicate leaves and ribbons, and a brocade blanket covered his back under a saddle for two.

Bregovi lifted her up as if she were as light as air, then climbed on. As she settled against him, he wrapped a warm arm around her waist and steered Odyssey toward the mountain.

After a steamy stop at the Kissing Bridge, he took her to their cottage.

The sight of the little cabin in the trees stole her breath.

Violets had been added to the wild display of forget-me-nots, and cozy firelight glimmered through the windows. It looked straight from a fairytale, making her feel even more like a princess.

Bregovi hopped off and held his arms up for her. She slid into them without hesitation, taking a moment or three to taste the lips she'd become so fond of.

When their kiss grew more steamy, he pulled back with flushed cheeks and dark eyes. "Inside."

Shifting her in his arms, he quickly headed toward the door, which flew open at his nod.

"You're certainly using your Gifts to full advantage," she said.

"I wouldn't want them to go dormant for lack of use," he said, carrying her across the threshold.

"I don't think you're at risk…" she began to say, but the words fell away as she found herself in the most lovely cottage imaginable.

It had been transformed. The cots had been removed, and in their place stood a grand oak canopy bed with wispy white curtains, lush lavender pillows, and a blanket of white and pink rose petals dusting the bed coverings.

As he set her down to look around, she noticed wild lavender in tall vases about the room, a fire blazing in the hearth, and candles burning everywhere. The floor had been covered with an elegant woven rug in the misty colors of sunset, and a table near the basin overflowed with delights, including fruits, breads and cheeses.

"It's beautiful," she said, smiling into his loving eyes.

"I'm glad you like it," he said, before dazzling her with another kiss that set her knees trembling. "What would you like to do first?" he whispered against her mouth.

"I don't know," she said with a saucy grin. "The fruit looks tempting."

"You want to start with the fruit?" he asked, glancing toward the table.

"Actually…" She pressed soft lips to his chin. When his clear green eyes met hers, she said, "I'd like to start with that beautiful canopy bed."

"Bless the gods," he croaked, sweeping her up and running toward it.

Laughter echoed about the room as they tumbled onto the plush bedding, sending rose petals flying in all directions.

A short while later, with gentle, urgent hands and, in one instance, teeth, they managed to rid each other of their wedding garments. Neither was able to get enough of the other. She knew it because she felt not only his touch, but his desire and his love and his need for her as well. Making love to him with her Gifts freed, with her ability to sense him, was far more intimate than anything she'd experienced.

Lying in his arms, she finally felt safe and loved and free. She had found a life and a love she had never thought possible. Pulling him close, she took his lips again and showed him exactly how delighted she was.

When they parted for air, his eyes met hers. "I love you, Kate. You are my perfect adventure."

Feeling the truth of his words to her soul, she rested a hand upon his dimpled cheek. "Knowing you is more magikal than anything I could have dreamed. I love you, Bregovi the Bandit."

Then she kissed his grinning mouth.

EPILOGUE

Kingdom of Florian — Weeks Earlier, Shortly After Sylvan's Ill-Fated Visit

Whipping out a handkerchief, Sylvan slapped the fabric in his palm and wrapped tight enough to staunch the bleeding, but not the anger. Months of searching all wasted. He still didn't have the means to unseat Zee.

A few strides before he reached an unattended steed, Elliana appeared in his path. Not unexpected.

"Where are you going?" she asked.

He stepped around her and mounted the horse. "Away to lick my wounds."

She reached up a hand. Within a moment, he'd pulled her up behind him and wished he hadn't. For with the touch of her arms around him, his frustration was now joined by guilt and sorrow. He'd failed.

"The seer was wrong," he said, directing the steed into the forest. "I can't fix this."

"She wasn't wrong," Elliana said, sounding frustrated herself. "You need to see with your mind."

"I know, I know and reason with my ass."

"Your *eyes*." Although she emphasized the word with a light smack to his leg, he could hear the smile in her voice.

"Unfortunately, my mind is the only part of my anatomy that does the reasoning, and my eyes are equally dedicated to seeing."

"Where are we going?" she asked.

"Does it matter?" he asked, taking up a path near a creek.

"We shouldn't get too far."

He couldn't be sure if it was her touch or the words, or perhaps the tone underneath, but another long-forgotten sensation stirred in his gut. *Hope.*

He halted the steed and shifted in the saddle so he could see her face. "Why shouldn't we get too far? I can't command Kate now and she's too Gifted to overpower."

Those amethyst eyes studied his, but her mouth didn't move.

"If you're going to help, then *help.*"

After a deathly long wait, she said, "What if...the seer...meant something...different?"

"Something different than the most powerful sorceress in Astonia?"

"What if the one you are seeking is not what we need?"

"Are you saying someone else can defeat Zee?"

Was it his imagination, or had her lips lifted at that?

"There's another? I've been after the wrong maiden?"

Her half-grin didn't falter.

Another? Dragging his good hand through his hair, he said, "If not her, then who is it? Is she here? In Florian?"

She didn't reply, just kept on as if he could read her pretty fae mind. As he gazed into those familiar eyes, wishing he *could* read her thoughts, he recalled a game they'd played long ago. One he'd devised when fishing to learn fae secrets she'd be punished for revealing.

"Elliana," he said, letting a lazy grin grow. "If she's here, blink once for *yes.*"

She laughed, tipped her head and blinked once.

THE TALE CONTINUES...

TAKE ANOTHER ADVENTURE OF SORCERY,
SACRIFICE AND SIZZLING ROMANCE...

FRACTURED

COMING SOON!

For more information about FRACTURED, please visit
Katrina Snow's website or sign up for her newsletter at
www.katrinasnow.com.

ABOUT THE AUTHOR

KATRINA SNOW writes renaissance-era fantasy romance, but also has in YA and contemporary characters in her head lobbying for stories of their own. She's a fervent traveler, avid photographer, and dark chocolate fanatic, and enjoys those pursuits when she isn't writing or earning her keep at her busy day job. Katrina lives in New York City with a neurotic tabby and eight million other people who might also be deemed neurotic.

For more about Katrina, her stories and the characters in her head, please check out her website. You can sign up for her newsletter there as well if you'd like to be alerted about upcoming releases. She also frequents Facebook and Twitter, and would love to say hello, if you'd care to stop by.

www.facebook.com/KatrinaSnowBooks
twitter.com/Katrina_Snow
www.KatrinaSnow.com